A Drop of Wizard's Blood

a novel by

Douglas Arvidson

CrossTIME
an imprint of the Crossquarter Publishing Group
PO Box 23749
Santa Fe, NM 87502

Library of Congress Cataloging-in-Publication Data

Arvidson, Douglas, 1946-
  A drop of wizard's blood : a novel / by Douglas Arvidson.
    p. cm. -- (The eye of the stallion series)
  ISBN 978-1-890109-90-5 (pbk.)
  I. Title. II. Series.

PS3601.R765D76 2011
813'.6--dc22

2011005321

Books by Douglas Arvidson

The Eye of the Stallion Series

The Face in Amber
The Mirrors of Castaway Time
A Drop of Wizard's Blood

Brothers of the Fire Star

This book is for my children,
Jennifer Arvidson Scarborough and Eli Arvidson

Who comprehends Time's swirling, twirling, whirligigs?
Neither the phantoms of dark regions nor the tides of reason.
Nay, only the gods.

Who apprehends the Time Vagabond's ways?
Neither I nor you, my dearest.
Listen at your peril to his wicked euphony.

Possession of our souls by the Vagabond's intentions
Shall cause dark passions to run amok,
And this is our greatest danger, Time Drifters, this is our greatest
danger.

For Time is the gods' handmaiden; its limits are uncharted and
it holds your ship in its embrace
And enchants thee forever, race after race, pace upon pace.

From the *Ancient Song of the Thrangs: Scraps' Lament*

Cast of Characters and Glossary of Terms

Astral — Astral the Ancient Boy begins life as Bum, a street urchin, but is transformed by Scrap's magic into a youthful wizard.

Captain Jarl — Dag-gar's adoptive father, he is the captain of the merchant ship, *Mother-of-Pearl* and becomes a prisoner of the Time Vagabond.

Captain Sorrow — Also known as the Time Vagabond

Dag-gar — At the beginning of Book III, Dag-gar is re-born and, as a babe in arms, taken away to sea. He is followed by the Time Vagabond and later possessed by him. Like Sonoria, Dag-gar is a Thrang and a Metacephala and his love for Sonoria is an eternal part of the fabric of Time.

Maximus — A race of war-loving technicians and scientists, the Maximus have, through selective breeding, removed any trace of color from their skin. They seek to conquer the world and enslave "inferior" races.

Metacephalas — A select group of humans, Metacephalas have special powers and so are considered to be small gods. A Metacephala is also the talisman these people wear around their necks—an amulet of their own heads shriveled and desiccated by Time, a symbol of their servitude to the cosmic plan.

Mother Mar — A wise crone, a sorceress, and healer, she is Scraps once-and-future consort. Mar, too, is a Metacephala who instructs young Metacephalas in the ways of life, Time and the Universe.

Scraps — His full name is Scrapius. He is an ancient wizard and Metacephala who wears clothes sewn together from multicolored rags. Like Mother Mar, his purpose is to pass the wisdom of the ages down to new Metacephalas,

	to keep the world on an even keel, and the Universe unfolding as it should.
Sonoria	Sonoria is a Metacephala, and a Thrang. She is the once and future Queen of the Stratus Valley, and the savior of her people. Due to the vagaries and whirlpools of Time, when we meet Sonoria at the beginning of Book III, she is again a child traveling across a desert with the great wizard, Scraps. It is her telling of her tale by the fire each night that causes our story to unfold.
Spiritus	Spiritus is Sonoria's half-wild, amber-eyed, blue roan stallion.
Stem, Pock, and Bor	Highway men Dag-gar befriends in a deep forest; they teach him the skills of bow and sword.
The Amber Teardrop	The Time-frozen blood of an ancient tree, the Amber Teardrop contains a mysterious sleeping face who is sometimes referred to as Time or as Eternity's mistress; it is the key to Time itself.
The Bird	Appearing in various forms—seabird, owl, or pelican, a man 'o war bird, hawk, or eagle—the Bird is the Metacephalas' spy, spirit messenger, and guide.
The Great Mystery	Also known as the Sacred Mystery, it is the unknowable essence of existence.
The Story	Also referred to as the Song, the Story is the history and legend of the Thrangs passed down orally from generation to generation in the form of an epic song.
The Stratus Valley	Ringed by towering, ice-covered peaks, the Stratus Valley is where Sonoria grew up, where, in Book I, *The Face in Amber*, she fought a bloody battle to free her people, and where she now rules.
Thrangs	Nomadic young men and women who travel the world astride half-wild horses, Thrangs live off the land as they seek the impossible: to understand the Great or Sacred Mystery.
Time	Consider time a living thing, a powerful, willful creature capable of whims and moods, and filled with vagrant energies and sucking whirlpools. Indeed, it moves this story backwards and forwards, folds it over on itself, and turns it inside and out: be ready, be wary.

Time Vagabond   A vagrant energy, the source of evil in the cosmic disquiet, the Time Vagabond is released by Sonoria and Dag-gar's eternal love feud.

White Kitten   Sonoria's avatar in animal form, the white kitten is a gift from Mother Mar to the young Dag-gar.

Prologue

A whispering: *Dag-gar is dead.*

The air is cold on his skin and there is the sound of wind howling across a desert and there is darkness; though his eyes are open, all is darkness. He tries to call out but there is no voice inside him; there is nothing inside him. He listens.

Again the whispering: *Dag-gar is dead, the arrow through his heart, his blood soaks the earth, his breath is gone from him, taken by the wind. Yet his spirit listens even now, as we speak.*

Then there is light, the flickering light of a fire, a fire without heat. Shadows move across the flames and still the desert wind is on his body but there is no voice inside him. He watches and he listens, watches the shadows on the flames and listens to the whispering and to the wind: *Dag-gar is dead. So what is to be done, then?*

The whispering answers itself: *He is wrapped now in the cold shroud of Time. It is over. He will lie forever in Eternity's bitter ice. Yet Time's song still must be sung—sung by the man called Dag-gar lying dead even as his eternal lover weeps over him.*

The flames rise and spread and he sees the shadows on the flames moving and he hears crying, a sobbing, coming from among the flame-shadows and again the whispering: *Shall Time's shroud-womb then suffer to birth him again, this Dag-gar? For if Time's song must be sung by him, his voice must be returned to him, his blood taken back from the earth, and his breath returned from the wind.*

Aye, aye, aye, all this must be done. Dag-gar the child must be birthed again unto the world to sing Time's song. And what is Time's song but the Song of Love, and he will learn it if he sings it.

But he will be followed through life by Time's ugly stepchild. Aye, yes, followed by the dark Vagabond. Beware and be wary, Dag-gar, be wary and beware.

He feels himself curl around himself, feels then heat and warmth and wet, and feels his breath come back into him; his blood is hot again in his veins, and strong hands grip him, and pull him from the sopping womb and there is no more sobbing, but the cry of joy at his birthing and the fire is gone and the whispering, too, and his first memory is of a night sky filled with stars.

* * * * *

An old man who was both very wise and a wizard, and a girl who the Ancient Songs said was destined to be a bold warrior but was as yet still a season from her womanhood, were traveling across a great desert. When the sun had dropped its blood-red heat behind the far-distant curve that describes the edge of the world, when the camel they had been riding had been set to grazing on thorn bushes, and when a fire had been built, they sat across from each other under a vast, cold, canopy of stars, wrapped in their blankets telling stories. This storytelling by the fire every night had been their habit since the beginning of their long journey, and the stories, though made up, were told slowly and carefully, for each one, once spoken, would become true.

"Begin, begin, begin—here," the man said, and he pointed his large, uneven nose up at the night sky and he raised his hand and gestured with a large, knobby finger. "When," he said, "that star there, the one with the reddish mist around it, was just being born, this tale also began—the tale of the Time Drifters."

The girl wanted to watch the man's face as much as she wanted to look at the star, for she never tired of sitting at the knee of the great sorcerer and making up tales about stars and dark heroes who drift through time as a bird's feather floats on a vagrant breeze. But, though a child, she knew enough to pull her eyes from the coarse-featured face with its ragged beard and to look upwards into the heavens and listen to the hoarse, high-pitched voice that seemed, despite its rasping, to be always filled with kindness and amused wisdom.

The wizard Scrapius, also called Scraps, looked to see if the little girl was doing as he had bid her. For an instant their eyes met and then the child Sonoria, whose hair was as white-blond as the desert sun and whose eyes were as blue as the tropical ocean-sea, looked away and upwards.

She raised a hand and pointed. "That one," she asked, "the one near the heart of the Scorpion?"

"Ah, yes!" Scraps said, "exactly that one. It is, in fact, the very heart of the Scorpion and we must learn to be wary of that Scorpion's sting, my young one. As one treads the great arc of the cosmos, we must watch where we step.

"But never mind that now. Here is the tale's beginning: A prince and his princess—a storybook couple if ever there was one—had a baby. It was a boy, a strong and lively boy with dark, curling hair like his father and piercing green eyes like his mother, with darkish skin like his father and aquiline features like his mother." Scraps paused for a moment and said, "Now that I think about it, the little boy bore not the slightest resemblance to any of his grandparents. Hmmm. I'm certain that did not please them one bit."

"What do you mean?" Sonoria asked.

"What do I mean?" the sorcerer responded. "Oh, just that grandparents like to be remembered in the features—but not necessarily the behavior—of their grandchildren. But, I'm getting sidetracked by spurious thoughts. It happens as one gets older.

"So," he continued, "as you look at the reddish star that is the heart of the great Scorpion, picture this: a large castle built of fine stone on a green island set in a gray sea not far off the coast of an ancient land. Can you see it, my child?"

The girl was quiet for a moment and then, when she was certain she actually could see it, said, "Yes, I can see it, Father Scrapius."

"Excellent. Now, picture this: A cool night filled with stars, much like tonight. The boy, just born and still in swaddling clothes, is placed in his cradle in the nursery high in a tower, a cradle that can rock to and fro so as to ease the baby's sleep. After she is certain the babe is sleeping, the princess leaves the nursery and the child is alone.

"Now, there are in this world certain whims and whimsies, vagabond energies generated by the spurious gravities of Time's passage, whose intentions, sadly, are not benevolent. And the moment the princess leaves the nursery, one of these Time Vagabonds, dressed in a black cloak and a cowl that hides his face, slinks into the nursery, appearing as if from nowhere—though in fact, he comes from everywhere. He leans over the baby, holds a candle close to it, and opening the baby's blanket, sees the birthmark in the shape of a certain starry constellation on the infant's chest. Satisfied that this is the child he is looking for, the Vagabond picks up the cradle with its precious contents and sets it out on a window ledge."

"But—" the girl started to interrupt.

"No," Scrapius said, "hold your questions for just a moment now. I'm just getting going here.

"So, the Time Vagabond sets the baby boy in his cradle on the window ledge, a window ledge overlooking the town built around the castle inside the castle walls, as they were then, and outside the big gates there was usually a moat or something, but in this case there was no moat because there was the ocean-sea instead, and the ocean-sea is a pretty good moat, when you get down to it."

"But," the girl started again, and this time she was not to be hushed, as it was in her nature to say what she wanted to say even to an ancient wise man. "But, wasn't that a bit stupid, Father Scrapius, to put a child out on a window ledge?"

"Well, yes, of course it would be stupid if you didn't know any better," Scrapius said. "But, believe me, the Time Vagabond is not stupid. Listen now, though, and look up again at the reddish star in the heart of the celestial Scorpion.

"Imagine this: a wind, a strong and sudden night wind pipes up, as if it has come from the reddish star itself. Down, down, down it comes until it reaches the castle. It swirls once, twice, thrice around the castle's walls, gathering up leaves and dust and then, in the middle of its fourth go-around, what do you think happens?"

The girl looked at the old man's rheumy eyes shining in the firelight and without hesitation said, "It blows on the cradle."

"Ah, but yes of course, my child! It blows on the cradle. Tell me, then, my little wise one, what does this night wind born of the fiery-red heart of the Scorpion do then?"

Again, the girl did not hesitate. "It starts the cradle to rocking," she said.

At this Scrapius could not contain his laughter. "Ha, ha!" he exclaimed, "You are a clever one! That is exactly what happens. That night wind sets that cradle to rocking. And now, precious girl, what happens next?"

"The cradle rocks and rocks and rocks until the little prince is asleep," she said.

"And then?" the sorcerer asked, "what next?"

The girl looked at the old man and realized it was her turn to spin the tale. So she looked back up at the stars as if she were reading the story up there.

"Down on the street below comes a hay wagon, just a clattery old hay wagon, clattering along, going through the gates, out of the town, and down to the harbor."

"Yes? And then?"

"And then the night wind rocks the cradle harder and harder until, just as the wagon is going along below the window, over it goes."

"And out..." Scrapius began.

"...falls the boy baby," the girl said, "down into the hay wagon into a pile of hay, where he is not injured in the slightest."

"Exactly," the sorcerer said, now whispering the words, "and away goes the wagon with its very special cargo, down to the harbor, where..."

"...where a ship's captain finds the little boy," the girl said.

"But, certainly," Scrapius said, "as soon as he finds the baby, this ship's captain sends out word and the baby is returned to the prince and the princess."

"No," the girl said, still reading the stars, "no, he does not send out word, because he has always dreamed of having a baby boy, a son, but his wife has died and he is getting old. So he knows that this one has been sent to him in some magical way from—from the stars. And so the ship and its captain and the baby boy prince sail away on the morning tide, gone to the ocean-sea even before the reddish star at the heart of the Scorpion is extinguished by the dawn."

Scraps sighed and thought, *Such is the way of Time and its Drifters. If you let them, they make up their own destinies, drawing them from the infinite light of the infinite stars. And then there is nothing left to be done but to let them live out those destinies.*

"And now," he said, "it's time you went to your own rocking cradle and your own dreaming."

"But Father Scrapius," she said, "I am much too old for a cradle. I sleep on the ground wrapped in blankets like a proper young woman. And we have to decide what happened to the baby prince."

"Oh, my, my, my," Scraps said, "I'll let you dream that, too. Go now, to bed, and get it done."

* * * * *

No sooner had the girl rolled herself up in her blankets and started breathing the deep, regular breaths of sleepers, than the old wizard stood near the dying fire and pulled his sword from its scabbard. He raised it up and with a sudden violence, spun it in a circle around his head. When the blade cut the air, there was a hissing sound and a track of blue flames came from the tip of the sword. With the flames forming a burning circle around him, Scraps then pointed the tip of the sword toward the northern night sky and spoke words from an ancient tongue, muttering them softly.

There was a soft commotion in the air, a nearly silent beating of wings, and a shadow passed across the firelight and landed on a rock ledge near Scraps' head.

"Hello, my fine friend," Scraps said. "I trust this excellent night is to your liking."

The owl—with the luminous, all-seeing eyes of owls—ruffled his feathers, settled himself, and then, ever so quietly, uttered a long stream of hoots.

The wizard listened, nodded, listened, and nodded until the owl was finished. "It's true, yes," he said, finally. "The girl-child is the other half of this tale about the Time Drifters, though she does not yet know it. Our precious, precocious, stubborn, willful Sonoria sat here and made up the beginning of the tale on this very night. Now that she has set things in motion, we must see how they play themselves out.

"And so we shall, my old friend. Let us see how the tale is dreamt this time around, for it is now out of our hands—or wings, as the case may be. All we can hope to do is follow the dreamers around and perhaps lend a hand here and there, tweak this, tweak that, and hope for the best.

The wizard pulled his own blankets over his shoulders. "Go now, fly on until the morning, Owl," he said, and he sat down on the ground and pulled his broad, floppy hat down over his eyes and stared into the last of the flames.

Chapter 1

The boy child, being willful from the start, was not an easy one and more than once the captain wondered if he had made the right decision. The captain called him Dag-gar, after a word in the ancient tongue his father had spoken that meant "the drifter," for this is what the boy seemed destined to be from the beginning.

Physically he was well ahead of other boys his age, and by seven months he seemed determined to be on his own, toddling around the moving deck as surefootedly as a goat, finding obvious glee in the challenge of moving from one place to another on wooden planks slick with seawater. Seldom falling, he set about exploring the various nooks and crannies one finds on such large, creaking vessels. For indeed, it was a ship made of heavy timbers and designed to sail the deepwater seas, its holds filled with various cargos such as cattle, timber, wine, tea, beer, wool, or bolts of fine silk. Ofttimes there were also interesting passengers aboard who wished to voyage from one exotic port to another.

And so it was that at the age of fourteen, when Dag-gar was a boy on the edge of his manhood and full of questions about the wider world beyond the decks of his ship, there came on board in the far eastern port of Eye o' the Sea an old woman bound for the distant town of Port o' Rue, a coastal city that sat tentatively, precariously, on the hip of a smoldering volcano.

The woman passenger was tall and gaunt and quite ancient, but not at all tentative in step or in thought. She said her name was Mother Mar and she was a silk trader by profession if not by choice, and she preferred traveling by camel or donkey but would voyage by ship when necessary. She always dressed herself beautifully in the fruit of her trade: long, silk robes of many colors that formed a cowl around her head and fell nearly straight down her long body to her feet, which, to the careful observer—a fourteen-year-old boy in this case—could be seen to be shod in blood-red silken boots whose toes turned up into sharp, tasseled points.

With her thick, gray-black hair and her powerful features, Mother Mar was an imposing presence. It was said among the crew that she was in fact a witch or a sorceress or a wizard—some such magical person—and not a silk trader at all. For the boy, who had grown up as wild and free and fearlessly arrogant as the son of the ship's captain could be, these rumors fed the fierce fires of his imagination; Mother Mar became an object of immense and endless curiosity. It did not take long for them to develop a relationship based on good-natured teasing.

"Why do your toes point up?" he would ask.

"Because imagine what would happen if they pointed down," she would answer.

She might be sitting out on deck taking in the sea air on a pleasant day. Great seabirds, the kind that can sleep while on the wing and that eat squid swimming on the surface of the water, would be sweeping around the ship's masts, never once flapping their long wings as they soared about the sails. The sea would be an endless blue with white clouds puffing along in the trade winds and the sun would be hot and good on their faces.

The boy, who would lean against the ship's railing in front of Mother Mar, staring at her feet or her face or her hands, would say, "If they pointed down, you wouldn't be able to walk."

"And then what would I do?"

"You could fly."

Mother Mar would raise her eyebrows and study the boy's face and say, "And what makes you think I, or anyone else, can fly?"

"Because you are a witch."

"Who says so?"

"Pommer, the cook. He says you are a witch."

"Well, you tell Mr. Pommer, the cook, that if I could fly, I would do so and not sail about like this having to eat the stale biscuits and sour gravy that come from his galley."

The boy laughed and said, "Mr. Steff says so, too."

"And who is Mr. Steff?"

"He's the mate."

"Is he also the navigator?"

"Yes. He and my father. They use the stars and the moon and the Amber Teardrop to steer us across the ocean-sea."

"Well then, you tell Mr. Steff to keep a sharp eye on all of them because he just might see me flying up there some night. And if he follows me, I'll take him and this ship somewhere he does not want to go."

"Where?"

"To Coddlesmooch."

"What is Coddlesmooch?"

"A place where all the witches gather and hang by their feet from the trees and brew up huge cauldrons of soup made from the blood and tears of sailors and the noses and toes of curious boys."

This pleased the boy and he laughed again, and asked, "Why are you going to Port o' Rue? There's a big volcano there, you know. It could blow up any moment."

"Of course I know that," she would say. "We witches love volcanoes."

"Why?"

"Because we can fly down into them, straight down to the middle of this fat, round earth, and collect the hellfires that burn there. Then we bring them back up to the surface and sell them to blacksmiths and wizards. It pays rather well, in fact."

The boy's eyes widened at this information but, because his father had taught him that a smart person keeps his fears to himself, his only reply was, "Oh," and he reached out and touched the tassels on the tips of her boots and was about to tell her that her toes did not go all the way to their pointed ends when his father, the captain, appeared.

"Mother Mar," he said, "I hope my son is not bothering you again with his endless questions."

"She is a witch, Papa. She says so herself."

The captain shot Dag-gar a warning glance and said, "I'm so sorry, Mother Mar, for the impoliteness of my son."

"Oh, not at all, Captain Jarl," Mar said. "He is a clever lad, after all, and handsome and will soon be a man. I always enjoy our conversations."

Then, after the captain had assigned the boy some duty and they had gone away and no one was left nearby on deck to see her, Mother Mar took out her pipe, lit it with a flame from the tip of her finger, and sat and puffed out billows of sweet smoke and thought about this boy named Dag-gar. Meeting him and talking to him was indeed the real reason she was making the voyage from Eye o' the Sea to Port o' Rue, and the real reason she sat out on deck. He was, she was now certain, like herself, a Metacephala, a small god, a Time Drifter, whose purpose it was to keep an eye on the worst impulses of the human beings who inhabit this world, and to try to keep things on an even keel. Yet, there was something about him....

She looked out across the vast ocean-sea and puffed her pipe and waited. It wasn't long before one of the great seabirds that had been floating on wide wings around the ship's mast, soared in closer to her.

Mar smiled and sent her thoughts out to the creature, for this is the way she spoke to her familiars: *So, there you are, and in the form of a lovely seabird, at that. I could not tell you from your companions. You all look the same to me.*

The seabird dropped a wing tip and floated around her in a tight pirouette, fixing her with a gaze from first one small orange eye and then the other. Mar waited for it to answer her, but heard nothing.

Never mind, she thought to herself, and then, to the seabird, she thought, *Our boy here, this young Dag-gar, is truly one of us. I am now certain of it. But, of course, you probably knew that, hey?*

Now the seabird clearly answered her thoughts with its own: *There was a night some fourteen years ago, Mother Mar, when I was visiting an island in the misty north, that a baby was born with the mark on his chest, yes, that is true.*

Mar puffed at her pipe and asked, *And so, what happened to this infant?*

The infant was in danger, the seabird said, continuing to fly in tight circles over the deck where she sat. *A Time Vagabond, intent on mischief, set the child in its cradle on a window ledge and made a night wind come down from the stars to blow the cradle off.*

What did you do? Mar asked.

Arrangements were quickly made and it so happened that a hay wagon passed by underneath the window just as the baby fell.

So, arrangements were made, Mar thought to herself and then to the Seabird, she thought, *Ah, such a business, stealing babies from their parents. Yet, you did what you had to do, for it would have been much worse for the world than even a plague had a newly minted Metacephala perished. And, as you can see, the lad is thriving out here at sea. Life aboard a ship suits him, it would seem.*

Yet, the seabird thought back, *you, Mother Mar, have your reservations about the boy named Dag-gar. Something amiss with his energy, perhaps?*

Mar stood up, walked to the ship's rail, rested her bony elbows upon it, and looked down into the water. *Yes, yes, yes. There is something amiss. But now, after hearing your story, I know what it is.*

And what, pray tell, might that be?

And Mother Mar answered the bird: *The Time Vagabond is still following him, I'm afraid. And, of course, bent on ill deeds.*

Having thought this to the seabird, Mother Mar puffed hard on her pipe, realized it had gone out, and rapped the bowl of it against the hard wood of the ship's rail.

And what can we do about the Time Vagabond? the seabird asked.

Ah, my old, old friend, Mar answered, *our boy Dag-gar is doomed to be plagued by the Vagabond's intentions—for that is the business of such vagabond energies—bad luck, misfortune, trials and tribulations, hardship and calamity. And there is little we can do about it. You see, in the swirling, folded measures of Time, the Vagabond is infinity and infinity is wickedness because there is nothing more dangerous than the absence of limits. So, my dear familiar, the Vagabond is the very source of the evils of the cosmic disquiet. We must only hope Dag-gar has the strength, the forbearance, the resilience to—to....*

To overcome? the Seabird offered.

Yes, to overcome, Mar thought, *to overcome and to still achieve his destiny. I think we can do something, though you, as a seabird, might not want to be a part of it.*

The seabird moved away from the ship, rising on the wind until it was again above the masts and the full sails. Mar could still listen to its thoughts: *I shall not, then, linger here, as I have my suspicions about your plan. And you are quite right—this is no place for a seabird.* And then it rose higher and higher into the air until it was just a white speck and then it disappeared altogether.

Chapter 2

When Mother Mar came on deck the next day, she appeared to be the same, still dressed in her flowing silk robes, still clutching the pipe in her teeth, still moving with her antique grace across the rolling decks, the sunlight shimmering on her silver hair. But now she carried something other than her pipe. Concealed within her robes was a small creature, a small, energetic creature, whose presence she was at pains to conceal until she could surprise the boy.

She sat in her usual place, just near the companionway to her quarters, and, as usual, it did not take long for the boy to find her. He came up from the main deck, looked for her, saw her sitting on her special chair, and immediately changed his attitude from one of eager curiosity to one of casual banter.

"Good morning, Mother Mar."

"And a good day to you, Dag-gar. What is the news about the ship? Any pirates been spotted? Any sea serpents?"

"Yes, I suppose so," Dag-gar answered, "but they really don't bother me. I'm used to them now, you know."

"Ah, of course, as you should be. A young man of your seagoing experience, growing up on a ship and all, what could a mere pirate or sea serpent mean to you?"

At that very moment, just when Dag-gar had looked away from Mar's eyes and down to her robes, the creature she held underneath them began to struggle in her grip. Dag-gar saw it and quickly looked away, pretending indifference.

"I think, though," Mar said, "it is a pity that, being so used to sea serpents and the like, you would not be interested in something I have here underneath my robes. I had thought to make it a present to you."

Now the boy stared unabashedly at the place on Mar's robes where he had seen the movement. Yet he said nothing, but looked up at her face and smiled slyly. "I am a little afraid of sea serpents, after all," he said.

"Well, of course," Mar agreed. "I would imagine even your father, the great captain Jarl himself, would be just a little afraid of sea serpents. I know I am, and, as you know, I'm a witch and witches aren't afraid of anything."

The boy kept his eyes on Mar's robes, which were now moving with a small violence as the creature she held began struggling again. "Is it a snake?" he asked.

"Oh, heavens no," Mar answered. "I may be a witch and love all the creatures of this fat, round world, but still, I would never hold a snake under my robes."

The boy thought for a moment, twisting his face up with concentration. "It is a monkey!" he finally said, looking up at Mar with a note of hopeful excitement in his voice.

"Now, my boy," Mar said, laughing, "that is a good guess, and I must admit that I almost wish it were a monkey. But, alas, no. Nothing quite that exotic. Yet, in a way, though this creature is common enough, it is exotic in its own way."

"A dog!" Dag-gar cried out and now he could not stop himself from reaching out for it.

Mar twisted away from his reach. "Again, no, and again, alas. I'm sorry, Dag-gar, because it is common enough wisdom that every boy needs to have a dog. But you are close. Think nemesis. A dog is the nemesis of this animal. Everyone knows that."

Mar hoped that this word would not be known even by a boy as gifted as the one who now stood before her and she laughed again as she watched him pretending that he did understand it. But a moment later their game was over, for the creature she held under her robes let forth a pitiful howl.

"A cat!" the boy yelled. "It's a kitten!"

"Ah, she gave herself away," Mar said, sighing, "just when I was beginning to have fun."

She withdrew the animal and held it out for him to see, and the kitten, for it was not yet more than two months old, stopped squirming in Mar's hands and blinked in the sunlight.

The boy reached for it and Mar let him have it. He held it close to him, squeezing it against his chest lest it wriggle away.

"Not too hard, now," Mar warned. "You're a strong boy and you don't want to crush it."

Dag-gar eased his grip, but still held the cat tightly to him. And now he was looking at it, examining it carefully. Its fur was long and white-blond and stuck out straight from its body, and its eyes were as pale blue as a desert sky. It looked up into Dag-gar's eyes and mewed fearlessly, as if it had known him forever.

"What's his name?" Dag-gar asked a little breathlessly, and trying not, at his age, to be too excited.

"What is *her* name," Mother Mar said. "She is a little girl."

"What is *her* name, then?" Dag-gar asked.

"Well then, I'm going to leave that entirely up to you."

"I'm going to have to think about it, Mother Mar. Is that all right?"

"When making decisions of great importance, such as naming a kitten, it is always best to do exactly that: think about it for a while."

"Can I show my father?"

"Oh, absolutely. He indicated to me that he would be glad to have a cat on board. Every ship, big or small, needs a cat."

The boy left, clutching the kitten to his chest, its tail sticking out from under his elbow.

Dag-gar had just disappeared down the companionway to the captain's quarters when Mar heard the seabird calling to her. She looked up and there, above the masthead, was the great white seabird, riding effortlessly on the wind. As they had before, they communicated silently, through their thoughts.

So, the bird said, *you have brought her to him.*

Indeed, Mar answered, *it was the only thing I could think to do. She might be some protection to him, I would think, even in her present form. Cats are good at sensing danger.*

Actually, the seabird said, *a cat was a clever idea. Imagine if you had given him a monkey.*

A monkey was never a serious consideration, Mar said. *There will be enough trouble as it is, I fear. In any event, my fine, feathered friend and familiar, they are together again, Dag-gar and his eternal love and fellow Time Drifter, Sonoria. There is nothing we can do now but hope for the best.*

* * * * *

The next morning they fetched Port o' Rue off the starboard bow. The tip of the volcano loomed first through the top of a cloud that had gathered itself around its peak, and by afternoon, the bottom of the island, green with trees and fields, could be seen clearly. Before sunset, the ship's anchor had been dropped into the calm water of the harbor and immediately the sailors set to off-loading the cargo.

It was here that Mother Mar disembarked, but not before seeking out Dag-gar. She found the boy in the galley, squatting next to the kitten, watching her drink from a bowl of fresh goat's milk.

"Has she got a name, then?" she asked.

Intent on the cat's eating, Dag-gar had not heard Mar approach and now he turned his head quickly toward her and then looked back down at the kitten. "Steff wants to name her Sola. Because she is the color of the sun. Father said to name her Blaouy, which means 'blue eyes' where he was born."

"And what do you think?" Mar asked.

"I'm still thinking about it," he said.

"Good. It's an important decision."

At that moment the kitten looked up from the bowl and gazed into Dag-gar's eyes with what could only have been a look of love. She then called out to him with a soft mew that had a peculiar and lovely trill to it.

Mar felt a shiver move down her spine. "There," she said, "maybe in her song you will find her name, for I have never heard a kitten make such a wonderful sound as that."

The kitten mewed again, and again it had an astonishing tune to it and Dag-gar scooped her up into his arms and snuggled his nose into her fur.

"She sounds like a tiny bell, one made of pure silver," Mar said.

"Sonoria," Dag-gar said softly into her fur.

"Ah!" Mar said, "Yes, 'Sonoria,' from the island of the silversmiths, famous for their bells. It means magical singer. Excellent." She sighed and said, "So, now that that is done, I feel ever so much better. Now I must go and get off this ship and take care of my business. Goodbye, Dag-gar. I hope we shall see each other again."

With that, she left the boy holding the kitten and went out on deck, where she checked to be certain her sea chest had been carried off by the stevedores, then walked down the steep gangplank and into the crowd on the bustling dock.

She had just taken the last step and was again standing on firm ground when someone brushed by her, bumping against her elbow. She glanced up at the figure, but he—or she, for by clothing alone it was impossible to tell—had already passed, not bothering to make an excuse or to nod in apology.

Mar took the figure in at a glance, and for the second time that morning a shiver ran down her spine; there was something familiar about the tall, gaunt frame and the smooth black boots peeking from the hem of the monk-like robe, something familiar about the limp that caused whoever it was to drag one foot. But there was something else: When she looked up to examine the face to determine if it was a man or a woman, she saw only a shadow inside the cowl where there should have been eyes, only darkness where there should have been a mouth. Mar watched the figure make its way up the gangplank and her shiver became a shudder.

And so, there it is, she thought, *Dag-gar's Time Vagabond, the shadow energy. Trouble, trouble, trouble is now a passenger aboard that ship—and there is nothing to be done about it.* And she looked up at the volcano, whose own shadow loomed over the town of Port o' Rue, and spoke to it. "From you, I suppose, it came, then, hey? From the very hellfires of this fat, round world. And so be it. But beware, oh great dark one! He is still just a boy, but very soon to be a man. He has his own strength and now the companionship of a warrior-goddess in the form of a white cat familiar. And he has us, too, and we shan't abandon him."

Chapter 3

The ship, called *Mother-of-Pearl* left Port 'o Rue the next evening with the rising full moon after having taken on a load of spices. The wind was fair from the west as they rode the outgoing tide through the harbor entrance and put the smoldering top of the volcano down toward the horizon.

Before darkness filled the heavens, there had been a strange sunset. Instead of the usual green flashing of light as the rim of the sun dropped below the horizon, something blood red seemed to explode from the top of the dropping orb. This was noticed by the captain and the mate, who were both on deck watching the sailors go about the business of getting under way.

The boy, who was standing next to the captain holding the white kitten tightly in his arms, noticed it too. "Father," he asked, looking at Captain Jarl's bearded face, "what is the matter with the sun?"

"Indeed, boy, I don't know. In all my years at sea I've never seen such a thing." He thought for a moment and, because he knew his son would badger him with questions until he came up with some sort of an explanation, added, "No doubt 'tis merely the effects of a cloud passing across its face."

"Oh," Dag-gar said as, gripping the kitten more tightly to himself, he moved closer to his father. Together they watched the ocean-sea transform itself from a shimmering evening blue to the rolling pitch black they would ride across all night.

* * * * *

It was that night, too, so soon after leaving the safe harbor of Port 'o Rue, that Dag-gar was awakened by a terrifying dream, a dream of twisting dark forms trying to suffocate him, wrapping themselves around his neck, covering his face with gaping, black mouths and shrieking their terror into his body.

When he woke up, gasping and tossing in his sheets, the sun-white kitten with the blue eyes was there, next to his head, purring and licking his face as if to comfort him. He pulled her closer. He felt the ship surging in the seaway and heard her great beams creaking and sensed her sails pulling, full and by. There was the sound of the watch calling out and the boy peered out his porthole and gazed at the stars. As he always did when he was frightened, he thought of his father and remembered his father's words: *We follow these stars across the sea because, though there is an infinity of empty space between us, we are together, this world and the stars above it.* With the voice of Captain Jarl in his head, he drifted off again, into his sleep.

The next night as he was going to his berth, Dag-gar noticed that the kitten, following at his feet, had stopped and was looking at the bottom of the door that opened onto the cabin in which Mother Mar had stayed when she was aboard. Little Sonoria stared at the small space under the door, ignoring Dag-gar's calls to follow him, and then, with a leap backwards, hissed and arched her back.

"Come now," he called to her, "Mother Mar is gone. There is no one in there."

But then a soft, scraping sound came from behind the door and Sonoria hissed again. Dag-gar reached down and picked her up and his eyes were caught by a small movement—the door latch had lifted itself up and then dropped down again. Dag-gar felt the cat arch herself in his arms and then he felt the hair on his own neck rise up. There was not supposed to be anyone in that cabin, no one at all. It was being used for storage; he himself had seen the stevedores fill it with provisions for the long voyage ahead.

He held Sonoria tightly in one arm, and with the other hand, reached out for the latch. Just as his fingers were about to make contact with the metal, a spark jumped from the latch to the tips of his fingers. With a yelp of pain, he pulled his hand away and stared at the latch. Again it appeared to move, to lift up ever so slightly.

"Who is in there?" he called out.

Nothing. No one answered.

Sonoria squirmed in his arms and Dag-gar stared at the latch. Again it lifted up and this time it fell with a soft click.

Dag-gar backed away from the door and moved slowly down the corridor toward his own cabin, when he heard footsteps and saw Captain Jarl walking toward him.

"Father," he said, "I think there is someone in that cabin."

"No," he said, "Mother Mar is gone and it's completely full of cargo. We needed the extra space, so we filled it up, right up to the door."

"But, I see the latch…."

But his father was distracted and interrupted him. "I expect some weather tonight," the captain said, "so you must be ready. We might need your help on deck."

Dag-gar went into his cabin, got into his nightshirt, climbed into his berth, and blew out the lantern. The clouds that had tricked the sailors' eyes at sunset had spread themselves across the sky from horizon to horizon, so now, though there was a full moon, there was little light coming in the porthole. Dag-gar lay still, listening to all the familiar sounds: the incessant creaking of the ship's hull, the lapping of the sea against it, the distant voices of the crew. He could feel the ship rising and falling on the seas, and feel the kitten warm against his neck. Still, though, he listened for something else. Closing his eyes, he pictured the latch on the storage cabin's door, lifting, lifting....

* * * * *

He was awakened by two separate things: a change in the movement of the ship, and the feeling that someone was holding his hand. He started to cry out, but there was a whispering, faint to his ears.

"Hush," it said.

He lay still. In the silence he could hear his own breathing and feel his own heart pounding. Very softly, very slowly, someone had taken his hand and was holding it.

Again, the whisper. "Hush. Be very quiet. We must ready ourselves. There is danger."

It was the voice of a girl, and in its gentle insistence he could hear music like silver bells. He felt for the kitten. It was not where it had been, curled up against his neck, and when he started to reach for it, he felt the hand tighten its grip on his and again heard the girl's magical voice. "Hush, there is danger. We must be quiet. Come, get up now and go with me."

"My kitten—I have to find her," he whispered back.

"She is well," the girl's voice said. "Do not worry; she is with us, always."

He pulled the covers away and slipped out of the berth. The wooden planking of the cabin floor felt warm to his feet. "Fire?" he asked. "Is there fire?"

"No," the whisper answered, "it is more than fire. Come now, quietly."

"But we must tell Father," Dag-gar said, "and tell the watch there is danger."

"Your father is not in danger," the whisperer said, "nor this ship."

"Who, then?" Dag-gar asked.

"Just you and I," the girl's voice answered.

"But who are you?"

"You have named me Sonoria, so that is who I am."

"You are my kitten?"

"And more, too, Dag-gar. Now come, quickly."

It was too dark to see anything but perhaps the pale outline of a figure standing next to him, but he could feel her hand in his, holding him tightly and pulling. He followed her. He heard her open the door to his cabin and felt the different air of the corridor on his skin and smelled the spices in the hold and the old reminder of supper coming from the galley.

"I can't see," he said. "Can you see?"

"Yes, yes, I can see. Come with me."

They went down the corridor, past the captain's quarters and past Mar's old cabin, but now when he listened for the scraping and the lifting and falling of the latch, he heard only his own breathing, and he realized the door to the cabin was open.

They went up on deck, out into the night air of the ocean-sea, and now he heard his father's voice. He was not in his cabin, sleeping, but was on deck with the watch.

"Aye," his father was saying, "'tis a strange thing, to be sure. Never have I seen anything like it."

Dag-gar could see the silhouettes of both men standing against the rail looking outwards toward the horizon at a brilliant glow that pulsed like a radiant heart against the surface of the ocean and the low clouds above it.

"That's the direction of Port o' Rue," the captain was saying, "but we're two day's sail from there."

"Then, Captain," the watch asked, "what could it be?"

"Ach!" the captain answered, "it could be a vessel afire. Or maybe the volcano that sits above Port o' Rue has finally blown its lid. We might see that, even from this distance. In that case, may the Gods have mercy on the innocents of that poor city-town."

At that moment, a whistling sound began to run through *Mother-of-Pearl's* upper rigging and then it came farther and farther down until the deck was being swept by a sudden and powerful gale. The ship began to groan and rolled nearly onto her beam ends. Captain Jarl yelled orders to turn downwind and run with it.

With the crew racing around them in the dark and the salty blast ripping at Dag-gar clothes, he felt the whispering girl's grip on his hand tighten. Then he heard her cry out and felt a great force pull her hand free of his—and her pale outline disappeared into the night. At the same moment another hand, this one rough and smelling of ashes, clamped itself over his mouth from behind and he was lifted off the deck. He kicked out and screamed, but with the captain and crew distracted by the change in heading, his struggles went unheard.

He was lifted higher and higher, as if in the grip of the wind itself, and then was flung far out beyond the rail of the ship until he was flying over the sea. He tumbled through the air, turning over and over, and then he was in the water and he felt it close over him, cold and black, and he was fighting to get his head above the surface even as the great, rolling seas lifted and dropped him.

Chapter 4

For long moments he knew he was drowning and then something grabbed his hair and lifted his head out of the water. He breathed in the air in a long gasp and at the same time his hands hit the wooden strakes of the side of a boat and he clawed at it, trying to get a handhold, trying to pull himself up.

He felt himself being lifted by the back of his nightshirt and then he was free of the water and dropped into the bottom of the boat. He lay choking and vomiting up seawater and crying out for the captain, and it was only after a long while that he became aware of the sound of oarlocks creaking and water splashing.

He sat up and fell backwards against a thwart. From here he could see that he was in a skiff and that there was someone sitting at the oars rowing, but in the darkness, the rower was just a shadow, a shadow blacker than the night.

"Who are you?" Dag-gar asked, still sobbing. "Are you taking me back to the ship?"

There was, at first, no answer and he asked again, "Are you taking me back to the ship? Where is the ship? Where is my father? He is the captain. He will not be pleased that you have taken me without his permission. The ship's name is *Mother-of-Pearl,* a well-found merchant vessel."

Then the dark form, who had been rowing steadily toward some unseen destination—for Dag-gar could see neither ship nor any lights that might indicate a ship—said in a sullen, rasping voice, "That's a good boy, then. You'll find out where we are going in good time. For now, we'll be making our way through the night and on 'til morn."

"Where's my kitten? Did you find her?" Dag-gar leaned over the side looking into the sea but saw nothing but the phosphorescence left by the blades of the oars. And, in fact, he could see nothing else, not the faintest glow of a horizon, not the moon, not a single star.

The figure worked at the oars in silence for a moment and then said, "A kitten was it this time? A little creature with wild white fur and blue, blue eyes, I suppose."

"Yes!" Dag-gar said, "Yes, just a little one. Mother Mar gave her to me and I named her Sonoria."

"Sonoria," the rower repeated, "A precious name for a precious puss cat. Too bad, too bad, too bad. But such is the way of the ocean-sea. It's a sad business, this sailing the deep blue swells of Time, and a lonely one, too."

"Well, I know she's not drowned," Dag-gar cried out. "Cats are good swimmers, even kittens! She must be right nearby." Again he pulled himself up so he could look over the sides of the skiff and again he saw nothing but the small explosions of the phosphorescence and heard nothing but the slop and gurgle of the sea. "I want to go back to the ship now," he said. "Father will be very worried about me."

The shadow rower laughed. "Ah, ha! Your father will not be worrying about you at all, boy. You see, you have left him behind, far behind in the long ago. As far as he knew, his son fell overboard that dark night. Disappeared at sea. Ah, such a tragedy! His pitiful laments could be heard for days. But those things happen, and not to worry, he's grown old and died by now. His pain is over, his anguish finished. And so then, he has no more use for this." The shadow figure held up something that glowed in the dark as if filled with its own heat.

Dag-gar recognized it immediately: the Amber Teardrop. "You stole the Amber Teardrop!" he yelled. "My father needs that to navigate his ship! Without that, they are lost forever!"

"Yes, yes," the shadow said, "That is true, they are lost forever and now I have it—the Amber Teardrop, the Sacred Blood of the Ancient Tree, the key to Time itself. And yes, your father and his ship are long gone. But why should that bother you? He was not your blood kin anyway. Nay. He stole you away from your real mother and father—a real prince and a real princess, in fact—when you were just a babe in arms and took you to sea. Your brave father, you see, was a kidnapper!"

"No, he wasn't a kidnapper," Dag-gar yelled, "you're a liar! You're the kidnapper, taking me away from him!"

"But of course," the dark oarsman said. "Time is the greatest kidnapper of all, for it takes all babes away from their mothers. And loneliness is Time's greatest sorrow. And so I am called and so may you call me, for I am a captain too, on the sea of Time: Call me Captain Sorrow."

But the boy was not listening. He jumped at the shadow rowing the skiff, the one who called himself Captain Sorrow, swinging his fists. But instead of hitting something solid, he hit only air and his momentum carried him forward and then he fell, hitting his head hard against an oarlock. In pain and with blood running down his forehead, he vomited and lost consciousness.

Chapter 5

When he woke up, his head throbbing with pain, there was just the first pearling of dawn spreading itself across the surface of the water. At first, remembering nothing, he looked around for the familiar things in his cabin; then, finding that he was alone, at sea, in a small skiff, he sat up terrified and began crying again.

Then he remembered the oarsman and glanced around: Nothing remained of him, neither shoe nor shadow. The oars, still in their oarlocks, hung in the water, sometimes banging against the hull. Finally, his throat too sore to cry anymore, the boy pulled his knees up against his chest, put his head against them, and again, escaped into asleep.

He was awakened by the sound of voices, the creaking of oars in their oarlocks, the bumping of wood on wood, and then he was aware that he was being lifted by rough hands—yet he could not pull himself out from the swoon that gripped him. He felt himself being carried, felt the sun on his face and the wind, and then these sensations were replaced by the smell of the inside of a ship and the sweat of sailors and the scent of a damp cloth placed against his face.

He reached his hand up to pull the cloth away but he had no strength. He felt his face being cleaned and the crust that was holding his eyes shut being washed away. He peeked out between swollen lids. Faces peered down at him, the familiar coarse, bearded faces of seamen.

"There he is now," one of them said. "Boy, can you see us?"

Dag-gar nodded and tried to speak but his voice would not come.

"Let's get some water in him," one of them said. "Hold him up, now."

His head and shoulders were lifted and a wooden mug was held to his lips. He smelled the foul water from the ship's scuttlebutt and then felt it running down his chin. He drank and then started to gulp, and the water ran cool down the sides of his mouth and trickled down his neck.

"Take it easy, now, boy," the voice said. "Slowly, or you'll choke and puke it all up."

After he had drunk all that he could hold, he began to see things again. His eyes darted around. Where was Father, where was Captain Jarl? He knew none of these sailors. Then it all came flooding back to him: the kitten called Sonoria; the hand in the night leading him from his cabin; the other hand, the one that smelled of ashes, clamped over his mouth; and him being lifted and thrown into the sea, nearly drowning; the shadow oarsman who said his name was Captain Sorrow....

He sat up, but now he did not cry but asked in a calm voice, "What ship is this?"

The sailor who was tending him said, "This is the *Talisman*, and you're lucky enough that we found you, that's for certain. You've been out there floating around for a while, by the looks of you."

"I fell overboard. My father is the captain of the *Mother-of-Pearl*, a merchant trader. Have you heard of her?"

The sailor's eyes widened and then he laughed. "Oh, the *Mother-of-Pearl* was it? Every sailor knows the old legend of the *Mother-of-Pearl*, sunk by the blast of the volcano that destroyed Port o' Rue. And if you fell off of her, you've been floating around out here for a while, lad, for it's been three hundred years or more since that sad day. The *Mother-of-Pearl* was a good ship that had bad luck, if the stories about her are true. But it all happened so long ago, who knows the truth."

The sailor laughed again and disappeared through a doorway and a moment later reappeared with a bowl and a spoon. "Now, boy, eat some of this fish stew to get your strength back—and your senses, too, it would seem, for I do believe you lost them, out there on the open sea. Ha! The *Mother-of-Pearl* is naught but a ghost ship now, and that would make you a ghost, and to be honest, you look real enough to me."

He blew across the spoon to cool it and held it up to Dag-gar's mouth. Again, Dag-gar smelled the foul smell of sailor's fare, but he did not argue. He sipped at it and then gulped the spoonful down.

"That's a good boy," the sailor said, pleased. "You'll be up and about in no time."

Dag-gar asked no more questions, but finished the bowl of soup and another mug of water and then fell into a deep sleep. When he woke, it was dark and he heard the familiar sounds of life aboard a ship: the creaking, the slosh of the seas, the sailors talking idly among themselves—and snoring, too, for there were sailors sleeping in berths next to him.

He had been wearing his nightshirt, but now that was gone; under a coarse woolen blanket he was naked. He wrapped the blanket around himself and stood up. At first his legs did not seem strong enough to hold him and he reached out and put his hand against a bulkhead for support.

After a moment the feeling of dizziness passed and he took a tentative step. His knees held and he shuffled forward, his bare feet sensitive to the rough planking of the cabin sole. By the moonlight streaming through the single porthole he made his way past the sleeping sailors to the companionway door. The ship rolled in a swell and he hung onto the edges of the bunks and then to the latch on the door.

He opened it slowly and looked out. There was the deck and the mainmast with lines and rigging and ratlines everywhere, and the capstan, and the dark silhouettes of sailors. But no sails were set. The sailors were climbing up the ratlines or lined up on the rail looking out across the water at a thousand lights that blinked in the distance. Dag-gar recognized it immediately: They were at anchor in a harbor and the men were watching the lights of a port town.

Wrapped in his blanket, he walked out on deck among the sailors. When he joined them at the rail, they made room for him without questions or even a glance. He looked out across the water at the town. There were fires lit here and there, and he saw the outlines of buildings and he could hear music and smell cooking.

"What port is this?" he asked.

Without turning to look at him, a sailor answered, "'Tis Port o' Rue."

Dag-gar began to cry out, but choked it back. *No more of that, no more,* he told himself. *I am a sailor, too, and near a man, and the son of a sea captain.* Silently he vowed that he would never cry again.

But he had just left Port o' Rue—when? Was it yesterday? No, the day before. Now it seemed like a long time ago. He would go ashore. Someone in the town would remember the *Mother-of-Pearl* and her crew. He had made friends with some boys on the wharf, and what of Mother Mar? Surely she would still be there. He would find them and ask them—for what? For help finding the *Mother-of-Pearl* and his father, because it could not be true what the sailor had told him, what the phantom oarsman who called himself Captain Sorrow had said: that the *Mother-of-Pearl* was gone, a ghost ship living only in the legends of sailors, and his father grown old and died.

Chapter 6

Now that he was up and about, no one seemed to take a further interest in the young castaway. A small, wizened sailor gave him a dirty pair of pants and a shirt, but no shoes could be found to fit his feet. So, when later the next day he walked down the gangplank and onto the dock at Port o' Rue, he was barefoot and wearing baggy, filthy, worn-out clothes pulled from the bottom of an old sea chest.

Nor, when he stepped again on dry land, did he know where to go or what to do. For indeed, this Port o' Rue did not resemble the town the *Mother-of-Pearl* had sailed away from just a few days before. He recognized none of the buildings; none of the boys he saw playing on the street had familiar faces. Still, the town was busy. Ships were offloading goods; people bustled here and there, intent on some business; horses, mules, and oxen pulled heavily laden carts and wagons through the streets; and hawkers sold pots and pans, potions, fruits and vegetables from the backs of donkeys or from stalls along the sides of the street.

But where the sailors on the ship had quickly accepted him, the people of Port o' Rue either ignored or abused him. If he wandered into a shop, he was stared at by the shop owner with suspicion and then, a moment later, asked what his business was. When he had no answer, he was booted out, sometimes with curses and a cuff on the ear.

On the street, people would take him in with a glance and either dismiss him as a street urchin and ignore him, or would vent some inner anger and swear and kick him. He quickly learned to watch the eyes of those he encountered and in them read their intentions as he asked his constant questions, "Do you know of the ship *Mother-of-Pearl*, a sturdy merchant vessel and well-found, too? Or an old woman called Mother Mar who they say is a witch? Have you seen her?" As soon as he spoke he was taken for a child possessed by something evil—a demon or a spirit, or a spell.

By afternoon he was hungry and thirsty and his feet, though toughened by running barefoot around the ship, were sore from the gravel and cobbles of the streets. He began to hungrily eye the partially rotted fruit that fell off the mongers' carts. Anything that suggested food or water began to catch his eye: a stale loaf of bread lying in the gutter, the stray peach that had rolled down from the fruit-seller's cart in the alley, the trickle of water from a leaking cistern.

Still, he could not bring himself to eat or drink any of it. He was the son of a ship's captain, and a proud sailor, born and bred—so he had been told all his life—and a boy well loved and cared for, too. What would Captain Jarl say if he happened around a corner and saw his son picking food up off the street? And he began to see and hear him, too, his father, in every grown man that caught his eye, in every manly intonation of voice, in every other father calling to his children to finish their chores.

As darkness began to gather, first in the alleys and then creeping out to form cold pools of darkness in the small town squares, Dag-gar's desperation grew, and it occurred to him that he could return to the ship, return to the *Talisman*. He would certainly be welcomed back aboard and given hot food and put back into his bunk.

Beyond the tops of the low buildings, the masts of the ships in the harbor beckoned, and Dag-gar began making his way back toward the water. As he thought about the soup the cook would probably be ladling out to the crew even at this moment, and the sea biscuits that he could use to soak it up, his hunger became a spike in his stomach and he began running.

He had just rounded a corner when he heard an angry male voice call out, "There he goes! That must be him, the bewitched urchin what's been wandering the streets casting spells! Someone grab him, he's made off with my money box!"

Dag-gar looked back. A fat man with a red beard and a bald head was standing in the shop door yelling and pointing at him. And then others took up the call and several of them gave chase. Dag-gar stopped and yelled back, but his voice, weak from disuse, would not carry his protests of innocence loud enough to be heard. He began running, but a moment later was trapped, surrounded by an angry mob of townspeople.

"Aye! That's him," someone yelled out from the crowd, "he's the one what's been asking about the ghost ship, *Mother-of-Pearl*! Says his father is the captain, he does!"

"Stone him," another voice said, "and throw him in the harbor for the crabs to eat!"

"Nay, nay," someone said, "we shan't befoul our waters with the Devil himself. We'll burn the monster, as is the proper thing to do. Someone get a rope on him and we'll drag him to the square."

"No!" Dag-gar yelled, in desperation and terror finding his voice. "I'm on the *Talisman*, a ship that's even now tied up at your dock!"

But his protests went unheard. "He is the Devil," someone said, "in the form of a youth! Get a rope on him, someone, quickly now!"

But no one dared lay a hand on the filthy, possessed boy that stood before them. As the crowd gathered around him, they had only the courage to taunt him. But then a rotten piece of fruit was thrown at him. Another followed and another, and then a rock struck him in his stomach and dropped him on the cobbled street, where he lay curled, writhing in agony.

Now someone ran forward and put a noose over his feet and pulled it taut. "Drag him to the square! We'll get the Fire Tree ready! Gather some wood now, and be quick about it!"

And so Dag-gar, the breath knocked out of him, was pulled across the rough stones of the street and up onto the packed dirt of the town square. Here, in the middle of the square, stood a tree, dead and leafless, its bark burned away by the countless fires set at its base, its branches yet reaching high into the sky.

Dag-gar was jerked to his feet and pushed against the trunk, where ropes were wound around him until he was tightly bound. And still the crowd grew, and some of them cursed him and some of them threw things: rotten fruit, stones, and sticks. A pile of wood was placed at his feet and built up around him until it reached his waist.

Then, when preparations were complete, the crowd was suddenly hushed by the appearance of a tall man dressed in black and wearing a pointed black hat. He carried a long staff carved from ebony into the form of a snake with some sort of symbol on the end. He held this in front of him and raised it into the air. Then, but for a dog howling in the distance, there was silence.

The silence deepened as the man, dragging one leg behind him, shuffled up to the edge of the woodpile. For long moments he peered at the boy bound tightly to the tree, then he turned to the crowd and spoke.

"It is the will of the townspeople that this—this boy—be subjected to trial by fire to determine his guilt or innocence, witch or not, demon or not. Is he an evil spirit sent among the good people of Port o' Rue to cast spells upon them and do them harm? His ordeal on the Fire Tree, the Tree of Judgment, shall tell us the truth. And well it is that this trial take place—and immediately, too, and that will not be too soon."

He pointed his staff at the great volcano that slumbered fitfully over the town, its peak gathering clouds like a white beard and its caldron even now spewing black smoke through the whiteness of that beard.

"For we know that in the past, when we have allowed evil to exist in our town, divine retribution has poured forth from this, our mountain, by the displeased spirits of our ancestors. 'Twas some three hundred years ago that hellfire and brimstone showered down upon our fair town and laid it waste, killing all who could not escape quickly enough. Yes, yes, yes! The spirits of our ancestors must be appeased!"

He turned to the boy and looked him over from feet to head, then fixed a cold stare into his terrified eyes. "And you—boy, demon, devil, witch, whatever you are—shall, of course, be afforded the opportunity to prove your innocence. For we of Port o' Rue are a fair and decent people, after all, and believe, as we must, in the basic goodness and dignity of mankind.

"So, you have been tied to the Fire Tree, the Tree of Judgment, a tree whose great roots descend into the very center of the world and connect there with the spirits of our ancestors, and whose branches reach upwards into the air of the present day to connect with the living. And by the element of fire shall you be judged: If the flames cause you no harm, so shall you be found innocent. If you burn, then you shall have received both judgment and justice and we shall have both cleansed the town of evil and assuaged the ancient spirits."

Smirking, he stepped closer to Dag-gar as his voice became soft with mock pleading. "You may also simply confess to being a demon—or whatever—and be set free, for no demon will linger in a body once it has been found out. So, then, do you confess to evil and witchcraft? Speak now. Simply whisper your confession in my ear and I shall have you set free."

But Dag-gar was frightened beyond speech. When he tried to talk, his voice was nothing but a low croak and he could not force himself to utter a syllable.

"Ah, yes, I hear a demon in your throat!" the man roared. He spun around and held up his staff. "Set the fire, good people, and we shall learn the truth!"

Chapter 7

The old wizard Scraps and the girl called Sonoria, whose hair was the color of the sun and who could sing the Old Songs in a bell-like voice, continued their journey across the great desert. Today the camel was restive and had taken to shaking its homely, ponderous head. With a flapping of its small, hairy ears and dangling lips the beast sent a spray of spit and mucous splattering on the face of the old man, waking him from his reverie.

Scraps, whose long, knobby limbs and coarse features closely resembled the camel but in a human way, shook his head and wiped the wet away with his sleeve. "Ah, you are a difficult one, you!" he said, and he gave the camel a withering look meant to chastise the beast for its wet transgression. When this seemed to have little effect, the old wizard sighed, looked at the sky, and then peered at the horizon, which was turning purple with the premonition of dusk. He studied their surroundings and then looked at the girl-child sitting atop the camel's hump.

"I suppose, my young friend," he said, "the time has come to end yet another day of wandering this miserable, hardscrabble, lizard-infested land—another day with still not, I'm afraid, even a hint that we are nearing our goal. I would hope, though, that by tomorrow night we shall have reached an oasis where we can bathe."

The child, whose white-blond hair poked out from under the cowl of her robe and whose blue eyes now looked down on the man, did not speak, but smiled a small smile.

"So," he continued, "prepare yourself for your dismount." He touched the camel with his leather-covered stick and, with a long, loud moan of complaint, the animal began the complex process of dropping to its knees. Once this was done, the girl swung a leg over the front of the saddle and slid to the ground.

"Now," the man said, "a fire." He cast his eyes about, seeking the dried thorn bushes and brambles with which to start a blaze.

The girl, who was slender and very tall, though only in her eighth season of growth, touched the man's shoulder. "Father

Scrapius, I shall be more than happy to gather the fuel for tonight's fire. My legs are ready to be stretched."

"Ah, good then," he said, "and my legs have been stretched quite enough. I will prepare the place for it and tend to Mrs. Camel."

So the girl set off in search of what small sticks and dried grasses the desert might offer. She came to a small ravine, a split in the bedrock through which ancient waters had carved a smooth channel. Protected from the wind, the ravine had become a gathering place for what sandy soil the wind might drop, so here she found a small abundance of dried bushes. These she gathered in her arms and carried back to where Scraps had built a small fire circle out of flat stones.

"So," he said as she approached, "you've had luck, I see, and good for us."

He took the tinder she had gathered and placed it next to the circle of stones he had prepared, breaking it into smaller pieces. This done, he stuck his hand into the bottom of the pile and, with a soft whooshing sound, a blue flame shot out from the tip of his long index finger. The fire quickly spread from stick to stick, and soon a lovely small fire crackled in front of them, forming a circle of flickering orange-yellow light against the gloaming.

"'T'will be a good, starry night, girl Sonoria," Scraps observed, looking at the first of the stars even now emerging from the darkening sky, "and a good one for continuing our tale—and a wonderful sky to dream under, once tonight's tale is told."

Again the girl smiled, a calm smile that belied her excitement at the prospect of yet another night of stories. "I want you to start tonight," she said. "I want some time to think."

Scraps laughed. "You've had all day to think, perched atop that infernal beast—but if you insist," he said. "And look, already the new stars are appearing. The Hunter, for so that constellation was called by the Ancients, is beginning his climb up from over the edge of the world. And he'd better not linger there lest the Scorpion sting him yet again."

As she spread her blanket, the girl, who knew well the legends that said the Hunter and the Scorpion were sent to different parts of the sky so that the Scorpion would not sting the Hunter, asked, "Why is it the scorpion stings?"

"Scorpions sting," the old man answered as he fiddled with the fire, "for the same reason people lie, cheat, torture, kill, and steal: because it is their nature to do so. And for the same reason, people love and cherish, offer succor to the suffering, and sacrifice their blood and their lives to save others: because it is their nature to do so. But this is not the nature of the scorpion. And so, you see, scorpions and people are not the same, no matter what some may think—though some people are more like scorpions than others. Beyond that, I can't explain it. The way the universe works—and why it works at all, for that matter—is a great mystery and it is that wonderful, unsolvable mystery—and love, too, of course—that makes life worth living."

Scraps settled himself down on his bony haunches and watched the fire. He went on. "For example, you love to sing, dear Sonoria, because it is your nature to do so. Why do you love to do so? Because it gives you pleasure. And then we must ask the final question—and this is where we bump up against the impenetrable stone wall of the Great Mystery—why does it give you pleasure? So we find ourselves beating our poor brains against the Great Mystery—we cannot understand the reason for either pain or pleasure. And I might add that scorpions are as good at stinging as you are at singing, as good at causing pain to animals and riling them up as you are at calming them down."

This compliment pleased the child and she began to sing. Her haunting voice seemed to answer any questions the fire might have had about the night and caused the camel to stop munching on thorn bushes and look at her from its place just outside the firelight.

When she finished her song, Scraps spread his blanket by the fire and lay down on it. He passed the child a large leather bag, from which she withdrew strands of dried meat mixed with dried berries that had been woven into a rope. She took a bite and pulled off a piece and began chewing.

"Shall I understand the Great Mystery when I grow up?" she asked, staring into the fire.

"Ah, my child, understanding the Great Mystery is not necessarily the point of it all. The point of it all is in the *effort* to understand the Great Mystery. For, if you ever give up on that, you have lost everything. If you ever believe someone who tells you he or she has the answer to the Great Mystery, you have lost your claim to your freedom and given it to that person. Always remember this: the path to your own enlightenment is yours alone. To be true to yourself, you must find it by yourself. No one can find it for you, no matter what they tell you. So, to answer your question: When you grow up, if you are lucky, you shall become a Thrang: that is, a wanderer and a seeker of the answer to the Great Mystery.

"But listen now," Scraps said, taking the food bag from the girl and helping himself to a bite of the meat rope, "it is time for tonight's tale to begin and I've been yakking long enough. It's your turn. Look up at the stars and see what you can read in their cold and distant twinkling light. Tell me, please, tell me."

The girl did as she was told. She lay back on her blanket and looked upwards, waiting for her eyes to adjust to the star-speckled darkness that spread out infinitely above her. At that moment a star seemed to drop from its place in the sky and streaked downwards in a short arc before disappearing. As if the star had carried the story down to her, she began her tale:

"The boy child grows up on the ship and is tall and strong even before he becomes a man. He is a good seaman and understands the stars and their ways and how to use them to travel across the ocean-sea. He loves to listen to the sailors' stories—even though the sailors curse a great deal and his father, who is the captain, does not appreciate this but there is nothing he can do about it. Because that's what sailors do. They curse a lot."

Scraps smiled and nodded and said, "And they've been known to drink a bit, too. But, never mind. Please continue."

"The boy knows about all the sailors' skills with knots and ropes and splicing and stitching up sails and is good with the shipwright's tools, too."

Scraps, chewing on the meat, interrupted her. "But what about the land? Does the boy know anything about the earthy parts of the world? About trees and flowers and hills and mountains and deserts and swamps—all those things that you know about?"

The girl thought for a moment, watching the sky, hoping another star would fall to inspire her. "No," she said, finally, seeing no star and depending on her own imagination. "No, he knows very little about those things. The only time he is not at sea and on the ship with the cursing sailors and the wild, blue water is when the ship comes into a port town. And then his father does not let him go a-wandering lest he get kidnapped or into some mischief. For the port towns are dirty and dangerous places where sailors not only curse and drink, but where they kill each other, too."

"Oh, my!" Scraps said in mock despair. "They do all that in port towns?"

The girl nodded. "Yes, they do. And worse than that, I would expect."

"Worse than that?" the old man said. "And what could be worse than killing someone?"

Now Sonoria had to think for a long time before she answered, for she did not, in fact, know what could be worse than killing someone. She studied the heavens, searching again for an answer in the patterns of the stars, but it was not until she looked into the fire that she spoke.

"What is worse than killing someone is the *reason* you kill someone: because you hate them. And hatred is worse than anything, because there is no hope in hatred and when you hate, you are really killing two people—the one you kill and also yourself."

At this, Scraps turned his eyes from the fire and studied the girl's face. The yellow-orange light had set her fine features to glowing and created shadows that moved around behind her like elemental spirits coming out from the night as if they, too, wanted to listen to her. He thought, *Where would a mere girl, a child, find such wisdom? Well, of course, I know the answer to that question even though she does not: She is a Metacephala, a small god, and she has been alive forever in some form or another, so her wisdom is the wisdom of the ages.* But he only said, "I think you are right, Sonoria. When we kill out of hatred, we are killing ourselves, too. Tell me, though," he asked, for he was curious to learn how ancient wisdoms are passed along, "where was the answer to that question, in the great stars or in the flames of our small fire?"

Sonoria shrugged. "I think maybe the fire, for there is no hatred in the stars. There is only the gift of the Great Mystery in the stars. But there can be hatred in fires."

"'Tis true, girl-child," Scraps agreed, "fire can be used to serve the purposes of hatred just as well as it can be used to cook our food and provide us with warmth."

He took another bite off the meat rope and put it back into the cloth sack. With some effort, he got his long legs under him and pushed himself up so he was standing over their small blaze. "I'll get some more fuel for the fire," he said. "You keep on with your story. I'll be listening."

And so the girl, who would one day be a great warrior, wrapped her blanket closer around her, looked into the fire, and began again. But before she started, she said, "Father Scraps, I'm going to put you in the story tonight."

"Me?" Scraps asked from out of the darkness. "An old man?"

"I'm going to make you a young man again," she said.

"Ah, good," he said, his hoarse, high-pitched voice sounding pleased. "Oh, to be young again. And tonight is my chance."

Chapter 8

And so, while the desert night reached for her with its chill and the stars swirled overhead, the girl continued her story:

"The tall man dressed in the black robe and the pointed hat disappears into the darkness, into the crowd, dragging his leg behind him. Eager townspeople, chanting 'Burn the demon boy! Burn the demon boy!' carry flaming torches up to the Tree of Judgment and throw them on the tinder-dry wood that has been stacked around Dag-gar. In a few moments, the small, individual fires join together to form a single large one, and then this fire rises up toward the boy, the flares of the blaze reaching for the edges of his ragged clothes.

"Dag-gar has no strength left to struggle against the ropes that bind him to the blackened trunk of the Fire Tree. He can only stare at the flames, feeling first their warmth and then their heat; he can only watch as the flames crawl onto his bare feet and touch the bottom of his pants. He is aware of a roaring in his ears, as if he were at sea again and the wind has come up strong and is ripping through the ship's rigging. He looks upwards into the sky now black with night, and sees the stars that he knows so well. As he watches them, he imagines that they are moving toward him. Descending from the vastness of space, they begin to dance around him, swirling and whirling and moving through him, and so, instead of the fire's agony, he feels only the coldness of the universe and then he is traveling among the stars, free of his bonds, flying and swirling with them."

* * * * *

He heard a voice, a hoarse, high-pitched male voice. The swirling stars disappeared as if instantly sucked away. When they were gone, there was nothing but darkness.

"Ha! Boy! Come, come now! Open up those eyes! Take a look around! 'Tis a fine morning, indeed!"

Dag-gar did as he was told. He saw the source of the voice: a young man, a very tall and awkward looking young man, with a thin beard, a big nose, and a tiny chin, wearing a hat with a wide, floppy brim and a baggy tunic and brocaded boots whose tasseled tips curled upwards and backwards. And this clothing, all if it—the hat and the robe, and the boots—had been stitched together from small rags of every imaginable color. He was leaning on an intricately carved walking stick that was as long as he was tall.

Behind the man, Dag-gar saw the town square, its air and hard-packed earth rosy with morning light. It was empty of the chanting, tormenting crowd that, it seemed, just moments before had been screaming for his death. Only a small, scabrous-looking dog wandered across it, sniffing here and there at the scraps of food that had been left behind.

"My name is Scrapius, though I'm usually called Scraps," the strange young man went on, "and this is my lucky day. I must say, *a very lucky day*."

Dag-gar looked down. The fire was out. All the wood had burned; not even a wisp of smoke curled up from the cold ashes. He saw that his feet were blackened and, moving his eyes up from there, he noticed that he was naked, his clothing having been burned away, yet his skin, though blackened with ash, had been left untouched by the flames.

"Yes, lad," the stranger went on, "you are a sky-clad youth, it would seem. Bare as a winter branch, naked as a worm. You see, the bitter flames consumed your meager garments while doing you no harm at all. A wondrous event, to be certain.

"And that is the fine irony in all this demon burning: Had you gone up in smoke with your shirt and pants, you would have been guilty of being one—a demon. Yet, for the good people of Port O' Rue, even though you were not being roasted meant that you were innocent, you were then more terrifying than ever, because, you see, it would take a very powerful magic indeed to protect you from the conflagration they set about you."

The young man who called himself Scraps laughed and said, "You should have heard the silence once the mob realized the flames would not consume you! You should have seen the panic of their departure from this burning town square as they all ran home to lock their doors. They are certain you shall seek some sort of divine retribution for their sins—and I'm not so sure you shouldn't."

He paused and then said, "Well, come on down from there, my boy. Walk away from that awful scorched tree and come with me. We have things to talk about. I have a proposition for you. You see, I'm quite serious when I say this is a very lucky day for me."

Dag-gar now realized that the ropes that had bound him tightly to the tree's trunk were no longer there. They had been burned away with his clothes. He took a small, tentative step, felt nothing holding him back, and then rushed forward toward

Scraps. When he reached his side, he stopped and looked back at the Fire Tree, and then at the young man.

Still he could not speak but watched as the man took a small cloth pack from his shoulder, from it removed a tunic and a pair of trousers, stepped away from Dag-gar, sized him up, and said, "These should fit you well enough. Of course, it would be nice to get you cleaned up before you put on these excellent silk garments." He paused, looked around, and said, "Ah! There is the town well. Let's have a bath."

Scraps led Dag-gar across the common to the well. He dropped the bucket into the well, heard it splash, and began cranking it up. When the bucket reappeared at the top of the well, it was brimming with water. "Stand still now, my friend, and I'll sluice this over you." Dag-gar held his hands out from his sides and allowed Scraps to pour the bucket of water over his head.

With the soot and filth washed away and without bothering to dry off, Dag-gar took the clothes from Scraps. They were the finest clothes he had ever seen, their smoothly woven blue and red colors gleaming in the morning light. As Dag-gar dressed, Scraps kept talking in his hoarse voice.

"You see, lad—uh, what is your name then?"

"Dag-gar," the boy said, his voice sounding hollow and far away.

"Dag-gar," Scraps repeated, "a good strong name. So, Dag-gar, let me explain to you why I see our meeting up like this as such good fortune, for you as well as for me."

He cleared his throat. "I, me, Scrapius, am nothing less than a wizard—a sorcerer, a conjurer. And what do wizards do? What is our purpose? Well, we wander about the countryside offering our services to the weak and the weary, the poor and the wretched, the hopeless and helpless, as well as the cowardly. You see, wizards are, in a way, warriors." With a swift movement he pulled back his robes and revealed a long sword in a scabbard at his hip. With another swift movement he withdrew the blade, pointed the tip of it toward the sky, and then swung it through the air in a great arc.

There was a swooshing sound as the blade cleaved the air, leaving behind a trail of blue flame. Dag-gar reflexively ducked. "Not to worry, my lad!" Scraps said. "While I have the ability to pluck a single hair from your head with this fine weapon, neither would I harm a single one. That's not the way we wizards work."

He looked at Dag-gar and smiled, revealing a mouth full of large, crooked, white teeth. "Now, my boy, you must finish dressing." With the tip of the sword, he pointed to a pair of blue brocaded silk boots and a brimless hat of the same material that lay on the ground near where they were standing. "Put those on, my friend, and we'll be the team we were always meant to be.

For you shall be my assistant, nay, even my apprentice. Perhaps one day you will be a wizard, for I noticed that on your chest you bear the Mark of the Universe—the brand of Forever. Whether you know it or not, you are someone special."

Dag-gar did as he was told and Scraps looked him over. "Excellent," he said, "and I might add that, considering what torments you have been through, you look fine indeed. Though, when we get back to my camp I'll put a poultice on those scrapes and bruises—for, being a wizard, I am of course, a skilled physician—a medicine man of the first order."

With that, the man swung around, waved his arm to signal that Dag-gar was to follow him, and began walking across the deserted town square. Dag-gar caught up with him and, walking next to him, said, "I should like to find my ship, the *Mother-of-Pearl*. My father is her captain."

Scraps stopped, looked down at the boy, and said, "I'm afraid that what the townspeople told you about the *Mother-of-Pearl* is all too true. While she was a vessel that called here often, and was a good and honest ship at that, the last time she was in the harbor of Port O' Rue was just before the volcano blew its own head off and smothered this town in hellfire and brimstone." He paused and added, "And legend has it that it sank the good ship *Mother-of-Pearl*—and that terrible event occurred some three hundred years ago."

He continued walking. "So, Dag-gar, while you and I know your tale to be true, it was impossible for the people of this town to accept it unless you were indeed a demon or a sorcerer or a magic boy of some sort."

"But," Dag-gar said, his voice now rising in its frustration, "I was just on the *Mother-of-Pearl*! Just—just a little while ago!"

"Well, of course you were," Scraps said, "and that's because you are a Time Drifter. In this swirling, twirling, whirligig thing we call Time, the *Mother-of-Pearl* is still out there sailing about, your father still the captain, for there is no beginning nor any end to things. But now you are here in this particular Time-flow eddy, not the one where the *Mother-of-Pearl* hangs out."

Dag-gar stopped walking. "I—I—I don't understand anything you are saying. I just want to be with my father again."

Now Scraps stopped too, turned around and looked back at Dag-gar. He sighed. "Yes, of course you would. Everyone would like to see their father again. Even I would like to see my father and I never did lay eyes on him at all. In fact—and this is a secret, so don't tell anyone—I may never have even *had* a father.

"But I know what your problem is. Your problem is that you, Dag-gar, are being followed by one of those pesky Time Vagabonds.

You remember that skinny, dark fellow with the bum leg? It was he who pulled you out of the Time-Eddy where you were and threw you into the Time River—he was rowing you along in the main channel that night—and now, here you are, in this Time-Eddy, having drifted quite a ways down the River."

"But why would he do that to me?" Dag-gar asked.

"Because it is his nature. That's what he does, that's what all Time Vagabonds do. They attach themselves to poor, unsuspecting souls and set about disrupting their lives, causing problems, big and small, causing grief and mayhem, on and on, *et cetera, et cetera*, to include the gnashing of teeth and the pulling of hair."

The boy looked up at Scraps with moist eyes—moist, though there were no real tears—and asked, "Why did he attach himself to me?"

Scraps turned away and began walking again. "An excellent question," he said, taking big steps now, and not looking back. "Time Vagabonds cannot exist unless they are attached to someone, you see. They are parasite shadows, really. Without you, he'd be gone in an instant—pop!—leaving nothing but a wisp of smoke and the faint echo of his departure. So, as you can imagine, he clings to you, holds on tight, doesn't let go, ever."

Dag-gar looked about himself—his legs and arms—and saw nothing. Scraps, walking and looking straight ahead, seemed to somehow have seen what the boy had done.

"Oh, don't bother looking for him," he said. "He's not riding on your back, not peering out of one of your pockets, not hanging on to one of your legs—nor is he buzzing about inside one of your ears as people so often think. No, he's just *there,* that's all. *Just there.* Like a headache or a bad attitude."

By this time they had left the town square and were walking along the same busy street Dag-gar had been on before. There again were the men and women selling their wares from stalls—the same applemonger, the same fishmonger, the spice man, the tinker, the candlemaker. But now they did not recognize the boy in the blue silk tunic and brimless hat as the one they had so lately stoned and dragged along the street to the square. Instead, recognizing wealth when they saw it, they called out, "Hey, now! Here they are, the best spices this side of the ocean-sea! Make that lamb stew you'll have tonight taste fit for a bishop!"

Dag-gar looked at them and heard his stomach growl. Scraps seemed to have heard it, too. "Ah, I'll bet you're hungry, then. So, we have a bit of a walk to my camp. Shall we have something to munch on? Look at that fish, cooked to a crisp."

He stopped, took some coins from the pocket of his tunic, and bought a whole mackerel that had been roasted on a stick. He handed it to Dag-gar, who studied it for a moment and then began to stuff it into his mouth, chewing hungrily and spitting bones out onto the street. And so they progressed through the town of Port 'O Rue, Scraps in the lead, talking constantly and stopping occasionally to buy something for Dag-gar to eat: a small loaf of black bread, a jar of honey, a haunch of meat.

When they finally came to a tavern, Dag-gar saw him: the tall, thin man in the black robe, the same who had bidden the people of the town to set him afire—Captain Sorrow. As Dag-gar watched, he pushed his way through the tavern door, dragging his leg behind him.

"There he is!" Dag-gar yelled. "Captain Sorrow! He's got the Amber Teardrop. He stole it from my father, and without it my father cannot navigate his ship!"

Before Scraps could stop him, Dag-gar was running after Captain Sorrow. A moment later, he had pushed his way in through the tavern's big door and disappeared.

Inside, there was a large, single room. A dark place, it reeked of wood smoke and tobacco, candle wax, cooking meat, stale beer, sour wine, and old sweat. Men holding mugs of beer sat around tables, smoking pipes and talking, while a heavy-set woman of middling age ran about serving them. Behind a counter, a huge man with a full gray beard and a flattened nose filled the mugs with beer from a tap set in the bung of a barrel and lined them up for the woman to grab.

When the door slammed behind Dag-gar, the tavern fell silent; suddenly he found himself the object of all the drinkers' attentions. With all eyes on him, he said, "I'm looking for the man who just came in through this door. He is a thief who has stolen something of great value."

"We've seen nobody come through that door but you, pretty boy," a man with food smeared in his beard said, his voice coarse and mocking, the words slurred. Dag-gar, used to the company of rough sailors, did what he had learned to do: he ignored him. He was, after all, the son of a ship's captain, and no sailor had ever dared do anything worse then taunt him.

The man looked him up and down and added, "And yer wearing a lovely silk costume there, boy. Where'd yer come from, then? Inside a rainbow, would be my guess."

Loud laughter burst from both the speaker and those around him. Dag-gar did not answer, but began to move backwards toward the door. Then he heard the crash of a stool falling over and felt a rush of air, followed by a powerful hand grabbing him by the back of his neck.

"Yer a bold and bothersome youth!" another voice said in a foul breath not an inch from his ear, "and I suppose that because yer rich and can wear silky clothes, yer thinkin' yer better than the rest of us, hey?"

Then Dag-gar felt the door open behind him and he heard Scrap's high-pitched hoarse voice. "Unhand him, you rascal, or I shall be forced to cleave your filthy body into two equal halves! And I shall not hesitate to do so!" He heard another crashing of barstools and a loud clattering of metal hitting the floor.

Dag-gar twisted his head around in the man's grip and saw Scraps sprawled on the tavern's rough, wooden floor. His sword, having been knocked from his grasp, lay just beyond his reach. There was much laughter from the drunken onlookers eager for such small entertainments.

But it all ended quickly. The big man behind the bar was out on the floor in a trice, clutching a thick wooden club, and in a moment he had thwacked Dag-gar's attacker smartly on his back, sending him running for the door. There was a general rush of patrons suddenly anxious to be out of the place; in a moment only Dag-gar and Scraps remained.

"You, too!" the big tavernkeeper yelled. "Get out before I knot yer's heads up good and proper, rich or not!"

Scrapius had recovered his sword, but his hat had been trampled by many boots. He now grabbed it from the floor and, taking Dag-gar by the hand, led him out the open door.

Once outside and squinting in the sunlight, Scraps dusted himself off, slid his sword into its scabbard, and said, "Now there's a lesson for you, lad. You'll need my protection until you learn how to fend for yourself. Nonetheless, we are a team, are we not? We cleaned out that nest of riffraff in short order before they could cause some real trouble. And having done so, my boy, it's time to be gone from this place. There is a world out there that needs our services." So saying, Scrapius turned on his heels and marched on along the street.

After a while, they had left the houses and shops behind and the street had become a road that led across a field and into a green forest whose canopy of branches formed a vaulted roof blocking out the sun. Within this cool and gloom, Scraps finally stopped, pointed to a narrow path that disappeared into the trees, and said, "Here we are then, at last—my camp."

He led the way in. After a few paces they emerged into a small, sunny meadow carpeted with green grass and small blue and pink flowers. On the far side of the meadow Dag-gar could make out a shelter, a tent made of the same multicolored patchwork cloth as Scraps' tunic and hat. The middle and the corners of this tent had been tied to the branches of the overhanging trees; underneath, it was completely open—one could simply duck his head and walk under it and be protected from the sun and rain.

Scraps spread his arms and said, "So, this is my home on the road. I suggest we pass the day and tonight resting here. We'll get a good night's sleep, and on the morn, begin our search—our quest."

He hesitated and after Dag-gar said nothing, added, "And what, then, you might ask, would we be searching for? What is our quest?"

Finally Dag-gar shook his head. "I don't know," he said.

"A horse and rider!" Scraps said, as if it were both the most obvious and most exciting thing in the world. "Yes, a horse. A stallion, to be precise, a marvelous stallion. And its equally marvelous rider. That, my boy, is what we shall discuss over our evening fire."

"I don't know anything about a horse and rider. I need to find *him*," Dag-gar said.

"Find him? Who's him?" Scraps asked.

"Captain Sorrow. He has the Amber Teardrop. I have to return it to my father so he can find his way across the ocean-sea."

"Oh, now, young Dag-gar," Scraps said, scratching his head, "I have a sudden suspicion that our two quests are intertwined. That is, when we find the horse and rider, we will find Captain Sorrow and when we find Captain Sorrow, we shall find the horse and rider, and only then can we return the Amber Teardrop to your father. It is obvious to me now that we cannot do one without doing the other, there being a reason for everything and everything having a reason."

Now Dag-gar turned toward Scraps and grasped his robe with one hand. He caught the taller man's eyes with his own and held them. "I will find him. I will find Captain Sorrow and I will get it back."

Chapter 9

Later, with the flames from their campfire shining in his eyes, Scraps spoke of the horse and rider they sought. His words seemed to get caught up in the heat and smoke as they traveled across the flames to Dag-gar's ears. The youth, well fed and wrapped in a silk robe, struggled to stay awake even though he was sitting up and looking directly into Scraps' eyes.

"Let me tell you about the wonderful pair we are seeking," Scraps said breathlessly. "'Tis a great and grand stallion and on his back, riding him eternally, a fierce young woman. Oh, they are a magical pair like no other! The horse has red amber eyes and a thick coat of shiny blue, and the proud woman warrior has hair the color of the sun and eyes the color of a hot summer sky. That, my boy, is our quest. We must find them.

"And let me tell you why: I have it in my knobby, wizardly head, based on recent coincidences and strange events, that she and you and you and she are meant to be together—together forever and ever. And longer than that, even. If fact, if my intuitions are correct, you already have been together for longer than forever."

He winked knowingly and set about stuffing a pipe with fragrant tobacco. He lit it in his usual way—with a flame from the tip of a finger—while he waited for Dag-gar to respond to the remarkable statements he had just made. With smoke rising and floating about his head, he sighed with pleasure and settled back against his small bedroll.

It was then, through his sleepiness and the thin veil of smoke and fire and before he could respond to Scraps' wild imaginings, that Dag-gar saw something white emerge from around the back of Scraps' neck. He realized it was a tail, a cat's tail, snow white and full. And then, as he watched, and as Scraps spoke, apparently oblivious to its presence, the entire cat appeared from over his shoulder, looked into Dag-gar's eyes with its own blue ones, and then slid down the front of Scraps' tunic and disappeared up one of his sleeves.

Scraps continued talking as if nothing had happened. When Dag-gar did try to speak, he could not utter a word. Nor could he raise his hand to point. He could only watch and listen.

"And that," Scraps said, giving up on the idea that Dag-gar would respond, "was why it was my very lucky day to find you. You see, when I came into this rat's nest of a town the other day, and while enjoying a cool beer at that tavern that sits just off the town square, I couldn't help but notice the ruckus that was just then beginning.

"Taking my mug with me—it had just been filled and I was loath to leave it for some scoundrel to drink for me—I ventured out into the street. And lo, what should I behold? A youth, dressed in a sailor's filthy rags, being dragged by a rope down the cobbles of the street and across the town square. That, of course, was you.

"Being a wizard, as I mentioned, I was curious as to whether or not this was a situation that required my services. The poor boy was entirely at the mercy of the mob. So, remaining apart from the crowd, I became a very interested observer. I watched as they took their whacks at him, as they popped this boy with rotten fruit and an occasional stone, and then tied him up to their so-called Tree of Judgment—the Fire Tree.

"I enquired of a passerby what this terrible small storm was about. 'Well, sir,' he said, 'the boy is a demon, for sure! He claims to have been on the *Mother-of-Pearl*. Imagine! A ghost ship that sailed these waters ages ago!'

"What's to become of him, then?" I asked.

"The *truth* is what shall become of him, sir," the man said. "And burning on the Tree of Judgment shall the truth reveal!"

"How so?" I asked.

"If he burns to ashes," the man told me, "he was obviously deserving of it and so, was a demon. If he survives unscathed by the flames, it means that the Tree of Judgment, the only living thing to survive the hellfire and brimstone that came from our mountain these many ages ago, protected him and he is innocent."

"Yes, yes, of course," I said, "I understand the simple logic of this method. Clever of the wise men of this town to devise such a test. Ingenious, really."

As Scraps related this tale, Dag-gar watched the white cat appear again, and again Scraps seemed to be unaware of its presence. This time it came out from the sleeve it had gone into, climbed up his arm, and disappeared around the back of his neck from whence it had first appeared. Again Dag-gar tried to speak, but could not utter a syllable.

"This is when I realized that I might have something here," Scraps continued. "That *you* might be the one for whom I have been waiting so I could fulfill my quest. The problem with that, of course, was it was necessary for me to let them set fire to you."

Scraps puffed his pipe, looked up at the stars, and gazed back into the fire. Dag-gar was so close to sleep and so entranced with the scene before him that he could not move at all. He felt the beating of his heart in his temples and heard the roaring of his breath in his ears. The words Scraps spoke seemed to become visible shadows floating across the fire.

"Alas," Scraps said, "a pity! I had to watch as they tied you to that black trunk and stacked the wood up. I finally could not tolerate it a moment longer and was about to come to your rescue. After all, you could have been just a poor, confused street urchin about to suffer the flames of outrageous fortune. But then I saw him—your *Time Vagabond*! That man dressed in the black robes who came from the darkness and spoke to you. What did you say his name was? Captain Sorrow? That was him, boy, that was him! Of course, I did not realize that at the time. Oh, if only I had known. I could have dealt with him then and retrieved the Amber Teardrop, too.

"In any event, I waited. I held my breath, and I waited. I watched the fires be set, I watched the flames climb and lick and lap at you, I watched as the inferno rose up around you—and then, miracle of miracles, I watched as you emerged from it, as pure as new steel, immaculate, vestal, virginal, cleansed of any further suspicions.

"And, of course, I watched with pleasure as that would-be killer mob realized what had happened and fled in terror—in terror of the very thing they had just proved was innocent. Imagine the irony! The rest, of course, you remember."

Scraps puffed on his pipe and the sounds of the night descended over them. An owl hooted, a dog barked, a cat howled, insects chirruped, and from somewhere in town, music drifted outward into the surrounding forest.

Despite his best efforts to stay awake, Dag-gar had finally fallen asleep sitting up, his chin resting on his chest. Scraps, however, did not seem to notice this any more than he had noticed the white cat crawling over his body.

"So," he continued, speaking to the sleeping youth, "why then, do I think you are the one I've been waiting for? Well, because after the fire, when your clothes had been burned away, I saw upon your chest the small discoloration that marks you for what you are—a Metacephala, a small god wandering through Time and tasked with keeping an eye on this mortal and deeply flawed human race. In fact, you're the same as I am and so, as I have said, we will be a team. A pair of Metacephalas! We go together like beer and sausage, bread and honey, mountains and sky."

Dag-gar, however, heard not a word of this. Instead, he slowly tipped over onto his side, his head coming to rest on a clump of grass. Scraps sighed, muttered, "Poor boy, poor boy." He stood up and covered the lad with a brocaded silk blanket and then returned to his pipe and the fire. "Ah, well then," he said softly, "you've had a rough enough time of it." He took a wineskin from inside his robe, pulled the bung out with his teeth, nodded at the sleeping boy, and said, "So, then, lad and fellow Time Drifter, here's to the fair adventure of tomorrow." Lifting the wineskin, he took a practiced aim and sent a thick stream of red wine shooting into his mouth.

* * * * *

Later Dag-gar knew he must have been dreaming—yet it was far too real to have been a mere dream: He heard the soft voice again, the same wonderful, bell-like voice that had awakened him in his cabin on the ship that night; then, he again felt a tug on his sleeve. "Come," the voice insisted, "come now. You must see this."

He opened his eyes. It was a dark night. The fire had burned itself out and he could smell the wisps of smoke from the ashes. Nearby was the long, lumpy form of Scraps asleep under his blanket, and above him, as if they were calling to him, was a heaven full of stars. He immediately recognized the pattern of the great Scorpion with its curling stinger tail. He saw the great red star that was the heart of this celestial creature, and its color and size made him gasp, for it seemed near enough to reach out and touch.

The voice called to him again. "Come, Dag-gar, before it's too late."

Yet, as on the ship that night, he could not see who was saying these words, could not see who was pulling at his sleeve so insistently. Only a gossamer white shadow seemed to hang in the night air next to him. He knew the voice, though: It was that of the white cat, Sonoria. There was no mistaking that.

"Where are we going?" he whispered.

"Over there," the voice answered, "just over there beyond that red star."

Dag-gar pulled back from her. "That's the Scorpion, you know," he said, "we should not go near it. Though it can't help it, it is the Scorpion's nature to—"

"Never mind," the voice interrupted, "as long as we stay close together we will be safe."

Dag-gar stood up and felt the familiar small hand take his. The fingers of the hand were cool and soft, yet their grip was strong. It pulled him along and he followed, though he could see nothing but the stars.

"Are you my cat?" he asked.

"Yes, yes," the voice answered. "And much more than that, too. Just as on the ship. I am Sonoria."

"Are we in danger again?"

"No. I'm going to show you something wonderful. Come with me before it's too late."

With the gossamer shadow leading him, he walked blindly into the night. After a few steps he felt the darker shadows of the trees, and with his other hand, he pulled aside unseen branches.

"Now," the voice said, "open your eyes."

"But they *are* opened," he answered.

"No, no they are not. I mean, really open them. Really *see* with them."

Dag-gar took his hand from hers and rubbed his eyes with his fists. He was about to say that he did not know what she meant, but when he took his hands away, it was no longer dark. It was as if what he now beheld was shining outward from his eyes themselves.

He saw that he was standing on the top of a mountain. He felt the cold wind and saw swirls of snow, and when the snow cleared away he saw, far, far below him, a great valley. It stretched out nearly forever, its green floor checkered with farms and forests. In the distance, on the other side, he saw more mountains, mountains with sharp peaks covered with snow.

He turned to look at she who had led him here, at the white cat, Sonoria. But she was gone. He was alone. Behind him he saw, in the side of the mountain, an ice cave, and from the blue mouth of the cave there was music flowing, a river of sound carried on a white fog that washed over him and pulled at him as his cat, Sonoria, had pulled him from his bed.

He looked down at himself and saw he was no longer a fourteen-year-old boy; he had become a man, a tall man dressed in a thick woolen tunic and leggings and a heavy shirt made of the skin of a sheep. He carried in one hand a long bow and on his back a quiver of arrows. At his side, in a scabbard, was a sword.

The music called to him. He followed it into the ice cave, through a narrow tunnel and then into a large chamber. As he passed into the chamber, the music died away with the white fog, diminishing until it became just the wind's low howling. In the center of the chamber he saw a large pedestal made of ice crystals and on the pedestal, encased in the same ice, were the bodies of two people.

He approached them. He could see them clearly, lying close to each other, their brocaded silk boots, their ermine robes, their hands folded across their chests—and then he saw that the bodies had no heads, that lying on ermine pillows where the heads should have rested were two gold crowns inset with amber cut in the shape of teardrops.

He heard a noise behind him. He spun around and saw, standing in the mouth of the cave he had just passed through, a very tall old man leaning on a long walking stick. He had a large nose and a gray, scraggly beard, and he wore a large hat with a wide, floppy brim, and a tunic sewn together from rags of many colors.

"Who are you?" Dag-gar heard himself ask.

"Oh," the old man said in a hoarse, high-pitched voice, "you know very well who I am. But are you not curious who *they* are?"

The old man raised his walking stick and pointed it at the pedestal of ice with its twin burdens. Dag-gar turned and again looked at the ermine-clad bodies frozen in the ice. He shook his head no but, instead, heard himself whisper, "Yes. I would like to know who they are."

The old man lowered his stick, leaned on it again, and said, "Good, and so now you understand our quest."

"Quest?" Dag-gar said, "I don't know what you mean. Who are you?" Then he looked back at the ice coffin. "And you didn't tell me who they are."

But when he turned again and looked back at the entrance of the cave, the old man was gone. Dag-gar ran back out the tunnel, back out into the mountain air, but the man had disappeared. Instead, some distance from him, standing on gravel moraine left behind by retreating glaciers, was a horse—a wonderful stallion with a blue roan coat and amber eyes that gleamed in the sunlight. Sitting on the back of the horse was a young woman, a young woman with wild, white-blond hair who wore, as he himself wore, a woolen tunic and a sheepskin shirt.

She had her sword out and was swinging it over her head and he could see her mouth moving as if she was yelling something at him but he could hear nothing. A moment later, they were charging toward him, the horse's breath steaming from his nostrils, the woman raising her sword above her head and swinging it down on him.

* * * * *

Dag-gar sat up and took in everything in an instant: He was in Scraps' camp where he had fallen asleep. It was early morning, the fire was out, everything was wet with dew. He heard Scraps' voice yelling a warning: "Watch out there, lad, we've been discovered by highwaymen! Prepare to do combat!"

Dag-gar heard horses, then saw them approaching from the road that led into the forest. There were three of them, each ridden by a man with a drawn sword. They were cantering easily toward the camp, but their intentions were obvious.

He again heard Scraps' voice and now he turned and saw the wizard calling to him from the thick trees that bordered the camp. "Come here, quickly!" he beckoned. "We must hide away here in the forest. Let them have what they want."

Dag-gar looked back at the riders, whose bearded faces wore grim smiles. Behind him, he heard Scraps' voice again. "Come on, boy, or they'll gladly relieve your shoulders of the burden of your head!"

But Dag-gar found he could not make himself move. As he stood watching the men approach, he felt a strange fire in his heart, a fire that spoke to him with a clear, human voice: *You have taken enough! It is time to give something back. You will not cry ever again, nor will you surrender—ever again.*

The riders came on. When they were upon him, they pulled up their horses, resting the blades of their swords across the pommels of their saddles in a gesture of deadly arrogance. For a moment there was silence and then the rider in the middle spoke. "Boy," he said, his voice barely above a whisper, "you would have done well to hide yourself in the forest like your cowardly, skinny friend. Now, I'm afraid, it's too late."

Dag-gar heard a strange and distant voice answer the man but it was not Scraps' voice—it was his own. The words came from his own mouth but sounded as if they were resonating from a deep well somewhere behind him. "If you try to kill me, I will kill you. You will leave me no choice."

There was silence again, and then the man in the middle began laughing while the others kept their grim silence. Then the man in the middle motioned to the man to his right and said, "Kill this insolent puppy and let's get on with it."

The man on the right moved suddenly, digging his heels into his horse's ribs. As the animal leaped forward, he raised his sword. But Dag-gar did not wait. Instead of reacting to the man charging at him, he jumped towards the man in the middle, rolled under the belly of his horse, and came up behind him. With another leap, he was sitting on the horse's back, behind the man. An instant later he had pulled the man's own dagger from his belt and had driven it into his neck.

The man tried to shriek but nothing came out of his mouth but blood. He raised his hands and clutched at his throat while

Dag-gar clung to his back and his horse danced in circles. The other two riders watched, mouths agape, as their leader struggled with his wound and the demon boy who had administered it so swiftly.

And while they watched, they missed another quick movement, this one from the forest. A tall, gangly man dressed in multicolored rags ran across the clearing, his thick walking stick raised. Coming up behind one of the highwaymen, he thwacked him hard across the back of his neck, sending him toppling from his horse. And then, before the last rider could react, he was on him, too, and that man went down, hitting the ground hard and lying still.

Dag-gar slid from the back of the horse, and the animal in its panic raced once around the small clearing and then, finding the road out, disappeared down it, his rider still astride and still clutching at his throat.

Chapter 10

"Horses!" Scraps yelled happily. "We have horses! A gift from the Gods. Grab that one there, lad. Be quick about it and let's leave this place before those gentlemen sprawled in the grass recover their senses."

Scraps did not wait for Dag-gar to follow his instructions but ran about the meadow chasing the highwaymen's horses until he had both by their hackamores and was leading them back toward the camp. Never having dealt with horses before, Dag-gar could only stand and watch. When Scraps approached, he took a step backwards.

"What's the matter then, boy? You act like you've never been near a horse before in your life. Here, take this one, I'll make him a present to you. He's a good one, too!"

But Dag-gar took another step back. "I've—I've never ridden a horse," he said.

Scraps looked at him with disbelief. "What's this? Never ridden a horse? Surely you must be joking. You just jumped up on the back of one like a circus rider!" Scraps paused and then said, "But, of course, you have spent the better part of your brief life rolling about the ocean-sea on a ship, then, haven't you."

Scraps looked about the meadow and down at the still-unconscious highwaymen. "Truth is, we have no time now to dilly-dally, even in the face of your understandable sailor-boy ignorance. Here, hold this horse like so." He grabbed Dag-gar's hand and pulled it up to the bottom of the hackamore. "Gather the reins like so, put your foot in this stirrup, and swing your other leg up and over, thus."

Scraps demonstrated, placing a long, silk-booted foot in the stirrup and then, with an ungainly bounce, swinging himself up onto the horse's back. "You see," he said from the vantage point of the saddle, his impossibly long legs hanging down nearly to the top of the grass, "it will take some practice to do it as gracefully as I, for I have had years of practice at the noble art of mounting a horse."

With a great heave of his body, he swung back down and stood next to Dag-gar. He handed him the reins. "Just do what I did, lad. I think you'll find it quite easy. And hurry now. We must be gone from here."

Dag-gar now set about doing what he had seen Scraps do. He took the reins, put a foot in the stirrup, and, facing the rear of the horse, swung his leg up. It worked. In a trice he was sitting atop the animal, a look of wonderment on his face.

"And bravo for you!" Scraps said, raising his hands toward the sky. "You did that like someone born to the saddle. Now, don't do anything else until I get my nag under me."

When they were both mounted, Scraps again looked down upon the men lying in the bright green grass, the yellow and blue flowers of the meadow sticking up incongruously around their bodies. "You would do well to remember this scene," he said. "There is a lesson within the drama of its still life. That lesson, of course, is 'never underestimate your enemy.' Now, let's be off!"

Dag-gar's horse seemed content to follow Scraps' mount as they trotted out of the meadow and down the path to the main road. Dag-gar bounced hard on the saddle and hung onto its pommel with both hands. After a while, Scraps turned around, looked at Dag-gar, and laughed. "Well then," he said, "your brains will be pudding if you keep that up. You must become one with your mount. Try to move with its rhythm, like so. You see, you hang on with your knees. Squeeze the horse between them."

He demonstrated. His elbows stuck out at odd angles and he kept one hand on his head to keep his hat on, but his example was good enough. A moment later Dag-gar seemed to have mastered the rudiments of riding, for his head stopped bouncing up and down and his bottom end no longer loudly flogged the saddle leather.

"Aye," Scraps yelled back at him, "that's the idea. You're a natural, as sure as I'm born. Whoever said sailors can't learn to ride horses? Ha ha! Sea horses, I suppose, is what you're used to. All these years you've been mucking about under the waves on the back of a sea horse!"

* * * * *

All that day and into the early evening they rode hard, traveling away from the sea and up into the hinterland that rose steadily from the littoral. By the time the sun was reddening and nearing the tops of the distant, wooded hills, Dag-gar felt at home in the saddle, though his legs and bottom parts were chafed and raw.

Finally, Scraps pulled his horse up. "Now," he said, "look there. What every weary traveler hopes to find at the end of an arduous day on the trek."

Dag-gar followed Scraps' gaze. Not far off the narrow road he saw a small valley, tucked down among the bottom of some low hills, and in the middle of that valley, a clearing that contained a barn and a small stone house, from whose chimney came a steady stream of smoke.

"It's a simple farm, would be my guess," Scraps said, nodding. "There we shall find a simple farmer and his equally simple wife; a simple child, maybe three; a milch cow, certainly, or at least a milch goat." He sighed at the vision of it all and went on. "There will be a loaf—probably two—of dark bread, and a pie cooling— at least one—on the window sill, a rack of mutton or some such succulence in the oven, and," he added, smacking his lips, "a keg of stout, perhaps—a simple farmer's beer is what I'm talking about."

His eyes seemed to grow misty at this thought. He slumped his shoulders and again sighed a heavy sigh. "Dag-gar, my boy," he said, "might I suggest we inquire as to the possibility of passing a pleasant evening wallowing in this uncomplicated joy?"

Dag-gar, who was standing in his stirrups to relieve the pain throbbing in his bottom, said, "Bread and mutton? Do you think they'll have bread and mutton, both?"

"Oh," Scraps answered, "I should think so. At least I cannot think of a single reason why they would not have both bread and mutton. And perhaps some gravy." He turned in his saddle and studied Dag-gar. "You would like that, wouldn't you? A growing boy like yourself? So, then," he yelled out to the valley itself, "here we come!"

But reaching the farm was not to be so easy. The way down immediately turned steep and narrow and then became both steeper and narrower, until finally they were forced to dismount and lead their horses as the animals picked their way down a rocky path. After an hour of this, when it seemed that they must somehow try to turn around and retreat back up the trail, they began to hear a roaring sound, as if a great dragon were blasting the air with its fiery breath.

A few steps later, the trail widened onto a small clearing and the source of the sound became clear: Where the trail stopped there was a deep gorge, down whose middle ran a torrent of water that crashed and tumbled over large boulders and sent a constant mist upward so that the rocks and trees that bordered the clearing were black with mold and lichens and dripping wet.

"Oh, the rotten luck of it," Scraps said, walking to the edge of the gorge and peering down into it. "I should have known.

Paradise awaits on the other side, yet, as is typical of any paradise, it is impossible to reach."

No sooner had he spoken these words than they heard another voice, a voice that perfectly mimicked Scraps himself, though the words came not from Scraps' mouth, but from the surrounding rocks. "La, la! Weary travelers," it said, "you would, then, cross this most violent of streams and sup with the Mother Goddess and her hunter husband?"

The source of the voice was not immediately apparent, for the sound of the water was nearly overwhelming.

"Who is that speaking?" Scraps demanded, casting his gaze about. "Where are you?"

"Away here," the voice said, "away from the obnubilation of the fog."

"Away from what?"

"Away from the befogging fogginess, the damp wetness, the miserable mistiness. 'Tis a constant sorrow, believe me."

Scraps threw up his hands. "I'm sorry, sir, but I cannot see you."

"Matters not, see me or not," the voice said, "for your only concern is to find a way across the rushing abyss before nighttime falls over us."

Scraps and Dag-gar looked up at the sky. They had forgotten the passage of time in their struggle to descend the path and now saw that it was nearly sunset.

"Yes, 'tis true, my fatigued friends," the voice said, "you really should find a way across the rushing torrent before the sun finds its way down to wherever it is it goes each evening. You see, where you are now is a miserable place, indeed, to pass the dark hours, it being cold, and damp, and filled with the gloomy spirits of those who have died here—and there are many, believe me."

"Died here?" Scraps said. "Died here doing what?"

"Why, trying to get across to Paradise, of course."

Scraps again peered over the edge of the chasm and quickly drew back. He looked at Dag-gar, who stood holding the reins of his horse. Dag-gar's robe was soaking wet and water was beginning to drip from the brim of his hat.

"Such a state of affairs," Scraps said, finally. "We can't go up, we can't go down, we can't get across, and we are being taunted by an elemental spirit—who sounds just like me, to boot. What to do?"

Now Dag-gar moved close to the edge and peeked over. When he looked back at Scraps, he was smiling. "I think," he said, "we need only take that bridge across. The trail will lead us directly to it."

Scraps eyes widened. "Whatever are you talking about?" he asked. "I'm afraid I don't see what you mean. A bridge? Point it out to me, exactly."

As they both gazed over the edge, they heard Scraps' own disembodied voice again, somewhere behind them. "La, la!" it said. "Some see it and others do not. What the difference is between those who do and those who do not, I do not know, I cannot say. Only the spirits of the dead know, and you will have to wait until after dark to ask them. And that, of course, is something you really do not want to do. Not worth hanging around for, if you know what I mean."

This time Scraps ignored the voice. "Dag-gar. Please, boy, be certain of what you behold. What is it, exactly, that you see, for I see nothing but raging water."

"There is a bridge," Dag-gar said, pointing. "Just there. A stone bridge with beautiful statues of winged seraphs and flowers all across it. And I just saw my white kitten, Sonoria, go across it. We need only follow her to Paradise. And look, over there is the stone house with the smoke coming from the chimney." He sniffed at the air and added, "And I can smell bread baking."

Scraps squinted at where the boy was pointing, and then he did indeed see the house, the same house they had seen from the top of the trail before they began their descent, the house with the pies and the bread and the mutton with gravy.

"I see the house," he said, "but my dear boy, I cannot for the life of me see the bridge. Are you quite certain you see it? There is a lot of mist billowing around, you know. And what white cat are you talking about? Have you gone mad, lad?"

"Of course he's not gone mad, and of course he's certain," the spirit voice yelled. "Only a fool cannot see it."

Now Scraps was getting angry. "Hold your tongue," he yelled back at the voice, "wherever and whatever you are! You are not dealing with just anyone here, you know. I'm a wizard!"

At this the voice laughed loud and long. "Oh, oh, my friend, I do indeed know exactly and precisely whom I am dealing with. And I should know, because I am dealing with myself—one and the same as me!"

"Confound it!" Scraps yelled, and now he began searching in the cracks of the rocks and behind the tumbled boulders for the source of the voice. "Where are you?" he demanded.

"You only need take a peek in your looking glass to see where I am," the voice said, its tone now definitely taunting. "Have you a looking glass tucked away in your tunic? I would assume your vanity would demand it."

Scraps again threw up his hands in despair and turned toward Dag-gar to ask for his help. But Dag-gar was not where he had been. He had disappeared. The clearing was empty.

Fearing the worst, Scraps ran toward the edge of the gorge and peered over. There, safely on the other side of the torrent, he saw Dag-gar, holding his horse by its hackamore and waving back at him through the rising mist.

For a moment Scraps was speechless and then, finding his tongue, he yelled, "How did you get over there?"

"I followed the white kitten across the bridge!" Dag-gar called back, his voice nearly overpowered by the roar of the swirling, falling water.

This sent Scraps into a fit of frustration. He pulled his hat from his head, threw it on the wet ground, and jumped up and down on it. He shook his fists at the darkening sky and shrieked, "What white kitten? What is happening to me? Am I to believe I am out of my senses? Am I now to understand that I have lost my grip on reality? That my own voice is mocking me, that my own eyes are deceiving me?"

He stopped suddenly, shook his head, and took a deep breath. He picked up his hat, wiped off the wet dirt as best he could, and then again looked carefully over the edge of the cliff. Again, on the other side of the rapids, he saw Dag-gar gazing up toward him. "I'm going to try to follow you," he yelled at the boy. "Just tell me where to step, because, though they must be there, for the life of me I cannot see the white kitten nor the bridge nor the path that leads down to it."

Dag-gar waved back and said something that Scraps could not understand over the tumult of the cascading water.

"What did you say?" he yelled back. "Is the path here?" And then to himself he said, "It must be right here." He was standing on the very edge of the cliff and, keeping his eyes on his feet, he tried to lead his horse along behind him, but the animal would not move. Instead, it reared its head back and pulled away. "Sorry, beast," Scraps muttered, still not looking back at it. "You act as if you see what I see—that there is nothing here at all, no path, no bridge. As if there is just a hundred-foot drop into a deadly turbulence. We both might think we are mad, but the boy crossed it and so shall we!"

He pulled harder on the horse's reins, putting his weight into the effort, but the horse jerked back and Scraps finally turned to eye it. There, sitting astride the animal, was a familiar figure dressed in a black cloak with a hood pulled down low so as to hide its face.

"You!" Scraps yelled, "I should have known. Captain Sorrow, the Time Vagabond. And I face to face with you, finally. Just let me get my hands on you!"

Scraps tried to grab the apparition by his cloak, but the dark rider drove his heels into the horse's ribs and the animal leaped forward, its chest smashing into Scraps' shoulders and sending him backwards over the edge of the gorge. Scraps reached for the horse's head but his hands clawed at thin air, and he could only watch the rearing horse and its black rider grow smaller and smaller as he tumbled downwards into the gorge.

Chapter 11

The small fire was burning low. The camel munched on the twigs of a bramble bush, the sound of its eating, soft and comforting against the night. The girl-child with the white-blond hair, sitting cross-legged, had just finished telling her tale. The old man regarded her carefully.

"So, that's it for me then?" Scraps asked. "I'm out of the story for good?"

The girl gazed up at the sky. Above them, amongst a million other stars, the pattern of the Scorpion wheeled its way around the heavens. For a long moment she looked hard at the red star in the middle of the constellation, as if she were getting her inspiration from its distant energy.

She then peered directly into Scrap's eyes. "For good?" she asked. "You mean forever?"

"Well, no," he said. "I know something about both good and forever, child. Forever is my territory, after all. No, I mean, for the sake of the story. Am I finished? I was rather enjoying being young again—though you could have made me a bit more heroic."

Again the girl gazed up at the night sky, at the Scorpion, as if drawing it down to her, as if commiserating directly with it. There was a long pause during which the old man waited patiently. He knew better than to rush her.

"I think you'll be back," she said, finally, "sometime."

The old man made to stand up, saying as he did so, "I would like to think so, too. The thought of disappearing forever into that cauldron of a river is a bit disconcerting. Where, by the way, do I end up? Because apparently I do survive my fall into the raging water."

The girl smiled at him, which surprised the old man since she was a serious child who smiled very little. "The stars will tell us that, won't they?" she said in her strange, bell-like voice. "Within them is everything that has happened and will happen again—always and forever."

Scraps stood to his full height and said, "I suppose I'll have to be satisfied with that explanation until tomorrow night's episode.

I am almost as curious, though, about what happens to our young hero, Dag-gar. He's followed his white kitten, who bears the same name as you, down an invisible path and across an invisible bridge, taking his horse with him. A substantial bridge made of stone, set about with lovely statues and festooned with flowers, if one is to believe your story, yet a bridge utterly invisible to the young me. And he's left me to deal with his own dark shadow, Captain Sorrow, the Time Vagabond. A bit unfair, I think. Nevertheless, it's your tale and my fate is to just sit and listen." He looked up at the stars. "That Scorpion that's floating around up there is a dangerous character. I'd better prepare myself for what is to come next. Meanwhile, I'll check on our friend the camel and then, to sleep. Another day's journey awaits us on the morrow. Lest we forget, we have our own quest, you know, you and I. And, I suspect, a great quest, too."

* * * * *

All the next day they journeyed, the gangly old man with the scraggly beard, the coarse features, and the ragged, floppy-brimmed, multicolored hat and tunic, and the girl-child with the sun-blond hair and eyes the color of the sky on a summer afternoon. Mostly the old man walked next to the camel, pretending to lead it, though he knew the camel would go where it wanted to go, and was in fact, leading them, for nothing can find its way across the desert like a camel. The girl would mostly ride atop the beast's great humped back, singing softly to herself and looking with no small curiosity at the country they were wandering through.

It was a lovely, strange country, too. Desert, mostly, but the kind of desert that offers visions and colors and untouchable, windswept mysteries that stretch out forever. From high atop the camel's back, Sonoria saw gazelles and lizards, hawks and desert rats, illusions and mirages of swamps and rivers and broad blue lakes that did not exist and never would.

Sometimes she would watch the top of Scraps' head. His hat bobbed and shimmered in the sunlight as he strode along, matching the camel's awkward, tireless gait as though they were an odd pair of twins, one human, the other not, yet both remarkable beasts conjoined by their dependence on endless, ungraceful wandering for survival.

And much of the time, she watched the horizon, sometimes a distant line of jagged, barren rock mountains, other times flat, watery misconceptions—hope where there was no hope, promise where none existed. But she was looking for something she knew was there and would at some time appear. Scraps himself had told her this and, somehow, she knew he was right: If she looked long enough, she would see something wonderful.

This, though, was not to be the day. It passed uneventfully. They plodded on. The sun rose, passed its zenith without celebration, and descended, slowly, toward a torrid, sand-parched reflection of itself. When it was about to bury its red mass again in the burning dunes, the camel began to complain. It stopped, lifted its head, and sang a most pitiful song.

Scraps stopped, looked at the animal's wagging head, and sighed. "Well, Mrs. Camel, friend and familiar, it took you long enough to decide a day was a day. I was ready some time ago. Now we'll have scant daylight left to make our camp and gather ourselves for another night in the wilderness. Yet, we have made good progress. I'm beginning to see signs that we have been heading in the right direction, after all."

He looked up at the girl. "I would think, child, that you are ready to stretch a leg—maybe both—and after that, a good night's rest? And we should take up that tale again from where you left off last night. Shall we find out what happens to the youthful me swallowed up by the river? To the young Dag-gar who followed his white phantom kitten across the phantom bridge? What did he find on the other side in the simple farm house? The bread, the pies, and the mutton with the gravy of Paradise?"

The girl looked down on him with eyes that were both patient and icy, profound and unfathomable. "He will find ever so much more than that," she said as she waited for the camel to finish the complex process of dropping to its knees.

When the beast had settled itself, she swung a leg over in front of herself and slipped off its hump and onto the ground.

"Oh?" Scraps said, "do tell."

"We need a fire," she answered.

"Of course we do," Scraps agreed. "No fire, no tale; no tale, no future; no future, no past. So—we must have a fire." He looked once more at the last fires of the dying sun and set off into the twilight to find the dried bushes that would provide the flames.

Chapter 12

That night, with the fire burning and the eternal stars wheeling overhead in the vastness of the desert sky, and the camel grazing with small satisfaction on the desert's sparse offerings, the girl-child continued her tale, thus:

Dag-gar watches as his friend—for so he has come to look upon the hapless Scraps—tumbles backward through an echoing eternity of air and vanishes into the white froth of the rapids. After that, though Dag-gar watches the surface of the water for a long time, there is no sign of him. Scraps is gone.

Horror-stricken, Dag-gar looks for a path that will allow him to move down along the river and help Scraps, should he manage to survive the tumult of the rocks and crashing water, but there is none, only sheer cliffs impossible to negotiate. He stands and stares in disbelief. One moment Scraps is there, yelling down at him, and the next, he has passed out of existence altogether. And what of the black-cloaked apparition that has appeared astride Scraps' horse and just as suddenly disappears after Scraps falls?

Dag-gar is now aware of how utterly alone he is. It is getting dark. The sound of the roaring water fills his ears, the mist rising from the rapids swirls around him, the black cliffs rise up and become forbidding mountains that tower above him. But when he feels tears begin to well up in his eyes he chastises himself. "You are near a man, now!" he says aloud in a harsh voice. "It is time you act like one! Your father is a brave sea captain who taught you to talk to yourself with words of courage when you needed to be brave. So now *be brave!*"

To his relief, at the sound of his own voice, the fear retreats. He turns away from the river and looks up at the farmhouse standing a ways up the slope where the steep river gorge gives way to a grassy terrace before again becoming forest. *I can get help there,* he thinks. *Someone will help me save Scraps.* Leading his horse, he begins to walk toward the humble structure set back at the far edge of the meadow behind a well-made fence.

As he approaches, he sees chickens pecking and scratching in the yard and hears a rooster crowing. A goat, tethered to a stake, eyes him; a donkey, busy eating grass near the goat, his long, hairy ears wagging and his little tail swatting at flies, stops grazing as Dag-gar draws near. The smoke wafting down from the chimney carries the sweet odor of applewood and baking bread.

When he reaches the gate, he stops and examines the house, wondering if he should go into the yard and knock on the door. But no sooner does he pause to think, than the door of the house opens and out steps a woman. Young and very tall and straight, she wears a plain, brown dress. Her long, dark-black hair falls thickly down past her shoulders; her features are strong—her nose arches outward and her deep-set eyes, as black as her hair, sparkle intensely. Dag-gar instinctively wants to bow down before her.

For a long moment he stands with one hand resting on the gate while she stares at him. He is about to speak when she holds up a hand and silences him.

"The supper is still hot," she says. "What's left of it. The sun has already left the tops of the mountains and it will soon be dark as pitch down here in the valley. You can put your horse in the paddock behind the house. Take the goat and donkey with you and put them in the shed. Toss them a little hay from the loft and then let yourself in the back door. And don't forget to bring in an armload of firewood and to take your boots off before you walk into my kitchen. As soon as you're finished, your food will be on the table."

Dag-gar does then bow, and murmurs, "Yes, ma'am. But ma'am, my friend fell in the river. I need to find him and help him. I wonder if you know a way down there past the cliffs?"

She looks at him for a long moment and says, "I am sorry. Pity your poor friend, then. The river is a tragedy where countless lives have vanished." She waves her hand in the air. "There is no saving him, be certain of that. The water disappears into a great hole—a bottomless whirlpool—just down there a ways. No one who has fallen in there has ever again been seen—not in this lifetime, at least." She turns as if to go back inside the house, but stops and says, "We must mourn him, though. Mourn his loss. It is what we humans do. Mourn those we love who have gone down the river. But remember this: mourning is one of the great seeds of wisdom and wisdom is the purpose of life." Then she turns and goes back inside the house, closing the door behind her.

Dag-gar stands transfixed, uncontrolled thoughts racing through his head. He has seen sailors swept overboard in storms, has known them to disappear while on night watches. Then there was a short period of mourning and the incident was recorded in the ship's log. After that, life went on. *This then,* he thinks, *is what I must do. Mourn my friend's death and let my life move on.*

64

Still, he feels weak with the shock of what he has witnessed, for he and Scraps had become great friends traveling up from the sea and into the hills.

Moving as if in a fog, he does his best to follow the woman's instructions. He leads the goat with one hand and his horse with the other and the donkey follows along. They walk around behind the house and find a small barn and a paddock with a watering trough and a hay rack. The donkey and goat walk into the shed of their own accord and Dag-gar shuts the door behind them. He puts his horse in the paddock and takes off its saddle and hackamore. Then he climbs a ladder into the haymow and tosses down a couple of armfuls of hay.

For a moment he sits in the open window of the haymow and surveys the farm before him—a house, a large woodpile, a small barn, a paddock, some pasture, and hayfields with tall haystacks looking like strange creatures born of the fields themselves. Behind him he remembers the dark gorge, the rising mist from the rapids, the sheer cliffs going up and up. He feels a shudder of despair start inside his heart and move through his body, but he fights it, shakes the feeling away. He murmurs to himself, *I am the son of a sea captain.*

At the back door, Dag-gar manages to balance an armload of wood while he pulls his boots off. Then he knocks lightly. A voice says, "Come in, come in."

He lifts the latch and pushes the door open. A great gush of warm air and intense smells greet him, washing over him, rushing into his nose and watering his eyes: spices, onions, baking bread, smoked meats, cheeses, and wood smoke reminiscent of the markets in the ports he has visited all his life. The fragrant richness quickens his heart and makes his mouth water.

He spies the young woman standing at a broad table near a wide hearth on which a pot of stew bubbles. She is kneading bread dough, pressing it down with her hands, folding it over on itself and pressing it down again. Next to her is a loaf of fresh-baked bread and a tub of butter. All around her, from the ceiling rafters, hang haunches of smoked meat, bunches of dried herbs, and cheeses—everything he had smelled.

"We honor the dead with feasting," she says. "Let us honor the loss of your friend. You may sit at the table and cut yourself a slice of that bread and put some butter on it. The stew tonight is rabbit and venison. Last night it was rabbit and venison, too. I suspect tomorrow night it will be the same." She smiles wearily, as if this complaining is a game she plays to amuse herself. "Do you like rabbit and venison?"

"Yes," Dag-gar says, nodding. "Yes, I do. Very much."

"I don't doubt that you would eat a leather shoe in the condition you're in," she says, appraising him with a shrewd eye. "You're a tad thin. And dirty, too. You need a bath. But eat first."

She takes a wooden bowl from a shelf and ladles it full of stew. She carries this to the table and sets it down in front of him and then gets him a spoon. "Go ahead now, cut yourself a slice of bread," she says. "Eat until you are full. Being full is a rare enough thing these days, what with the starvation all around."

Dag-gar cuts himself a thick slice of bread and smears butter across it. He bites off a mouthful and chews while he listens.

"Life is a burden, what with the remembrance of past war and pestilence, the current state of war and pestilence, and the fear of future war and pestilence," she says, and now she sets the dough aside, wipes her hands on her apron, and takes a clay pipe from a pocket in her dress. She stuffs the pipe with tobacco as Dag-gar looks down to get a spoonful of stew. When he looks back up a moment later, the pipe is already lit, though he has seen no taper, no burning straw by which she could have ignited it.

Smoke from the pipe now spirals around her head and the perfume of it reaches Dag-gar's senses, mingling with the stew and the bread and everything else. "But," she goes on, "it is fear, mostly, I think, that gets in people's hearts. Fear makes people do what they do, both good and bad." She pauses and then says, "Don't you think so?"

Dag-gar, chewing hard, tries to think. This woman, young but somehow seeming very old, is someone he has known—but no, he is certain he has never seen her before. He steals a glance at her face, brown from working in the sun, at the calloused hand holding the pipe, the fingers thick from hard labor. Pipe clenched in her teeth, she smiles, still waiting for an answer.

"Yes, ma'am, I suppose you are right," he says, finally, after swallowing.

"Yes," she says, "I suppose I am." She puffs at her pipe and studies Dag-gar unabashedly. He glances at her surreptitiously, then his eyes dart away and he attends to his bowl, making a great deal of getting another spoonful, sensing that she is watching him.

"You reek of it," she says. "Of fear."

Dag-gar looks at her and stops chewing. He sniffs at himself and gazes down at the bowl.

She smiles. "The smell of fear is not there," she says, "not in your armpits, not in your feet. It's here." She touches the front of his chest with her fingers and as she does so, Dag-gar feels a small, sharp burning. "It comes from your heart," she says, "as of course it should. Now, tell me about your friend. What happened?"

"I—I walked across the bridge," he says. "I looked down and saw my white cat going across it—she's just a kitten. Her name is Sonoria. So I followed her."

"I see. And where is your white kitten now?"

"I don't know. She is always disappearing and then, suddenly, there she is again."

The woman smiles. "But that is very much like a cat, isn't it?"

"Yes, I guess it is."

"And your friend?"

"He could not see the bridge. I don't know why. I tried to show him—but he...."

"He fell into the raging torrent," she says.

"Yes—yes. His name was Scraps. He was very good to me. He was a wizard."

"Ha! A wizard, you say? His name again?"

"Scraps."

"Was he kin to you?"

"No. He helped me like a brother, but he was not my kin. I met him down in Port o' Rue after—after my ship..." He stops, not knowing how to explain the unexplainable.

The woman's eyebrows rise and she smiles. "Don't worry. You've been through a great deal and you're but a youth. But now don't stop eating. You'll need your strength. I suspect your adventures are not yet finished."

She watches as Dag-gar puts another spoonful of stew into his mouth. "This man, Scraps," she says, "was he old or young? Tall or short? Tell me about him."

Dag-gar chews quickly and swallows. "He was a man, but he was not old. He was very tall, with long, skinny legs, a scraggly beard, and a big nose. He wore a tunic he'd sewn together from rags of many colors and he had a hoarse voice and he loved to make up jokes and limericks." So saying, Dag-gar feels tears begin to come into his eyes again and he brushes them away with his sleeve.

"That's fine," the woman says, "he deserves to be sent off with sadness. He sounds like the kind of person whose loss should be mourned, but whose life should be celebrated."

The room is lit with brown beeswax candles, but now, after Dag-gar finishes eating, the woman stands up and takes a white candle from a shelf. She holds the wick to the flame of another candle, lights it, and sets it down in front of them. "This," she says, "shall be the candle of his life. Watch it and think of him. It will give his soul some peace as it travels home."

They sit together at the table for a long time, watching the candle burn down until the dying flame sputters in the pool of wax in the bottom of the candle holder.

"We were on a quest," Dag-gar says, breaking the silence. He looks away from the sputtering candle and into the woman's eyes. "That's what he told me. A quest to find a horse, a great stallion who is blue and who has red-amber eyes, and we were to take that stallion to a place where a warrior goddess lives, a place encircled by snowy mountains like an icy crown, a place called the Stratus Valley." He stops, breathless, and looks back into the candle. The flame diminishes, struggles, and then, with a small wisp of smoke, goes out.

Chapter 13

As soon as the candle was out, the woman, who still had not spoken her name, stood up. "There, then, the mourning is finished. Time for your bath."

In the corner of the kitchen sat a large metal tub. Above it, a spout hung down from the ceiling. She walked over to this spout, reached up, and pulled a rope, whereupon water poured from the spout and into the tub. She stepped to the hearth, lifted a large, steaming kettle of water, and poured this hot water into the tub. "Now," she said, "for modesty's sake, I shall avert my eyes while you bathe. And while you make yourself clean, I shall find you clean clothes. Indeed, what you are wearing smacks a bit of wizardry. In fact, you look as if you might have been that wizard's apprentice. Wherever did you come by such multicolored silk robes?"

"Scraps gave them to me. You see, the people of Port o' Rue tied me to the Tree of Judgment and set me afire. All my clothes were burned. After that, Scraps gave me these."

She listened to Dag-gar's tale and then smiled a small smile. "The Tree of Judgment, was it?" she said. "And so it is for all of us. We must all be burned at the Tree of Judgment and we then survive or we perish. Now, into your bath."

She disappeared out the back door and Dag-gar stripped down and slipped into the tub. He lathered himself with the bar of harsh lye soap she had given him and then sat soaking. After a while, her voice came from outside the door. "Enough," she said, "now get out and wrap that blanket around you. I've got something for you."

Dag-gar did as he was told. When the woman came back into the kitchen, he was standing in the middle of the room draped in a long blanket knitted from coarse wool.

She looked at him appraisingly. "You are tall and strong for your age. As big as a man and you shall be a man soon enough," she said. "These should fit you." She held up flannel undergarments, a brown wool tunic with long breeches, and a short supertunic made of tanned sheepskin, reversed so the wool was toward the inside. "There is a pair of hunter's boots for you, too," she said, "good ones with proper soles."

When Dag-gar could only stare in wonder at these gifts, she said, "They are hunter's clothes and should serve a warrior, too. Put them on, then. I'll turn my back. But before you do, let me have a look at your chest."

"At my chest?"

"Yes, boy. I'll do you no harm."

Dag-gar hesitated and then opened the top of the blanket. The woman came close and pulled apart the folds of cloth, exposing him from the waist up. She moved her face even closer and then said, "Ah, just as I thought, the sign of the cosmos. But let's see if it's real or just an anomaly of your birthing."

Raising her right hand, she pointed her fingers at the mark on his chest. Then in a sing-song voice she muttered something Dag-gar did not understand. As the last syllable left her lips, blue sparks flew from the dark constellation on his skin to her index finger. Dag-gar felt a sharp burning and jumped back.

"Yes," she said. "It is as I had hoped."

"What do you mean? What am I—I don't...."

"Your friend the wizard did not bother telling you, hey? Didn't tell you about stars and their constellations? About the Hunter and the Scorpion? But you will learn soon enough. Be strong and be brave and you will fulfill your destiny. Now, get dressed."

When Dag-gar had dressed, she again looked him up and down and said, "One last thing. What is a hunter without his bow? And what is a bow without its arrows? And what is a warrior without his sword?" She moved across the room and opened the lid of a great chest. "Here," she said, "come and take these things."

He moved next to her and looked down into the chest. There, lying in the bottom, were all the things she had spoken of: a long bow, a quiver of arrows, and, under them, a belt with a sword. When he hesitated, she reached in and took out the bow and arrows. "First, the warrior's girdle. Lift it out."

Dag-gar lifted out the belt with the sword. The belt was dark brown leather with the pattern of the cosmos sewn into it with gold thread. It was, he realized, the same pattern as the marks on his chest. Evenly spaced around it, on the sides and in the middle of the back, were two precious stones set in gold, and in the middle, a setting that was empty, its gem gone.

"It is a very special girdle and sword," she said. "It belongs to you, the Hunter. Yet the most precious jewel—a lovely piece of amber in the shape of a teardrop—is missing from it."

Dag-gar stared at the belt, touched the vacant setting, and then looked up at Mar. "I am just a boy from a ship. I'm a sailor, not a hunter. Not at all. Nor am I a warrior. But I'm searching for an Amber Teardrop. I must find it. Captain Sorrow stole it from my father, who is a ship's captain and needs it to steer his ship across the ocean-sea." He stopped himself and then said, "Why are you giving this to me?"

"Because," she said, "despite what you think, you *are* the Hunter. I'm certain of that now. So, it is yours and has always been yours. And therefore, you shall have it." She placed her hands on Dag-gar's shoulders and said, "I have been waiting for you to come to claim it. You say that you are seeking this 'Captain Sorrow' to get the Amber Teardrop back? Then you are on the path to that destiny, and my farm on the edge of this forest was a roadhouse along that path."

"But Scraps said we were on a quest to find the blue, amber-eyed stallion."

"Yes, of course," the woman said, "that's exactly right. The paths of your quests joined together at Port o' Rue, for in truth, your separate quests are indeed one and the same; when you have completed one, you will have found the key to the other."

She leaned forward and kissed him on both cheeks. "Now, you have eaten and bathed and have a blanket, a shelter, soap, a flint and steel for fire making, and new clothes fit for your journey. I have even given you a small sack of gold coins. Sleep in the hayloft, but when you hear the cock start his crowing, be gone from this place."

Dag-gar nodded and said, "I don't know where I shall go."

"When the rooster crows, look up towards the north. You are a sailor and I expect know your stars. Follow the Pole Star, called by some 'The-Star-That-Does-Not-Move.' Keep it on your nose, always."

* * * * *

There was little sleep that night, though the hay was sweet and Dag-gar's exhaustion overwhelming. It seemed that no sooner had he drifted off into fitful dreams than he heard the rooster's first crowing. He sat up and rubbed his eyes. It was still dark, though the late moonlight streamed in through the open door of the loft and struck him full on the face. As if carried on the moonlight, memories flooded back: Scraps falling, falling helplessly, silently, into the terrible water; the vision of the dark apparition of Captain Sorrow sitting triumphantly atop Scraps' horse; the good farmhouse with its unnamed and unearthly mistress who told him he was the Hunter; the sword and girdle with its missing jewel—now the object of his quest.

North, she had said; he must follow The-Star-That-Does-Not-Move. Indeed, he well knew this star used by all ship's navigators to steer across the ocean-sea.

He gathered together all those things she had given him and, as quietly as he could, climbed down from the loft. The rooster crowed again as he slipped the hackamore over his horse's head, and then crowed a third time after he had cinched the saddle on and was opening the gate to the paddock.

It was then that Dag-gar, seeing a light in the farmhouse kitchen and being certain the farm's mistress would be awake, led his horse to the window to thank her again and bid her goodbye. But when he drew closer, he saw that the glass in the window had been broken out, and when he looked inside, he saw an empty room that smelled not of baking bread, stew, and smoked meats, but of dust and mold. The hearth that had been the warm heart of the kitchen was cold and fireless, the roof beams were falling in, the thatch rotted away.

He called out, "Mistress, are you there?

There was no response but the crowing rooster as the dawn overtook the night. Yet the shadows in the house were deep and from them came a scurrying sound, as if the place was now infested with rats.

He called again. "Mistress of this house, are you there? It is I, Dag-gar. I wish to thank you for you many kindnesses—"

Before he could finish his sentence he heard a groan and saw a whirlwind rise up from the floor of the kitchen. Where last night he had sat in front of a warm fire and eaten bread and stew, now a dark windstorm lifted the detritus of abandonment: dead leaves and ash, straw and dust whirled about inside and then moved toward him as he peered through the broken window.

From the middle of the storm came a voice. "Abandon your quest. You are lost. I have him, your father!"

The blast hit Dag-gar full on the face and he fell backwards. He scrambled to his feet, grabbed the hackamore of the rearing horse, and jumped on its back. He gave the animal its head and it raced away from the house, found the road, and headed blindly toward the forest.

Dag-gar did not attempt to control the panicked animal. They galloped toward the black shadows of the woods, the road no more than a dim trace before them, the branches of the trees arching over them forming a roof through which the morning light was reluctant to enter. For a long time they ran, until Dag-gar felt his mount begin to tire. He pulled the horse to a walk and continued, often looking behind to see if they were being pursued. By the time the early sunlight found its way through the leaves and intertwining branches, they had reached the other side of the forest. Here the country opened up to rolling fields and the road made its way across green pastures where sheep and cattle grazed.

Now Dag-gar remembered the woman's instructions: North. But which way was north? The guiding star had long since faded from the sky. Coming out of the woods on the road that ran across the fields, he saw the rising sun to his right; north lay more or less in the direction the road was taking him.

They made their way through the day, a day neither hot nor cold nor cloudy nor sunny. In this country, it seemed to Dag-gar, it was neither summer nor winter nor any other season. The trees had leaves, the grass was green, but the air was hard with a cold, dry bitterness that fell harshly on his eyes and forced him to squint.

They passed through a town where no one was about—no milkmaids, no farmers' wives, no farmers, not even a farm dog yapping at the horse's heels. Then they entered another forest where there were neither birds nor squirrels, and not a bee or a butterfly. The thick-branched pines blocked out the sun and pressed a feeling of gloom into the air; Dag-gar began to whistle to relieve his growing feeling of dread.

He followed an old road through this forest, whose low branches occasionally forced him to dismount and lead his horse. Gradually the forest closed in even more until he was hemmed in on both sides of the road by the reaching limbs of black-trunked trees. Ahead of him he could see nothing but more forest, a forest that became darker and darker.

Then, out of the darkness, a male voice, coarse and deep. "Come on then, Hunter," it barked. "Let me feel the sting of your bow!"

Dag-gar pulled his horse to a stop but did not answer. He waited, his hand now on the pommel of his sword, his heart pounding in his ears. The voice had come from nowhere and everywhere, from the trees, from the earth itself.

For a long time there was nothing but the muffled silence of the deep pine woods. Then, when he was about to urge his horse on, the voice spoke again. "You! The great false Hunter! Astride your stolen horse and wearing your stolen girdle and sword, a sword with a missing jewel in the belt, and a sword that belongs to the true Hunter. Yes. You!"

Dag-gar twisted around in his saddle seeking the source of the voice, for now it sounded very close indeed. But he could see nothing but dense thickets and the narrow trace of road that lay before him. Finally he called out, "Where are you? What do you want? I am no hunter, but a sailor born and bred to the sea."

"Ho? No?" the voice answered, and then there was a rustling in the branches just ahead of Dag-gar and a man stepped onto the path in front of him. Short and powerfully built, he held a long sword in one hand and a dagger in the other. He was dressed all in deerskin and he smiled through his words. "My name is Stem, and you are, my boy, naught but a common thief and murderer, know it or not, like it or not. Your reputation precedes you, indeed it does. To deny such a thing is to deny your own face. Your dagger, it seems, has been well felt, I can assure you."

Dag-gar could only stare. He did not comprehend a thing.

"Nor are you as dumb as you now look, I suspect," Stem said. He planted the tip of his sword in the earth and again smiled his gray-toothed smile. "A rider, a sour-looking nobleman dressed in a black robe and riding a weary horse, came through here not long ago. He told me you were coming, told me what you looked like, even the color of your horse, and told me about your deadly deeds—and the gold in your purse. So, I challenge the great hunter to a battle. 'Twill be a feather in this cap, I can tell you, to have the head of a rogue like you on my platter—if you know what I mean."

Dag-gar did not withdraw his sword from its scabbard, for he was now filled with terror at the thought that he had never fought with a sword before and here, standing before him, challenging him, was a man who was obviously a seasoned fighter. Finally, in response to the man's silence, he said, "I'm just a boy, sir, truly. I'm lost in this forest, nor have I stolen anything or murdered anyone."

"Oh? Murdered no one? And what of the gentleman in Port o' Rue? The dark nobleman said your knife made a bloody hole in that fellow's neck easily enough, and this after knocking his compatriots senseless and leaping on the back of his horse."

Dag-gar's eyes widened at the tale. "I was just defending myself," he said, and heard his voice rising with the pleading. "And it was Scraps who did in the other two, not I."

Stem ignored this. "And then, just last night, there was a certain widowed farm wife down near the river got nearly the same treatment when someone broke into her home, ate her food, and made off with her poor dead husband's best sword and girdle."

"No, that's not true!" Dag-gar yelled. "She invited me into her house. She fed me and gave me this sword as a gift."

"Enough of this!" the man said as he pulled the tip of his sword from the ground and pointed it at Dag-gar. "Now, Sir Rogue, do you accept my challenge or not?"

Dag-gar's mouth was suddenly dry and his hands sweaty. "Sir," he said, "I am no warrior. I know nothing of fighting. It is true what I said—I am a sailor and was, until a short time ago, aboard a sailing ship of which my father was the captain."

At these words, Stem's face changed expression. His grim smile dropped to a questioning frown, his shoulders relaxed, and he again lowered his sword, sticking its tip into the earth. "So," he said, "you want me to believe that you're a sailor?"

Dag-gar nodded.

The smile returned to Stem's face, this time with a look of shrewdness. "Tell me then, sailor of the ocean-sea, what is the mizzenmast on a ship?"

"It's the third mast from the bow," Dag-gar said without hesitation.

"And what is a capstan for, then?" Stem asked.

"A windlass, sir, for pulling up the anchor or putting up sails."

Stem's smile faded, but just for a moment. "And the scuttlebutt?" he asked, and the grim smirk returned.

"The water keg, sir."

Now Stem frowned. He thought for a moment. "And Mother Carrie's chickens?"

"Seabirds," Dag-gar said, again without hesitation, "storm petrels."

Stem sighed and slid his sword back into its scabbard. "All right then," he said, "those are the first true things you've said to me. All the rest were lies. But you are a man of the sea, no doubt. And though I'm landlocked here in this desperate forest, so am I, too, a man of the sea."

He turned his back on Dag-gar and began walking away down the road. "Come along then," he said over his shoulder. "We'll need to spend some hours telling seamen's lies and then we can eat. I've shot a sizable buck—one of the bishop's finest—just this morning."

Dag-gar watched Stem move along the road, walking heavily, swaying side to side with each step, the scabbard of his sword sticking out behind him and his broad back nearly filling up the hole the road made through the forest. He wondered whether he should turn around and ride hard back the way he had come to escape this highwayman. But where would he then go? There was nothing but the haunted farm by the river. He looked down at the jeweled belt and sword, remembered his quest, took a deep breath, and urged his horse onward.

Chapter 14

There were three of them: Stem; a man named Pock, a small, skinny man with filthy clothes; and another who Stem said was called Bor—a mute, incapable of speech. They were, Stem said, all sailors, able seamen, and had become highwaymen after they had mutinied and were forced to flee Port o' Rue. So now they made a living as highwaymen.

They all sat around a fire in front of a small, thatched-roof hovel built at the intersection of two roads, and talked and ate hunks of roasted deer meat until the sun was dropping from the sky. The forest was dim enough at noon, but as night fell, it was pitch black outside the reach of the fire's small circle of light. Stem and Pock were anxious to talk of the sea and sing shanties and tell bawdy jokes, and it was enough for Dag-gar to sit and listen; hearing them talk was like being back aboard *Mother-of-Pearl* and listening to the sailors tell their tall tales.

Then, as Dag-gar was beginning to grow sleepy, his eyelids drooping, Stem and Pock fell silent. This silence brought the boy out of his stupor. His head came up and he saw Stem's bright eyes on him.

"We've spoken long enough, my brother and I," he said. "Tell us, then, your story. How did you come to be here on a horse, in the middle of a forbidding woods such as this?"

Dag-gar sat up straight and rubbed his eyes, and as he did so, he saw something familiar: the fluffy tail of a white cat. It appeared from around the back of Stem's neck, slowly lashed from side to side, and disappeared. Yet, as with Scraps, Stem seemed not to be aware of its presence, nor did Pock or Bor seem to see it. They all continued to watch Dag-gar and wait for a response.

"My father was named Jarl," Dag-gar began. "He was the captain of the merchant ship *Mother-of-Pearl*. All I can remember of my life is being aboard her. Except for going ashore in the ports we visited, I had never spent any time on land—until I was taken off the ship one night by a wicked stowaway. He threw me into the sea and I swam until I came upon a small skiff. But the stowaway himself was rowing it. I had no choice but to climb up into it. After a while, I fell asleep and when I woke up, there was another ship close by. They rescued me and took me back to the port *Mother-of-Pearl* had just left—Port o' Rue. But everything had changed. The streets had changed, the buildings were different, the people I had known, gone."

As Dag-gar spoke, the white kitten appeared again. Now she was on the ground and came out from behind Stem. She walked in front of them—Stem, Pock, and Bor—and around the fire to where Dag-gar was sitting. Dag-gar reached out and ran his hand over the cat's back. None of them seemed to notice. They were listening to Dag-gar's story, all of them watching his eyes.

Dag-gar went on, stroking the kitten's back all the while. "I walked around the town looking for something I would recognize. I asked about my ship, *Mother-of-Pearl*. The people said *Mother-of-Pearl* was a dead ship, a ship long gone. They thought I must be a ghost, a demon. They were frightened and they beat me and dragged me to the town square. Then they tied me to a big tree, a tree with a black trunk and no leaves. They called this the Fire Tree, the Tree of Judgment. They stacked wood around me and set it on fire and waited to see if I would burn. When I did not burn, it meant I was not a demon, but this frightened them even more and they ran away."

As Dag-gar spoke these last words, the cat walked back around the fire and again disappeared behind Stem's back. Dag-gar called her. "Sonoria! Come here, girl. Where are you going?"

Stem looked around him. "What did you say?"

"My kitten," Dag-gar said. "She has followed me here. Her name is Sonoria. She just went around behind you."

"A kitten?" Stem said. "I saw no kitten."

And then there was silence as the highwaymen considered what they had heard. The boy had seen a cat where there was no cat. They looked at each other and then back at Dag-gar.

"Where is this kitten?" Pock asked.

Dag-gar saw a look in Pock's eyes that went beyond sudden mistrust to something much more dangerous—fear. "No," Dag-gar said quickly. "I did not see a cat. I was just thinking of my little white kitten. I'm very tired. I must have been dreaming."

Stem interrupted them. "Never mind that, now," he said, and he fixed Dag-gar with hard stare. "My lad, you have a fine sword and a fine bow. And you also have a fine problem: If what you say is true, you have not been trained in the use of these weapons."

Dag-gar shrugged. "Yes," he said softly, "that's true."

"Well, then, if you want to join us and be a gentleman of the road—and I make this offer only because you are a fellow seaman—

you will have to learn to use them. We can start your instruction tomorrow. Now, though, it's time to sleep."

With that, Stem stood up and disappeared into the hut. Pock and Bor watched him go and then they too stood up, and without ceremony or so much as a goodnight, followed him, leaving Dag-gar alone by the dying fire.

He wrapped his blanket around him and his eyes searched the dark margins of the camp for a white tail. But there was nothing and he dared not call out for her lest the highwaymen hear him. Then it started to rain, at first just a small pattering on the overhanging branches, and then harder, until the wet found its way through the thick foliage and he felt it on his head.

He looked at the hut, now just a shadow in the night. Should he go in there and find a place to lie down? No sooner had he thought this than he heard Stem's voice calling to him. "Come in here, then, sailor boy. This place is filled with lice and other vermin, but better, I should think, than being out in the cold rain."

Dag-gar stood up and walked to the doorway of the hut. He could see nothing inside. Again, Stem spoke to him from the darkness. "Just find a place in the middle. There's nothing but dried grass for a bed, but good enough for the likes of us—and now for you."

Dropping to his knees, Dag-gar felt the floor with his hands. It was covered with dry hay. He moved in from the door a few feet and, finding enough space to lie down, spread his blanket and closed his eyes. It was then that he felt her next to him. She was purring softly and then she touched him with her cold nose and licked his cheek with her coarse tongue. He felt her warm fur and he pulled her close. In the blackness of the hovel he thought he could see her, just barely, a luminous white cloud hovering over him. Then he heard her voice—not the voice of a kitten, but the clear, bell-like voice of a young woman. "I love you, Dag-gar. We are together, always. We must be brave and strong."

Now, for the first time, Dag-gar understood that he should not question this, not wonder. He felt the kitten curl up next to him and he said, "I love you, too, Sonoria."

* * * * *

It was a sodden morning of overcast skies and flat light that cast no shadows. The forest was dripping wet, the grass soaking, the air cold—perfect, Stem said, for instruction in the use of sword and bow. And so, after a breakfast of cold venison, the lessons began.

Poor Pock. The skinny little man with the filthy, torn tunic smiled bravely through his rotten teeth when Stem told him he was to demonstrate the use of the shield. From inside the hut

Pock produced a light shield that was nothing but a wooden frame covered with thick leather. He held it out in front of him protectively and backed around the clearing in circles, desperately fending off the blows from Stem's heavy stick while Stem alternately lunged at him, battered him, and scolded him for not standing his ground. Finally, he knocked Pock off his feet with a tremendous blow.

When Stem had worked up a sweat and Pock lay on the ground panting, Stem handed the stick to Dag-gar. "Now you've seen how it's done. You must be fast, you must try to get your opponent off balance, find an opening, and, of course, when you have the advantage, you must show no mercy."

Dag-gar took the stick from Stem and tried to do what Stem had done. Pock, once again on his feet, danced this way and that, trying to avoid Dag-gar's blows. It quickly became apparent, however, that Dag-gar had an advantage Stem had lacked: speed. As fast as Pock moved, Dag-gar was there with a thrust of the stick; when Pock dodged one way and then the other, Dag-gar's stick found him before he got there.

Stem at first yelled encouragement and advice to the unschooled Dag-gar, but then, realizing what was happening, that Dag-gar was far faster than Pock and far faster than he himself, he fell silent. Dag-gar, too, soon realized that no matter how or where Pock ducked and feinted, he was able to strike him at will. The tip of the stick-sword had soon left its history on Pock's body, written in red welts and swelling bruises.

Finally, Stem called the practice to a halt. "That's good, very good, young Dag-gar. We must not beat poor Pock into a sodden pulp." He stopped, cleared his throat, and said, "You are very fast. You have potential. In fact, I should say you are a natural warrior."

Chapter 15

So the days went, the mornings spent in training in bow and sword, the afternoons hunting for food, the evenings sitting around the fire telling the lies sailors tell. And each evening, they were visited by the white kitten that only Dag-gar could see. Now, though, instead of calling out to it, he knew enough just to watch it and wonder.

"I was once a rich man," Stem said. He was stretched out next to the fire, his head resting on a log. His fingers combed through his long, graying beard as he spoke. But no sooner had he begun than the now-familiar fluffy white tail appeared over his shoulder, unseen and unfelt.

"A very rich man with three servants—a cook who could make a king drool, a manservant who tended my clothes and my bath, and a jester who kept me laughing while I dined."

He scratched his belly and yawned. The kitten walked across his chest. "I fell in love with a woman who was much younger than I. The fox-beautiful daughter of a nobleman—a nobleman from the far corner of this world, to be precise. We had sailed there to take on a cargo of spices—I owned the ship, and two more like her—and the moment I saw her—the woman, that is, she was performing for us after our evening meal, singing and playing a lute—I was terribly smitten. Hopelessly infatuated. I'm certain you know what I mean."

He winked at Dag-gar from across the fire and went on. "There was a problem, though, and it became apparent to me immediately. I would have to fight for her love. For you see, there was also present at this meal, sitting directly across from me—cross-legged on a wonderful carpet of gold and red thread as was the custom in the country—a handsome young man with great moustaches and a large dagger at his side. As men will do, he immediately understood my attraction to this beautiful young woman and became madly jealous.

"So there was a sudden tension in the air as she played for us. Her voice was lovely, her playing exquisite, her beauty by the light of the paper lanterns, beyond a dream. Yet the air became as chill as if a north wind had come in through the walls of the tent. Did I hesitate at this sense of dread as another man might have? No! After all, I was young and rich and had three servants. A man like that—like me—takes what he wants. And I wanted her."

Dag-gar had been absorbed both by Stem's story and the adventures of the kitten. She had now moved over to Pock and Bor. Both men had been abused pitilessly that day by Stem's demonstrations and Dag-gar's growing skill with the wooden sword. Pock, one eye swollen closed, sat listening, his mouth open, his beard greasy with food, while Bor, who could neither hear nor speak and who had a large purple welt across one cheek, had fallen asleep sitting up. The kitten climbed, unnoticed, up each man's arm and across each man's shoulders, whipping its tail playfully under their noses. First Pock sneezed and then Bor. Dag-gar smiled. The kitten, he understood, was both flirting with him and teasing the men.

"Yet," Stem went on, "I knew I would have to work carefully. After all, I was a guest; the beautiful woman, who I was determined would be my mine, was my host's daughter; and the dangerous looking young man across the fire from me, her suitor."

The kitten walked around the fire, curled up in Dag-gar's lap, and began purring loudly. Stem, oblivious to the cat, sat up, spat into the fire, and listened to the satisfying hiss it made. He rubbed his nose with one hand and said, "I understood the custom in those parts of the world was to offer the father of the maiden a large price for the privilege of marriage. This I now set about to do. I looked at the dangerous young man, challenging him with my eyes, and smiled in a meaningful way so there would be no misunderstanding my intentions. I then turned to my host. 'I am prepared,' I said, 'to pay ten thousand gold pieces for the hand of this wonderful musician—your daughter.'

"At these words, translated by a eunuch who sat by my side for that purpose, the dangerous young man reached for his dagger. Was this the time for polite negotiations? Apparently not. Did I have a moment to consider options? Absolutely not. Was I willing to forgo the favors of this goddess of a woman because I was afraid of this exotic young warrior? Never! Indeed!

" 'Swain!' I said, pulling my own dagger from my belt, 'I shall feed your ears to this fire ere the night is over!'

"My dagger was sharp and my threat triumphant. The dangerous young man hesitated. I again met his eye with mine and held it. He blinked. When I realized my advantage, I sneered at him. 'I take her, then, as mine—as my bride,' I said, and I signaled my manservant to fetch the gold."

Now Stem leaned back on the log and looked up into the night forest. He smiled at the memory of this tale. "The lesson, young Dag-gar? The lesson is this: If you have three ships and a pot of gold, be satisfied. Leave well enough alone; abandon other ambitions such as humiliating young men with long daggers and big moustaches and spending that gold on exquisite maidens playing lutes."

He sat up and poked at the fire with a stick. "We had no sooner left the harbor, all three of my ships heavily burdened with spices and sandalwood and ebony, than we were attacked by what turned out to be the dangerous young man's small navy. They had many guns and we had but few; they had many ships, we but three. The fight, such as it was, was soon over. My ships were seized, my crew taken prisoner, and I? I was whisked away to a dungeon where I languished for years—who knows how many?—before managing my escape by throttling the jailer one night when a great storm swept in from the sea and flooded the city and put us up to our necks in seawater."

Now Stem stopped and finally looked at Dag-gar, who was petting the kitten. "I'm sure, young seaman, that you have similar tales to tell, for there isn't a mariner I know who doesn't. But there will be other nights for such stories. I'm weary in my very bones. I must to bed." He stood up and went into the hovel. Pock soon followed him, while Bor slept on, his chin on his chest.

Dag-gar, too, went into the hut and took his place on his blanket on the straw. Immediately he felt Sonoria's soft fur against his face and heard her bell-like voice. "I love you, my Dag-gar. Sleep well, for tomorrow we begin another adventure. You shall be called upon to use all that you have learned from these men."

* * * * *

And so, the next part of the girl's story ended. She came out of the reverie her imaginings had spun for her and looked across the fire at Scraps. He was asleep. But it mattered not. The tale was told, and so it would be. She lay down on her blanket and went to sleep.

In the morning, the desert presented a purple dawn. Clouds, gathering in the east above the night-cool sand, filtered the light of the rising sun and scattered it about the sky in violet streaks. Playing on her face, the waves of this light woke the girl. As was her custom, she did not open her eyes, but lay listening and feeling the world around her. She smelled the familiar things: the cold ashes of the dead fire, the peculiar odor of cold rocks, the faint perfume of some desert flower carried on the breeze. And, of course, she smelled the camel.

She opened her eyes slowly and, without moving in her blanket, looked about her and above her. She saw the clouds and watched the dance of their changing colors and then looked at the horizon to the west where the black night could be seen still retreating. Finally, keeping her blanket around her, she stood up and walked to an outcropping of rock and climbed up to the top of it. She looked toward the north.

"Do you see anything?" It was Scraps. The old man was still lying where he had fallen asleep, still wrapped in his blankets.

"Yes," she said. "There they are."

She heard Scraps sigh. "Good," he said, "I'm exceedingly tired of this desert trekking."

He stood up and stepped up on the ledge next to her. She pointed toward the north and he saw it, too. They could have been merely more clouds, but no, these were something else, something vast and sharp and permanent: mountains.

"Your once and future home," the old man said, "and lovely they are, indeed." He grunted and turned away and addressed the camel, who was still resting in the sand in its awkward camel way, legs under it, head stretched out on its long neck. "I'm certain you can't behold the distant promise that we can, my humpy-backed friend, yet it is cause enough for celebration, for the goal, at least the very tops of the goal, are in sight."

He touched the beast on its rump and, with its usual bellow of complaint, it began the involved process of getting to its feet. Once up, it cast its head about looking for something on which to breakfast. Finding a dried thorn bush within reach, it pulled some branches into its mouth with rubbery lips and began chewing.

Scraps looked on with satisfaction and then found his own breakfast in a coarsely woven bag he had set by the fire. He offered it first to the girl, who took a bite of the dried meat and handed it back to him. "It will be," he said, "still many days before we reach the foothills with their lovely green meadows and running streams. We will have just time enough to finish your story. And this we must do if the quest we are on is to play itself out as it should. Quest meeting quest, as it were, Dag-gar's and ours, joining at just the right moment, past, present, and future mingling together. It shall be, I suspect, a powerful spectacle. Something worth the wait—and worth the miserable slog across this wilderness."

He began to gather things up and to pack them on the camel's back. The girl, though, continued to look across the far distance at the mountains. Not until the sun found her and illuminated first her hair and then her features did she step down off the ledge and, without a word, begin walking toward them. And as she walked, her head once again was filled with the story the stars had given her during the night.

Chapter 16

Dag-gar was awakened, not by a purple sunrise, but by the hard voices of approaching men. He heard them and then, as if part of his dreaming, Sonoria's bell-like voice was again in his ear. "Beware, my love, beware."

He was up on his feet and so too, were the others. They had all slept with their weapons next to them and now the four of them stood in the dark of the hut holding their swords at the ready.

Stem put his finger to his lips to signal silence and then he stepped alone out the door of the hut. Three men, all carrying short swords and bows, were just coming down the path and entering the small clearing. When they saw the hovel and the horse, they stopped.

A tall one in front said, "And look here, then. A house and a horse in the middle of the dark wood."

Stem came out of the doorway. "Greetings, gentlemen," he said, "and a good morning to you."

The men scrutinized Stem, noting his sword, now back in its scabbard, and the bow and quiver of arrows he carried on his back. "You must be the peasant that owns this lovely little farm," the tall man said and the others laughed.

Stem smiled at the joke. "Yes, of course," he said. "I was just about to milk my cow." He nodded at Dag-gar's horse.

"Is that cow for sale?" the tall man asked and now the three of them had all moved into the clearing and had spread themselves out around it. One of them approached the horse and looked it over.

"No," Stem said, "I need the milk."

"Such a pity," the man said, "for I surely could use a good milch cow." He pretended to think for a moment and then said, "Listen, my peasant friend. As there are three of us and just one of you, and we are all alone out here in this deep forest, I think we can reach an agreement on the sale price of the cow. How much will you take for her?"

Stem forced his smile to stay on his face, but his hand moved to the pommel of his sword. "Oh, certainly then," he said, "a good cow, where there are no other cows, is worth a great deal—a king's ransom, in fact. So, let's say," he scratched his chin thoughtfully, "a thousand gold pieces. And for that, I'll throw in the saddle and hackamore, for this cow has both."

"Indeed?" the tall man said and now the second man moved slowly around behind Stem while the third moved to the other side of him.

Stem watched this and said, "I have a better idea. Instead of negotiating a price, why not have a contest of strength? The winner takes the cow." He raised his hand and motioned. This was what Pock and Bor had been waiting for. They moved to step out through the door, their bows at the ready—but Dag-gar pushed out ahead of them, his sword in his hand.

Without hesitating, he stood in front of Stem and said, "That is my horse and I'll not sell him at any price."

The tall man's eyes widened, but just for a moment. A smile played across his face and he rested his hand on the pommel of his sword. "Ah," he said, "a youth with a good horse and a magnificent sword. Makes a man wonder where such a boy would come by such treasures. Perhaps he has the blue blood of a nobleman—or perhaps the black blood of a thief."

As the men began to laugh, Dag-gar felt his face redden. He raised his sword and pointed it at the tall man and said, "Or perhaps both bloods run in my veins—blue and black. And both, sir, I find to be rank insults."

"Oh, do you?" the tall man said. "And, of course, you are a brave lad and willing to challenge the man who speaks such calumny."

Dag-gar felt his mouth go dry and his hands begin to sweat, but he would not allow himself to back down. He heard Stem's voice behind him. "Don't worry about the other two, Dag-gar. We have them under the eyes of our bows. You are free to deal with this one."

With a quick movement, the tall man withdrew his sword from its scabbard. "Good," he said, moving forward, and then his face twisted into a snarl and he said, "I haven't yet had my breakfast. I may as well start with you."

He jumped at Dag-gar with a quick slash of his sword. But Dag-gar leaped away and the sword cleaved thin air. For an instant the tall man seemed surprised; this instant was all that Dag-gar needed. He spun around and sprang at the tall man, the tip of his sword slicing through his cheek.

The man staggered backwards, blood pouring down his face. He stared at Dag-gar for a moment and then, with a scream, charged at him in a rage, swinging his sword in great arcs.

Dag-gar danced around this attack, moving backwards and then to the side, stepping over the ashes of last night's fire, ducking and feinting. He waited, surprised at how easily he could dodge the man's blade. Then, when the man stumbled on a piece of firewood, Dag-gar was on him. With a quick, hard thrust, he felt his blade enter the man's chest, heard the gasp of surprise, saw his eyes widen, and watched the blood pour from his mouth, mingling with the blood running from the wound on his face. The tall man stood this way for a long moment and then went straight down in a heap in the ashes of the dead fire.

There was a long silence and then Stem said, "Well done, boy. And quick, too. Never have I seen such speed with a sword. You have learned your lessons well."

The other two were now disarmed, stripped naked, and sent scurrying back up the path the way they had come. Then Stem said, "Now, of course, we must quit this place. Dag-gar, you may join our small band of land-bound pirates if you so choose. We can use a good swordsman, and, by my word, that is what you have become."

Dag-gar looked at them, at Stem, and Pock, and the silent Bor. They were what his father, Captain Jarl, would have called scoundrels of the first order and, he would have added, doomed to be hanged.

He shook his head. "I am grateful," he said, "for your instruction in the use of sword and bow. I hope I have repaid the debt I owe you. But I am on a quest and need to go my own way."

* * * * *

So they separated. Stem, Pock, and Bor, trudging along under the weight of their collected arms, left Dag-gar behind at the hovel. When they took leave of each other, Stem said, "We shall take the road that leads back to the coast. There are enough small towns down there to keep rascals such as us busy for awhile." Pointing at the road Dag-gar would now follow, he added, "Where that road leads, I know not. Upwards, I expect, toward the higher country.

"There is a rumor of a great grass prairie that stretches forever and is populated by wandering bands of a wolf-like people who can run like deer and who eat horses. Also, it is said, there are great mountains covered with eternal ice and snow, whose passes are guarded by filthy trolls with magical powers. Perhaps that is where you will end up.

"Good luck, then, and do not rest until you have fulfilled your quest—no man should do less."

They turned away then, the three of them, and Dag-gar watched as they disappeared around a bend and dissolved into the forest.

So he found himself alone with the dead highwayman. The dark forest now reeked of raw death mingled with the damp rot of the sodden woods. He looked at the body, and at the hovel where he had slept. It was pitiful enough, this corpse, this filthy, lice-ridden hut. Captain Jarl, in his great dignity, would have said—what would he have said? Dag-gar could not imagine his reaction.

Once, aboard *Mother of Pearl*, a sailor had killed a shipmate with a belaying pin. Blood had flooded the deck from the dying man's ears and mouth and nose. Dag-gar had seen it all—first the argument between drunken seamen, the cursing, the rising violence, the surging desire to kill. And then, in a trice, it was over. *So fast these things happened*, he had thought later. *A man is alive and then he is dead.*

What had his father done then? He had had the killer clapped in irons and thrown in the brig. The dead man was buried at sea with some ceremony and then, as captain, his father had handed down judgment. The guilty sailor was hanged from a yardarm, and then he too went to the dark depths—and with the same dignity as his victim, for, after death, we are all the same, victim or killer—or so his father had said. And so the convicted and the murdered were both released to the same deep ocean mansions.

Witnessing those events, Dag-gar had felt something happen to him, though he did not realize it until later: a small hardening of his heart. These tragedies were part of the affairs of men and he, soon to be a man, was part of them. He must prepare himself. He gathered his few possessions and rode away.

Chapter 17

There was little else to do but think as he rode along the dim forest trace. And yet he could not allow himself to do this lest he sink into dreadful and fearful daydreams that came at him from the shadows of the woods like red-eyed demons. He let the horse have its head and it picked its way along the road.

He whistled all the sailors' songs he knew, and sang them, too. And when he could remember no more, he tried to concentrate on the horse's ears as they moved back and forth seeking the source of the various sounds a forest makes, for now the forest seemed filled with life: squirrels chattering, a crow cawing, branches cracking, wind disturbing the quiet corners of thickets.

Time, measured by the arc of the sun, its light broken and diminished by the trees, was metered out by the rhythm of the horse's hooves on the road. When the squawk of a raven pulled Dag-gar from his fearful reverie and he realized that night was again approaching, he looked about for shelter.

There, where the road emerged from the trees, he found himself moving along the edge of a meadow, a meadow bordered on one side by a small river and on the other side by a sheer cliff whose rock face cut up suddenly from the meadow's grass. At the base of the cliff, less than a man's height from the ground, was the entrance to a cave, a dark hole in the rock face from which a small stream ran, its water coursing across the meadow to mingle with the wider river.

He stopped his horse and analyzed the scene before him: a meadow green with young grass and speckled with blue and yellow blossoms; a stream that flowed with a small, calm dignity untroubled by rapids; a low escarpment into which water had carved, with eons of patience, a hole big enough for a man to walk into.

Here he could rest, let the horse drink and graze. He could collect himself, decide what to do, think about what lay before him. He dismounted. The horse immediately started pulling at the grass and Dag-gar took off the saddle and blanket and set them on a log. He went to the stream and bathed, using a bar of soap the mistress of the farm had given him.

Though the sun was now gone from the sky, enough light remained in the early dusk to let him do what he knew he must: enter the cave. He felt its presence as if it were a great eye staring at him from the center of his fear. Hobbling the horse so that it could not wander far, he made himself a torch of bundled dried grass and twigs tied together with a piece of cloth. When he was nearly ready he caught, out of the corner of his eye, a movement at the cave's entrance. He spun around, but too late. If there had been anything there at all, it was gone.

Dag-gar felt fear twist his stomach. *Perhaps he has followed me here,* he thought. *Somehow, he has followed me.* But, as always, he heard his father's voice in his head: *If you try to ignore your fears, they will come to possess you. You must face them, grab hold of them, and you must kill them as a warrior must kill his enemies.* Dag-gar lit the torch with his flint and steel, blowing on the spark until it ignited.

The entrance to the cave was narrow, dripping with water, and he had to step around the various pools the stream had carved in the rock of the cave floor. But then, just as the flames of the torch were at their highest, he found himself entering a larger room. The ceiling arched upwards and the walls fell away so that his footsteps and even his breathing created an echo. Though he held the torch up high, he could not see the cave's ceiling. When he looked down, there in front of him was a great, wide pool of water, a spring that was the source of the small stream that flowed out from the cave, a spring that bubbled like a hot cauldron though its water smelled cool and sweet. Then the torch began to die down and he had to quickly retreat, picking his way back toward the circle of light that marked the cave's entrance.

Once outside, he gathered firewood and kindling and, carrying as much of this as he could and lighting another torch, set off again into the cave. This time, when he entered the big room, he found a clear, dry place on the floor next to the bubbling pool and made his camp. In a short time he had a fire blazing and had curled up next to it. Before he could understand how tired he was, he had fallen asleep.

He was awakened in the middle of the night by the sound of gurgling water. When he opened his eyes, he could see nothing and, for a moment, could remember nothing. Where was he? How had he gotten here?

The feeling of not knowing where he was when he woke up at night, though, was now a familiar one. He had been traveling hard and meeting many adventures and so now here was another one. He lay still and he thought and then he remembered, he remembered everything.

He did not move. He found the handle of his sword and lay on his blanket and listened. There was the sound of the water that had awakened him and there was another sound: a squeaking and with it a fluttering as if a thousand wings were beating the air around him. Bats. He remembered them from one night when he and Scraps had passed a night in a cave. They were tiny winged creatures, like flying mice, but, Scraps had assured him, harmless enough.

So he dismissed them and listened again to the water and how its bubbling echoed within the depths of the cave's chambers. It was a deep-water sound, not light, as a small, bold stream would sound flowing over rocks. There was a depth to this water's voice. His father had told him that water was the blood of the gods, very ancient and very alive; it had a voice, listen to it—and for all his life at sea, he had. Somehow he understood that this water was speaking to him of another place, another time, and yet he could not fathom its message.

He turned and, in the pitch blackness, sought some source of light. There, behind him, he could see the entrance to the cave, and through it, the lighter shadow of the night forest with its moon and stars. He held his breath and fought back his panic and then choked on a sob. There was no one here. He was utterly alone in a dark cave in the middle of a black forest.

Then he heard a voice. "Boy," it said, and the voice was light as a whisper but it joined the water, echoing off the walls of the cave. "Boy, you are in a pitiful way. So sad. You are lost and frightened—nay, you are lost and terrified. As terrified as if the demons of the Nether Regions were at your throat."

The voice sighed and took in a breath that rattled in its lungs like a death rale, and then again it spoke in its whispering way. "And that is true. They are here, all of them, for you have found their home here in this forest in this cave by this sacred pool of water that rises from the bowels of Time."

There was a scratching sound and then the light of a taper, dim and yellow, and Dag-gar could see the outline of a figure standing some distance away on the other side of the pool. The water was bubbling, rising, and Dag-gar knew his father had been right—it, too, was alive.

Dag-gar could not see the figure's face, but the hand that emerged from the sleeve of its robe held the taper with long, bony fingers, the flesh dried and shrunken around them. Through his terror, Dag-gar found his voice and when it came from his throat, it came with a hollow shuddering. "What do you want with me?"

The figure held the burning taper out before it as if to allow Dag-gar to see it better. "I am, as you know, a mere vagabond, a Time Vagabond, wandering here, wandering there. You call me Captain Sorrow. Either will do, for both are true. What do I want from you? Remember this: Sorrow is as necessary to this world as that opposite thing, that thing called happiness. Indeed, they come in proportions, one equal to the other.

"And you, a mere youth, have achieved a certain infamy, too, for word of your deeds now spreads rapidly throughout the countryside: You are called the Hunter, and possessor of the magical three-starred belt and sword. But more than that, you are also a killer of men. So, my callow youth, you and I could be considered brothers in that we are both dispensers of sorrow and misery." A rattle of laughter from Captain Sorrow shook the taper with a tremor.

Dag-gar knew he must face this terror if he was to live, for if he died, this evil would take his spirit with it, would possess it forever. He stood up and held out his hands, beseeching Captain Sorrow, "Give me the Amber Teardrop. It belongs to my father, Captain Jarl, the master of the ship called *Mother-of-Pearl.*"

Captain Sorrow laughed again and the echo from his laughter drowned out the winging of the bats and the gurgling of the water. "Oh, oh," he said, "such conceit! That your father should have it and not I! The Amber Teardrop, the frozen blood of the Ancient Tree, and so the blood of the gods, belongs to Time, not to your father or to any other man, mortal or not. And so, by that logic, I may as well keep it." Again laughter rattled from his lungs and the light from the taper shook.

Dag-gar drew his sword, the light from the taper gleaming from its blade. "I will have the Amber Teardrop," he commanded. "Without it, my father cannot navigate across the ocean-sea. It will mean his life."

Now Captain Sorrow sighed. "A pity," he said, "but, alas, your father is doomed—as are you, my young Dag-gar. But, come now and try to get it if you must—and if you are as brave as you would like me to think! Come and get the Amber Teardrop! I have it right here." He held out a glowing gem that swung on a gold chain, a gem that glowed a rich brown in the taper's light.

Dag-gar felt something rise inside him, something he had felt only once before—when the highwaymen had attacked him and Scraps at their camp outside Port o' Rue: a cold, unthinking rage. And so he lifted the sword like a spear and threw it across the water at Captain Sorrow. The blade of the sword struck the specter in the middle of his chest. He shrieked and with a loud hiss was gone.

Dag-gar watched as the taper, the sword, and the Amber Teardrop for an instant seemed to float in the air above the water. Then they fell, all three, into the pool, and the flame on the taper went out and again there was utter darkness. But this Dag-gar did not see, for as the Amber Teardrop hit the water's surface, he leaped in after it.

Chapter 18

Then there was darkness, a complete blackness that seemed to come from the water itself, and he was engulfed by it as the pool swallowed him and took him down. He tried to swim, but found that the rising effervescence in the water made swimming impossible, for the water was, in fact, mostly air. He thrashed around, struggling to reach the surface, but felt himself falling, slowly at first and then faster, until he was tumbling downward feeling the water rushing around him as if he had fallen into a great, foaming waterfall.

He held his breath, but when he could hold it no longer and finally gasped for air, he found he could breathe and that the air tasted soft and sweet and familiar. He felt something under him, something powerful, something carrying him, something that moved with a wonderful rhythm.

He continued to fall, and as he fell, the darkness began receding, like a dawn at sea when the pearling of first light seemed to be not there at all, like a poorly kept promise. And then, like that promise of dawn which must be kept after all, there was light all around him and he saw he was moving over an earth green with tall grass, an endless horizon of grass that went on forever, rising on the backs of low, shimmering hills as if the sea and its restless waves had turned to solid ground.

At the same moment, he felt the bubbles of water that had rushed against his face and body turn into a wind, a wind that blew through his hair and carried the wild perfume of the grass. Below him, the surging, powerful rhythm became a horse on which he was riding, and he looked forward and saw the horse's great head stretched out, its ears laid back, and in front of the running horse's head was the green ocean of an endless grass prairie.

He was then aware of something next to him and he turned his head and saw another horse and rider close by, keeping pace, stride for stride. The horse was a big, blue roan, its rider a tall, slender young woman with white-blond hair. Her clothes were made from the fur and skins of animals and she carried a long bow and a quiver of arrows across her back and a short sword at her side. She rode easily, at one with the smooth movements of the horse beneath her, her body balanced, barely moving. When she felt Dag-gar's eyes on her, she turned and looked at him and smiled. He saw that her eyes, as blue as the bright sky above them, were filled with some wild spirit that came from the prairie and from the horses, too. *It's them,* he thought, *the blue horse and its wild woman rider, the ones Scraps told me about, the ones I saw in my dream that first night Scraps and I spent together talking by the fire.* And then he remembered what else Scraps had said that night: *You are meant to be together—all of you—forever and ever. And longer than that, even! If fact, you already have been together for longer than forever.*

Then Dag-gar saw the object of their mad race across the prairie: Ahead of them a large herd of horses moved as one immense dark cloud of animals, brown and black and bay and dappled, all running hard, the pounding of their hooves a low rumble he could feel in the air. Beyond the charging herd he saw a vast beach and on the beach a great walled city, a city that seemed to rise out of the sea, its ramparts immense and gray and topped with turrets. It was a strange sight, but somehow a familiar one.

Among the horses were other riders—young men and women, all dressed the same in furs and skins and all with the same bows and quivers of arrows across their backs, and all with short swords at their sides. But they did not all look the same. Some were black-skinned with black hair, others were brown-skinned with reddish hair; all shades galloped along together.

The young woman riding next to Dag-gar came closer, bringing her great blue roan stallion shoulder to shoulder with his mount, and when she was close enough, she reached out and Dag-gar saw she carried his sword—the sword the mistress of the farm had given him, the sword he had thrown at the phantom called Captain Sorrow. She passed it to him and then began pulling away, moving quickly so his horse could no longer keep pace with hers. He wanted to ask her if she also had the Amber Teardrop, but as he began to form the words he felt the water and its effervescence around him again and the darkness increased until it was blackness and then he was struggling in it, trying to swim.

As he thrashed his way upward, he felt someone next to him, someone struggling beside him in the foaming, bubbling torrent. They alternately clutched at each other and pushed each other away, kicking and grappling, and then they were at the surface, choking and sputtering.

He was now back in the cave, struggling to stay afloat in the middle of the pool, but this time the cave was lit by torches and fires, and the people sitting by the fires jumped up and reached into the water for Dag-gar and his companion and threw them ropes to grab.

Dragged gasping from the water, Dag-gar lay on the stone floor of the cave, breathing hard. A moment later, his fellow swimmer was also pulled from the pool. Though they lay within an arm's length of each other, for a moment Dag-gar did not recognize who was sprawled out next to him.

It was an old man, a long, thin old man with a scraggly gray beard. He wore a tunic sewn together from rags of many different colors, and beneath his tunic, which now clung to his body, his spindly arms and legs and his bony hips and shoulders were all akimbo. In one hand he clutched a big hat made from the same rags as his tunic; with the other hand, he wiped water from his face.

For a long moment Dag-gar stared at him, certain that he knew him, but, as with the gray-walled city, unable to remember from where. Then he looked at the people who had pulled them from the bubbling pool and he did remember them; he remembered exactly where he had seen them before: He had just been riding with them, galloping with them across the great grass prairie, taking a herd of horses toward a distant city.

They were young—fifteen or sixteen seasons of the sun, none more than eighteen seasons. They wore animal skins and furs and they themselves were all colors. Some had bright yellow hair and others had reddish hair. Some had black skins and some had brown. They all now stared at Dag-gar and the skinny, gangly old man who lay next to him.

Dag-gar sat up and stared back at them. He felt for his sword. Somehow it had gotten back in its scabbard and the scabbard was on the belt around his waist. He remembered something else: The young woman with the white-blond hair and the blue eyes who had returned the sword to him. He looked around for her but did not see her among the others.

Dag-gar searched the faces of the young nomads for some sign of their intent. They had obviously made themselves at home in the cave—they were cooking haunches of meat over fires and had spread sleeping blankets on the floor.

The old man spoke first, seemingly unaware of the presence of the others. "Ayee!" he said to Dag-gar. "What a commotion. Such a drenching. But thank you, thank you, Dag-gar, for saving me. It took great courage for you to leap into that raging river and haul me out. I thought for certain I was doomed!"

Dag-gar stared at the old man. His voice sounded familiar—hoarse and high-pitched—and his face with its large, uneven nose and his tiny chin and scraggly, curly beard—he was certain he had seen it before, too. And the multicolored tunic... Scraps? But Scraps had been a young man, no more than twenty seasons of the sun.

The old man spoke again. "By the look on your face, I can see you have been stunned out of your senses by the violence of our experience. Never mind. I'll remind you. I am your traveling companion. We met at Port o' Rue when the kind citizens tried to roast you alive. My name is Scrapius, though I am commonly called Scraps. I just fell off the cliff and into the river. Surely you remember that? Somehow you and your horse had crossed the raging torrent on a magnificent bridge that I, for some reason, could not see. When I tried to convince my horse that there was actually a bridge where none could be seen, he refused to budge and then... ." His voice trailed off as he remembered something else. "... And then there was a voice—my own voice coming from nowhere and everywhere—and then, just when I was pulling hardest on my horse's reins, there, on his back, appeared a black-robed phantom... ."

Again the old man paused and began scratching his chin through his beard as if the better to think. A moment later he continued. "He kicked the horse, the horse bolted forward, and I was pushed off the edge of the cliff and fell into the maelstrom of the raging water. And then, just when I was certain I would drown—I don't swim well, you see—I felt you and, together, we managed to make it up to the surface."

He stopped talking and looked around. "But what is this? This is not a riverbank. We're in a cave!" Then for the first time he seemed to notice his young rescuers, who were now staring at him. He stared back at them and then looked at Dag-gar. "Well, I can see the hand of the Gods in all this. Look at them, Dag-gar, look at them. Such a lovely sight. Thrangs! We have fallen in among a band of Thrangs!

But Dag-gar could not take his eyes from the old man. Now he knew who he was, but... . He shook his head as if to get cobwebs to fall away from his brain. He rubbed his eyes and looked again. Finally he was able to say, "But—but Scraps, you were young, and now—now you are... you are old!"

The old man who called himself Scraps looked at Dag-gar for a moment and then down at his hands and then he put his hands to his face and said, "Indeed, it would seem that is the case. I am now old. But, never mind, it happens like that, you know. One moment you are young, and the next moment you are old—perhaps in another moment I shall be young again. Why, take yourself, for example. As I remember, before we took our dip together in the furious water, when you traipsed across that invisible bridge all la-de-da, you were a beardless boy not more than, what—fourteen seasons of the sun? Now look at you: a full man—though still a very young one—with a fine beard!"

Dag-gar put his hands to his face. It was true: his cheeks and chin were covered with curling brown hair. He pulled his hands away and examined them. They were no longer the slender hands of a boy, but the thick-fingered hands of a man.

Dag-gar looked questioningly at Scraps. Scraps shrugged and said, "I have my suspicions that this unintended swim of ours was taken in one of Time's swirling eddies and that the Time Vagabond, your Captain Sorrow, was somehow mixed up in it. But in any case, there is nothing to be done about it. We may both end up as squalling infants needing a wet nurse before he is done with us." Scraps motioned at the young people who were still watching and listening to them. "But you must understand, Dag-gar," he said, raising his voice so it would be obvious that he was speaking to them, too, "we have had great luck in our time drifting. Have you never heard of the Thrangs?"

Dag-gar shook his head.

"Ah, well, they are a wonderful idea—that is, they live by a wonderful philosophy—credo, creed, doctrine, if you will. You see, all they do is wander this fat, round world seeking the answer to the Great Mystery. What could be better than that? They hunt, they fish, they ride their great shaggy horses and do little else, all in the name of their particular quest: to understand the how and why of Existence. But why should I tell you this? Let's let them tell you all about it."

With some effort, Scraps gathered his legs under him and got to his feet. He put his soaking wet hat on his head and held his hands out toward the gathered Thrangs. "I am Scrapius," he said, "known as Scraps by those who know me. Do you understand my language?"

One of the Thrangs stepped forward, a young man of perhaps eighteen seasons of the sun, tall and with a magnificent beard. He was dressed like the others in undergarments of coarse wool and a tunic and leggings made from animal fur and skins. His boots were also made from skins and had intricate, multicolored patterns sewn into them. He held his hands out toward Scraps in what was evidently a mutual gesture of peace. "Yes, of course," he said, "we understand each other. And you are right. We are Thrangs. Every year we come to this cave. It is a sacred place. The water that flows from this spring is magical. We believe it is connected to the Great Mystery itself. It has the power to heal wounds and make well the sick."

He peered closely into Scraps' eyes and said, "But answer me this, old one. Are you the great wizard by that same name, Scrapius? Our Ancient Song sings of such a man, a magician of great power."

"Ah!" Scraps said, and he winked at Dag-gar. "I suppose that is true. I am that very same cranky, finger-wagging, self-righteous old sorcerer that's mentioned in your Song. You see, on occasion the Great Mystery—which I think of as the workings of the Gods and their handmaiden, Time—allows me the pleasure of traveling with you, though I am as surprised as you are when I find myself plopped down among you. But believe me, I have no idea how it all works either, this Great Mystery-Time thing. Nevertheless, I'm always hoping to be of some small assistance in your business of understanding it. Then, you see, we would all know what is going on."

Scraps paused and smiled. "However, who cares about the Great Mystery? For the moment, anyway, let us forget it exists. I am, in my current Time, very old and very cold and very wet. Dry clothes, a good meal, and, perhaps, if you are real Thrangs, you would have a small dram of plum wine handy? That would be just lovely."

The big Thrang who called himself Calip laughed. "All that, great wizard, and more, we shall make certain you have."

But Dag-gar interrupted. "Where is she?" he asked. "I don't see her here. The young woman with the white-blond hair. She was just with you—down—down there." He nodded at the water. "She was riding a blue horse. She... ."

"What is your name?" Calip asked.

"My name is Dag-gar."

Upon hearing Dag-gar's name, Calip's eyes widened and for a moment he was speechless. The other Thrangs had also heard the name and moved closer, murmuring among themselves. Finally, Calip found his tongue. "Dag-gar," he said, and the syllables were a little breathless. He looked at the water in the well, bubbling and swelling upwards and glittering orange and yellow in the reflected firelight, and then back at Dag-gar. "Can this be?" he asked and he looked at Scraps and then again at Dag-gar. "Can we have here the ancient wizard Scrapius and Dag-gar, too, the eternal lover of our warrior-goddess, Sonoria?"

Dag-gar now looked as confused as those who stared at him. He felt their eyes on him and blood rose in his face. "I—I only know my name. I am Dag-gar, son of the great sea captain named Jarl." Then he remembered his cat. "I—I do have a kitten. I named her Sonoria, but she—was just a cat. She is gone, lost at sea."

No sooner had he spoken these words than the familiar fluffy white tale appeared around Calip's neck, yet the young Thrang seem not to notice it at all and neither did any of the others. Dag-gar bit his lip to stop himself from calling out.

But now Scraps interrupted. "Ah, so, my wonderful and hardy youths, we can discuss all this later over a goatskin of wine and spit of roasted hare or, better yet, venison. Again, I must insist; I'm old and I'm cold—a deadly combination. Have you a dry blanket I could wrap around myself?"

A Thrang brought two thick wool blankets and wrapped them over Scraps' and Dag-gar's shoulders and led them around the edge of the pool to a log set by a blazing fire. All through the long evening that followed, while their clothes dried and while each of the Thrangs shared the stories of their adventures, Dag-gar watched the white kitten cavort among them, unseen.

* * * * *

And so the girl's tale had continued as she and the old wizard made their tedious way toward the beckoning distant shadows that they knew were mountains—a great mountain range that exploded from the dryness of the desert and promised green trees and flowing streams. Yet they were still many days off from this goal and the camel was becoming peevish.

When it seemed the beast would soon decide to move no farther, when a harsh wind lifted the fine desert grit and sent it stinging against the skin of their faces, when the water bags were near to empty, there was, of a sudden, a breath of freshness in the air. The camel, of course, sensed it long before the old man and the girl. Its head went up, its nostrils flared, and there came a spring to its step.

Scraps felt the camel's gait change and he looked out across the rocks and dunes toward what had been for days a merciless horizon. There he saw what he was certain was yet another mirage—a lake where there was no lake, shimmering water where there was but baked sand. But he understood camels and their peculiar genius for finding water and forced himself to believe: They had come upon an oasis.

At this increased pace they continued, and soon they could see trees silhouetted against the sky, and the dark smudge around them became a bright green, and the wetness of a marsh, complete with splashing, quacking, honking water birds, sparkled under the sun.

"We shall have a bath!" Scraps said, more to himself than to the girl. "And feast on ducks and dates. Perhaps there is a goat or two. I do love roast goat! And we can sleep on beds of soft grass." He smacked his lips and started to sing as he jumped in the air and made a clumsy attempt to clap his heels together, his long, bony legs flailing in the air.

The camel now began to run. With the girl laughing and bouncing on its hump, it pulled free of the old man's grasp and galloped toward the sanctuary of date palms and the refuge of bubbling springs.

By the time the sun was sagging toward a skyline a-dust and baked, they had set up their camp. Intending an extended rest, they put up their small individual tents and inside them laid out the carpets and blankets that had been stacked up high on the camel's back. Then the camel was set to grazing while Scraps and Sonoria went off to different ends of the oasis for their private baths.

When the sun was about to lose itself in the bruised haze of evening, Scraps built a fire and set about roasting the ducks he had shot with his bow. The girl, freshly scrubbed, her hair a great white-blond corona around her head, emerged from her tent wearing a silk robe of bright blue. She settled on the grass at the edge of the fire and watched Scraps turn the ducks on the spit.

"So, my lovely young one," Scraps said, smiling at her, "you sparkle with anticipation. What shall tonight's tale bring us? The stars shall be especially brilliant tonight, the dust having left the sky. Perhaps you can convince a great red-orange one, the one at the heart of the Scorpion, to join us at our fire and partake of the feast of your imagination?"

"I must go to him again tonight," she said, watching the flames lap at the grease that dripped from the browning skin of the cooking ducks.

"Oh?" Scraps said. "And him, I assume, would be this Dag-gar who has been so wound up in your story."

"Yes, Dag-gar. I was just with him—during my bath in the bottomless spring of this oasis. I found him. We were riding together toward a great city built on the edge of an ocean-sea."

Scraps, realizing that the evening's narrative was even now beginning, did not speak. Instead, he settled back on his haunches and listened to both the fat sizzle in the flames and the girl's unfolding story. For he knew that as it was told, so it would be, for nothing is more true in the whirls and folds of Time than a dream.

Sonoria spoke, her words soft against a night that was seeping in along ridges and valleys of the distant mountains. "I had to leave him then," she said, "but I must go back. Captain Sorrow is still near him. He has something else we must take from him, something he has stolen from Dag-gar in a far, forgotten time, something Dag-gar must not be without. We can face him together, but not alone—neither one of us can face him alone."

Oh, my poor, poor child, Scraps thought, *to think that eternal love can defeat such an eternal energy as the Time Vagabond and his message of bitter truth. You and your eternal love can only hope to soften the pain of his inevitable victory. But never mind. I'll let you get on with it—get on with it, child, get on with it.*

Chapter 19

Dag-gar was awakened by the soft touch of the white cat, Sonoria. All evening while the Thrangs had sat around the fire next to the bubbling well talking with him and Scraps and feasting on venison and hare, she had tormented him with her presence, first there on Calip's shoulder, then walking serenely across the circle of firelight to crawl into the lap of another Thrang and then another. And yet no one was aware of her presence. She was a ghost of a cat, a spirit visible only to Dag-gar, and she kept her wide blue eyes on him as she purred and rubbed herself against their legs and arms.

Finally she came to Dag-gar, sitting cross-legged on his blanket, and curled up on his legs. He dared not respond to her, dared not speak to her or stroke her lest he be thought possessed—which indeed, he realized, he was.

When the need to share their stories was overwhelmed by the need for sleep, the Thrangs, one by one, fell asleep, leaving on duty at the mouth of the cave a guard whose job it was to keep at least a small fire burning and a torch blazing. Finally, only old Scraps, Calip, and Dag-gar were left awake and then they, too, began yawning and the conversation flagged.

It was a relief to Dag-gar, who was determined to stay awake as long as Scraps and Calip, when Scraps yawned and stretched and bade them good dreaming. Only when the old man had stretched out on his blanket and immediately begun to snore, did Dag-gar spread his blanket out and lie down on it. This seemed to please the kitten, who curled up under Dag-gar's arm. He could hear her purring and feel the warmth from her body coming through his tunic and spreading through him.

* * * * *

He did not feel himself drifting off into sleep, did not sense the coming of it, and so, when he heard the white kitten's mewing and felt her licking at his face, it seemed to him that he had just closed his eyes. Yet when he opened them and looked about, things had changed—time had passed. But how much? The fire had burned low, the cave was filled with the sounds of multiple sleepers as well as the sound of the bubbling spring, and the guard at the cave entrance was gone.

Sonoria licked him again, then walked away from him and went to the edge of the pool. She stood for a moment gazing at the rising water, which had begun to glow as if far below in its depths there was great light shining upwards. Then she turned and looked at Dag-gar, staring into his eyes as if to draw him into her.

He stood up and walked to her and peered into the water. "What is it?" he whispered. "What do you see?"

Sonoria mewed a clear, bell-like mew and leaped into the roiling effervescence, disappearing among the bubbles. Following her intently with his gaze, Dag-gar saw swirling colors—greens and browns and blues—that he did not at first recognize. After a few moments, however, he began to apprehend the moving colors as images, images of horses running across a vast green prairie under a blue sky. They seemed to be right in the water, just below the surface, yet they were running in bright sunlight, their shadows chasing them, their manes and tails flying in the wind.

A horse with a rider appeared. He recognized her immediately: it was the young woman with the wild, white-blond hair. Her eyes sought out his and when she found them, she held them and he felt her pulling him toward her. At first he tried to break away, but then he yielded and felt himself falling forward.

The water closed over him but this time he did not struggle. He let the rider's eyes take him down into it. As before, he felt a surging power under him and the wind against him. Once more he had reins in his hand; once more below him a great shaggy horse galloped across the endless green prairie.

And she was riding next to him dressed in animal skins and furs, a bow and quiver of arrows slung across her back, a short sword at her side. They were running neck and neck together, his horse keeping pace with her big blue roan stallion, and again they were chasing a large herd of wild horses, and among them were what he knew now were the Thrangs: Calip with his long beard whipping madly in the wind, and the others, all the others astride their large, shaggy horses.

Then he saw it again: the familiar city that seemed to come up from the sea, the great, gray-walled city that floated above the waves. They were all racing towards it, the horses and the Thrangs, and it rose up to meet them, a forbidding citadel, vast and unspeakable.

He glanced over at the young woman who rode beside him. She smiled at him as she had before, and she urged her blue roan stallion on and now Dag-gar's horse held the pace. They came to the end of the prairie and rode down a long sandy incline, following the herd, and then they were all galloping on a wide beach, the waves lapping at the horses' hooves.

When they were still some distance from the city's walls, the Thrangs stopped the herd, bringing them up and gathering them together, circling them constantly.

For the first time, Dag-gar heard the young woman speak and her voice was a woman's voice, but as pure and bell-like as the white cat's. "This is an ancient city, built and ruled by a race of people long gone. It looks forbidding, but it is now a peaceful seaport. Its gates are always open."

Dag-gar nodded and he realized that he knew where they were. He had been to this city before, had sailed here with his father on *Mother-of-Pearl*. He had been inside the great walls, had seen its people—amazing people of many colors, many shades, a people of much music and laughter. He looked at the woman who sat on her horse next to him. "What is your name," he asked, "and what is the name of this city?"

She laughed, and in the laugh Dag-gar again heard the echo of a person he had once known. "It is called," she said, "Eye o' the Sea, and it is a very wonderful place."

"Then it is true," he said. "I have been here before. I have sailed here with my father on his ship."

"Then you'll understand what I mean when I say I am excited to be back. All the Thrangs are excited. Today we shall be rewarded for gathering these wild horses and delivering them to the city's horse traders. Then we shall feast and dance. There will be a full moon tonight. There is much to celebrate."

"Please, then," Dag-gar said, turning in his saddle and looking directly into the woman's face, "how are you called? What is your name?"

"My name is Sonoria," she said.

Dag-gar eyes must have widened and his mouth must have dropped open, though he did not realize it; he *did* feel blood rush into his face. The young woman who had just called herself Sonoria laughed and this time it was a long, loud laugh that was carried out on the wind. Some of the other Thrangs turned and smiled at them.

"But," she said, finally, "it is not, I think, such a terrible name as to cause you such discomfort."

"No, no, not at all," Dag-gar said, struggling to come up with an explanation for his reaction. How offended would she be if he told her he had somehow managed give his kitten the same name? How could he tell her that this kitten was invisible to everyone but himself? That this cat he had named Sonoria had white-blond hair and blue eyes just like hers? "It is a beautiful name," he said after a moment. "I was surprised because I have heard it before. It comes from an island we used to sail to. The silversmiths there make beautiful silver bells. Sonoria means 'beautiful singer.' "

Sonoria tossed her head in a vain attempt to get her wild hair out of her face. "I didn't know that," she said, "but your story must be true. I was given this name because I can calm wild horses with my singing."

Dag-gar did not want to take his eyes from her face. Scraps' words again came back to him: *You are meant to be together—all of you—forever and ever. And longer than that, even! If fact, you already have been together for longer than forever.*

He wanted to reach out for her and put his fingers in her hair. He longed to say things to her that he did not know how to say or why he wanted to say them. He felt his face growing red again and he looked away, out toward the sea.

It was then that he saw something he had not noticed before: a ship lay at anchor in the small harbor on the seaward side of the walled city of Eye o' the Sea. She was far off, but Dag-gar was certain that he knew her rigging, knew her wonderful lines, her fine sheer: It was his father's ship—it was *Mother-of-Pearl.*

He stood in his stirrups, the better to see, and he noticed something else. A skiff was approaching *Mother-of-Pearl,* a black skiff, with a single rower at the oars. The oarsman appeared to be wearing a black cloak. He worked steadily at his task, moving slowly against the wind. A moment later, the skiff was by the ship's side. As Dag-gar watched, the cloaked figure climbed up the ship's boarding ladder and disappeared aboard her.

"What is it?" Sonoria asked.

"I see—I see a ship. I need to go there right now. Is there a way to do this?"

"Of course," she said. "We'll bring the horses into the city and then you can go through the city down to the harbor."

Even as she said these words, Dag-gar saw Calip ride forward and disappear into the city. He was gone for only a short time and then reappeared. He rode out a short distance and signaled for them to begin to bring the horses in. With great skill, the Thrangs now moved the herd slowly toward the gate and into Eye o' the Sea.

Dag-gar and Sonoria rode side by side, bringing up the last of the herd. When they passed through the gates, Dag-gar was flooded with memories. How long had it been since he had been here? It seemed a very long time and he must have been very young, yet he recognized the tree-lined streets and the odors of the market place. There were merchants selling all manner of spices and vendors and hawkers selling all manner of food. Musicians played on street corners, sending sweet sound out to join the din and clamor that was life in Eye o' the Sea.

The streets were lined with people eager to watch the parade of horses and the wild youths bringing them in. Old people stared, children called out, their voices shrill with excitement, dogs barked, and chickens squawked. The sound of hooves on cobblestones set up a great clatter; dust rose upwards and swirled away in the wind.

They followed a straight, broad boulevard until it opened up on a large common area, in the middle of which was a big corral. The horses were guided into this corral and the gate shut behind them. This done, the Thrangs sent up a loud whoop that was answered by applause from the watching townspeople. The riders then slid from their saddles and each accepted a large schooner of drink ceremoniously presented by several young women of the town.

When Dag-gar and Sonoria had dismounted, they were swallowed up by the crowd and Dag-gar found himself being handed a flagon of foaming liquid. "No," he said, "I need to get to the harbor."

"Do you remember the way?" Sonoria asked. "I can show you."

"Yes, come with me," he said, though he did not know why he wanted her next to him. Leading their horses, they set off on foot.

They made their way through the crowds away from the big corral until they came to a side street that seemed to lead to the water. Here the open square gave way to wooden buildings built close together with only the occasional narrow passage between them. Here, too, the streets were paved with cobblestone; through gutters along their edges, water carried the effluent of the city. Above, laundry dried on lines strung between the buildings; children shrieked and women called to each other across the space.

They picked their way along, the smell of human waste and garbage strong, the clopping of their horses' hooves echoing in their ears. Gradually these smells and sounds were joined by the salt scent of the ocean and the sloshing of seawater against pilings.

A short time later they reached the waterfront, a broad, open area where ships were unloaded and from where they had a clear view of the port. Beyond the few ships tied up at the dock, they could see *Mother-of-Pearl* swinging at anchor in the larger outer harbor.

The first thing that Dag-gar noticed was her condition. Her furled sails were gray and hung in tatters; her wooden sides were stained with a greenish mold. Once proud and noble, she was now a rotting hulk.

He looked about for a way to go out to her. Skiffs were tied up along the seawall and in one of them, sitting on a thwart, he spied an old sailor mending fishing nets. "Sir," he called out, "I need to go out to that ship—to *Mother of Pearl*. Can you take me?"

The old seaman peered up at Dag-gar with rheumy, cloudy eyes, studied him for a moment, and said, "I'd rather play a blood sport with a demon than go near that ship, my boy. What business could you have on her?"

"She is my father's ship. I grew up on her."

The old man, squinting in the sun, looked more closely at Dag-gar. "You did, did you? Grew up on her, you say? Well, either you are a very old young man or you are possessed by some dark spirit that has caused your mind to go astray. For I tell you, boy, that ship is indeed called *Mother of Pearl*, but she has been there since I was a young man, and you can easily see that some time has passed since the hot blood of youth ran in my veins."

"But I must go out to her. My father may still be aboard. He may need my help."

"Heh, heh," the old man cackled, shaking his head and showing toothless gums. "Get along, then. There's a smart boy. Your good sense has all leaked out your ears! I tell you, no one has been on that ship in living memory. How she still floats is the great mystery of this harbor, yet no one will go out on her to find out."

"That's not true," Dag-gar said. "I just saw someone row a skiff out to her and go aboard."

The fisherman now spat into the water and looked away from Dag-gar and at Sonoria. "My pretty," he said, "please take this poor lad home and keep him safe from harm, for I do think he will come to no good. Such people who have lost their senses can come to grief in this town."

Without hesitation, Sonoria said, "I will pay you handsomely to take him where he wants to go." She held out a gold coin.

The old man's eyes widened at the sight of the gleaming metal. He spat into the water again, wiped his mouth with a dirty, calloused hand, and looked out toward the ship. When he looked back at Dag-gar and Sonoria, he shook his head and sighed. "That is a cruel thing you do, girl," he said. "For I cannot turn away from what you offer, and yet I dare not row out to that ship."

"Then," Sonoria said, "you need not go yourself. I will pay you to let him take the boat."

The old man thought for a moment and again smiled across his raw gums. "Now there you go, making some sense," he said. "But we will wait here together for him and if he does not come back, you will buy my old skiff for the price of a new one."

Again, Sonoria did not hesitate. "Agreed," she said.

The old man rose from the thwart, collected his net, threw it over his shoulder, and climbed up the ladder to the dock. He squinted up at the much taller Dag-gar and said, "And if it's trouble you find out there, there's no reason to call for help. No one will go near that demon ship—she is filled with the gloom of evil, for certain." He took the coin from Sonoria's hand, sat down on a wooden crate, and began to fill a pipe with tobacco.

Chapter 20

The outgoing tide quickly carried the fisherman's skiff out of the inner harbor and toward the sea. She was a well-found little vessel, full-keeled and stiff, and Dag-gar, having handled such boats all his life, was able to steer her easily. As he rowed, he looked back at Sonoria. Holding both their horses, she was watching him, as was the old man sitting on his crate smoking his pipe. Behind them Eye o' the Sea unfolded herself, this harbor her squalid underbelly, the rank seawall her soiled petticoats.

He looked over his shoulder and watched as he drew closer to *Mother-of-Pearl*. The ship he had called home all his life, the ship whose essence had become a part of him, had been transformed by neglect and time into an apparition draped with a sinister moodiness. Her lightness was gone, the hot, moist, sense of adventure that had formed the heart of her soul was now desiccated and twisted. There was little left of her spirit save the wondrous lines of her sheer that spoke of her former beauty. And there, tied up to her side, was the black skiff he had seen being rowed out to her by the cloaked figure.

When he closed the final distance with her, he brought the bow of the boat around to face the tide, grabbed the bottom of the rope ladder, and tied his skiff up next to the other. He looked down into the black skiff and remembered, remembered the terrible night he had spent lying in her foul bottom while the specter he had come to know as Captain Sorrow rowed them over the face of the ocean-sea.

He shuddered and found himself gasping, and his mouth went dry. But he remembered his father's words: "When you face terrible things that cannot be ignored, stop, take a breath, let your soul accept what needs be done—and then do it."

He closed his eyes for a moment as he pictured his father standing tall and straight on the deck; then resolutely he took his sword from its scabbard and swung himself up the rope ladder and onto *Mother-of-Pearl*.

When he stepped onto her broad wooden planks, there came two powerful and conflicting understandings: He was home again, where he had lived since infancy; yet the feel of the wood under his feet brought no comfort—merely dread. The familiar now was alien, the intimate unknown; the longing to again belong here was powerful, the horror of being here overwhelming.

His eyes darted around, surveying the features that he knew as well as he knew his own face—the capstans and belaying pins, the lines and blocks, and the huge masts. Here was his past, the beloved country of his youth.

He heard a soft creaking. The door to the companionway stairs that led down to the captain's cabin was ajar, swinging slowly open and closed as the ship rocked on the swell. A foul odor rose up the companionway from the blackness within the cabin, carried to him on the small breeze that ran across the ship.

His sword up and ready, he strode to the companionway, all the time watching the moving door. It was as if the ship were breathing, as if, despite everything, she still lived. Yet the smell that came up from her innards was the stench of something beyond death.

When he reached the door, he put his hand on it and stopped its swinging. He looked down the steps. He could see nothing but darkness. The smell of rot was nearly overpowering, and with it came a sense of doom that made his mouth go dry. He shuddered. Whoever had rowed that black skiff out to the ship was down there, listening and waiting. It would be, of course, Captain Sorrow.

Dag-gar stepped down into the companionway. He felt the wood of the steps yield slightly under his weight. There was a soft moan. He took the next step and then the next and the next. The darkness gave way to a dim illumination: the glass of the portholes, filthy from the years, still allowed some light to pass in. He saw more objects, objects that made his heart race: his father's things, Captain Jarl's possessions. A telescope lay in a corner. How many times had he and his father looked out to sea with that? Looked at the stars? Searched the ragged face of the moon? Papers and books were scattered about, everything strewn as if a great blast of wind had torn the place asunder.

Dag-gar stopped and listened. He heard breathing. From a dim corner of the cabin came a rasping intake of air that was released in a harsh rush of sound. Then again the rasping and then again the release. Dag-gar waited, his blood pounding in his ears, his hands sweating, and the sound of his own breathing filling in the empty moments, spaces in time when there was no other sound.

He took the last step down and turned.

A voice rasped on the rough exhalations. "Thank you for coming out to my ship. It is ever so lonely here." The voice was a gasp, the syllables of the words a coarse retching as if the speaker were gagging on the unspeakable truth of his own tongue.

"Where is my father, Captain Jarl?"

"In which fold of Time?" the voice asked. "For in one he is dead and gone to dust—as are you all. In another, he is a young ship's captain plying the fair ocean-sea. In another he is as ancient as the stars, yet still lives. You can see him if you wish."

Dag-gar stepped forward, holding his sword before him. In a dim corner of the cabin he saw the black-robed figure that had come to haunt his dreams. The phantom lifted its arms and the sleeves of the robe fell back to reveal hands... not gaunt and wasted, but the tiny, fat hands of an infant.

"Your sword," the phantom said, "is powerful. It is, after all, Saiph, the sword of the celestial Hunter. But, boy, consider before you attack me with it again, for you will be astounded to see who I am."

The fingers of the small hands motioned to him to come closer. The voice rasped again. "You call me Captain Sorrow. Such a thing. A specter like me knows no sorrow. Indeed, only where there was once hope can there be sorrow, and I can tell you, for the eternity of my existence, I have never known hope."

Dag-gar stepped closer, raising his sword. "Where is my father?"

"Do you want to see him?" the specter asked. "Of course you do. Well, then, here he is." The baby hands reached up and pulled the cowl of the robe away from Captain Sorrow's head and there, bearded, skeletal, and emaciated, was the face of Captain Jarl.

Dag-gar cried out, "Father!"

"Yes," the specter said, now hissing the words through Captain Jarl's dried and lifeless lips. "Here is your father."

"You've killed him," Dag-gar screamed, looking into the empty sockets of his father's eyes.

"Nay, boy," his father's mouth said, and yet it was not his father's voice that came from it, "'twas Time that killed him. For Time is death and death is sorrow and all that ever was, hangs on Time's gallows. To all that is, we shall bid farewell, and all things unborn are yet doomed."

Dag-gar stared, unable to speak.

His father's mouth spoke again. "So, call me Sorrow. Yes, I am Captain Sorrow. Yet all is not lost. Things may yet be saved and this long-dead face that now speaks, the face of your father, may again be filled with the juice of life.

"Listen to me—listen: There is a place in Time's swirling where everything is as it once was, where you are still a child running barefoot on the clean, new deck of this ship; where Captain Jarl yet plots the course of your voyage across the ocean-sea and across Time itself using the secrets locked in the Amber Teardrop.

"And I tell you, boy, I can return you there to that very time and you will be with your father—happy forever. You see, I have her—the Amber Teardrop, the missing gem from the Hunter's belt, a belt that even now hangs on your waist. And locked within the amber is the inscrutable sleeping face—the very face of Time. I have her here, close to my heart.

"Yet, alas, my heart beats not, for I am without life. And as I am without life, I am without hope, and so—I am powerless to use her. So I need you—you and the hot blood of your living flesh. Do you understand? Together we can control Time itself. Our power will be infinite—greater than the gods themselves."

One of Captain Sorrow's small hands disappeared inside his robe and when it re-emerged, the hand was no longer that of a babe, but was as dead and skeletal as Captain Jarl's face, and in its grasp was the Amber Teardrop. "See now, lad, here it is: the key to Time itself. The frozen blood of the Ancient Tree, a tree that spans the three planes of existence: its branches, the celestial home of the gods; its trunk, the present where you and your kind exist; and its roots, the underworld where the spirits of the dead await their fates. But you know the Teardrop well, I'm certain, having seen your father use it to unlock the mysteries of the cosmos. Perhaps you, too, know how to do such things, hey?"

Dag-gar stared at what the specter held before his eyes—the familiar glowing, teardrop-shaped piece of amber that he had known all his life. And within the Amber's dark, honey-colored matrix was the sleeping face of Time, inscrutable and immaculate. Now Captain Sorrow reached out and offered it to Dag-gar and Dag-gar lifted his hands and accepted it. The Amber was light and warm and its energy ran through his body and he began to shake.

"Yes! Yes," Captain Sorrow said, "you feel it, don't you? And you may have it and keep it forever. But beware! By accepting it, you give yourself to me. Even as the power of the ancient blood courses through you, so too will I be a part of your blood and your bones—part of your living flesh."

"Where is my father?"

"Far from here," the specter said. "He is my prisoner in a forgotten castle on a forgotten island whose shores are washed by the cold ocean-sea. He is very ancient now, blind and toothless and pitiful. You see, when I took the Amber Teardrop from him on his ship—this very ship—he refused to reveal to me the secret of its use despite my promise of eternal youth. So until he does so, he will travel with me, suffering the pain and the cold and lonely miseries of infinite old age.

"But you can save him, even if he refuses to save himself. If you indeed know the secret of the Amber—how to use it to navigate across oceans and across Time—you may also use it to find your father. Reveal the secret of the Amber Teardrop to me and I will release him to eternal youth. He will be forever happy sailing the ocean-sea."

As Captain Sorrow spoke these words, Dag-gar stared at the perfect face in the gleaming brown amber. And then he looked up. No longer did the specter's robes hold the empty, desiccated face of his father. Now within those dark robes Dag-gar beheld the face of a young woman, a young woman with white-blond hair and eyes the color of a clear desert sky.

"Sonoria," Dag-gar said, and he whispered her name.

Again, though, it was the specter's voice that came from the woman's full, red lips. "Yes, Sonoria," Captain Sorrow said. "Despite your bloody, murderous ways with men, you are a young man who loves blindly, blind to the vagaries, insults, passions, and madness of it. In your case it is eternal love. For, my good and foolish Dag-gar, you have loved her forever, and she you."

Then, before Dag-gar's eyes, the face folded in on itself. Sonoria's fine young features collapsed and disappeared as if sucked into a hole, a black tunnel that led nowhere. Dag-gar stared into it and understood that this infinite emptiness was the true face of sorrow, the true face of the Time Vagabond.

The voice now came as an echo, not from the hole, but from all around him inside the ship. "You need me to find your father and you need me to save the love you have for this woman. Without me you will lose both, for I shall destroy both. What say you then? Do you accept my offer?"

"Yes," Dag-gar said, and he bowed his head. "Yes, and so I must."

Dag-gar felt himself being lifted from the floor and drawn upward into the cowl of the specter's robe, into the lightless place where Sonoria's face had been. He reached out for something to hold onto but there was nothing, and he began spinning as if caught in a whirlpool, not of water, but of something between air and water, something that was thick and wet and icy cold. He closed his eyes and felt himself spinning and falling and felt the cold, hard bitterness of the Vagabond enter his mouth and his nose and his eyes and he started choking, gagging, suffocating, and then, when he could no longer struggle, he surrendered to it.

* * * * *

The fine teak boards of the cabin floor were cool on his face, the rolling of the ship a balm to the pain in his bones; the smell of old linseed oil and tar brought back floods of memories. But they

114

were dreams, illusions. He opened his eyes. The dreams faded, the memories drifted away.

He rolled onto his side. The light from the filthy glass in the portholes was diminishing, the darkness of the ship's interior increasing. He pushed himself onto his hands and knees and stood up. The specter was gone. There was only the smell of the ancient wood and dust as the motes drifted in the still air.

He felt for his sword. It was there in its scabbard at his hip, hanging from the belt, the heavy leather girdle of the Hunter. He ran his hands over it. He found the stones. There were the two and now, a third. The empty setting had been filled. He unbuckled the belt from around his waist so he could look at it. There was the Amber Teardrop with its sleeping face. The Hunter's belt had been restored. He tried to remember everything, tried to replay it in his mind, but as with a dream looked at too closely, the visions he had witnessed began to fade. He remembered, though, Captain Sorrow's face, the face of the Time Vagabond, and the horror of its emptiness.

Around him the old ship sang its ancient song: its timbers creaked, the wind moaned through its spars, and the sea sighed against its hull. He saw his father's telescope lying in the corner amongst the yellowed, rat-chewed papers. He picked it up and felt the cool of its bronze and the solid weight of it. A last ray of sunlight was coming in a porthole. Dag-gar pulled his sword from its scabbard and smashed the glass. He held the telescope in the stream of light and brought the beam to bear on the papers on the cabin floor, and then he adjusted the telescope so the beam of light was concentrated on them. Soon they began to smoke and then, with a flash, burst into flame. He threw the telescope onto the fire, turned away, and went back up the companionway steps and out onto the deck.

The land breeze brought the odors of the town of Eye o' the Sea out to him: horse dung and human waste, cooking food and wafting smoke. And there were sounds, too. Distant voices cried and laughed and music drifted out over the water, arriving at his ears as if the players were somewhere nearby.

On the dock, he could see Sonoria waiting, standing between their horses. She was looking out across the harbor at him and when she saw him, she waved. He did not acknowledge this. He went to the side of the ship and climbed down the rope ladder and stepped into the skiff. As he pulled on the oars, the ghost ship that had been *Mother-of-Pearl*, had been his home and safe refuge, seemed not to be floating on a swelling ocean, but hanging over it, the sky become a gibbet. Smoke was beginning to drift up from the companionway as the fire inside quickly spread.

The wind pushed against him and the tide, too, and it took all his strength to row against it. It was nearly dark when he reached the wharf, tied the skiff up, and climbed the ladder onto the dock.

The fisherman sat on the wooden crate smoking his pipe, watching and waiting. Sonoria, holding the horses by their reins, had moved away from the old man, but now, as Dag-gar came up on the wharf, she approached them.

The fisherman eyed him, looking disappointed. "So," he said, "what'd ya' find out there aboard the demon's ship?"

Dag-gar stopped and stared at the old man, but did not speak. The old man looked into his eyes and his toothless smile faded. He looked out to *Mother-of-Pearl* and saw it was now ablaze; great orange flames and black smoke rose from her decks and were spreading to her rigging. He took the pipe from his mouth, gathered up his nets, and limped away.

"I was worried about you," Sonoria said. For a moment she watched the burning ship and then she handed Dag-gar his horse's reins.

Dag-gar took the reins and, with the other hand, reached out and touched her cheek. "I saw you out there," he said, looking at her face as he stroked it, "on my father's ship—in the face of the Time Vagabond. He is with us now. Captain Sorrow is a part of me, and so, a part of us."

Sonoria looked back out across the harbor. "The ship..." she said.

Dag-gar did not look at it. "Now we must find my father."

Part II

Chapter 21

They remounted their horses and rode up from the harbor and back toward the center of the town of Eye o' the Sea. But now, Dag-gar and Sonoria found the narrow streets jammed with people, all moving toward the town square. They were carried along by this flood and felt the great excitement that pulsed through it and heard what the collective voice of the mob was saying: A great magician has come into town! A true wizard who is doing wonderful things. Lead becomes gold, fire becomes water, noise is transformed into beautiful music. Bring something, they said, any piece of rubbish, any scrap of food, and he will make it what you want. A fat beefsteak from gristle, a golden goose from a piece of eggshell! So Sonoria and Dag-gar were rushed along in a throng so dense that they pushed against the horses, and the great blue roan stallion, Spiritus, pranced against them and snorted his complaints.

In a short time they emerged from the alley into the broad, open square, and here a huge crowd had already gathered around the Great Tree, a living temple whose branches reached upwards and spread outwards forming a broad, green arch. Torches and fires had been lit and the air was illuminated with red-orange flames that cast shadows that danced among the people like spirits of the dead come to join in the joy of the sorcerer's deceptions.

Under the Great Tree, in the middle of it all, surrounded by the mob's fiery exuberance, was a donkey, a small gray ass whose long, gloomy face hung down nearly to the ground, and whose thin tail swatted at imaginary flies. Atop the donkey's back, perched on its withers, was a large, homely seabird, a pelican with an immense bill and small, black, disconsolate eyes.

Next to these dejected-looking beasts stood a tall, gaunt, coarse-featured man with a long gray beard, dressed in a patchwork tunic of many colors, as if it had been sewn together from the tattered shards of a fallen rainbow. On his head he wore a broad hat cut from the same cloth with a flapping brim that nearly covered his eyes. But his eyes were visible. Moist and aglow, they held the gathered citizens of Eye o' the Sea in thrall.

"Come now!" he said, in a hoarse, high-pitched voice that carried out over the upturned faces like an irresistible spirit wind. "Behold Admiral Penance, my donkey, my poor *equus asinus*—a wise little brute with a large appetite. He is in need of fodder, my kind friends. Cannot one of you manage a piece of hay?—nay, even a coarse stem of straw would suffice."

A boy stepped forward and offered the magician a yellow stalk of straw. The magician's face lit up. "Ah! Now you will see how a wizard feeds his ass!"

The crowd laughed. He waved the stalk in the air and spoke an incantation in a tongue that sounded like guttural gibberish. Nothing happened. The stalk remained a stalk. The crowd murmured and the magician sighed. "I forgot the most important element in any magical trick and that, of course, is fire." he said, "I'm always forgetting something, forgivable in someone as old as the moon. Someone come forth here and bring me a small blaze."

He called to the same boy who had brought him the straw. "Bring me some fire, lad, and be quick about it!"

The boy shrugged his shoulders. "I don't have any," he said.

"Ah, then," the wizard said, "bring me that stick that lies next to you on the ground there."

The boy looked down and saw the stick. He grabbed it up and brought it to the wizard.

"Now," the wizard instructed, "hold on to the end of it and reach it out towards me—and whatever you do, do not flinch!"

The boy did as he was told. He held the stick out and the wizard reached as if to touch it. But when his hand drew close to the stick, flame shot from the tip of his index finger and set the stick on fire. The boy's eyes widened but he did not pull back. The crowd murmured.

"Now touch the flame to the straw," the wizard instructed, holding the straw out toward him, "but once you have done so, step back quickly."

The child hesitated and then touched the straw with the fire. There was a great puff of smoke and a small clap of thunder. The crowd gasped. A moment later, hay began to fall from the night sky, at first just a flurry of it, and then clumps of it as if someone were pitching it from a hayloft. Everyone looked up into the darkness but could see nothing. The donkey cast his head about for a moment and then began munching.

The wizard, too, looked up and held his long arms out as if in supplication to a higher authority. "Oh, gracious gods, our many thanks for your munificence!" He again turned to the crowd. "Now take pity, if you will, on this poor seabird you see roosting on the Admiral's back, its inelegant countenance dismal and dispiriting. A fish, my friends, is what he needs. Does anyone have something from a fish? A mere scale or a bone would do nicely."

The boy now found the skeleton of a fish in a pile of garbage. He again stepped forward and offered it to the wizard.

"Excellent," the sorcerer said, grasping the naked spine between his thumb and forefinger. He winked at the boy. "A smart lad! But let us not again forget the—"

But the boy was still holding a burning twig in his other hand, and before the magician could finish his sentence, he held it up to the bones. Now there was a loud crackling sound as they began to burn. A small trail of smoke rose up past the magician's hand and when the flames, too, were about to reach his fingers, he tossed the bones out over the crowd. Again there was a small thunderclap and living, flapping fish began to fall out of the darkness and down amongst the people.

There were shrieks of terror and wonder and everyone began scrambling, clutching at the slippery prizes. "Please!" the wizard called out, "let's not forget the poor bird!"

A woman stepped forward, her eyes wide, her mouth agape. She was holding a wiggling fish and offered it to the pelican. The bird studied her suspiciously, its eyes moving from her face to the fish and back again to her face. Finally, it opened its bill and allowed her to drop it into the sack that hung from its underside. It flipped its head up and down, worked the fish into proper position, and swallowed it whole.

This seemed to satisfy the magician immensely. He doffed his hat, revealing a huge bush of gray hair, bowed, and said, "Our heartfelt thanks at your generosity. Now, I shall return the favor." Scrutinizing the crowd for a moment, he picked out a man dressed in rags, a man with withered legs who dragged himself about through the dirty streets by rocking on his hands. "You there!" he called, "stand up and come here then. I've something for you."

The crowd, grasping their struggling fish, fell silent and opened up a circle of space around the filthy cripple. Uncomprehending, the man gazed up at the sorcerer.

"You! Get up and come here to me before Time's passing robs us of this opportunity. For that is from where these wonders unfold—Time itself, the handmaiden of the gods."

The man started to push himself along by his hands as usual, but now, when he exerted pressure on his palms, he rose from the ground as if levitated by some force, and underneath him his legs straightened themselves out. A moment later, he was standing up, tall and unbent.

"That's the spirit!" the magician exclaimed. "Now, come here to me. Come. Come!" He peered up at the sky as if the large, full moon, now rising from the ocean-sea and poking up over the tops of the buildings, held the key to the success of his conjuration.

The man took a tentative step forward. In disbelief he looked down at his feet and then up at the sorcerer. His mouth moved, but he was incapable of speech. The people of Eye o' the Sea parted before him, making a clear path to where the donkey, the seabird, and the wizard waited under the Great Tree. A moment later he was standing alone in the middle of a large space.

"Stop right there," the wizard instructed. "That's close enough or we'll all be in hot water!" The man stopped. The wizard looked for the child who had been so quick to bring what he had asked for. "Where's that boy? Can he bring me a flagon of water?"

In a trice the child appeared, now carrying a pitcher of water. "There's a most excellent lad!" said the wizard. "We'll have a bit of magic for you, too, my boy. Just be patient. In the meantime, pour that water over this man's head, again being careful to step away quickly. By the way, what is your name?"

"I don't have a real name," the boy said, "but they call me Bum."

"Bum," the magician said. "How sad a name for such a sterling lad. But never mind. Pour away, Bum, pour away."

Bum did as he was told. Stepping up to the man, he heaved the flagon back and then quickly forward, sloshing a big dollop of water onto his face. The crowd laughed at the cripple's sputtering, but an instant later there came a great booming from the sky and, though the moon was moving through cloudless heavens, it began to rain. In a moment it was a deluge, and someone yelled, "It's hot water! The rain is hot!"

The wizard laughed a loud, hoarse laugh. "And soapy, too, my dear friends, for as the gods' teeth are as dazzling as the sun, so are you people as filthy as gutter snipes."

And down it came, hot rain and soap, and soon the town square and all the people in it were dancing about, dripping with suds. For a long, joyous time, the citizens of Eye o' the Sea bathed together, hugging and sloshing and stripping down to their undergarments, the gleeful, shrieking children running about naked.

Then, for a time the rain ran clear and the soap was washed away. The people stood in their sopping clothing wondering what would happen next. The wizard, who, along with the donkey and the pelican, had remained dry under the protection of the Great Tree, looked out upon them and said, "Now that cleanliness has been established and food provided, I'm afraid the good news is over. For I have something terrible to tell you—all of you, all the citizens of this fair and lovely seaport."

He stopped and waited for the meaning of his words to sink in. The laughing quickly subsided; the crowd turned to him and stared. Still he waited, and while he waited he looked up at the moon, which had climbed high over the town and turned from orange to a bright, pale yellow. Then he removed his sword from its scabbard and swung it in a circle around his head. As the blade of the sword sliced through the air, its tip left an arc of blue flames behind.

This sight caused a great silence to descend over the crowd, and when the murmuring of the distant ocean-sea and the dripping of water from the deluge was all that could be heard, the wizard spoke. "Oh, great moon! 'Tis not you on whom our expectations fall, but rather your passage across this perfect night sky. For as passage is Time, so Time is mindfulness, and mindfulness is spirit, and spirit is all we have, we mere mortals, clinging so urgently to this, our fat, round world. So now, Time, you are the gods' handmaiden, moving the moon and the vast firmament itself, and moving us, as well, toward our graves. Tonight I ask only one more gift from you: Give these people of this town called Eye o' the Sea the wisdom and the strength to do what they must now do."

The wizard lowered his gaze toward the crowd. He held his arms out toward them. The light from the torches caused shadows to dance across his face and his eyes seemed to burn with their own internal fire. "People of Eye o' the Sea, listen and hear what I must tell you. Listen and understand. Listen, I beg you, for the magic you have seen tonight is but a mere ghost of the power of Time, of the cosmic spheres and their infinite motions. What you have witnessed comes not from me, but from the spirit of the cosmos *through* me. And, too, this we must always remember: We can borrow from Time, but *we must repay the debt.*"

The people of Eye o' the Sea stared up at the wizard, their wet hair clinging to their heads, their drenched clothing revealing every crease of their humanity.

The wizard went on: "On this night of the cross quarter, you have been cleansed of your wickedness and now is your chance for deliverance. For as I speak, as you stand before me in your new purity, there approaches this town an immense evil—an army vast and implacable."

He waited for these words to have their effect. He looked out over the upturned faces, at the myriad features, plain and lovely, at the eyes that looked at him with such unabashed wonder. They were his now; they belonged to him. "We must, on the morn, as the cock begins its crowing, abandon this place, your home by the sea, this portal, this cervix on the sacred womb of the Earth. For those that come would defile it, my brethren, would tear it asunder, would poison its wells, salt its earth, pillage its riches. And more than that, and much worse, too, they will likewise tear you and your babes asunder, limbs from limbs, eyes from sockets, bowels from bodies, heads from necks.

"So go now, back to your homes and prepare. Gather your treasures and clothing and what food you can carry. For come the first pearling of the new day, we shall leave. Should you choose to remain, as you certainly may, be advised you will not survive the scourge that will overwhelm this place."

Yet again, he gave his words time to be understood. There was, after a moment, a muttering. A man, a stout man with long moustaches still drooping with wet, stepped forward. "You are but a sorcerer," he said, "A mere magician. We have had such as you here before. M'thinks 'tis but trickery. You may be a demon come to lead us astray."

"Ah," the wizard answered immediately, "yes, that is the possibility. So, stay then! But, reason would dictate you hedge your bet just a tad. Come with us for a time and then return and see if what I have foretold is not true. If it is but chicanery, you have lost naught but time. If not, if I tell the truth, you have saved yourself and your precious loved ones."

Before the man could say more, the wizard added, "But I see that what I have done thus far has not convinced you to believe in me. Where is that boy who is called Bum?"

As usual, the boy was ready. He stepped forward into the circle of light that glowed around the wizard. While the townspeople watched, the old man studied him, walking around him, looking him up and down, nodding and murmuring to himself. Finally he said, "I can tell that you, lad, are an orphan, yes?"

The boy, suddenly embarrassed, nodded and looked down at his dirty bare feet.

"A street urchin?"

Again, the child nodded.

"But a smart boy, a clever and canny one?"

Now the boy looked up and smiled.

"Ah," the wizard said, "living on the street by one's wits tends to make one cagey and shrewd, and that, I suppose, is good. But you deserve better, boy. Much better. What say we start with a new name? Let's see, let me think."

The sorcerer made a great show of scratching his chin, tugging his beard, and looking upwards as if deep in thought. The crowd and the boy waited. There was the sound of dripping water, and now a breeze rustled the leaves and branches of the Great Tree and the moonlight's shadows joined those made by the torches' flames.

"Astral," the wizard said at last. "Of course. That's it! On such a night as this, it would have to be Astral—a boy of the stars, a boy of another dimension. And now that we have renamed you, let me give you something very special."

He waved his hands over the boy's head, snapped his fingers, and the child began to rise off the ground, lifting straight up, water from his bath dripping from his ragged pants. He tried to run, his arms and legs flailing in the air, and the crowd laughed. But then he stopped struggling and accepted the force that carried him upwards, even smiling as if he now trusted everything the sorcerer might do to him.

As the boy hung suspended above the crowd, the wizard spoke to him. "Astral, I am going to send you on a small journey. But you need not worry, for soon you will be back among us poor mortals safe and sound and very much the wiser. Are you ready?"

The boy was looking down at the townspeople, who had stopped laughing and now were staring up at him, open-mouthed. The wizard repeated himself. "Are you ready, lad?"

Now the boy nodded and apparently what he was feeling was not unpleasant, because he continued to smile.

"Good," the wizard said. "Close your eyes and imagine… uh, let's see, what would a boy like to eat? Ah! I've got it. Imagine the taste of honey."

The boy closed his eyes and his smile got wider. Then he began to spin as he hung in the air. Slowly at first and then faster he spun, until he had been transformed from a whirling ragamuffin into a blur of color and there came a humming sound, soft at first, and then louder and louder the faster the boy spun, until people began putting their fingers to their ears. Finally he was spinning so fast he seemed to become nearly invisible. Indeed, the moonlight passed through him as if he were but a vapor.

Then the spinning slowed, the humming diminished, and the vapor resolved itself once more into solidity. Turn by diminishing turn, the boy appeared again until he was, as before, suspended motionless above the people of Eye o' the Sea.

But now he was no longer dressed in his filthy urchin rags; indeed, he was not dressed at all, but hung above the crowd skyclad—naked as if he had just been born.

This drew a gasp from the upturned faces. The wizard cleared his throat. "Oh my," he said, "I had forgotten that this would happen. But never mind." He reached behind him somewhere—no one could see exactly where, though it seemed to be just into the darkness itself—and brought forth a brand new suit of clothes. He held them up and the cloth from which they were made gleamed softly and richly in the firelight. "Here you go, my boy. Put these on."

He tossed the gleaming outfit into the air, where the boy caught it and, in mid air, managed to dress himself in new pants and a tunic and boots, too, made from soft leather.

"I suppose now I need to get you down from there," the wizard said, mostly to himself. "I hope I remember how." Again he made a great show of scratching his chin and tugging his beard as if thinking very hard and then he said, "Ah, yes, that's it!" He waved his hands in the air, said something that, as before, sounded like guttural gibberish, and the boy began to float slowly back toward the earth.

When Astral was again standing amongst the crowd in the soapsuds and dying fish, though still in the space they had created for him, the wizard said, "I would like to introduce to the good people of Eye o' the Sea, Astral, who is now a brand new boy but will also be called the Ancient Boy. For you see, he has been away traveling through Time, and Time has been so kind as to have stuffed as much knowledge into his young head as if he had been living for ten thousand years."

Scraps then moved to the donkey and took up the lead rope tied to its halter. He turned to the crowd, doffed his hat, and said, "So now my job is done. Those who choose to heed my warning should now retire to their homes, gather up what they can carry, and follow their noses along the coast to a new location where you will build another Eye o' the Sea. You have enough horses now to carry all your possessions, and it's a much nicer location, believe me. You will most assuredly know it when you see it, for it has been chosen just for you. Those determined to remain, go home and prepare yourselves for death or for slavery, for I'm afraid you shall have little choice between the two."

Then, with Admiral Penance following along behind him and the pelican flapping its wings to maintain its perch on the donkey's back, he began to walk off into the darkness.

He was stopped by a small voice. It was the former ragamuffin, now the finely dressed Astral the Ancient Boy. "I wish to go with you," he said, and he hesitated and added, "please, sir."

The wizard stopped and looked back. He studied the boy for a long moment as if considering the request. "Do you eat much?" he asked.

The boy shook his head. "No, sir."

"Hmm," the wizard said. "Can you walk all day without resting?"

Now the boy nodded. "Yes, sir."

"I see," the wizard said, and he began scratching his chin and tugging at his beard. "But can you use a sword?"

The boy's face fell. He shrugged his shoulders and gazed down at his feet.

"That, I suppose, means 'no,'" the wizard said. "Well, never mind. Besides, who knows what skills and abilities you might have gathered while you were spinning through Time for an eternity. You might be surprised. In fact, we both might be very surprised." He thought for another moment and said, "For example, try this: face the moon, lift your hands in the air, and snap your fingers."

The boy did as he was told. He looked up at the moon, raised his hands, and snapped his fingers. There was a loud popping sound and a great sheet of sparks flew from under his fingernails and disappeared into the night sky. The boy's mouth dropped open in wonder and he brought his hands close to his face and looked at them in amazement.

The wizard laughed. "Just as I thought. Time has presented us with a little wizard. Now you must come with me. We'll be partners, you and I! So, come then, let's be gone from this place."

Chapter 22

The magician, the donkey, the sea bird, and Astral the Ancient Boy made their way through the nighttime streets of the fortress town of Eye o' the Sea and out through the gates, leaving behind a great hubbub of excitement. When they were outside the walls and there was silence and they could again see the stars without the interference of flaming torches and bonfires, they stopped. Scraps looked up and spied the small cluster of stars the ancients called the Seven Sisters. Respectfully he spoke to them. "Ah, yes, Ladies of the Night—and you, all of you, are certainly the loveliest of them all, I might add—I stretched my luck tonight with you and your companions. Asked a great deal of you and your velocities, gravities, and variegated energies. Forgive me. But the mean and tiny affairs of humankind demanded this small intervention on my part. For, you see, the town of Eye o' the Sea, in ancient times a war garrison but now a place of peace and of art, music, and human freedom, too—as messy as human freedom tends to be—must exist somewhere on this fat, round earth, and this one here is about to be destroyed by a great evil. So, as it was you who chose me to be a Metacephala and wizard and gave me such discretionary powers, I hope you are not displeased."

He reached into the front of his robe and withdrew the small object that hung around his neck on a chain woven from many threads of fine gold. He held it up as if to show it to the stars. "You see, here it is, my own head, desiccated and shrunken by eternal Time, the gods' handmaiden herself—and the symbol of my servitude to the cosmic plan."

He sighed. "If it's any consolation, I'm exhausted and shan't be doing anything like that again anytime soon. You can be certain of that." He hesitated, looked at the shadow of the donkey with its feathered burden and the boy who stood watching silently, and added, "The Admiral, the Seabird, and Astral, this newly anointed ancient child of the universe, and I too pray not, in any event. We certainly pray not."

Then he heard a horse snort and in the moonlight saw the shadows of two riders approaching from down the beach, coming up fast upon them. Scraps and his small entourage stood still and waited. Swords drawn, the riders were laughing raucously, as if they had been drinking. Too late, the wizard realized they were soldiers, lead elements of an approaching army.

They did not see the wizard and his companions until they were nearly on top of them, and then they pulled their horses to a stop. "So, then, what have we here?" one of them asked, peering down in the bright, ivory moonlight.

The other one answered his question. "It's an old tinker, I think, with a boy and a donkey, and we have caught them outside the walls of his city. It's too bad for them, too, for we have orders to destroy such subhuman trash wherever we find it. And these look like Inferiors, for certain."

The first one laughed and said, "The donkey first, though. I hate those ugly little beasts, though he is probably smarter than the one who leads him. Watch while I leave his head on the sand, and then we can play awhile with the others before we drain their blood into the dunes, too."

"Ah!" the wizard cried out, "Stop this nonsense, or I'll send you to lower regions forthwith, and with your hair on fire, to boot!"

"Listen," one of the soldiers said, "the tinker speaks. Threatening us, I believe! No, old man, we are Maximus, rightful rulers of the Earth, and it'll be mercy you'll be begging for and for your boy, too, and soon enough. For I intend to cut off your toes one by one and work my way up from there! If its mercy you want, you'll have to ask for it from the demons themselves, for it's you who shall be going down with the red-eyed monsters of the nether world. And you can be certain of this, too, old man—you'll be glad enough to be down there and away from us when we're finished with you."

He laughed and raised his sword and, while the wizard watched the moonlight play off its blade, he began to bring it down toward Admiral Penance's neck. But when the downward arc of the blade had just begun and before the wizard could conjure up some magic in his own defense, there was a small, hard rush of sound and the soldier's breathing seemed to get caught in his throat. He dropped the sword and reached for his neck. He began gurgling, as if drowning on the air itself, and his horse bolted, carrying him forward. They smashed into the donkey, sending the pelican flying off in a great flurry of feathers and wings, and knocked the wizard and the boy to the ground. Admiral Penance kicked once with his hind legs and ran off toward the grass-covered dunes.

The wounded soldier's horse, its rider still clinging to its back, galloped off down the moon-bright beach. The other soldier, struggling to reason through his drunkenness, hesitated and then, with a curse, pulled his sword from its scabbard and rode down on the wizard, who was trying to get back on his feet. Before he could strike, however, there was another small, hard rush of sound and then this soldier, too, dropped his sword and his reins and reached for his throat. Now the wizard could clearly see the black shaft of an arrow protruding from the soldier's neck. But this soldier could not stay mounted. When his horse leaped forward, he toppled backwards. There was a heavy thudding sound and the gasping release of air as his body hit the ground and lay still.

The wizard slowly stood up and dusted himself off. "Astral," he said, "are you injured, boy?"

"No," the boy said, knocking the sand off his new clothes.

The wizard knelt over the soldier and again a flame shot out from one of his fingers, revealing the soldier's white-blond hair and his pale blue eyes staring, lifeless, into the night. Scraps studied him for a moment and said, "Dead." Then, still kneeling, he peered out into the darkness. "Whoever you are out there, you have earned our eternal gratitude. I trust, however, that neither I nor this child will cause you displeasure, having witnessed the results of your moonlight-and-shadows marksmanship."

Two riders came out of the darkness cast by the city's walls. Slowly they closed on the wizard and the boy and then a low male voice said, "Scraps, I'm Dag-gar, your traveling companion."

The wizard narrowed his eyes, attempting to see the man's features.

Then, a woman's voice: "And I'm here too, Scraps—Sonoria, who has also been traveling with you."

The wizard peered up at the two riders, who now dismounted and, leading their horses, approached on foot. The old man stood up, took off his big hat, and scratched his head. "Forgive me, my young saviors, for you have this night indeed saved our skins, but I have no recollection of either of you. It is my habit of long standing—until tonight, that is—to travel quite alone, except for my familiars here, living the solitary life of the itinerant sorcerer. Magic tricks, you know, for the entertainment of the common people—and the occasional king and queen. Once even for a group of monks who afterward suspected I was in league with the underworld and threatened to burn me. But, never mind that, come closer; let's have a better look at you."

Dag-gar and Sonoria drew closer and the wizard studied them in the moonlight. "So sorry, my dears, but you are complete strangers." He thought for a moment and added, "Dag-gar and Sonoria, you say? Indeed, those are ancient names sung in certain ancient songs, but is it possible we have traveled together?

Certainly even a man as old and forgetful as I am—and I am very old and very forgetful, rest assured—would remember two such lovely young people as yourselves. Perhaps we were traveling with a large group of pilgrims?"

"No," Sonoria said, "we were traveling across a vast desert. Just the two of us. I was then a young girl and you had a camel, not a donkey."

"Oh no," the wizard said, "a camel? I cannot stand camels. Nasty, moody beasts. I hope it never comes to that—traveling with a camel. But we must figure this out and I have an idea. You, Dag-gar, when did we travel together? Was there also just the two of us?"

"Yes, Scraps, just the two of us. You found me tied to a burning tree in a harbor town called Port o' Rue. We traveled together into the mountains. You fell into a waterfall and were swept away. We found each other again in a wellspring in a cave—"

The wizard now interrupted him. "Ah! Yes! Yes," he said, his hoarse old voice crackling with excitement, "waterfalls and wellsprings! The bubbling effervescence of Time itself! And tell me, Sonoria, did we find an oasis whilst wandering across that desert?"

"Yes, and I went to bathe in it and the—"

"And then—you were here?"

Sonoria nodded. "Yes," she said, "then I was here."

"And each of you left an old wizard called Scraps waiting for you, Dag-gar in the cave, and you, Sonoria, at the oasis."

It was a statement, not a question. There was then a long moment of silence while the wizard looked up at the stars. "Look now," he said, pointing at the night sky, "see the great Hunter with his belt and sword. See there? There are three stars in his belt, and there, where his left shoulder would be, is the bright and lovely star called Bellatrix. The ancients named it after a great woman warrior." The wizard extended his hand to Dag-gar and said, "Let me see your sword."

Dag-gar took it from its scabbard and handed it to the old man. The wizard held it up and let the moonlight play off its blade and its hilt and pommel and then he looked back up at the sky. "Saiph," he murmured and then he regarded the young man and said the word louder. "Saiph—the sword of the Hunter. This is it, it could be no other. Let me see the belt in which you carry this."

Dag-gar turned around and Scraps bent closer, the better to see. The gems set in the belt gleamed in the moonlight. Scraps nodded and grunted. "Eh! Yes, that's it then. And a small miracle it is, too—the Amber Teardrop, the key to Time itself, lost these many years, right here under my nose. Many men—and women, too—have given their lives to possess that precious bauble, for it is none other than the frozen blood of the Sacred Tree."

Scraps then looked at the soldier dead on the sand while the surf pounded against the shore not fifty paces away. "Let us be away from this place," he said. "Lovely as it is, it is cursed by death." He gazed at the walls of the city that loomed over them, casting black shadows across the shining night. "Let us hope that the populace of that place heeds my warning and gets away from here before the rest of these monsters arrive. First, though, I must find my donkey. Just when I need him most, he's run off into the dunes."

He made as if to begin walking away, stopped, turned, and said, "One more thing, though. Can't be too safe, you know, so please forgive me. Dag-gar, dear boy, open up the top of your tunic and let me have a look at your chest."

Dag-gar hesitated, then untied the leather lace that closed the front of his shirt. The wizard leaned close, held out a finger, snapped it, and flame shot out from his fingertip. In the light of this small, blue fire it was clearly visible: a small discoloration in the middle of Dag-gar's chest.

"Good, good," Scraps muttered to himself, "yes, that's it." He turned to Sonoria and said, "Not to demand immodesty from you, dear, but please, let me have a look."

Sonoria did as he requested and there too, a hand's width below her throat, was the same mark. Again the wizard muttered to himself, the fire from his finger went out, and he turned away and began walking toward the dunes. "Come then," he said without looking back. "I have a camp hidden in the tall grass far out on the prairie. There is a thicket of willows, a small, freshwater stream, and some pasture for the horses. We will be hidden from further depredations by other roaming bands of the barbarians we just encountered. We can rest and talk story, as the people of the blue-water islands say. And I am certain you have much story to talk, too, as it is obvious from what you have said and what I have seen that you are on a quest of great importance."

Chapter 23

They sat under an immense night sky with a bright full moon and brilliant stars, smeared like milk across the heavens. They hobbled the horses and the donkey nearby, and with the sound of grazing soft in their ears, the four of them huddled close and told their stories.

The old wizard, Scraps, was the last to speak. "So. I have listened long and well to your tales and I am now, more than ever, certain of one thing: We are, as we speak, together in another whirligig of Time—each of us separately, Dag-gar and I, and Sonoria and I. And now, due to yet another vagary in the cosmic whirlpool, we are all together.

"But you may be certain, my young friends, that all this is not without purpose. Aye, no indeed! Always remember, there is a purpose to every snap, gurgle, and burp this universe makes, and all are interconnected, one affecting the other. And now I must explain something to the both of you, something of utmost importance to you, to me, and to this fat, round earth itself: I am more than just a magician of some skill, more than just your wandering sorcerer. Indeed, you see, when I make it rain from a clear sky, 'tis no illusion, no trickery: it really does rain from a clear sky. When I change a chicken feather into a chicken, it is a real, egg-laying hen. When I lift a street urchin off the ground and give him a new name, send him spinning off into the universe for an education, and provide him with a new set of clothes, it is no underhanded caper. No, he really does fly into the air, disappear into Time. For I am, you see, what you will someday be and in fact are in the process of becoming.

"For you, Dag-gar, and you, Sonoria, are, like me and like Admiral Penance the donkey, and like the sea bird—and Astral, the Ancient Boy, too: we are, all of us, Time Drifters. The identical marks on the skin of our chests attest to this, you see."

He opened the top of his tunic, snapped a flame from a finger, and showed them his own mark, and then he pulled out the strange object that hung around his neck on a chain of woven gold. "This," he said, "is what you are now preparing for. This is my own head, a gift to me from the End of Time, and the symbol of the Metacephala—the small gods that are in charge of the day-to-day workings of the world. In another Time, and who knows when that is, you all shall be presented one.

"For now, understand that our names have been sung throughout Time, sung in the ancient songs of the Thrangs, those young people who search eternally for the answer to the Great Mystery and with whom you found yourselves riding. And so it is absolutely clear to me that we have all been brought together for a purpose: We are on a quest—and it could only be a great quest, the kind of quest that stirs the soul and gets you memorialized in the Ancient Songs.

"Dag-gar, you have completed the first part of it: you have found the Amber Teardrop. We must find Captain Jarl and return the Amber to him, for he is the great and ancient Time Navigator, and without the Amber Teardrop, he is lost—and so is the very world on which we stand."

Scraps held his hands out to either side and said, "Now let us join together and engage the force of our combined magic—for we are all powerful here, each of us in our own way."

They did this and when Dag-gar had taken Sonoria's hand in his and Astral had taken Scraps' hand and all were joined at their fingertips, a brilliant streak of light raced across the night sky above them. "Ah, yes," Scraps said happily, "our union has been consecrated. Good for us. And now, to sleep, for I am old and drooping with fatigue. We'll leave the Admiral on watch, for he can sleep with one of his great flapping ears listening and he will sound the alarm should danger find us."

There was little else said. Scraps rolled himself up in his blanket, and before the others could sort out their sleeping kits, he was snoring with a peaceful intensity. Astral found a place near the magician and curled up inside his blanket. But Sonoria was restless. She heard her stallion whicker in the darkness and went to check on him. She was singing softly to him when she heard Dag-gar's voice behind her.

"Too much has happened to me today. It's impossible to sleep."

Sonoria stopped her singing and turned to him. "I know. What is this? What is happening? I was a girl riding a camel, traveling with an old man called Scraps, across a desert. We stopped at an oasis. I bathed in a wellspring and everything changed. I became a young woman riding a beautiful horse. I even knew his name: Spiritus. And I know everything else, too. It is as if I belong here, as if I have always been here, riding this stallion." She paused for a moment, and then said, "And I have always been with you. I know you, Dag-gar. I don't know a thing about you—you are a complete stranger—and yet I have always known you. We, too, have been riding together—forever."

Dag-gar moved close and put his hands on her shoulders. He kissed her and she did not resist him. "We are Thrangs," he said, "and like all Thrangs, we are seeking answers to the unanswerable. We must only accept that. And we must accept that we have been together forever, strangers or not, and we must understand this: Forever is not a destination; forever is the place we are now and always have been."

Now, as when he had come back from the ship, Sonoria felt a powerful sense of both dread and longing at the sound of Dag-gar's voice and the nearness of his body, and both feelings came together at a single, sharp point of awareness. She turned away from him and began rubbing the stallion's withers. "What happened to you on the ship? The man who came back from it was not the man who went out."

She waited a long time for him to answer and when he did not speak, she turned back to him and said, "That old fisherman, he saw the same thing I did. It was in your eyes, in your face, in your movements. It was as if you had seen something terrible."

"It was as I told it tonight at the fire," he said. "There was nothing out there. The ship was rotting away. I found the Amber Teardrop in my father's quarters, lying in the dust." .

"You set the ship afire."

"Fire purifies as it destroys.

"But what needed to be purified?"

Dag-gar ignored this question. "We need to find my father. Traveling with an old man and a boy riding a donkey will slow us down. Together on our horses we can move much faster."

"But we don't know where he is."

"I have the Amber Teardrop. It will lead us to him."

"How can we make it speak to us?"

He put his hands on her shoulders and pulled her to him again, but this time he did not kiss her. Instead, with his face close to hers, he whispered, "We will wait. In time that old wizard or this Ancient Boy will unlock the Amber's secrets and the sleeping face will tell us where my father is. Then we can leave them behind and go there. We will not need them anymore." His whispering voice was hard and without pity.

Sonoria looked up into Dag-gar's face, pale and cold in the moonlight. "I think you are wrong," she said. "It is as Scraps said, we will need our combined powers to rescue your father."

Now Dag-gar's hands squeezed her shoulders and again he spoke in his harsh whisper. "All we need, my love, is each other. Nothing more." He released her and dropped his hands to his sides. "It's time to sleep," he said, and he turned away and found his own place in the tall grass to spread his blankets.

Left alone, Sonoria turned back to her stallion and spoke to him as if he were her familiar and would understand. "Nor did I tell the truth tonight," she whispered in his ear, "the truth that this—all of this that is now unfolding—is part of the story that I'm telling Scraps out on the desert around our fire, a story sent to me from the ancients in the stars. Yet, though I speak the words, I have no control over them. The story is inside of me and I am inside of the story."

Chapter 24

They awoke before dawn and rose to the smell of smoke. At Scrap's bidding, Astral climbed up on Admiral Penance's back and looked out over the prairie toward the ocean.

"Eye o' the Sea," he said in a loud whisper. "I fear it is burning! There is a big plume of smoke."

"Can you see the town from there?" Scraps asked.

"No, but it is a very great fire, no doubt," the boy said, "and what else could it be?"

"Ah," Scraps said, "this is bad news indeed. There was no time for the people to leave. I'm afraid my warning came too late." Then he saw something else in the sky, something flying high, circling them. "Now this is bad news to compound the first. My friend, that homely pelican, left us last night and now there he is, far above us doing his birdie thing. Yet he is no longer a mere pelican. He has transformed himself into a Man-o'-War bird. It is a warning, preparing us for the mayhem and devastation of battle."

They all looked upwards and saw a great seabird soaring, turning first on one wingtip, then the other, never flapping his wings but riding the air currents, his head turning this way and that.

Sonoria and Dag-gar had their horses saddled and they now mounted them. "There is little we can do here," Sonoria said, looking down from Spiritus' back. "We must not be captured by these soldiers. We should move deeper into the prairie."

"But," Scraps asked, "in which direction should we move? For this is the beginning of our quest to find Captain Jarl and we must make the right choice. Dag-gar, do you remember how your father used the Amber Teardrop to find his way across the ocean-sea?"

"I watched him many times," Dag-gar said. "He had maps and drawings of the world and its oceans, and a machine to spin the Amber Teardrop. But I was too young to learn how it worked."

Astral had dropped down so that he now sat astride Admiral Penance. The donkey lowered his head and his ears drooped, but the Ancient Boy seemed oblivious to the animal's apparent misery at its new burden. "I can assure you," Astral said with an impish smile, his voice that of a boy but his words those of a wise man, "that we shall find out. For there is more than one way to unlock the powers of the Amber Teardrop. Tonight we shall have moonlight aplenty and by combining moonlight with the Amber's energies—and a drop of wizard's blood—we can make Eternity's Mistress, who is locked in the Amber's matrix, speak to us."

Scrap's cleared his throat. "A drop of wizard's blood, you say? And however shall we acquire that? Well, never mind and good for you then, Astral. Your journey through the Universe was time well spent. You have learned your lessons well. Tonight we shall speak with Time's Mistress. Until then, I agree with Sonoria: Let us move back away from the danger of this Maximus horde."

So they finished breaking camp and set off. Scraps, striding in his long, awkward gait through the tall grass, managed to keep pace with Admiral Penance and his burden of the skinny Ancient Boy. But Dag-gar and Sonoria, mounted on their big horses, went on ahead, loping off across the prairie, moving upward but keeping within earshot of the others.

When a small deer broke cover and raced away from them, Sonoria gave out a whoop and kicked her stallion into a gallop. She had her bow ready and now, with the deer leaping and bounding through the tall grass, she allowed Spiritus his head and the horse seemed to understand. He followed the deer's path, not gaining on it, but not losing ground.

Sonoria notched an arrow. Letting go the reins so they hung across Spiritus' withers, she brought the bow up and, without hesitation, aimed and shot. The arrow caught the deer behind its shoulders. The animal leaped up and then came down kicking in the grass. When Sonoria reached it, it was dead.

Dag-gar rode up next to Sonoria and reached out to pat her stallion's neck. "A fine shot," he said. "Where did you learn that?"

"I don't know. Perhaps I have always been able to do this," she said.

"Apparently," he said, "but I don't know if I could have."

"You're next," she said and she tossed him a challenging look.

When Scraps and Astral had caught up with them, they were dressing the deer.

"So," Scraps said, smiling his big, yellow-toothed smile, "venison. I dearly love deer meat yet have it so seldom. After all, how is an old wizard supposed to come by something so lovely, wandering about with a pelican and an old donkey? Mostly I eat rice and beans I buy in village markets. And roots—I'm rather good at gathering roots."

They traveled on. The sun, until midmorning dulled by high clouds, now presented itself full of heat in a bright blue sky. The grass prairie sloped down toward the ocean-sea behind them and imperceptibly upwards ahead of them. Yet the prairie was its own sea, a great, undulating plain sweeping away toward a far distant horizon as if the ocean's swells had been frozen and painted green and brown. They saw many animals: hare broke cover and leaped away before them, deer and antelope bounded off at their approach, and there were always hawks and eagles high above, some of them mere specks in the blue vastness of the heavens.

By late afternoon, when the sun's heat was easing and its colors were changing from white-yellow to orange as its light was collected and diffused by prairie dust, they came to another small stream. Its banks were flanked by willows and here and there it gathered itself into small, limpid pools filled with tiny fish.

"A good place," Scraps said, surveying the surrounding area. "There is a small rise from which to keep watch; here is a smooth, flat place to put up our shelters; and there are dead willow branches for our fire." He looked up at the sky and added, "It will be a fine night tonight for consulting the moon and the mysterious sleeping face in the Amber Teardrop. We must prepare for that."

So it was done. By the time the sunlight was merely a red-yellow streak on the western horizon and the brighter stars were appearing in the ink-blue sky to the east, animal-hide shelters had been set up and a cooking fire started. The horses and Admiral Penance were hobbled for the night, and with the sound of the animals' grazing blending with the buzz and whine of insects, the four of them gathered around the fire and each cooked their own meat impaled on a stick of green willow.

For a long time no one spoke. It was a time for listening, a time to allow the tranquility of dusk to penetrate their minds and the sky to bring together the celestial beings that would guide the evening's journey.

When they had finished eating, Scraps spoke, and though he spoke softly, his hoarse, high-pitched voice was startling as it cut through the quietude. "Now is the time," he began, and he withdrew his sword from its scabbard, pointed it toward the heavens, and then swung it around his head, cutting a circle in the air. As the blade sliced through the night, it left behind a trail of blue flames. He then stuck the sword into the earth in front of him and said, "The heavens have gathered above us, the Earth-World is below us, and the fire offers us its elemental blessing of purified warmth and light. We now only await the arrival of Sister Moon."

As if on this signal, the sky to the east brightened and all eyes turned to watch. Slowly, a gloriole of soft light increased and intensified on the horizon. The fire crackled, the night creatures rustled through the grass, the horses whickered softly, and overhead the stars formed once again in their ancient patterns.

Of a sudden, there it was: the moon. The top of it, orange and huge, rose as if the black earth itself were birthing it. It appeared to move quickly, anxious to be a part of what would transpire next. As it rose, its face changed from orange to a dark yellow and then, when it had emerged fully, this yellow paled until it was nearly white and the dark air of the grass prairie was suffused with a milky substance that was nearly palpable.

Scraps spoke to it. "Welcome! We are gathered here to bear witness to your power and to ask of you no small favor."

There was another moment's silence as if, given the opportunity, the moon would speak back to Scraps and acknowledge his greetings. And in some way it must have, for when Scraps spoke again it was as if they were conversing. "Astral, also now known as the Ancient Boy, has traveled infinitely far in Time. Now he has come back to us bearing the knowledge of the very spheres and energies which comprise the heavens. He shall now use this wisdom to harness their powers."

There was again silence, a long silence, an extended moment necessary for Time to unwrap itself and open itself up to the desires of such as now sat hunched by the diminishing flames of the small fire.

Then Astral spoke, and again he was a boy speaking as an ancient soothsayer. He raised both his eyes and his hands to the moon. "Oh, great lunar sister! Such eager greetings we send your way! 'Tis a great quest we are about to set out on, we tiny energies you now look down upon, gathered as we are around our poor fire. Yet we can assure you that we are true, that our intentions are noble, and that what we will now ask of you is worthy. Indeed, Sister Moon, our quest is as necessary to the smooth workings of the universe as is your regular orbit around this fat, round, Earth-World."

Astral paused for a long moment to give the moon time to digest what he had said. Then he looked at Dag-gar and said, "Now, take off your sword and belt and lay it out here in the grass near the fire."

Dag-gar hesitated, but just for a moment; then he untied the sword and its belt and, leaning forward, stretched it out between himself and the flames. Exposed to both moonlight and firelight, the Amber Teardrop seemed to come alive in its setting on the belt's black leather. The fire pulled from it a luster that grew as they watched. The rich brown of the Amber's matrix began to glow.

"Ah," the Ancient Boy said, "so the magic begins. And so quickly!" He turned to Scraps, who had rested his bearded chin on his bony knees as he watched. "We have fire, we have moonlight, and now all that's required to draw out the spell is a drop of an old wizard's blood." Astral reached into his belt and withdrew a small dagger whose tip glimmered in the light of moon and flames. "Give me your hand."

Scraps looked at the Ancient Boy. "Why not a *young* wizard's blood? You are now, apparently, a wizard, too."

"No, no," Astral said, "this specifically calls for the blood of an old wizard." He reached out for Scraps' hand. "Come now, or you will break the spell."

But Scraps was not forthcoming. "I don't understand," he said. "Wizard's blood is wizard's blood, young, old, in the middle—what could be different?"

Astral smiled a bit condescendingly. "The accumulation of ancient fluxes, legends, and bodily humors would certainly be different in an old wizard like you than a young wizard like me. You must admit that, at least, Scrapius. Now, come on, give me your hand. It will be nearly painless."

"You forgot to mention the accumulation of wisdom, too," Scraps said, still withholding his hand.

Astral sighed, and as with the smile, a bit condescendingly. "Yes, fine, and the accumulation of wisdom, too." He held out the knife. "Come then, let's get it done."

Scraps hesitated a moment longer and then held out his arm. Astral took his hand and turned it over so that the palm was up. With a quick movement, he jabbed the thick part of it and a bead of blood surged from the wound, black in the moonlight.

"Hold your hand over the Amber Teardrop," Astral instructed. Scraps leaned forward and to the side, stretching out his long arms.

Astral lifted the belt so that the Amber was directly under Scraps' hand. They waited and they watched. As the firelight and shadows played off the growing drop of blood, it seemed to seek out the Amber and the Amber Teardrop seemed to be waiting for it, seemed to be opening itself up to receive it.

They all held their breaths. The whine of insects waxed and waned, a breeze began to build, the fire lifted and pulsed. Only the moon was steady.

Then the blood drop fell, a large dollop, and when it touched the Amber Teardrop there was a sound like a sharp intake of breath, as if something sleeping had been startled awake, brought out of a dream. For a moment afterwards there was nothing, no sound, no movement, but then there was a rising, smoking glow from the Amber and from inside the glow, a voice and then, from inside the voice, a face.

The face shimmered above the Amber. The eyes were open, the mouth moved, but there was utter silence. Still, all who listened heard what the voice said. "Walk North toward The-Star-That-Does-Not-Move. When it is nearly overhead, you will come to a cold, gray sea and there, in a house covered with fogs and mists, you shall find an old woman. Do her bidding and do not fail."

The voice trailed away so that the last of the syllables it spoke were nearly unintelligible. The glow began to fade, the fire to diminish, while the breeze became a wind that sent the fire's ashes off and up into the sky.

But then from the middle of the glow came a hiss and the face rose again from the Amber and the face expanded and from the Amber's matrix came a body—a naked, yellow-brown body that writhed as if in agony—and the face hovered above it and a hand emerged and from the hand a finger pointed at Dag-gar. The hissing became words that spat on the fire and cut the night, bearing no forgiveness. "He is there! That is he! The one called Dag-gar! He is the Hunter and has been stung by the Scorpion, Time's Vagabond. He is possessed and deadly is he, yes! Deadly is he! Oh! Covet thy lives, pilgrims of Time, or scant shall be your remaining days!" The face clutched at itself with its vaporous hands and curled up, retreating back into the blood and the Amber, while the moonlight covered everything with its pallid luminosity.

Then there was nothing but those eternal sounds, wind and fire. And more than that, human breathing. Eyes turned toward Dag-gar. Dag-gar clutched suddenly at the sword and its belt. He screamed, "No! The Amber lies!" and he grabbed the belt and with his knife he pried the Amber Teardrop from its setting and threw it into the fire. He sprang up, buckled his belt and sword around his waist, and backed off into the darkness beyond the firelight.

Sonoria jumped up. "Dag-gar!" she called and she ran after him and she, too, disappeared into the darkness.

Without hesitation, Astral scrambled to the edge of the fire on his hands and knees. He reached into the flames, plucked out the Amber Teardrop, and dropped it into the grass. A moment later, there were the sounds of horse's hooves running on the prairie grass.

Chapter 25

She could not stop him. He would not speak. Working fast in moonlight shadows, Dag-gar threw the blanket and saddle on his horse, pulled the hackamore over its head, and with a single motion, untied the leather thong that hobbled its front legs. When Sonoria touched him as he was about to mount, he ignored her and swung his leg over the animal's back, gathered up the reins, and galloped off into the darkness.

Her only thought was, *I must stay with him.* With a glance back toward the camp and the fire, she saddled her stallion, released its hobble, and rode after him. She leaned forward and whispered in Spiritus' ear, "Catch them! Catch them!" and the horse seemed to understand. She let him have his head and, with his nose up testing the air, they were off across the grass prairie.

It did not take long to find them. Though Dag-gar must have known she was there, he ignored her presence. She followed him through the night. She soon understood what he was doing. Despite his rage at the words of the Amber Teardrop, he was following its instructions: riding toward the Star-That-Does-Not-Move. Even as the night wore on and the other constellations traveled across the sky, east to west, the star he followed did not leave its place in the north, did not vary in its position, but rather held steady as if it were a bright gemstone fixed in an internal setting.

Toward morning, the approaching dawn caused the stars to wink out one by one, and when the Star-That-Does-Not-Move faded away, Dag-gar stopped. For a long time he sat on his horse and looked out across the plain. Sonoria stopped some distance behind him and watched his silhouette against the morning sky. She waited, not knowing whether to approach him or not.

Finally, when the first rays of the sun had reached him, setting him and his horse aglow above the still-shadowed grass, she urged Spiritus on until she came up beside him. For a while, they sat their horses next to each other, shoulder to shoulder, looking out across the endless grass.

He spoke first. "There is a stream down there." He nodded toward a small vale below them where a dark, meandering line of trees marked the course of a small creek. "We'll need to rest the horses." Without looking at her, he urged his horse on and they began the gradual descent toward the distant valley.

By midmorning they had reached their goal. Here the grass was short but lush, and the bright sound of the moving water was comforting. In silence they made a rudimentary camp without shelters or blankets. After watering the horses, they hobbled them, set them to grazing, and then lay down in the grass close to each other, but not touching.

They slept through the remainder of the morning and well into the afternoon. The cry of a hawk soaring above in search of a meal woke them. It took each of them a moment to remember what had happened and where they were. When Sonoria opened her eyes, she saw first the high-flying hawk and then the blue sky above it and then, from the corner of her eye, Dag-gar.

He was sitting up and she knew he had been watching her, but now he pretended to have been looking at the horses. Then he turned to her and said, "I'm going to leave now. Come with me if you must, but I'll not wait for you."

Sonoria smiled. "Nor I for you," she said. "We both know where we are going and how to get there. We are on the same quest and so we'll be on the same path. We may as well travel together. Anyway, as you said, the ancient songs say we have been together forever and will always be together, so it would seem we have no choice."

Without answering her, Dag-gar stood up and began getting his horse ready. Sonoria did the same. Soon they were again riding across the great prairie, but it was beginning to take on a different appearance. Sonoria noticed that the grass was shorter and the thickets of trees more numerous and larger. Still, though, the undulating prairie itself spread out before them, seemingly without end.

In silence, and with Dag-gar for his own reasons maintaining a constant distance ahead of Sonoria, they traveled through the afternoon and into the evening without stopping. When they came to another stream, this one deeper and wider than the last, Dag-gar pulled his horse up.

"We'll swim them across," Sonoria said. "There is a good place, down to the left."

But instead of looking where Sonoria was pointing, Dag-gar brought his heels sharply into his horse's ribs. The animal leaped ahead and into the stream. Sonoria watched as they sank nearly out of sight into the current and then, with the horse swimming powerfully and Dag-gar hanging onto the pommel of the saddle, began to make the crossing.

When they emerged on the other side, Dag-gar came out of the water next to the horse. The animal surged up onto the bank with powerful strides and immediately shook itself, sending a shower of water off in all directions. Without looking back at Sonoria, Dag-gar remounted and again set off at a trot.

Sonoria rode Spiritus down the stream bank until she came to a place where the water was shallow. She urged the stallion off the embankment and, with the water only up above his fetlocks, they walked across.

Again Sonoria kept a small distance between herself and Dag-gar, and for the remaining daylight they traveled this way, Dag-gar ignoring her, she watching his back and watching the country around them, too, as it continued to rise up and change nearly imperceptibly from prairie to forest.

Then—and it seemed to happen of a sudden rather than gradually—it was dark again. Yet Dag-gar did not slow his pace nor stop to rest. The night was clear and cool and the wind light. The stars came out before the moon rose; among the others was The-Star-That-Does-Not-Move, ever constant in its celestial position. The moon, now a waning gibbous, was beginning to move toward the end of its lunar cycle; as its light lessened, the stars grew in brightness.

They had not eaten now since the night before but they were to spend another night—a long night—without food and without rest. Sonoria was beginning to feel dizzy from fatigue and hunger and she knew that Dag-gar must soon stop. They would need to find something to eat, need to sleep. Yet he kept moving, his body stubborn and straight in the saddle, his horse's gait steady and its nose always pointed at that great star that hung so far above them.

She knew what he was struggling to do, for he was living out her story, a story she had received from the stars themselves—and from the red heart of the Scorpion itself: He was defying the will of the Time Vagabond that now possessed him. He was struggling to deny the Scorpion's power over him. But here the tale she was telling ended, and she did not know what would happen next.

* * * * *

In the early morning, as the sun was just rising above the rolling hills, Sonoria came upon a large hare. Rather than running, it sat and looked at her, and so she understood it to be a gift from the gods. It continued to watch her as she notched an arrow, aimed, and let it fly. Nor did it twitch when the arrow pierced its spine; instead it leaped once and lay still.

Sonoria dismounted and gathered it up. When her feet and legs took up the weight of her body after she had sat so long in the saddle, pain shot up her thighs and into her hips. Still, it felt good to walk, and now, carrying the dead hare by its hind legs, she strode towards where Dag-gar had pulled his horse up.

"I've got breakfast," she said.

Now, for the first time, he turned and looked at her and Sonoria was stunned by what she saw: His eyes were hard and angry, his thin face with its thickening beard looked gaunt, even desperate.

"Dag-gar," she said, "there's a large thicket of larch and pines down there and a river of willows growing around what must be a river of water. Let's stop there together and eat and rest. We must rest."

"You must rest," he said. "I must not. I know how to find my father and I will."

"But you no longer have the Amber Teardrop that you were supposed to bring to him. What—"

He cut her off, his voice harsh with scorn. "The Amber Teardrop can burn eternally in the Dark Places! We'll need it not, my father and I. We can sail the ocean-sea without it." So saying, he brought his heels into his horse's flanks and again rode off.

Sonoria watched him go. She felt the warm, dead weight of the hare in one hand and the warm breathing of the exhausted stallion on the other and she felt a weakness of her body. The sun was now full on her face and she wanted to lie down in the grass and sleep. She made her decision: let him go. And then she began leading Spiritus toward the promised shelter of the trees.

* * * * *

She set up her camp among the thick, intertwining branches of the thicket. She let Spiritus drink his fill from the clear stream and then hobbled him so he could graze on the thick grass growing nearby. It was dark and cool under the canopy of leaves and boughs and soon, with her flint and steel, she had a small fire going. She dressed out the hare and set it to roasting while she bathed in a pool in the cold, slow-moving stream.

Then she dressed again and set about making her bed, gathering hemlock boughs and covering them with grass until she had built up a soft nest. She looked at the sky and saw what she knew were the telltales of approaching rain: streaks of high, thin clouds moving in from the east. Now she used her sword to cut thicker branches from the surrounding trees and built a small shelter over her bed, covering it with a thick layer of leafy branches.

When she had finished, she checked on Spiritus again and while she did this, she ate most of the hare, wolfing down the dark, stringy meat almost without chewing it. Then, with the sun high in the sky, she crawled into the shelter, wrapped herself in the stallion's saddle blanket, and was immediately asleep.

Chapter 26

The chill in the air woke her. She peeked out from the shelter. Through the branches of the trees above, she saw a sky thick with clouds and spitting rain carried on a cold, fitful wind. It was nearly dark but there would be no stars tonight and there would be no traveling. She looked at the dead ashes of her fire and then sought out Spiritus. The horse had finished eating and now had turned his back to the weather and was sleeping. Sonoria withdrew into the shelter and, ignoring the damp and the cold, escaped once more into a deep sleep.

She was awakened again, this time not by the cold but by warmth. It was dark. Someone was lying next to her in her small shelter. She lay still and waited. She heard breathing and then a soft sob.

"Dag-gar," she said.

"Yes, it's me."

"I'm… I'm so glad." She turned to him and put her arms around him and pulled herself closer.

"No, don't be glad. I can't stay. I'm here to warn you. You mustn't try to follow me. Don't try to help me."

"Oh, no, no, Dag-gar. That cannot happen. I—"

"I am, my Sonoria, as we speak, a prisoner. I cannot escape. The Time Vagabond is the Scorpion. He is taking revenge on me because I destroyed the Amber Teardrop. I'm gone, gone forever."

Sonora buried her face in his chest and began crying. "No, it will be good, you and I, as it has always been. Just stay here with me tonight, and tomorrow we will continue our quest to find your father."

But she felt him slipping away, and though she held on to him, somehow he was gone as if he had melted into the darkness.

* * * * *

When she awoke again, it was still dark. Despite the thick blanket, she was wet and cold. The sky had cleared and just the scattered remnants of the storm drifted overhead. Through them she could see the star-filled night sky. Then she remembered Dag-gar, the feeling of him, his warmth and his arms around her.

She felt for him but there was nothing next to her. She pressed her face into the grass, seeking out his smell. But it all had been a dream and he a mere apparition. She told herself this and then said aloud, "It is time to move."

She gathered her sword, her bow, and her quiver of arrows. Spiritus seemed happy to see her and eager to be off. She saddled him, pulled the hackamore over his head, untied his hobbled front legs, and mounted him.

She gazed up at the night sky. There they were, all the old ones, the ancient and eternal constellations locked by their gravities in an aeonian struggle: the Hunter, the Sisters, the Bull, and the Bears. And there, as always, was the Star-That-Does-Not-Move, placid and perfect. She pointed Spiritus toward it and urged him on with a soft whisper of encouragement.

Now there was something different about the journey. Somehow she had hardened to it, hardened to traveling alone, at night, across a vast emptiness where no other human being existed. She was rested and had eaten what was left of the big hare. The stallion felt strong between her knees and she, too, felt light and powerful. There was even a measure of satisfaction: If this was the way the ancient songs said it must be, if this was how *her* story had been told, she was eager to get on with it.

Dag-gar was out there somewhere, ahead of her in the darkness, looking at the same stars and taking his bearings from the same steady pinpoint of light. He, too, would be cold and hungry, and he would be desperate, his heart burning in the flames of his silent rage.

And Time's Mistress, awakened by wizard's blood and moonlight from her slumber in the Amber Teardrop? What had she meant? She had called Dag-gar "the Hunter," had said he had been stung by the Scorpion, Time's Vagabond, and that he was now possessed—was now deadly. Sonoria shuddered with dread. The Vagabond had done more than possessed her love, he had stolen the tale from her lips and would change the Ancient Song.

* * * * *

The blue roan stallion, Spiritus, carried her through the night, through the long darkness. Only occasionally did they stop to rest and drink from the clear, sweet-water streams that carved their meandering ways through the prairie. While the heavens wheeled in their huge circle above them, the one true star held its place and it was this they followed.

When again the sky began to brighten in the east and the stars to fade away, Sonoria found that they had arrived in a different country. Indeed, the increasing light revealed the prairie's end. A forest rose up before them, vast and black in the dim pre-dawn, and when the wind shifted, it carried the scent of the woods: thick pine, flowering trees, damp, rotting vegetation. And with the new day, there was the sound of birds, a cacophony of chirping and twittering.

She pulled Spiritus to a halt and for long moments watched and listened. As the sun drew closer to its rising, the forest's smells and sounds intensified and the immense spirit of an endless woods rushed out toward her. She took in big breaths of it and she felt Spiritus do the same as he snorted and stamped his front hooves.

Then the first rays of the sun broke over the forest, illuminating it, and she saw spread out before her a vast land of trees in the sea of grass. *How,* she thought, *will we ever find our way through this? The branches will block the sun by day and the stars by night.*

And yet she knew that Dag-gar must be in there by now, maybe deep into it, maybe lost, maybe… . She swung a leg over Spiritus' back and dismounted. It felt good to stretch her legs, and she led the horse down the last low hill of the prairie until they came to the very edge of the woods.

It seemed impenetrable, a solid wall of trunks and interlacing branches that within twenty paces blocked all light. Before her, the forest's infinite features dissolved into darkness.

But then there was something. As her eyes and her mind accepted the idea of the forest, it seemed to open up to her. Where before she had seen nothing but heavy foliage, she now perceived an opening, a small path, a trace, a track opened up by the habits of some animal. She soon realized that the seemingly solid face of the forest was scored by such opportunities.

Choosing one, she led Spiritus forward. The passage was like a tunnel. It had walls and a roof of branches and leaves and it meandered like a prairie stream. She followed it farther and farther back until the forest closed in behind her. Before her, the path curved deeper into the woods and then disappeared.

For the first time in her life, she felt a surge of panic. She had never been closed in like this. She was a person of open spaces, a person of sun and wide skies. Now she was about to be swallowed up by something that seemed to clutch at her, something that seemed alive and intent on pulling her down into it. She found that she was gasping for air, struggling to breathe.

She clutched at Spiritus' hackamore and moved her face close to his, feeling his warm breathing on her cheeks and imagining how her familiar's fearless strength would be imparted to her. He allowed this and whickered in her ear.

"We need to get out of here," she whispered. "I don't want to get lost."

With some effort, she managed to turn the big horse around in the narrow trace and together they worked their way back the way they had come. It was with great relief that she finally saw the glimmer of strong sunlight through the foliage ahead of her—and then, almost without warning, they burst from the last of the trees and were once again in the open.

Sonoria lay on her back, staring up at the sky until she caught her breath. Spiritus immediately began grazing, his head near hers, the sound of his pasturing close by her ears. Then she noticed something beyond the stallion's head, high above them—a mere speck in the bright morning sky. It was a bird, a high-flying hawk or an eagle. It soared on the wind, never having to move its wings, wheeling around on its wingtips as if challenging the Earth to dare to pull it down.

Somehow she thought it was watching her, and then she realized that of course it was. Even from that distance its powerful eyes could spy a mouse running in the grass, never mind a woman and a horse. As she watched the bird, her breathing became easier and she was able to sit up. She continued to watch the hawk. She knew it was a spirit of the air and was trying to tell her something—but what?

The sun was warm on her face and on her body and the sound of Spiritus' grazing was comforting. She felt herself dozing off and at first she fought it. Finally, though, she allowed herself to drift away and let the deliciousness of exhaustion guide her down into her kip.

She slept until the sun was high overhead. When she awoke, she found she had curled up in a ball in the grass and that Spiritus had wandered off in his grazing. Sitting up in a near panic, she saw him a hundred paces away near a clump of trees. She got to her feet and walked down towards him and when he heard her, he lifted his head and regarded her. He still wore his saddle and the reins of the hackamore dragged at his sides. Chewing a mouthful of grass, he began walking toward her and when they met, he nuzzled her stomach.

She stroked his head and his ears, hesitated, and looked toward the forest. She had been avoiding this, for in her dreams the endless trees had appeared as a vast living creature, looming dreadful and horrific. Again she asked herself how she could navigate through this infinitely complex maze.

Then there was a soft rush of air by her ear. It was nearly silent—she felt it more than heard it. At first she thought it was the shadow of a cloud. But when she looked up, she saw it was a bird. Not the high-soaring hawk that had drifted above her as she had fallen asleep, but rather a night bird, an owl with a broad, wise face and large, luminous eyes.

It had flown close enough to her to brush the wild ends of her hair with its wings and then had swooped upwards and now was coming back at her. For a moment she thought it meant to strike her with its talons, but instead, it passed by again, and as it did so, it spoke to her—or seemed to, although because its speech was as silent as its flight and she heard nothing, she had understood it perfectly: *Follow me,* it had said, *follow me.*

Chapter 27

She knew she must now do this, must allow herself to be led into the dark confusion of the woods by this forest bird. She spoke to Spiritus. "Come then. We'll try this again. We have no choice, other than turning around, and so we have no choice."

She gathered up the stallion's reins and, rather than ride him into the wilderness, she led him. She scanned the sky and there was the night bird not far above her, leading her toward the trees. It swooped down and rose again in its flight and then disappeared into the foliage.

Sonoria and Spiritus walked after it. Again, after just a few steps into the forest, the prairie disappeared behind them and the trees closed in around them. Yet now there was a way discernable amongst the tangle of branches, fallen limbs, and logs.

With a sudden whisper of wings, the owl passed right by her head and shot through an opening in the darkness ahead of them. Sonoria tugged at Spiritus' hackamore, and together they committed themselves to the unknown, following the bird wherever it might lead them.

The path narrowed and the trees closed in until they scraped the saddle on the horse's back and rubbed against the animal's chest and withers. Sonoria walked ahead, holding the reins behind her in one hand and holding her other hand up before her face to ward off branches. How the owl had flown through this she did not know, but then there it was again, as if to encourage her. She felt its wings before she saw it, and again, though its flight was silent, she heard its voice: *Follow me. Don't despair. Follow me. He needs you.* By some magic, the bird wove its way through the impenetrable branches, its wide wings folding and extending in perfect synchrony with the will of the forest, as if they were but one creature, bird and woods, together.

So Sonoria and Spiritus followed the bird, the stallion's immense body driving its way through the trees. After a long time, when the scant sunlight diminished as evening approached and it seemed the horse could go no farther, when it seemed that the very solidity of the woods must stop them, they stepped into a clearing. It opened up in front of them like a sudden void and Sonoria felt the urge to step back, to pull away lest she fall into some open pit.

But no, it was but a clear place in the woods where nothing grew. The moist, black earth was mostly covered with dead and rotting leaves and branches; there was no grass, no flowers. Not the thinnest ray of sunlight could find its way in and now, as the sun set, the shadows of the surrounding thickets were quickly sucking out what light remained.

It had been a hard day. Now, when they must stop, there was nothing for Spiritus to eat and Sonoria was far too exhausted to build a fire. Instead, she left the hackamore on the stallion, unsaddled him, spread his thick horse blanket on the ground, and lay down on it, wrapping herself in its warmth. She tied the stallion's reins around her ankle, rested her head on his saddle, and drifted off to sleep.

It seemed as if she had just closed her eyes when she awakened, knowing she had been sleeping for a long time. Her face was pressed into the smooth leather of the saddle and her body was stiff with the chill of the wet soil that seeped through the blanket. Yet, though she was certain she was awake, she might still have been sleeping, for the darkness was utter and complete. She could see nothing, not the silhouette of a branch, not a glimmer of the night sky, not a star nor any hint of the moon.

She lay still, knowing that *something* had awakened her. She listened. She felt Spiritus' presence next to her and heard the sounds of a forest at night, carried on the cold, pitch-black air: Insects and frogs buzzed and croaked; branches snapped; leaves rustled; in the distance, a wolf howled—yet she could see nothing. She took her sword from its scabbard and held it next to her; she withdrew her dagger from its sheath and clutched it in her hand. She curled up deeper into the blankets as if they could offer some protection from the unknown dangers that lurked about her.

As she lay listening, she must have fallen asleep again and then again awakened, because she knew more time had passed and the night sounds had changed. It was early morning now. She sensed this even though there was no easing of the darkness, no emerging shadows to indicate the coming of some light.

Then she heard what had awakened her this time: a soft singing, and then murmurings, and soft clatterings and bustlings and footfalls and even laughter. It was all barely perceptible, as if she were sitting amongst an invisible crowd of spirits. It came from everywhere; the air was filled with it, though it was so faint it may well have been merely the music of a random zephyr drifting through the leaves and branches, or the hum of the forest itself.

But she was hearing it, she was certain of that: words carried on a melody of unseen humanity, unintelligible words, but bearing the discernible rhythm of syllables.

Then there was the smell of a fire. Sonoria lay clutching her weapons and her blankets and sniffing the invisible air that now brought to her the pungency of newly lit tinder. Sweet smoke wafted over her, yet she could see no flames. She sat up, gathered the blanket around her shoulders, and cast about for a flicker of light.

There it was, beyond where she knew Spiritus was standing—just a quick glimmer and then gone, and then there it was again and gone again. Sonoria stood up, trying to remember the boundaries of the small clearing. She touched Spiritus and his broad, warm body felt comforting. She gathered up the reins and felt him nuzzle her and she whispered to him, "Let's find the light, Spiritus. Let's find the light."

Sonoria's eyes searched the blackness for the illusive glow and there it was again. Leading Spiritus by his hackamore, she moved slowly toward it, holding an arm out in front of her face to protect herself from unseen branches. When she felt the first leaves, she knew she had reached the edge of the clearing. With her free hand she parted the branches; then one of them broke with a loud snapping sound.

Spiritus pulled backwards but Sonoria held onto the reins. She stopped and listened. She was about to move forward again toward the flames clearly visible through the branches, when she realized the singing and the sounds of bustling had stopped. She waited, wondering if she should call out to whoever was by the fire.

But before she could do this, someone called out to her. "Come, come, then, my dear. Don't be shy. Come to my fire and bring your lovely horse with you."

It was an old woman's voice, so old it seemed to crackle and waver with age. Sonoria hesitated. The old woman spoke again. "I've got some bread here, newly baked, and you've not eaten in—in how long now? Come, come! You must be starving."

Sonoria pushed through the branches and Spiritus followed her willingly enough, seeming eager to get closer to the fire and the smell of the bread. A moment later they found themselves standing in another small clearing where, from above them, the morning light was just beginning to set things aglow. Sonoria could now begin to make out details: A fire burned in front of a small, comfortable-looking, thatch-roofed house, and the shadowed figure of someone tall and thin stood at its door.

"Don't linger, now," the figure said. "'Tis the magical time of day, this, the time between night and day, and it is brief enough without wasting it. You'll miss the show if you dawdle." The old woman took a step toward them. She lifted her arms and said, "You see now, all around you, there are, gathered in the dim light of dawning, the energies of the many dimensions of this universe. It's the only time you can rub elbows with our unseen neighbors. When the light gets too strong, they vanish—poof, back to their own planes of existence. Like the stars, you can't see them during the day, but they are there, nonetheless."

Now Sonoria could begin to make out the woman's face. Her nose was long and bony, her cheeks hollowed out with age, and her snow-white hair seemed to hang all the way to the ground. Sonoria was about to speak, about to say, "My name is Sonoria and this is my horse, Spiritus," when she was bumped by something and turned to see what it was. Just for an instant, she saw a man walking past her, a man dressed oddly in strange pantaloons and a baggy shirt. But before she could say something to him, he vanished, as if into the air itself.

"There now, you see?" the old woman said, "a passing citizen of another time and place. Had you been quick enough, you might have asked him a question or two. They often like to stop to chat. Watch me, now, I'll grab the next one."

No sooner had she said this than another figure emerged from the air in front of them. It was a woman who in one hand carried a chicken and with the other led a young girl. The child had very curly brown hair and was clutching a small doll made of corn husks. Before they could disappear as the man had, the old woman spoke to them. "Hello, then," she said, "what are you seeking?"

The woman stopped. Both she and the girl looked at the old woman. "We are just going here to the market," she said, "and we can't be late. It's quite busy, as you can see, and we need to trade this old hen for some salt and get home for dinner."

Then, for an instant, it seemed to be true: They were all standing in the middle of a busy market with throngs of people rushing about. "Ah, yes, yes," the old woman said. "Go along then, please. We shall not hold you up with idle chatter." With that, the woman, the little girl, and the market with all its shoppers and merchants vanished and the air in front of the old woman was empty again.

She smiled at Sonoria. "You see, they are there—here, there, everywhere—all around us all the time, living their busy, busy lives, layer upon layer of them, time folded into time, their time into our time, past time into present time into future time. But it is only the magic of the earliest morning when night and day hang balanced between each other that we can visit with them.

It is called the Portal of Convergence and it is as ephemeral and transitory as a breath."

She seemed about to say something else when they heard a gasping sound and the rattle of chains and a man appeared in the clearing. He was stumbling, trying to keep to his feet, but he was very weak and he staggered and fell. As he lay on the ground, a man in a black cloak appeared. Standing over the fallen man, the cloaked figure lashed at him with a short leather whip. Cut and bleeding, the beaten man struggled to his feet and they moved away. Just as they were about to vanish into the air as the others had, Sonoria recognized the prisoner who was being beaten: It was Dag-gar. She gasped and looked at the old woman but they were all gone—Dag-gar, the black-cloaked man, the old woman, and the house and fire, too. Sonoria and Spiritus were alone again, standing in a small clearing.

But where the fire had been, now, instead of ashes and soot, was a large loaf of bread, set carefully on a bed of fresh, green leaves. Sonoria picked it up. It was still warm and smelled of corn and wheat and herbs. Behind her, Spiritus whickered and his head came around and he began eating the bread from her hand.

While the sun rose and the forest slowly filled with light, Sonoria and Spiritus ate the bread, the horse taking pieces of it from one of her hands while she stuffed her mouth full with the other. When there was enough light to see clearly, Sonoria retrieved the saddle and looked about for the trail they had been following the evening before.

She turned around and around, again and again, searching for the break in the wall of forest that would be the way out of the clearing, yet this turning only served to confuse her more. There was no way to tell which direction was north or south or east or west, no way to tell from which direction she had come the night before or in which direction they had been moving when darkness forced them to stop.

Then, their savior appeared again—the great forest bird. It swooped in from the trees, passed close enough by her head for her to feel the brush of its feathers, and flew directly into the wall of trees. But it did not smash into the impenetrable tangle of branches; again a pathway opened up before it and it disappeared into the shadows.

Sonoria stared after it, unable to move. Stunned by all she had seen, she clutched at Spiritus' head, holding onto the stiff leather of the hackamore, the horse's smell and the hot moisture of his breathing her only connection to reality. As if to urge her on, as if he understood, the stallion nudged her with his nose, pushing her ahead.

She took a tentative step, stopped, and then took another. The layer of moist, rotting leaves was soft under her feet. She moved silently, the horse behind her. When they reached the edge of the clearing, she again hesitated. There was no sign of the owl, nor was there any sign of other birds—no chirping or twittering as there had been the day before. The forest loomed before her, vast and silent.

She felt the chill of fear run through her body and she scolded herself aloud. Her voice was immediately absorbed by the woods. She yelled again, and again her words were drawn away from her as if the silence of the wilderness was hungry for them. She began walking down the path opened up by the owl. With one hand she held Spiritus' reins; with the other she drew her sword and held it before her.

The path wandered and turned and at times seemed to curl back upon itself, so by the end of the day she was certain they were moving only in circles. But then they came to a small stream they had not seen before, and nearby was a clearing where sunlight had allowed a large patch of grass to grow. Spiritus would not be stopped now; he pushed past her and, ignoring even the water, began eating. Sonoria let loose of the hackamore and allowed him to graze. She drank her fill and found a place where a ray of sunlight had warmed the earth and where the grass was thick. She lay down and stared up through the branches at the blue sky.

All day long she had relived the image of Dag-gar, had relived the vision of the man in the black cloak beating him, of his falling and his staggering to his feet. And what could the old woman have meant about time, about layers and layers of it, folding each on the other, each filled with busy lives? Had it really been Dag-gar lying there bloody and filthy and exhausted, or was it merely some trickery of the haunted dawn?

The sky seemed to be watching her as she lay in the little forest clearing in her rough woolens and leather tunic, her sword at her side, her bow and quiver of arrows beside her on the grass. *The stars,* she thought, *are out there even now, though we cannot see them. Just as, if what the old woman said is true, the people in the visions I witnessed this morning are always there, always, time folded upon time, living and dying forever and ever.*

Warmed by the sun and having slept little the night before, she was soon asleep, the familiar sound of Spiritus' grazing filling her ears. When she awoke it was nearly dark. She had dreamt of Scraps and the Ancient Boy and Scraps' wonderful magic as he had lifted the Ancient Boy into the air and, in front of the entire town of Eye o' the Sea, sent him whirling away through Time to gather up the wisdom of the cosmos. The memory of it gave her a warm feeling, but this was soon replaced by the chill the creeping night shadows spread toward her.

She searched in her kit bag for her flint and steel and the soft dry grass of the mouse nest and birch bark she carried for tinder. With some patience, she was able to strike a spark into the nest and blow on it softly until a real flame rose upward. She gathered some larger sticks and branches, and soon she had a sizable blaze going. She had saved a hunk of the bread and now she bit off small pieces of it, savoring the coarse flavor of its hardened texture and the leathery toughness of the crust.

When she finished eating, she hobbled Spiritus to prevent him from wandering off, took off the hackamore, and then again wrapped herself in the saddle blanket and lay on the ground. This time when she lay down and looked up, the stars were there, released from their invisibility by the absence of light. The stars were, she was certain, the eyes of the universe and they were watching her. Maybe they were even judging her, deciding her worthiness for the task that lay ahead.

She fell asleep again and while she slept, the moonlight cascaded through the trees and onto her face. The fullness of it did not disturb her sleep, nor did the cry of foxes or the howl of wolves nor the hooting of the great owl who sat in the hollow of the giant oak tree and watched her sleep.

Chapter 28

She was awakened by a kicking and stomping and she sat up clutching her sword, trying to bring it up to defend herself. And yet there was no need. She was lying in the middle of a busy road; the thud and dust that had roused her out of sleep was caused by the passing of oxen and horses pulling heavily laden wagons. And there was the cursing and grunting and yelling of wagon drivers and the smell of them, too, the reek of unwashed humanity mingling with the steady raucous hubbub.

She scrambled to her feet and stood among them, watching them pass, a parade of them: wagons burdened with hay or casks of beer or gourds or wood, and tinkers with their wares hanging, swinging and clanging. Dirty, ragged, barefoot peasants trudged alongside them. Some carried chickens or ducks; some led small, bony goats; and a family—a mother, a father, and five filthy children—came along herding a gaggle of honking geese before them.

Sonoria backed off the road and stared, open-mouthed. She had never seen anything like it. What had been a quiet forest clearing when she lay down to sleep was now a busy thoroughfare, and the passersby seemed intent on ignoring her. Had she not gotten out of the way, they would have been content to trample her into the earth.

And there was a babble of tongues. She could not understand a word of what they were saying. Their speech was all blather and gibberish, a great honking and gurgling that make no sense to her at all.

Then she remembered Spiritus. She felt her heart leap, and her head spun around as she looked over the crowd for him. There he was, surrounded by four men. They had put his hackamore on him and untied the hobble. Two held him by the hackamore's cheek straps and the other two by his reins. They were yelling loudly at each other as if they were fighting over him.

Sonoria pushed her way through the crowd toward them, forgetting that she still held her sword up and at the ready. When she stepped in among the men, they at first ignored her and continued to argue, each trying to pull the stallion's head around in his own direction. Finally, Sonoria screamed at them and they stopped yelling and looked at her.

"He is mine!" she screamed. "He's my stallion!"

For a moment the men hesitated and she felt their eyes move up and down along her body. Then one of them spoke to her, and though she could not understand his words, it was clear by the tone of his voice, the squint of his eyes, and the movements of his arms that he was dismissing her. He turned back to the other men and they started arguing again.

With a quick movement, Sonoria put the razor-sharp tip of her sword against the man's neck just below his ear. "He's mine, you fool!" she yelled again.

The man swung around to face her and as he did so, the sword nicked his skin. He put his hand up to the wound and, with blood oozing through his fingers, stared at her in disbelief. The other men, too, turned to face her and Sonoria knew what they were looking at: She was as tall as the tallest of them and a head above the shortest. She was dressed in a rough-tanned fur tunic and leggings under which she wore coarse woolen undergarments. Her white-blond hair was wild and matted and festooned with sticks and leaves from sleeping on the ground. But in the end, it was her eyes that held them hostage for a moment too long: they were a fierce blue, the color of a hot, clear sky.

While they gaped at her, she jerked the reins out of their hands and started to lead Spiritus away. The men who had a grip on the hackamore's cheek straps, though, refused to let go; one of them pulled out a long dagger and lunged at her. Sonoria saw this out of the corner of her eye and she spun around, swinging her sword. The tip of it caught the man's wrist and lay it open to the bone. He yelped and dropped the knife. The other men now backed away and Sonoria again had full possession of her horse.

Then, as she led Spiritus off the road, she heard her name being called. She saw a wagon drawn by a team of black oxen, and in the wagon's bed was a cage made of heavy wooden poles lashed together with leather thongs. In the cage was a thin young man. He was ragged and dirty and emaciated, his face covered with a thin beard. He was looking at her through the bars of the cage and crying out to her.

The terrible truth that her eyes brought to her took a moment for her heart to accept: *It was Dag-gar.* Pulling Spiritus behind her, Sonoria ran to the wagon and reached up for him. He put his hands out between the timbers and for an instant their fingers touched. At that moment, Sonoria heard a guttural snarl and something grabbed her arm and spun her around.

She found herself looking into the face of a specter, its features shadowed by the cowl of a black robe. Its eyes were mere sockets, its lips pulled back from sharp teeth. The voice seemed to be an echo rising from some infinite and hollow depth. "He is mine!"

Sonoria stared into the unspeakable face and as she did, it faded away and she was looking at a dawn-dim forest and feeling the damp chill of dew. She spun around. They were all gone, the ragged families, the carts and wagons, the dust and noise—and Dag-gar.

She still held Spiritus by his reins and she looked at the horse and held her breath, waiting. But he did not disappear. She touched the velvet of his nose and felt the warm moisture of his breathing. The stallion, at least, was real.

She heard another familiar voice calling to her from the edge of the clearing. She turned and saw the old woman, the same coarse-featured old crone she had met the morning before. "Sonoria, dear," she said, "they are gone. The dawn is growing old, as even dawns must do, and Time is now quickly moving past the Portal of Convergence; our planes of existence are moving away from each other. I, too, must go now. But here, I've left you some food. Eat. You will need your strength. It should be enough until we meet again."

With that, the crone, too, faded away as if she had melted into the woods behind her and become one with the shadows. Where she had been standing, in the very place her feet had touched the earth, a small feast lay spread on fresh, clean leaves: bread, a large meat pie, a yellow pear.

Leading Spiritus by the reins, Sonoria took a tentative step toward the food. Yet for long moments she could not bring herself to reach down and touch it lest it, too, fade into nothingness. When she did pick it up, the bread was still warm, as was the pie, and the pear was soft and filled with juice.

The dawn was now full and the woods aglow with its new light. The clearing where they had spent the night gleamed with dew; songbirds filled the air with their chirping. She felt overwhelmed by it all and she struggled to understand that which she knew was beyond understanding. Then she remembered what Scraps had told her once when she was a girl—it seemed only yesterday, but could that be?—and they were traveling across an endless desert. She had been trying to explain to him all she could see from high atop the back of the camel, trying to tell him the reason for the wind, for the lovely russet sands, for the irrational beauty and the senseless complexities of everything she saw and felt.

He had stopped her with a wave of his hand and then, as he continued walking and leading the camel, had said, "Child, you must learn the truth about wonderful things. It is this: Nothing exists by itself. Everything, the wonderful and terrible, the lovely and the strange, the possible and the impossible, are made of many parts joined into a oneness that is greater than the many parts themselves. And so the beauty of a sunset is more than the elements that make it beautiful: It is the sunset itself, in its entirety, that is beautiful. It is better that we not try too hard to understand beauty, lest the wonderment that comes from it fade away." She had responded to this small wisdom by wrinkling up her nose and saying that she did not understand what he was talking about.

She was now, though, despite everything, of a sudden very hungry. At least this she could understand. She tore off a mouthful of the bread and as she chewed, she pictured Scraps as he had been then, walking along in front of her day after day on his long, bony legs and endlessly, tirelessly, spouting his strange sapience.

As she ate, she waited and watched. Soon the forest bird, the great owl, appeared again, and again he came from behind and brushed her with his wing. She watched as he flew toward the impenetrable wall of trees and, as before, just as he seemed about to crash headlong into the branches and leaves, a way opened up and he disappeared into it. As before, the bird left behind a trail, a trace through the forest as a ship might leave a wake. Still eating and leading Spiritus, Sonoria left the clearing and followed the bird.

So it became the pattern of life. All day Sonoria and Spiritus followed a path through the forest created by the bird, and every evening, as darkness engulfed the woods, they would somehow come to a small meadow or clearing where there was pasture for the horse and a stream for them both to drink from. And in the morning, at dayspring, she would wake up among throngs of people churning up swirls of dust as they passed by her herding their animals or selling their wares. Then the old woman would appear and leave enough food for Sonoria for the day, before vanishing with the others.

Chapter 29

And there were many others. The farther into the woods she went, the more numerous and strange they became. Every morning at earliest light, though she had fallen asleep in a quiet meadow, she would wake in the middle of some madness—a goat nibbling at her feet; a pig rooting around her head; a group of children yelling and chasing each other, swinging a dead rat by its tail; fat peasant women bellowing at each other over the price of a chicken; brainsick old men singing and talking to their hands and dancing in circles as they passed over her.

Each time she was awakened this way, she leaped to her feet, her sword at the ready. She had learned to keep Spiritus tethered to her ankle so that he could not wander off. Now she would stand in the middle of the din and clamor holding him by the hackamore and waiting for what would happen next.

Sometimes it happened and sometimes it didn't. Sometimes she would hear her name called and turn to see Dag-gar. Always he was gaunt and desperate, and always he was in the company of a tall specter in a black cloak and cowl, and always when Sonoria approached Dag-gar, the specter turned on her, hissing the words, "He is mine!" But sometimes she could hear him calling her and yet could not see him, as if he were just out of sight, just around some corner. Always his voice came to her filled with pain.

Then it came to this: One morning she was, as usual, awakened by the turmoil around her and she heard Dag-gar pleading with her, begging her to help him. But she could not see him, and then when the scene began to fade and the quiet forest again emerged where a moment before all had been dust and fury, the old woman appeared. Sonoria ran to her and put her sword up to the crone's face and said, "You will stop this! Dag-gar is dying! What is this? Where are we going? Why are we being tormented so? Tell me, old woman, or I'll cut you in two!"

The old woman did not pull back, nor did she show fear. She put her hand on the blade of the sword and Sonoria felt a powerful energy coming down its sharp steel and through the handle into her hand and then into her body. The old woman's face seemed to glow with a faint aura and when she spoke, her voice was a hoarse whisper. "Girl, you are nearing the end of your journey. Be brave, be strong, do not yield. You have but one more test to pass through and you will be where you need to be. If you are to survive, if your eternal lover is to live, you must be ready to face what is next: the Unspeakable."

As the final syllables left the woman's lips, a ray of peach-colored morning sunlight came through the trees and for just an instant played on her face. Sonoria saw there, in the blood flowing through the paper-thin skin of her cheeks, the lives of all those who had passed by her in the forest—the dogs and children, wives and soldiers, tinkers, murderers, and horse thieves, and on and on; the endless procession she had so recently witnessed played out on the crone's benign expression. And then she was gone, leaving not a breath of her being in the air. Sonoria reached out for her, to touch her, but her fingers found only sunlight. She pulled her hand back and looked at it and then sat down in the meadow and cried.

After a long time, when the sun was directly overhead and the forest shadows small, Sonoria found she had been sleeping. She was awakened by Spiritus tugging at her ankle by his tether as he reached for fresh grass. She sat up. The meadow was peaceful in the warm noon light. Insects floated in sunbeams, spider webs woven across branches glowed, a young deer fearlessly shared Spiritus' pasture.

But it was quiet. There was not the movement of a branch, the stirring of a leaf, the twitter of a bird. Sonoria held her breath and felt the beating of her heart in her chest and the pulsing of her blood in her throat. She looked for her sword. It was lying next to her, as were her bow and quiver of arrows, and next to them, as always lying on a bed of fresh leaves, was the old woman's daily gift of food: a haunch of roast meat, a loaf of bread, and a large green apple.

Sonoria glanced about. The old woman was not to be seen. Sonoria then remembered what she had said: "You are nearing the end of your journey... if you are to survive, you must be ready to face the Unspeakable."

But where was this unspeakable thing that she must face? When would it appear? How would it present itself? What would it look like? She felt a chill run through her.

* * * * *

This time the bird was not an owl. It was an eagle, a war bird with a white head and a broad span of wings and talons curled up beneath its body. It came in from on high, directly from the sun, down through the space the meadow had opened up in the trees. Instead of flying into the forest and opening a path as the owl had done, it landed on a branch directly in front of her.

Sonoria held onto Spiritus' hackamore and moved closer to the horse for protection. From its perch, the big bird eyed her with its fierce gaze. Its curved beak was open, its tongue visible as it breathed. For long moments they stared at each other within the silent forest. Then the bird leaped off the branch, spread its wings, and rose once again into the air.

Now the silence was broken, however gently, by the flapping of the eagle's wings. Sonoria watched it rise, begin to circle, and then, when it had cleared the tops of the trees, disappear into the sun as suddenly as it had arrived. When it had gone, it left behind no trace through the forest, no path, no trail however faint. There could be only one meaning in this: She was to remain where she was. The Unspeakable would come to her. And the bird-of-war's message was this, too: She must be ready.

Chapter 30

And she was ready—as ready as she could be with what weapons she had: her bow and quiver of arrows, her sword, and her dagger. Yet she had no idea how to use them; at least, she did not remember ever being instructed in their use. How had she so expertly and with such facility dealt with the men who would have stolen her horse? She had done it spontaneously, without a thought, without effort. Once—perhaps just a moment ago—she had been but an innocent girl riding a camel across a great desert led by an unearthly old wizard. Now she was alone, a warrior, a soldier, and there had been no time between the two lives for one to become the other.

Still, the sword felt easy in her hand, as if she had held it forever, as if it were a part of her. And the bow and arrows—had she ever practiced with them? No, but when she notched an arrow and let it fly, it went true to where she intended it to go. Hare, deer, and even birds on the wing fell before her effortless skill. It was like her love for Dag-gar, the perfect stranger she had known forever.

So she must only wait; the Unspeakable would come to her in its own time. She knew this was true, for she believed what the old woman had said. For a while, she jumped at every sound: a branch snapping off a tree, an animal rustling in the leaves—these sounds tormented her. She kept her sword out of its scabbard, her dagger in its sheath at her hip, her eyes on the edge of the clearing where the forest closed in on her and from where the Unspeakable must come.

Time passed slowly, measured by the changing shadows. As the sun moved, the shadows grew, seeming to ooze out of the spaces between the trees and creep towards her across the clearing. She watched their progress and wondered what would happen when day was done and they had filled the clearing, when there was no more light, when the fingers of darkness met each other and held her in their grip.

She built a fire. She found a birch tree and peeled off a great quantity of its bark. From a thicket of hemlock, she broke off an armful of the small, dead twigs on the low branches. She found an abandoned bird's nest and from its woven matrix took bits of grass and a small clump of dried thistle seedpod. She knelt over this with her flint and her dagger, striking the flint with the steel blade until a spark flashed off and fell into the seedpod. It lay there glowing and pulsing. She blew on it gently and from that point of spark, a small flame rose and spread, first to the grass of the nest, then to the shredded birch bark, and then to the dried hemlock twigs. Her small fire flared up and she carefully placed larger and larger twigs and dried branches on it until she had a real blaze.

Tending the fire would keep her busy into the night. She searched the edges of the clearing, gathering armloads of fallen branches and throwing them on the flames, building them up until the night shadows had retreated into the forest and the clearing was filled with flickering orange-yellow light.

How could the Unspeakable approach her now? she thought. No, it would stay back in the darkness with the demons of the night—the purity and heat of the fire would protect her. And if she could stay awake until the sun came back to the clearing, there would be no Portal of Convergence through which the Unspeakable could reach her, for she understood now that it was sleep, when the soul was unprotected, that allowed the wanderers from other worlds to gather around her.

* * * * *

The night passed but she was uncertain how quickly. She constantly searched the small patch of sky above the clearing for some sign that dawn was approaching, realizing it would be the stars that would tell her when morning was nigh. Their fading away before the advancing light would be the signal: The Portal of Convergence was opening—beware Time Drifter, beware. It was then, in those few moments, that she must stay awake if she was to prevent the Unspeakable from leaping at her from its furtive dimension.

Then it happened: Time delivered to her that which she most feared. She was standing near the fire, her sword hand gripping the handle of her weapon. She had closed her eyes only for an instant, squeezing them shut to stop their burning from fatigue, but as she did this there was a sudden and powerful stink of rotting flesh.

Before she could open her eyes, she felt something slip around her neck and tighten and then she was strangling, unable to breathe. She dropped her sword and reached for her throat. As she did this, she twisted around and saw her attacker. He was a short, powerful man with matted hair, dressed in rags, his skin covered with oozing sores. He had slipped a leather thong over her head and pulled it tight around her neck and now stood back laughing and smiling through rotting teeth.

Sonoria tried to pull away, to run, but was jerked to her knees. She reached for her dagger but felt the thong tighten and she reached for her throat to try to loosen it. But he was too strong for her and he pulled it tighter and tighter and then she was choking and felt herself dying.

* * * * *

But she did not die. As consciousness returned, she found that she was no longer in the forest clearing. Instead she was in a place of drifting fog and rocky outcroppings. Water dripped from crags and the bare branches of dead trees and there was nothing visible more than ten paces away. In the distance, she heard a soft thundering, a roaring, as if a great ocean-sea was breaking against an unseen shore.

The monster who had strangled her was standing over her. He held the leather thong around her neck, but had loosened it so she could breathe. He looked around as if he was waiting. And then something emerged from the fog in front of her. It was someone wearing a black robe with a cowl that covered its face with shadows—it was the specter, the phantom she had seen before, the one that had been holding Dag-gar prisoner. The mist swirled around it as it stopped coming towards her; it now seemed to be watching her, studying her.

Then it spoke, but not to her. It spoke to the man who held her. "Prepare her for her battle. Release her. Give her her sword."

He did as he was told, releasing the thong and dropping her sword onto the ground next to her. Then he stepped back and was gone, dissolving into the fog, leaving Sonoria alone with the phantom.

She could not see his face and the sleeves of his robe covered his hands. But then he lifted an arm and the sleeve fell away, revealing the hand of a baby. The hand motioned towards something hidden by the fog and there was a rattling sound. The mist cleared away to reveal a man crouching near a fire, a man nearly naked but for a leather loincloth. He was staked to the earth, a chain running from his ankle to the root of a dying tree.

He looked up at Sonoria: It was Dag-gar, but Dag-gar as she had never seen him. His body was covered with sores, welts, and bruises. His dark hair was matted and filthy, his teeth were black—but it was his eyes, so filled with hate, that made Sonoria swoon.

With a snarl, he leapt at her and the chain brought him up short and jerked him back down onto the earth. For a moment he lay there writhing in pain and while he did, the specter spoke. "I am the Time Vagabond, Lord of all this—this fog." He waved his tiny, baby hand around. "And all of this cold and miserable country. 'Tis my place, you see, a place abandoned by Time. Nothing really can grow here, and if something does, it soon dies. The sun is a stranger to my land, as are stars and the moon. It is, you might say, a place of perpetual gloom."

Sonoria now was able to take her eyes off of Dag-gar for a moment and look at the Vagabond. She raised her sword and took a step toward him. "You are killing him—"

The Vagabond cut her off with a snarl of words. "He has chosen to kill himself, fair warrior, for he has betrayed my trust. I presented him the Amber Teardrop so he might find his father and rescue him from his doom; in return, I entered his body so that I might have life, and therefore, hope—and so learn the secret of controlling Time. Yet, in a fit of rage, he tossed the Amber into the fire, from which it was rescued by a wizard.

"So what is to be done? Dag-gar must be punished. And as I do not comprehend Time, his punishment will be, for him, eternal. What you see now, will be his fate forever. A pity, really, that you must both pay the price for your eternal love. But as you are eternally precious to him, I will punish him by forcing him to fight you to the death. And as I will not allow him to die, you, my dear, will be the one whose life blood shall soak the dead soil of my empty earth. Dag-gar will be forced to kill that which he loves—and he will continue to do so forever.

"He is ready. Look at him. He will kill you when I let him loose and give him a sword. Unless you kill him. It will be a fine battle; I know, because I have seen you both fight. You are experts with your weapons. Prepare yourself then, my dear—prepare yourself."

Sonoria leaped at the Vagabond, her sword flashing in the cold, misty air, but when the blade should have cut him in half, he was not there. Instead, there was the cool, clear air of the forest and Spiritus grazing and the sunlight weaving its way through the branches of the trees—and on a bed of fresh-cut leaves, there was a loaf of warm bread and a freshly roasted rabbit.

Chapter 31

Scraps and Astral the Ancient Boy were not getting along. Their disagreement about which wizard's blood to use on the Amber Teardrop was the beginning of a chronic discord, and in any event, two wizards traveling together on the same road means trouble.

They quickly moved on from wizard's blood to other disagreements. There was dissension about which path to be followed, the way the food should be cooked when they stopped and made camp at night, the best location for the camp, and the way the camp itself should be set up.

Which direction their shelters should face mattered a great deal to both Scraps and to Astral. Scraps insisted their feet should face south, their heads north toward the very star they were following. Astral was certain the position of the rising moon and the nearest water source should determine in which direction sleeping heads should point. They bickered and pouted and grumped about it and finally each did it his own way so that every night the camp was a helter-skelter affair.

Fire building, too, was a great concern about which they could not agree. Build it on a rise and there was no shelter from the wind, build it in a low spot and the smoke might settle down around them and cause discomfort. So, often as not, Scraps built his own fire up high and Astral his down low and each sat by his own flames, by his own shelter, pointing in different directions throughout the evening, keeping his own company.

And then there was Astral's choice of a familiar—a toad. He found it one day as it sat by a pool of water in the path and, to Scrap's disgust, toad and boy became inseparable.

"A toad?" Scraps said, looking down his long, lumpy nose at the wriggling creature that the Ancient Boy held up for his inspection. "With all manner of lovely creatures available to you, why would you choose—a toad?"

Astral smiled. "It called to me. I had no choice."

"It will wet all over you every time you pick it up."

"I'll keep it here, in my tunic. It will get used to being handled."

"You'll get all manner of warts."

"I have a potion that cures warts."

"It's ugly as the underworld from which it was spawned."

"You?" Astral said, and now his voice was rising in irritation. "You are calling something ugly? Of all people."

"I'm not that bad. I have some redeeming features."

"No, I suppose you're not that bad," Astral said, "compared to a toad—or even a donkey."

At that point the conversation ended and for the rest of the day's walk they kept a distance and a long silence between them.

None of this mattered even the smallest bit to Admiral Penance. The sad-eyed donkey, if he thought anything at all about the matter, kept it to himself, setting about grazing for at least half the night and sleeping standing up in the manner of donkeys the other half. In the morning, at the first hint of dawn, he was always standing at the doorway of Scraps' shelter, his long face poking in, his breath steaming out on Scraps' head.

This would awaken the old wizard with a start and a curse. "A pox on you, you muddle-headed ass! The smell of your cabbage breath and sight of your floppy-eared, hairy countenance is no way for an ancient sorcerer to reenter the world every morning! Be gone now, or I'll... ."

But by then the donkey would have gotten the reaction it sought, would have backed out of the shelter, and would be standing patiently, swatting at imaginary flies with its scrawny tail.

One morning, when Scraps poked his head out of his shelter, through the donkey's legs he could see Astral down in his hollow place, squatting over the remains of his last evening's fire, which he had coaxed back into a blaze.

"What are you doing?" Scraps asked.

"I'm making tea."

"From what, pray tell? We have none."

"I found elderflower and wild mint that will do just fine. I've been drying them. A hot drink made from them is excellent for constipation and heart flutters and tastes rather nice, too."

Scraps grunted his disapproval. "You and your cures! You've one for everything, I suppose. Gout, constipation, dropsy, warts, dyspepsia, and now heart flutters. Whoever heard of such a thing?"

"You have them," Astral said.

"How do you know that?"

"It's very clear to me. I have had no end of training in affairs of the heart—and yours is definitely fluttering—no doubt due to some bad humor floating through your veins."

"Affairs of the heart? What would a mere boy know about affairs of the heart? Posh! I can't feel a thing. My heart is rather jolly—happy in fact, and doing its job just fine."

"Nonetheless, take my word for it. A cup of this tea and your heart will beat true once again."

Scraps harrumphed and strode off into a thicket to take care of his morning business. When he came back, Astral had the tea ready for him, steaming in a dented tin cup he had found lying beside the path.

"No, thank you. I think not," Scraps said, though the steam rising from the cup carried a wonderful aroma.

"If you don't drink it, I may as well throw it away. I've had mine already. It was very nice. Quite nice with the bread."

Scraps grunted and harrumphed again and then said, "Well, if you insist. Just set it there in the grass and I'll get to it when I have time." Then he hesitated and said, "Bread? What bread?"

"I used the last of the flour and a pinch of salt, made a paste of it, and wrapped it around a stick in front of the fire. It should be ready presently."

Scraps looked in the direction of Astral's fire and sniffed the air. "Well, it would be a pity to throw it all away."

And so they shared a meager breakfast in spite of themselves and then set to packing up their kit—shelters, damp blankets, the odd pot, some clothing, and an expanding sack of strips of tree bark, leaves, roots, and plants that Astral called his medicine bag—and tied them to the Admiral's back.

Then there was a brief squabble about which trail to take and they were off. Scraps took the lead, Admiral Penance followed closely on his tether, and Astral brought up the rear, stopping now and again to study an insect or listen to a bird or to smell or taste this plant or that.

Yet despite these inconvenient incompatibilities, they did see eye to eye on one thing: they must follow, at least in a general way, and not varying off the course too much, The-Star-That-Does-Not-Move. And they understood the extreme importance of reaching that goal, for they had, in a small leather bag tied on a leather string and worn close to Scraps' heart, the Amber Teardrop, inside which resided the sleeping face of Time.

Chapter 32

And so they traveled, plodding across the grass prairie that, after a while, seemed endless indeed. Instead of having to travel at night so as to keep The-Star-That-Does-Not-Move in sight, Astral invented a way of traveling during the day and staying on course when the star was not visible. The last thing he would do before going to sleep was look up at the star and then, from one place to another in front of his shelter, draw a straight line in the dirt that pointed toward the star. Then in the morning, he would sight down that line to a landmark—a hill or a copse of bushes— in the distance and they would then proceed to that landmark. Upon reaching it, he would simply make another sight straight out from it. This seemed to be working well; at night they could see the star was again visible directly ahead of them.

Though he was impressed with Astral's ingenuity, Scraps never said so, but stayed in the lead as he thought was his right as the elder wizard. Finally—and because he had no choice—he was able to swallow his pride and take directions from the Ancient Boy, who would yell up to him from behind, his voice filled with a maddening tone of condescension, "Take the path on the left," or "No, not that bluff, the one to the east of it," or, "This will be a fine place to camp, as it's getting dark and I have already lined up the goal for tomorrow morning."

One day at about noon, with the sun high overhead, they crested a rise in the great grass prairie and beheld, stretching to the distant horizon, a vast forest. Its trees had grown so thickly together that it seemed from their vantage point to be utterly endless and impenetrable.

"I suppose," Scraps said when Astral came up beside him and they stood looking out over the scene together, "you know your way through this darkling woods?"

Astral was silent. For a long time he stared out ahead of them and said nothing.

"Well?" Scraps said, sighing with impatience. He turned and looked at Astral, who was standing on the other side of the Admiral, his head visible over the bundle tied to the donkey's back.

"We shall," Astral said finally, "have to put our wizardly heads together and come up with something."

"Indeed."

"Yes, indeed."

"Well," Scraps said, "I've had enough of following your directions. I shall, henceforth, be the pathfinder.

With that, he withdrew his sword, stepped away from the donkey and the Ancient Boy, and, muttering something under his breath, swung the blade in a wide arc over his head. He then stood for a moment, waiting, but nothing happened.

"You used the wrong incantation," Astral said.

"I don't think so," Scraps said, and now he was clearly irritated.

"Let me try," Astral said and he withdrew his sword and, stepping off the path and muttering something under his breath, swung the sword around in a great arc as had Scraps. As the blade cut through the air, a great trail of blue flame came from the tip of it.

"There," Astral said, "I think that should do it."

Before Scraps could reply, a swift shadow crossed them and they both looked up. A great bird, a night bird, a bird of the forest, swooped down, nearly knocked Scraps' hat off, and then swooped up and dove down the grassy slope toward the trees. A moment later it had diminished to a speck and vanished into the woods.

"The Bird!" Scraps said softly, and then he took off his hat and waved it in the air and yelled, "The Bird! I had wondered where that feathered chimera, that blasted winged fiend had gotten off to. But I'll have to compliment it, first chance. It came in the nick of time."

"Of course it did," Astral said. "I just called it."

Scraps pretended not to hear him and said, "Our troubles are over, my little wizardly friend. Trust me. My magic worked!"

"I believe," Astral said, "it was my magic that worked. Your bird was a pelican. This was an owl."

"If you'll recall," Scraps said, "my bird was also a man-o-war, harbinger of battles, herald of our fates, soothsayer, and now, as an owl, our guide through the wilderness. It changes form to meet our needs."

And so, it seemed, it was true. Astral gave up the argument and said nothing more. They went down to the edge of the forest where the owl had disappeared and there, opened up in the tangle of branches, was a path just wide enough for a man or a donkey to pass. They peered in.

"It's quite dark in there," Astral said. "Can we trust your bird to take us all the way through? I fear we will not be able to see the Star-That-Does-Not-Move through the tops of the trees."

"Ah, yes, never worry, little wizard. My bird, in its various forms and variegated guises, has been my companion, my intimate, my familiar spirit for the longest time. I will admit that it can be a bit trying. It is usually late for appointments and has a rather low sense of humor; it enjoys sneaking up behind me and giving me a start and I end up cursing it and... but never mind that. Yes, it will take us through, you can be certain of that. Let's go now. We must not linger."

They proceeded, and to Scraps' satisfaction, Astral no longer seemed to have the obnoxious, condescending self-assurance he had had out in the open. In fact, he seemed quite timid—even, perhaps, a bit frightened by the enclosing gloom of the deep woods. This, of course, brought out the very same behavior in Scraps that Scraps had found so annoying in Astral. The old man began addressing the boy in exactly the same patronizing tone of voice the boy had used on him.

"Watch for that branch now. When walking in the woods one must be careful of branches whipping back and striking one in the face—or even in the eye." And, "When walking through the woods, it is better to step over a fallen log than step up onto it. Much less tiring for the legs." And he took no little pleasure in putting small fears in the boy's heart. "Don't let that howling frighten you. No doubt it's just a half-starved old wolf looking for an easy meal."

By the time darkness was descending on the already dim woods, they were exhausted and ready to make camp. Just at this moment they came upon a clearing, where Admiral Penance began sniffing around in a curious manner. Then Astral found a hair from a horse's tail and a bit of cloth caught on a branch.

"Ah," Scraps said, examining both, "they have been this way. No doubt this is something from either Dag-gar or Sonoria. We can make an excellent spell from these. Let's spend the night here and in the morning get an early start. Perhaps we can catch up with them."

So they made camp and, as was their habit, Astral used his fire-making skills to get a blaze going, while Scraps unloaded Admiral Penance. Once those chores were finished, Scraps opened his leather sack and took out a small vial.

"What's that," Astral asked.

"Olibanum. A special oil made from frankincense and dragon's blood."

"Really?" Astral said.

"Yes, of course, really," Scraps said. "I'm surprised you haven't heard of it. I use it quite often." He then took the horsehair and the bit of cloth they had found hanging from a branch and put them in the vial, muttered some words over it, and then sprinkled the oil onto the fire.

"That ought to do it," he said.

"Do what?"

"Come dayspring, it will bring us to whoever's clothing that small piece belonged to—or to their horse. We hope it was either Sonoria or Dag-gar. But be ready, it is powerful magic."

That night all past animosities were forgotten, at least for the time being. The two wizards sat close together, as near to the flames as they could get, and set up their shelters as close to each other as they could, too, and Astral did not complain about Scraps' snoring, rather taking some comfort in the old man's noisy breathing.

At the first hint of dawn they were awakened by the sound of hooves, the cries of men, the honking of geese, and the laughter of children. A great cacophony greeted them when they looked out the doors of their shelters. They were no longer in a small, damp clearing in a deep forest, but rather in the middle of a busy road filled with the dust and din of a great throng of rabble.

They scrambled out of their shelters and to their feet and Scraps immediately found the Admiral, looking perplexed, wandering among a herd of sheep. He led the donkey to the side of the road, where Astral joined him to watch the parade of animals and peasants.

"What in the name of the gods is going on?" the boy asked and Scraps noted that he was clinging to his tunic as a properly frightened child should.

"Oh? Just my magic, that's all. I warned you it was powerful. My guess is that we have been caught up in a Portal of Convergence. We're in another Time dimension, my young friend. Don't worry, it shouldn't last long. These portals only open up at dayspring and only very briefly. By the time the cock crows thrice, it shall close up—"

But something stopped him in mid-sentence. There before them passed an oxcart drawn by a team of black oxen. On the cart was a wooden cage and in the cage was a young man, battered, bruised, and nearly naked.

It was Astral who managed to get the words out first. "That's Dag-gar! In that cage!"

And then something else: A young woman with white-blond hair leading a big blue roan stallion ran up to the cage, calling out Dag-gar's name. She reached up to him and he out to her and for a moment their fingers touched. Then the driver of the oxcart, who wore a black robe and whose face was concealed within the folds of a cowl, approached the woman and began speaking to her.

But in the great bleating and yammering that was going on all around them, they could not hear what was said. And then it was over. In the snap of an eyelash, Astral and Scraps were back in the clearing in the forest, where the first pearling of light spoke of the coming dawn and somewhere close by in the trees a bird began twittering.

The wizards looked at each other, for a moment unable to speak. But a voice came from the trees behind them. "Yes, Scrapius. That was Dag-gar and Sonoria and they are in great danger."

Chapter 33

They spun around and there, standing just outside the edge of the clearing, was an old woman whom Scraps apparently knew. "Mother Mar," he said softly, and in the tone of his voice there was real affection.

"You have witnessed the terrible thing that is happening across the Time dimensions," she said.

"Yes. That was him, heh?"

The old woman stepped back into the darkness and began to fade. "Yes, it is he—the Time Vagabond."

Scraps was about to respond when, of a sudden, she too disappeared and Scraps, Astral, and Admiral Penance were again alone.

"Wha... wha... who was that?" Astral stuttered.

"That was, in fact, a very old friend of mine. Her name is Mother Mar and you shall have occasion to get to know her, if you are lucky, for she is very wise and filled with love—and in my case, out of necessity, with patience. I am, to be honest, very glad to see her. It means we are not alone in all this. She is very powerful and is with us and she is with Dag-gar and Sonoria, too.

"We can be certain of one thing: There is mischief afoot. The Time Vagabond is stirring things up. He has Dag-gar and, I'm afraid, will soon have our Sonoria, too. We must proceed at all haste through the forest, and at dayspring tomorrow, be ready."

They spent another day following the path that the owl created for them through the foliage. They saw wild animals—a great cat leaping across their trail, and a deer, and Scraps was able to shoot a large turkey-like bird that strutted out from a thicket— and found plentiful small streams. Late in the afternoon, just as it would have been impossible to go on and as if it were being presented just for their pleasure, they came to another clearing. This not only had a stream running through it, but an open area where the sun reached and where lush green grass grew in great abundance.

"Ah, thank you, Mother Mar," Scraps said and he began unloading the Admiral and set him to grazing while Astral built the fire and got the turkey roasting. Then, after gorging on the dark, moist meat and feeling content with full bellies, they sat around the fire while Scraps played tunes on a small mouth organ. They were, in fact, a bit nervous and were doing their best to pretend they were not, for now it was necessary to wait through the long night for the coming of dawn—and what adventures it would bring.

"What do you suppose will happen on the morn, then?" Astral asked. He was picking his teeth with a splinter he had carved from a stick.

"I suppose," Scraps said, "we are all caught up in this Portal of Convergence business. We are in a great wood where the light is dim on the sunniest of days. This compounds the effects of dayspring, that magical time of day when we citizens of this plane of existence have access—at least for brief moments—to the citizens of other planes of existence. And because the forest is eternally dim, the dayspring lasts much longer. We can visit with our brethren in other dimensions for longer periods."

"Brethren?" Astral asked. "Brethren? Those people were but a mob of dirty peasants. Uneducated, filthy, loud, and as dumb as the beasts they were leading along that dusty road."

"Now, now, dear Astral," Scraps said. "It was not such a very long time ago that you, the dirty street urchin of Eye o' the Sea, would have been described in the same terms. They are, in fact, your people. You must not forget that. Don't let a little education separate you from you roots. For, like the mighty oaks we passed by today, no matter how lofty one becomes, without our roots we die."

This seemed to cause Astral some consternation and to set him to thinking, for he was quiet for a long time while Scraps continued playing a slow, sad tune on his mouth organ.

"The point is," he said finally, "what are we going to do? We at least need to have a plan."

"Indeed," Scraps said, and he knocked the spit out of the mouth organ, returned it to its pocket in his robe, wrapped his long arms around his bony knees, and stared into the fire. After a moment, during which Astral was obviously waiting for an answer, Scraps said, "Now, we are wizards, after all. We have wonderful and powerful energies at our disposal—namely, our magic: legerdemain, illusions, deceptions, spells, and conjurations. If need be we can even go beyond those small parlor tricks and do something really wonderful. But it takes great energy and the full cooperation of the gods and other elemental celestial energies. I'm certain you are familiar with them: gravities, time warps, vacuums, cosmic synergies such as eclipses, exploding stars, supernovas, falling stars, comets, *et cetera, et cetera.* And how do we gain access to these marvelous forces? Why, we have the key to it all—the key I suspect the Time Vagabond so desperately wants—the Amber Teardrop."

"But remember, we need moonlight and wizard's blood to do our conjuring—to ask the help of the face in the Amber," Astral said, "and it is a new moon tonight—there will not be any moonlight."

"Hmm. You're right, of course. The light of the full moon is best, but any moonlight will do in a pinch. Well, so then we'll have to hope we don't get involved in anything too difficult at dayspring tomorrow."

Astral was pensive for a moment and then, the firelight playing off his boyish face, said, "I have heard of the Time Vagabond, but had never seen him. What are his powers?"

"Oh, limited powers, very limited," Scraps said, "unless he has taken up residence in a living body. For you see, the Vagabond is not alive, per se. That is, he is an intelligence-energy and can take human form—sort of, more or less, hence the robe and cowl. And I think I'm beginning to have an idea about what he is up to."

Scraps stood up and began walking around the fire, tugging at his beard. "Yes, yes, it's coming clear to me now: The Time Vagabond, in fact, exists outside the realm of Time as we know it. He can choose it or not. Now he is choosing it for some reason. Now, what could that reason be? Well, the control of Time itself. He wants nothing less than to be able to tell the gods what to do—to be able to push them around."

"But why?" Astral asked. He was seated by the fire and had been watching Scraps pacing about, but now he looked into the flames as he spoke.

Scraps stopped walking, picked up a stick, and set it carefully on the fire. "There could be only one reason," he said. "It is simply his nature—he is pure energy and his energy is pure evil." Scraps pulled at his beard and added, "and he is bored—and evil and boredom are a terrible combination."

"Bored?"

"Of course. Why wouldn't he be? He's been pulsing and floating and zipping around out there since forever and, having a sort of intelligence, he became bored—world weary you might say—or cosmos weary, to be more precise."

"I never became bored," Astral said, poking at the fire.

"No, probably not. You were too busy being a street urchin trying to survive in Eye o' the Sea to be bored."

"Have you ever been bored, Scraps?"

"No. I'm a wizard, after all, and at times when I might become bored, I practice my art. I conjure up a rabbit—or something better. I might conjure up an animal that is part rooster, part snake, and part camel."

"Really?"

"Absolutely. I recommend it, in fact. Nothing worse than boredom and nothing cures boredom better than having something like that running around. But, as they say, intelligent people are never bored."

"Are you bored now?" Astral asked. "I'm not, certainly. In fact, I think I might enjoy a little boredom right now."

"One thing you can be certain of: We will not be bored at dayspring. Now, let's get ready by going to sleep."

Scraps yawned, bent over, and disappeared into his shelter.

"But," Astral asked, "what is our plan? What do we do when we meet the Time Vagabond?"

From inside his shelter, Scraps said, "Until we have sufficient moonlight, we can't use our ultimate power—the Amber Teardrop. So until then, we can only do what we can. Maybe we can catch him by surprise. My advice to you is, while you're drifting off to sleep, think of your best magic."

"Of course," Astral said. "We won't know what we are up against until we are up against it."

There was no response from Scraps at this small wisdom but a snort and then a long intake of air as he began to snore.

Chapter 34

The wizards were awakened by a loud clatter of swords and a blast of cold wind. When they crawled out of their shelters, they found themselves in a land of heavy swirling fog. Before them in the fog, two people were locked in mortal combat. Disbelief at what they beheld instantly dissolved and reformed itself as horrible truth: Dag-gar and Sonoria were trying to kill each other.

Dag-gar was nearly naked despite the fog and cold. His skin was covered with cuts and bruises, his beard and hair were matted and filthy. But his eyes carried a message of utter hate and desperation. They glowed with a dark light and glinted with a deadly will. As he attacked, he snarled, snarled words that were not comprehensible, spitting them out in venomous bursts as he swung his sword downward toward Sonoria's head.

But Sonoria seemed to be too quick for him. With graceful expertise she blocked his blows and dodged his thrusts, and all the while she spoke to him, pleading with him, "Please, Dag-gar, please. I love you. You are me and I am you—we are one, together always."

For a moment, all the wizards could do was watch as the moving fog drifted through the scene of battle and the sound of steel on steel clashed against the wet rocks that formed their arena. Then Scraps, without looking at him, grabbed Astral by the collar of his tunic. "Now is the time for our magic."

"Yes," Astral agreed in a whisper.

"Now!" Scraps said.

"Yes!" Astral said, now speaking louder.

"Together! Our magic will be stronger together!"

"But—what magic? What shall we do?"

"I suggest we turn Dag-gar's sword into wood."

"Excellent, yes, that's excellent."

"Get your sword out! Point it at Dag-gar's sword! I'll count, and on three...."

Scraps began counting. Dag-gar seemed to be waiting, gathering himself, and then, with a cry of rage, he leaped at

Sonoria again, his sword held high. He swung it downward, the blade flashing, its razor edge gleaming.

"Now!" Scraps cried out, and a jagged blue light arced out of the tips of his sword and Astral's and ripped into Dag-gar's descending blade. For an instant, Dag-gar and his sword glowed together in the fog and then both of them fell to the earth. Dag-gar lay on the ground writhing, while the sword began burning with bright, white flames.

Astral looked at his sword and then at Scraps. "What did we do?"

"Intention, lad. It's called intention. Now, grab Sonoria, hold onto her. I'll hold Dag-gar. We must take them with us back to the forest."

But before Scraps could reach Dag-gar's side, a snarl of rage pierced the air and there, squatting over Dag-gar's body, was the specter, his black robe flying about him in the wind, the black cowl hiding whatever face might have been inside it. Fog swirled around it as it spoke, its voice guttural and choking. "He's mine! No one shall take him. He cheated me. He shall suffer eternally."

Sonoria began to speak, but Scraps held up his hands and cut her off. "Nay, sad Vagabond," he said, his voice nearly sympathetic, "he is ours, of our world, flesh and blood, and of our love, too."

The specter rose to his full height. "You, wizard! You have the Amber Teardrop. Give it to me and I will make you a present of this sick and mangled youth. Even now I'm having trouble keeping him alive. I'm growing tired of it."

But Scraps appeared to have had enough of talking. He lifted his sword, pointed it at the specter, and said, "Begone, Vagabond. Without the benefit of human blood and bones and consciousness, you are but a soulless energy, doomed to drift through Time's dimensions—begone."

Scraps muttered some words from a language long dead, syllables from the beginning of time, and then pointed his sword at the specter. The specter shrieked and raised the sleeve of his cowl, which fell away to reveal the hand of a baby. Then there was a moment when the air was filled with such violence, such energies as to bring Sonoria and Astral to their knees, and yet the old wizard did not flinch but held his sword outward, the wind blowing his robes against him and against his hair and beard, and nearly lifting him off the ground.

The specter's baby hand began to wither and while all watched, it shrank and shriveled until it was but small bones and the specter himself began to fade, and then, fog swirling around him, he disappeared.

Scraps quickly moved to Dag-gar's side and grasped his wrist with a tight grip. "Astral, hold tight now, hold tight to Sonoria! Be ready!"

The words were not long out of his mouth when, as suddenly as they had left it, they were back in the forest, in the quiet clearing. Birds were chirping, dew glistened on the grass and flowers, and the day's first beams of sunlight had found their way through the leaves and branches and settled in warm patterns on the forest floor. And there was Admiral Penance, his tail working at imaginary flies, and there too, was the great blue roan stallion, Spiritus, grazing nearby.

Still they held onto each other, Scraps to Dag-gar and Astral to Sonoria. Dag-gar lay still and appeared to be unconscious.

"Now, young wizard, is the time for your medicinal magic," Scraps said. "I fear Dag-gar has been sorely abused and may be near to leaving us. Quickly now, mix your potions."

Astral set about building and lighting a fire. He lashed the handle of his tin cup to a stick, filled the cup with water, stirred in his dried herbs and roots, and held it over the fire. While this tea was brewing, Scraps and Sonoria bathed Dag-gar, cleansed his wounds, and wrapped him in a warm blanket.

"What will happen now?" she asked Scraps as they worked.

"Now? Now is a grand illusion, child. There is no such thing as 'now.' All is past or future. But I quibble. Now is good enough—for now." He felt for the small leather bag that hung around his neck. He withdrew it from his robe and opened up the drawstring that held it closed. He turned it upside down and the Amber Teardrop fell out into his hand. "There it is," he said. "I am holding Time in the palm of my hand. Imagine such a thing.

"We must understand, too," he continued, "that the Time Vagabond exists still, even as we speak. He is out there somewhere, raging, raging, raging against us. For the moment we are safe, yet who knows on the morrow? Who knows what the next dayspring will bring?"

Astral stood up from the fire. He held the cup close to his nose and sniffed. "We should let this steep for a bit," he said, "and cool. Then we will need to help Dag-gar drink it. It's a powerful medicine but he will need food, too, if he is to recover. He's very weak. We should stay here until he's strong enough to stay on a horse."

"No," Scraps said, "this is not possible. We must leave this forest before the next dawn or we may well have to face the Vagabond once again."

Sonoria was sitting in the grass beside Dag-gar, holding his hand and stroking his forehead. "How, then, will he be able to travel? He is too weak to even move."

"I have seen certain peoples travel with their sick or wounded," Scraps said. "Their method will work for us. We will cut two flexible, but strong branches and make a harness by which we can tie the branches to the Admiral's back. We will then lash a frame across these branches and lay Dag-gar on it, wrapped in his blankets. This way we can travel through the forest. It will be slow, of course, but it's our only choice."

So they set about hacking at small trees with their swords and skinning bark to make rope, and before the sun had reached its apex, they were ready. There was, however, no path that led out of the clearing and through the forest: They were hemmed in on all sides by trees.

Scraps grew impatient. "Come on then, bird," he said, casting his eyes about and finally calling out loudly. "Where are you, you feathered hoot?"

A moment later, a large night bird appeared from nowhere, flew three times around them on silent wings, and then made for the edge of the clearing at a spot where the trees seemed the thickest. As before, when it seemed the bird must crash headlong into the impenetrable foliage, the branches parted and a trail just wide enough to accommodate a donkey opened up before it. Then the owl was gone, disappearing down the very opening it had created.

"It's about time!" Scraps called after it. "Why must you always keep me waiting? Dangerous things are afoot here now, and you're forever dilly-dallying!"

They set off with Sonoria in the lead, her bow ready with an arrow notched. Scraps led Admiral Penance—or rather, the donkey, who had a mind of his own, decided to follow Scraps—and Astral followed the Admiral.

It was difficult going. Every time they came across a log, they had to lift the end of the frame lest it drag and jar poor Dag-gar. At times the path was rocky, and then Scraps and Astral were forced to carry the end of the frame until things improved. Still, at times the path was smooth and straight and they made progress.

After many hours they stopped to rest. Dusk was fast approaching. Scraps called out again to the bird, who was nowhere to be seen. "I hope, my big-eyed friend, that you understood we need to take the shortest way out of this leafy maze. I feel that you've been taking us in circles." When they started again they could feel the first coolness that presaged the dropping of the sun and the coming of the night. The path before them grew dimmer, and still there seemed no end to the woods.

"We'll have to expect to be traveling through this at night—in the pitch blackness," Scraps said finally, stamping on the ground in his frustration. "We must try to get out of it before the morrow's dayspring."

But then, when the unseen sun was lowering itself past the unseen horizon, when the shadows of the surrounding forest were joining together across their path to weave the night, Sonoria, who had moved well ahead of the others, called back to them, "Come and look! Here it is! The end of it!"

Chapter 35

They emerged into a different land from the one they had left behind on the other side of the forest. Instead of an endless grass prairie, there were rocky outcroppings and small hills with sharp, rocky peaks. These small mountains were covered with scrub and wind-dwarfed bushes halfway up their sides and then the bushes gave way to smooth rock cliffs that rose vertically into what seemed to be a low ceiling of fog and swirling mists. The air was cool and damp and filled with a peculiar smell that was not unpleasant.

"It seems," Astral said, standing on the edge of the forest, "that we are back in the land of the Time Vagabond."

"No, we are near the great ocean-sea," Scraps said, sniffing the wind. "We are in the land of the misty isles. That briny smell is the salt from the waves breaking on a rocky coast. We are, then, nearing our goal." Then he looked at Astral. "So, Navigator, can you still lead us toward the Star-That-Does-Not-Move, despite the fog?"

Astral thought for a moment and then said, "Of course this is possible. We have the Amber Teardrop. We only need… " and now he looked meaningfully at Scraps, "…we only need some moonlight and a drop of blood from an old wizard."

Scraps continued looking up at the little mountains and the fog that covered their tops. "Moonlight, hey? There will be precious little moonlight tonight, from the looks of it."

"Hmmm," Astral said, "perhaps you're right. I know of a type of wood, though, that when properly dried, burns with a flame that produces a light that reacts with amber."

"And where," Scraps asked, "are we to come by some of this wood?"

"In the forest we just left."

"So you say we need now to reenter the forest and seek this magical wood?"

"We could do that if it were necessary," Astral said, "but it is not necessary. As we walked, I recognized one dead tree as being precisely this kind of wood and I gathered some just in case—enough for us to navigate through the fog for some time."

"You're a good lad—very forward thinking," Scraps said and he looked at Sonoria, who was kneeling beside Dag-gar. "How is he, my dear?"

"Weaker," she said. "This day has not been restful for him. We need to stop. He needs food and time to gather his strength."

"Indeed. We'll find a place," Scraps said. "We are out of that confounded Time-warping, spook-filled forest and now we can spare a few days to let him recover."

With darkness nigh, there was little time to waste and they set off again, now heading downward into a small valley that promised a stream and protection from the weather. Just before it became too dark to move farther, they emerged into a level area that had some grass and was surrounded by thickets of pine trees. Astral found a path through the pines and followed it while the others waited. When he came back, he announced that at the end of the path there was a shallow cave that would be a fine place to camp until Dag-gar was strong enough to move again.

Before long, they had a fire going in the mouth of the cave and Sonoria had cut enough pine boughs to make a soft bed for Dag-gar. While she did this, Scraps began roasting two ground birds—a grouse and a pheasant—that Sonoria had shot earlier in the day, and Astral boiled water to make a broth in his cup.

When all was ready, they lay Dag-gar on the bough bed and began feeding him small mouthfuls of the soup and then while they shared the remains of the birds, they made their plans.

"Once we have eaten," Astral said, "I will burn a stick of the magic wood and we will, with the help of a drop of blood, again beseech the sleeping face to help us find our way."

"Agreed," Scraps said, "but this time, you shall nick my earlobe, not the palm of my hand."

"Agreed," Astral answered. "Old wizard's blood is still old wizard's blood, whether it comes from an old wizard's hand or an old wizard's ear."

Scraps muttered something under his breath and took the Amber Teardrop from its leather pouch around his neck. As he held it in his hand, they gathered around to look at it. In the light of the fire, the brown matrix of the Amber gleamed with a warm light; within the matrix the sleeping face was visible, serene and inscrutable.

"We cannot mingle the light, though," Astral said.

"Meaning?" Scraps asked.

"Meaning we must light a stick of the magic wood from this fire and take it out away from here where this fire is not visible.

Any light from another flame will ruin the magic. I'll go find a place and prepare the fire."

When Astral had left the cave, Dag-gar called out from his bed. Scraps and Sonoria gathered at his side.

"My father," Dag-gar said.

"We are on our way to him," Sonoria said again, taking his hand in hers. "We are going to stop here until you are strong enough to travel."

Dag-gar pushed himself up onto his elbows. "The Amber Teardrop," he said. "Is it lost?"

"No," Scraps said, "we have it. Look here. Astral plucked it from the fire before it could be damaged. We will use it to find our way through this new land to wherever your father may be."

Dag-gar looked at the Amber Scraps held in the palm of his hand and then up into Scraps' face. His eyes glistened in the firelight. "Captain Sorrow—the Time Vagabond," Dag-gar said, "he was on my father's old ship in Eye o' the Sea. He has taken possession of me. He is with me, even now, in my blood and bones."

"No, Dag-gar, he is gone," Scraps said.

"Gone?"

"Yes, gone—but who knows where? Back to one of the variegated planes of Time, I would think. He has been forced to release his hold on you. But... " Scraps paused for a moment, "... he still has your father, it seems, somewhere. And we will have to face him yet again, I'm afraid, for he certainly will not give him up without a fight."

"Where is my father?"

Now Sonoria spoke. "We still don't know. But we're getting close. Tonight we will ask the Amber Teardrop the path we must take to complete our journey. First, you must be well enough— strong enough—to travel with us."

Dag-gar studied her and for the first time since he was rescued from the Time Vagabond, he seemed to actually be able to see her. "Sonoria," he said softly, and for a moment she again saw the young man she had known forever.

"What does he want?" Dag-gar asked. "What is it Captain Sorrow seeks?"

"To take Time all for himself, I suppose, to use it for his own satisfactions," Scraps answered. "And who knows what those might be. What is it the power-hungry seek? Eternal life? Great wealth? What good would those things do a creature that is pure energy? Or perhaps to strut down the street worshipped by the peasants? No need for it in his case—the peasants can't imagine he exists. No, we decided awhile back that he does this merely because he is bored and it his nature to be evil. And why is it his nature? Because that's the way the universe works: all goodness must be counteracted by evil, else Time, and so the universe, and so life itself—lose their balance."

Astral returned to the cave and announced that the fire with the magical flames was burning and all that was needed was the Amber Teardrop—and, of course, a drop of blood from an old wizard.

Scraps sighed. "I do hate the sight of blood, you know, my own in particular. But, nevertheless, what must be done, must be done."

He stood up and then looked down at Dag-gar and Sonoria. "Best, perhaps, Sonoria, that you stay here and tend to Dag-gar. Astral and I will have our chat with the handmaiden of the gods when she is again released from the amber. I would recommend that your patient eat as much of that stew as he can and get some sleep."

"No," Sonoria said, and her voice carried a note of defiance, "I will come with you. I want to be there. I want to meet her again. I want to hear her words."

The look on her face made Scraps clear his throat. "Well, yes," he said, "I suppose that it is only right that you should. Dag-gar will be safe. Come, then. We'll be back presently."

Scraps and Sonoria followed Astral out of the cave and he led them to a clear place on the other side of a thicket of pine trees. Here a small fire blazed with a cold luminosity, its flames the same pale color as the light of a full moon. They squatted around it and Scraps once again took the Amber Teardrop from the small bag around his neck.

Astral took it from him and held it up so the flames played on it. "Good," he said, and he handed it to Sonoria. "Hold it in your open palm and be ready to put it under Scraps' ear. When a drop of blood hits it, quickly set it down on this stone." He pointed to a flat rock he had set near the fire. "Now, Scraps, lean over here so I can get to your ear."

Scraps did as he was told. Astral withdrew his dagger from its sheath on his hip, grasped the old wizard's ear, aimed, and jabbed with the tip of the knife. A large drop of blood, black in the light from the fire, immediately formed on Scraps' earlobe. Sonoria reached up and held the Amber Teardrop under it. The blood hung on Scraps' ear for a long time and then, with a sudden release, fell onto the Amber. Sonoria turned and set it down on the rock and they all stepped back and waited.

Chapter 36

For long moments no one breathed and for long moments there was no stirring from the Amber. And then, as if human breath itself was the key, when the three of them exhaled as one, the Amber, too, began to breathe.

There was a soft sigh and then another, and from the Amber came a golden light that at first slowly and then quickly became brighter until there was a halo around the rock on which the Amber sat. The halo began to pulse as if it were a beating heart and with the pulses came a sound unlike anything any of them had ever heard: a child crying, a woman sighing, the wail of a hungry baby, a chant, a wish, a prayer—all came from the Amber's halo and mingled and rose up among them, growing in intensity until the watchers were forced to step back, dumbfounded and deafened.

And from the sound, from the vibrations themselves, a human figure, life-size, formed itself before their eyes. And yet it could not have been human at all, for it shimmered and rippled and undulated and transformed itself into a glowing nebula and then back into its human conformation. Then it held out its hands as if offering them something, and they could see in its palms the drop of Scraps' blood, still intact and, like the Amber, teardrop-shaped as if it were perpetually falling through the air.

And then, though there was no sound, the human-like vision spoke to them and they understood its words. "There is destiny to protect, the eternal wisdom to defend, the darkness to keep at bay. This you must do—or you will certainly perish."

The vision pulsed and transfigured itself but before it could speak again, Scraps spoke to it. "And, please, how do we do this and in which direction should we now proceed?"

The vision's voice came at them again, pulsing like the halo that surrounded it, and its words, though silent, were bell-like in their clarity. "You need now only follow Sister Moon for a night, and there, by the ocean-sea, you will find her. But you must go now. Do not hesitate nor linger here."

Now Sonoria spoke to the vision and her voice was pleading. "But Dag-gar—he cannot travel. He is injured and weak... ."

She had not time to finish her sentence when the vision reached out and pointed toward the cave. "He is ready now," the vision said and the three of them turned to look and saw Dag-gar standing in the path to the cave holding up a flaming torch. He was dressed in the rough woolens and leather and fur tunic of a Thrang. His sword hung in its scabbard on one hip, a dagger rested in a sheath on the other, and a bow and quiver of arrows were slung over one shoulder.

Sonoria stood and faced him and he held his arms out toward her. "I am ready now," he said. "I am strong again and can travel."

Sonoria turned back to the vision, who now smiled at her and said, "And you, too, must be powerful, Sonoria, for you are the chosen—and you must join the man you love and prepare for desperate combat."

As the vision spoke these words, it swirled upwards and expanded and the light that was the vision throbbed outwards and engulfed Sonoria and Sonoria fell to her knees and the luminosity entered her through her eyes and her nose and her open mouth. Then she was lifted upwards into the air, where she turned once, twice, thrice, and then she fell back to the earth and lay still.

The vision and its energy then withdrew from Sonoria's body, swirled once around the fire, and, with a flash like a lightning bolt, returned into the Amber Teardrop. When the vision was gone, the fire quickly diminished. In a moment the magical flames went out and the night was dark.

Something caused Scraps to look upwards. A strong wind was gusting through the trees, taking away the clouds, and, floating above the treetops, a gibbous moon waxed bright and pale. "There," he said, "the gods' handmaid has given us a great gift. We have the moon!"

But while Scraps looked at the moon, Astral turned back to Sonoria, who lay outstretched on the grass of the small clearing where she had fallen.

He knelt at her side and asked, "Sonoria, are you fine or are you injured?" He did not know what else to say, so he looked into her eyes and asked again. "Sonoria? Are you injured?"

"No," she said calmly. "I am not injured." Astral stood up and stepped back as she got to her feet. He looked up at the tall young woman towering over him. "I am ready, too," she said, and she again faced Dag-gar who was still standing in the path to the cave.

"Excellent!" Scraps said. "Then we are all ready. And as I recall, the gods' lovely handmaiden's instructions were quite clear: We are not to linger here. Let's gather our kits and be off—for we are chasing the moon, my friends, we are chasing the moon!"

* * * * *

Now Admiral Penance, his long, hairy ears sagging and flopping, led the way. He was, Scraps explained as they walked, an excellent nighttime navigator—hence the title Admiral. And then Scraps added, "To understand the Penance part of his title, one must only look at his face—such a face! And the only thing about a donkey that is sadder than its face is its voice. For, while its face is a face of long suffering, its voice is a song sung in the key of mourning and anguish—and makes us all suffer."

As Scraps talked, they followed the Admiral's dark silhouette along the narrow path. Scraps walked behind the donkey, Astral the Ancient Boy behind Scraps, Dag-gar behind Astral, and Sonoria, leading her great blue roan stallion, Spiritus, was last. Around them, illuminated by the moonlight, lay a land of scattered thickets of hemlock trees and small, sharp-pointed hills from which the shadows of jagged cliffs jutted outwards. The path the Admiral followed, his small, round hooves clomping with a light thudding sound, meandered through this wilderness, but went generally in the direction of the moon.

When they came to a fork in the path and had to decide which branch to take, there was no bickering as there had been between Scraps and Astral. Now Admiral Penance was allowed to choose. He seemed not to hesitate.

The moon moved quickly across the sky and before there was any hint of dawn, it was dropping toward the scraggy horizon. It was about to drop behind one of the small mountains and disappear completely, when Dag-gar said, "I smell smoke." They all three stopped as one; Admiral Penance paused and looked back at them.

Scraps sniffed the air. "He's absolutely right, my friends. That is smoke. A wood fire—and methinks, perhaps bread baking, from the lovely odor carried along on the smoke." He wetted his finger in his mouth and held it up into the breeze. "Ah. It's from over there, just to the east of us—a hundred paces or so, I should think. And, in this moonlight, I think I can make out a small path leading off in that direction. Let's go." Before the others could speak out for or against this decision, the old wizard was gone, striding away into the darkness.

Astral, though, was muttering, half to himself, half to the others. "Ah, that crackpot old sorcerer. No doubt this is a goat trail or something carved out by a million generations of rabbits. He could have at least waited for us so that we might all proceed together. Now he is gone, who knows where, and we'll probably have to rescue him after he stumbles into some tar pit or some such thing."

But instead of a cry for help, they heard Scraps' voice not far off, calling for them to come along. They had happened upon a great thing—nay, he said, hollering out into the darkness, they had happened upon a wonderful thing.

And it seemed he was right, for when they came around a rocky outcropping, there before them was a scene of no small comfort: in a broad flat meadow stood a small stone house. From the windows of the house came the soft light of candles and, from the chimney of the house, even in the moonlight, one could see smoke puffing out.

And there was Scraps standing in the open doorway beckoning them to hurry with a long, bony arm. When they were standing before him, they could see the pleasure in his eyes. "My children," he said, and he smiled his huge-toothed smile, "behold!"

The wizard stepped aside, allowing them to see beyond him into the house. Inside, it was the picture of coziness: a fire blazed in a stone hearth and before the fire was a large wooden table laden with food—a leg of lamb, a roast goose, several large loaves of bread, a jug of drink, a bowl of apples. A large night bird, the same owl who had guided them through the woods, was perched on a ceiling beam surveying the scene with huge, round eyes.

"Come in, now," Scraps said, "and be assured that we are welcomed. For we have happened upon the home of a very dear and very old friend of mine that you have met before—out in the dim and dangerous forest."

At that moment an old woman appeared at the door and stood next to Scraps. She was as tall as he and equally gaunt. She wore a long black robe and had strong features and thick gray hair that hung in braids nearly to the floor. Sonoria realized it was the same old woman who had been haunting the forest at dayspring, the same old woman who had provided her with sustenance, the same old woman who had faded away as dayspring passed.

"My dear friends and boon companions of the road," Scraps went on, clearly very pleased with this turn of events, "pray, make the acquaintance of Mother Mar, grand old sorceress of the forest, ancient witch-mother of this fat, round Earth, as old as the stars, as young as the dawn—"

She interrupted him. "Quiet now, you foolish old man. Your friends are exhausted and famished and no doubt would benefit from hot baths and warm bread." And then to the three waiting in the dark, she said, "Come in, please. Sonoria, Dag-gar, and Astral—I already know who you are as I've been watching your progress. I've set the table for you and prepared the bathwater. Eat, and then to bed with you, for you are all exhausted. I've a warm loft that will accommodate all of you."

"But," Astral said, "how did you know us? How did you know we were coming?"

Scraps laughed a big laugh and said, "And you call yourself a wizard? Come, come, boy, Mother Mar makes it her business to keep an eye on the likes of us. Besides, she could probably smell us coming since yesterday."

But Dag-gar hesitated. He studied the old woman and then said, "I know you—from on board my father's ship. I was a boy. You gave me a cat, a white cat I named Sonoria."

The woman Scraps had called Mother Mar had turned her gaze on Dag-gar when he had spoken and now she continued to study him with her deep-set eyes. There was a long pause and then she said, "Yes, yes, that is true. And yet, the boy on that ship has become a young man—and nobly so, it would seem. As for the white cat, never question great mysteries that please you—'tis bad luck."

And so, without further questions, they entered into the small paradise that was the witch's home. They sat by the fire and ate and drank and when they were finished, and Scraps, who had had several long pulls on a goatskin of wine, and Astral, who had stuffed himself with pie made from sweet, red berries, were beginning to nod off, Mother Mar announced that it was time to bathe.

One by one they soaked in a metal tub of hot water and washed themselves with a strong lye soap, and when they were finished and all dressed in clean undergarments provided by Mother Mar, she pulled on a rope that hung from the ceiling and a ladder came down from a trap door. "Now, to bed," she said, waving them up the steps. "It is past dawn. Sleep all day, for tonight we make our plans."

Chapter 37

It was dusk when they awoke. The sun, having completed its arc, was dropping behind a veil of clouds in the west. When they were again gathered before Mother Mar's fire and again eating bread and roast meat, she said, "Now, before the sun is gone, you must see something."

She led them out the door and across a front yard where chickens scratched and pecked and ducks waddled. Where the yard ended they found themselves standing on the edge of a high cliff overlooking the rugged coastline of the ocean-sea. Far beneath them, waves broke against black rocks, sending blasts of white foam upwards.

"Look," she said, pointing not downward but out across the water toward the horizon where a cloud, silhouetted a bright pink by the dying sun, rode high on the surface of the waves. "Watch, now," she said, "watch the cloud."

As she spoke, the cloud momentarily parted to reveal the top of an island rising high above the water. "The cloud sits perpetually upon this place, this island of mists and damp," she said. "It is an island of dark spirits, an island with little hope, an island where dreams are spun from tendrils of the blackest night."

Then she looked at Dag-gar. "On this island there is a castle, an ancient ruin whose walls are tumbling down, whose ramparts can no longer shield it from its enemies, and whose bold knights have long ago turned to dust." She now met Dag-gar's eyes and held them. "And this castle's dungeons hold terrible secrets—for it is the castle of the Time Vagabond, the dark Prince of Forever." Then she looked away and back out toward the distant cloud-shrouded land. "There is still, however, within its walls—life. And where the pulse of life still beats, so does the pulse of hope—for they are one and the same. And Dag-gar, that life within the walls of that castle is your father."

Dag-gar took another step forward so that his feet were on the edge of the precipice. He looked down into the breaking waves far below and then out across the water to the island. "How can we get there?"

"There is only one way," Mar said. "There are things in this natural world little understood and soon you will witness one of them." She cast her hand out over the sea toward the island. "For what you see below you now, the ocean-sea crashing and smashing against unyielding rock, will soon change. The moon will cause these terrible waters to recede on a swift ebb tide, leaving behind them solid earth—solid from here to that distant island, solid enough to ride a horse on."

She turned to Sonoria. "Your wonderful stallion, the magnificent Spiritus, is a fast horse, hey?"

"Yes, Mother Mar. He has never been beaten in any race with any Thrang horse."

Mar smiled. "Good, then. But let us hope that Spiritus is not only faster than the Thrang horses, but faster than the tide, for if you are to save Captain Jarl, my brave young friends, you will have to outrun it."

Scraps then spoke up. "Now, dear Mother Mar, I must understand this: The only way out to the island is by riding across the dry sea bottom after the tide has receded. And that would then, most logically, be the only way to return. So once on the island, we must wait for the tide to again leave the sea's bottom dry and race its flood back here." He then fell silent for a moment and said, "And we must win that race or... ."

Mar finished his thought for him. "Or you drown."

"Or," Scraps said, perking up at his own idea, "perhaps a boat?"

"Ah," Mar said, "a boat would seem to be the solution, and so, many have tried, but alas, an equal number have perished. You see, there is no boat fast enough to reach the island before the tide recedes and leaves it aground. And then, when the tide returns, it does so with such violence, with such powerful whirlpools and overfalls, that the boat is destroyed, its crew overwhelmed. Carried to this shore, their bodies are smashed against the rocks."

"When is the next low tide?" Dag-gar asked.

"As we speak. Look below you. Even now it is beginning."

They again peered over the cliff and saw that what had moments before been crashing surf was now mild waves and as they watched, these waves pulled back from the cliffs, leaving behind the hard-packed sand and rock of the sea bottom.

"You see now," Mar said, "how fast it goes? Faster and faster, my friends. And yet you must keep pace with it when you ride to the island for there is scant time between its ebb and its flood. Should you fall behind its seaward progress, you will be swept up when it returns."

It was now Astral who spoke. "And yet, Mother Mar, among the three of us there is only one horse—and one donkey."

She laughed her loud laugh and said, "Oh, I have horses enough. It seems that over the years I have picked up a horse here and a horse there until I have a small herd out in the pasture behind the cottage. Indeed, just last year a band of Thrangs passed by during the early spring. One of them was quite ill and all of them were cold and exhausted. In return for bringing them all back to good health, they made me the gift of a horse—with a hackamore and saddle, too. In any event, all my horses are quite young and a bit wild—barely broken in, I should say—but, nevertheless, they look as though they would be fast."

* * * * *

That night they again ate their fill, climbed into the loft, and again slept deeply and dreamlessly. They were up before the first cock-crow, and were again provided a meal of meat, cheese, and loaves of fresh-baked bread.

"So," Mar said as she sat at the table watching them eat, "you have rested well and eaten plenty. The day promises fair; the next ebbing tide begins when the sun is just past its highest point. But before we prepare the horses and go down to the sea, there is one more thing I must tell you."

She stopped, broke off a piece of the dark bread, smeared it with butter, and then, before eating it, said, "The Time Vagabond—Dag-gar's Captain Sorrow—he is there, on the island. His darkness of spirit, his morose and moody energy, his sour voice, his dismal desires, rule that sad place. But of course you, Scraps, are not without your own tricks and conjurations, nor is Astral as harmless as he might seem. And I sense great power in these two young warriors, Sonoria and Dag-gar. Perhaps the handmaiden of the gods, the Lady of the Amber, has bestowed upon them something that will give the old Vagabond pause. "

Mar smiled at Sonoria and Dag-gar. "Regardless of our fates, my children, we must strive to do what is right, always."

There was nothing more to be said; they were ready. Each of them, Dag-gar, Sonoria, Scraps, and Astral carried his weapons: a sword and a dagger on his hips and a bow and a quiver of arrows across his back. They went to the stable behind Mar's house and gathered up the horses.

Chapter 38

Mar led them down a steep path that emptied onto a narrow beach of rocks and cobbles. The sea was still frothing and pounding on the littoral when they stopped at its edge and looked out over it toward the cloud-covered island. The peak of the mountain rose through the low-hanging cloud for a moment and then disappeared again behind its swirling veil.

"So now," Mar said, "you must be ready, for the tide will change of a sudden and then you must go immediately."

They all mounted their horses. From the herd of seven, Astral had picked a skinny, fast-looking bay mare; Scraps chose a black gelding with a white star on its forehead and legs long enough to match his own; and Dag-gar found a small, wiry gelding that looked as if it could run. From among the collection of dusty old tack in Mother Mar's stable, they were able to find saddles and hackamores.

Now, as they waited, no one spoke, each lost in his own thoughts. They watched the sea for any sign that it would relinquish its hold on the land; they watched the distant island, too, as it emerged from inside the cloud and then was again swallowed up by it.

Then there was silence. The sea stopped its endless pounding and its eternal roar dissolved as if into the sky. The waves flattened themselves to ripples and the water began to move backwards, away from the land. In a few moments, a sandy beach interspersed with smoothly rounded boulders lay stretched out before their eyes.

"Go now!" Mother Mar shouted. "Do not hesitate. You must keep pace with the water!"

Sonoria gave a yell and brought her heels into Spiritus' ribs. The stallion leaped forward and they were off, galloping out across the ocean floor, chasing the fast retreating water. The others immediately followed her and in a few moments they were all racing neck and neck outward toward the cloud-draped island.

At first it seemed the pace of the horses was faster than the ebbing tide and that soon they would be up to their fetlocks in the sea, but then, as Mar had said it would, the ocean's speed increased until the riders were hard pressed to keep up with it. Yet keep up with it they must, or they must perish in the returning flood.

They had gone not half the distance to the island when Astral's horse stumbled on a rock and fell. Astral flew out of the saddle, over the animal's head, landing on his back in the sand. He was up immediately, but his young and wild mount, now spooked, raced away, leaving Astral standing alone in the middle of the channel.

Scraps was the first to notice that Astral was not with them. "Sonoria! Dag-gar!" he called out, "Astral has fallen. I'm going back to pick him up. You go on ahead. You must make the island."

Sonoria and Dag-gar pulled their horses up and looked back at Scraps, who had already turned around and was galloping back to where Astral stood calling after his horse. For an instant, their eyes met and they understood each other: They could do nothing but continue.

Again they brought their horses to a gallop. Eight thundering hooves pounded and clattered on the wet sand and cobbles. The island was quickly rising; now it seemed to loom over them, its trees and cliffs clearly visible through the tumbling mist of the cloud. But the receding sea, now far ahead of them, seemed to be moving even faster. They urged their horses on with Mother Mar's words loud in their heads: They must win this race—or die.

* * * * *

Scraps yelled at Astral the Ancient Boy, for it seemed that once again the child was refusing to obey his elder out of pure stubbornness. "You eternal pee-wee of a wizard. Do you have to choose this moment to argue with me? Your horse has run off. He's not listening to you any more than I am. You need to get up here behind me and we need to head back to shore! Now!"

Astral looked up at Scraps but his eyes did not seem to focus. He then looked back out across the wet sea bottom toward the distant dark speck his horse had become. Still he continued to call after it, his voice growing weaker and weaker.

Scraps dismounted. He grabbed Astral by the shoulders and shook him. "Listen to me! Wizards or not, we are going to perish if we don't make it back to the land. Come now, up with you and onto my horse. He can carry both of us—I hope."

Still, Astral did not move. Scraps stooped down and, with a grunt, lifted him to his feet and Astral was able to stand, but was wobbly.

"You've been winded and stunned by your unsightly dismount, I'm afraid," Scraps said, pulling his horse around. "Now, up we go."

Astral was able to grip the pommel of the saddle and with Scraps' help, slide up onto the horse's back and swing his leg over.

"Good boy. Now hold on, I'm coming up behind you."

Scraps swung himself up, brought a long, bony leg over the horse's back, gathered the reins in his hands, and with his arms around Astral and a quick look behind them, kicked the horse into a gallop.

The land was right there ahead of them, for they had no choice but to go back to where they had started. Scraps could see the rocks, make out their cracks and crevices, could see the branches on the trees and even a large hawk perched high in the leaves—and yet they could not seem to get there. As in a dream, they seemed bogged down, the horse striding through some thickness of air, its legs struggling with some invisible muck that sucked at its hooves.

Then Scraps glanced back over his shoulder and saw it: the sea was returning. A great froth of water curled and spouted behind them, carrying all before it. His first thought was about Sonoria and Dag-gar. Could they have possibly made it to the island? And then he looked ahead of them at the reluctant shore. It seemed it had not moved, or had maybe even—impossibly—pushed back farther away. He pounded at the horse's ribs with his heels and yelled encouragement, but now the animal was tiring. A foaming sweat was gathering about its withers and its pace slowed to a lope.

Then a fast-moving shadow crossed the sand and rocks in front of them and Scraps heard the familiar cry of a war bird. He looked up. There above them, rising up and turning sharply on one wing, was a big hawk.

Wonderful, Scraps thought, *this one time, when I need help the most, who shows up on time? The one who can help me the least.*

The hawk made one more close pass as if to gain time to make a decision, and then rose again, folded its wings, and dove hard toward the horse's rump. Just before it would have crashed headlong into it, the bird spread its wings and broke its fall. At the same instant, it extended its talons and sank them into the horse's backside.

Thus encouraged, the horse came out of its lethargy and resumed its gallop. Now the land did seem to move toward them but Scraps heard a roar and looked back. The water was rushing toward them, the leading edge of the flood tide a huge standing wave. In just moments it would overtake them.

Then Scraps felt Astral go limp in his arms and begin to slide sideways off the saddle. Scraps struggled to hold him up against the renewed pace of the horse, but it was impossible. The sea broke behind them. Scraps heard it first and then felt the spray on his neck as the foaming surf engulfed the horse's hooves and then the horse went down, falling and tumbling over itself, and Scraps, still clutching Astral to him, was dragged under the thundering water.

There was no time for Scraps to think anything but the worst possible thoughts: *We will now die such unwizardly deaths, drowning in the froth of this deadly tempest, our bodies then washed, without ceremony, upon the rocky beach, or smashed and broken against the bottoms of those black cliffs—the small gods of such hard-earned magical genius reduced to the common elements from which we were born....*

Together they were swirled and spun and dunked and finally carried downwards into a deep tidal pool, and Scraps struggled against it with one arm as he held Astral to him with the other. He held his breath, he searched for footing with his long legs—but it was useless. He fought, he groped for life, and finally, he had to breathe. The dead air came out of his lungs in a rush and then, helpless to stop it, he inhaled.

Chapter 39

Sonoria and Dag-gar rode together, neck and neck, the horses' hooves kicking up great sprays of wet sand behind them. Yet they could not gain on the retreating sea, and then, with the island still some distance off, they could see that the water had stopped its outward race and was rushing back toward them.

While Dag-gar flogged his horse's flanks with his heels, Sonoria merely had to whisper encouragement to Spiritus to feel him surge under her. Then, with the fast-approaching torrent sending spray into their faces, they found themselves racing up onto the sloping sand beach of the island, where a shroud of fog took them into its wetness and dampened the sound of the breaking seas.

When the tidal race had passed the island, there was only the sound of the surf hissing across the beach and the cry of seagulls carried on the chill wind. They pulled the horses up and looked behind them. In the far distance, the land they had come from was visible through the mist and between them and that land, the sea had returned.

The island rose above them; high on the flanks of the mountain, the broken ramparts of the castle could be seen floating in the endless fog. The castle's walls were hidden by the drifting vapor, but occasionally, when it momentarily cleared away, a turret was visible, and it was during one of these brief moments that Dag-gar saw a black-cloaked figure standing at the battlements looking down across the sea. Had they been seen?

"There he is—Captain Sorrow," he said. "Look."

Sonoria looked up in time to see the figure disappear again in the moving fog. She said nothing, but began walking Spiritus down the beach to cool him off.

Dag-gar followed her. After a while they found a place where dripping water from the eternal condensation had formed a permanent, freshwater pool. Nearby, in a small clearing, grass grew in abundance.

"This will be a good place to leave the horses," Sonoria said.

"Good, we'll hobble them."

"No. It will be best to give them their freedom—in case we do not return."

Dag-gar looked around and said, "You're right. They can survive here. There is pasture and water enough."

They unsaddled them, slipped the hackamores off their heads, and set them free. Sonoria paused, reached for Dag-gar, and took him by the sleeve. "Scraps... ." She hesitated and then, fighting the sudden despair she felt in her heart, she said, "He has the Amber Teardrop."

Dag-gar stared at her and then at the ground. For a moment there was silence between them. "Nevertheless," he said, finally, "I must find my father. I can take him away from this place. I can take him to Scraps, to the Amber Teardrop—if they have—"

"They are back with Mother Mar, have no doubt about that," Sonoria said quickly.

Dag-gar took Sonoria by the shoulders, held her for a moment, then dropped his hands and turned away. "Why are you doing this with me?" he asked.

"Because I am you—and you are me. I love you. My heart tells me this, so it must be true." She made a fist with one hand and placed it over her heart.

Dag-gar turned back to her, took her fist and opened it up so that he could touch her fingers. They were red with the cold. He lifted them to his mouth and breathed a warm breath on them and folded them closed again. "You have your bow ready, I, my sword. We will be ready for attacks from far away or close up."

They both looked up toward the castle that loomed above them. The island was a mountain rising steeply from the sea floor into the cloud; its sides were covered with tumbled boulders between which grew thick stands of brush and small trees. Paths were worn, helter-skelter, among these boulders—they seemed to lead everywhere and nowhere. Dag-gar chose one and they began moving upwards along it.

Slowly, silently, they climbed toward the invisible ramparts of the castle. The path was precipitous, filled with loose rock and crossed by roots and fallen branches. They had to stop often to rest. Soon they had climbed to the bottom of the cloud and moved up into it. Now it was impossible to see more than a few paces ahead.

From off to one side came a scratching sound. They stopped and raised their weapons, waiting. It approached them slowly. Whatever—or whoever—it was moving unhurriedly, rustling the branches of the low bushes as it came. Then, out of the fog came a huge sow, followed by six small piglets. They were all rooting and digging with their snouts as they walked.

Sonoria lowered her bow and eased the tension on the bowstring. They glanced at each other and then watched as the pigs moved past them, oblivious to their presence. When the animals had disappeared down the path, Dag-gar and Sonoria stepped back onto it and again began their upward climb.

After what seemed like a long time they reached the bottom of the ramparts. But where was the entrance to the keep? The rolling, swirling fog made it impossible to see for more than a few paces. They would have to work their way around the bottom of the walls until they found the road that must lead up to it.

It was impossible to tell the passage of time. The cloud blocked any sight of the sun and created a flat light that cast no shadows. They could sense the mountain rising above them and they could hear the sea below them. They followed the bottom of the ramparts until they felt they had nearly made a complete circle of the castle. There was no road leading up to a door, nor any broad path that might lead to a gate.

Then Sonoria put her hand on Dag-gar's shoulder. She whispered, "There it is. Look, down there." She pointed at a hollowed-out area that dropped down toward the wall. A narrow path led down to it and disappeared into it. "There is no need for a great gate," she said, her voice soft. "No wagons would be able to come out here. Only horses, singly, with their riders, could make it—as we did."

Dag-gar nodded and began to move down the path. In a moment he turned and motioned for her to follow. Catching up with him, she saw a heavy, nail-studded wooden door with several large iron latches. Wide enough for two big men to enter abreast, it stood ajar, emitting a smell of wood smoke and mold and other things she could not identify.

Dag-gar came up behind her and put his hand on her shoulder. "Let me go first," he whispered.

Sonoria had put the arrow back in her quiver and hung her bow over her shoulder. She pulled out her short sword. "Why?" she asked.

Dag-gar squeezed her shoulder with his hand. "Because," he said, "as you love me, so do I love you."

"Then," she said smiling a small smile, "it matters not who goes first. Love is equal in all things—or it is not love. That is a very ancient rule."

Dag-gar shrugged and started moving past her. "He is my father... ."

But before he could finish and before he could get around her, Sonoria had slipped past the door and disappeared into the castle.

Chapter 40

Scraps did not drown. When he breathed in, his gasping took in not water, but air. He lifted his head and saw darkness with, here and there, glimmers of light. He gasped again. The air was cool and pure and damp. He still held Astral by the collar of his tunic and now he pulled him up and lifted his face out of the water. The boy fought against him, trying to pull away. The weight of their swords and bows and quivers tugged them downwards.

Scraps looked about. They were in an enclosed well of some sort. The space was dimly lit by openings in the stone walls that rose around them. He saw a set of broad steps carved into the rock that led up from the water and began thrashing toward them with one arm, dragging Astral with the other. He kicked hard, fighting the weight of their weapons.

When he reached the bottom step, he grabbed it with his free hand and pulled Astral to it. The boy was now sputtering and choking, but when he felt the solid rock, he gripped it with both hands and hauled himself up onto it, where he lay breathing in long, powerful sobs. Scraps crawled up next to him and for a long time they both lay on the steps, unable to move.

But Scraps was listening. There was the sound of water dripping into water and the separate sound of water dripping onto rock. There was sometimes a low moan, as if wind were passing through an opening. And there were smells, too: the smell of decay, of mold, the cool odor of moss growing on wet stone.

His eyes picked out things in the scant light. A ceiling rose from the walls in a half arch and met another wall. The openings in the wall were arrow slits through which archers could shoot. There was another set of steps that went up from the room and curved out of sight into the darkness, and an archway that led to an open passageway.

"Astral," he whispered, "are you with me yet?"

There was a pause in Astral's breathing and then he said, "Yes, yes I am. I'm here. But—where? Where are we and how did we get here?"

Scraps rolled over, pushed himself up to his knees, and stood up. He looked around again. "Who knows, my friend? We could be anywhere—and I mean anywhere in Time. I think we got caught in a whirligig—a Time water spiral. Difficult—nay, impossible to navigate in one of those. You go where it puts you."

Astral now stood up next to Scraps, holding onto the old wizard's tunic for balance. He wiped his hair out of his face and turned his head as he looked about. "I think it's a well, a water source for something—maybe a castle. I saw one like this once."

"Impossible," Scraps said.

"Why is it impossible?"

"Because, my ancient young companion, this is not a fresh water well. It is salt water. And notice that it rises and falls, surging and dropping away again. It is attached to the sea from whence we came. Nonetheless, I believe we may have arrived, after all, at..."

"...the Time Vagabond's castle?" Astral asked.

"Indeed, lad, indeed. Come on then, let's proceed, but cautiously." Scraps shook the water out of his bushy hair, squeezed it from his beard, and climbed the steps to the floor of the chamber.

Astral did not immediately follow him. "You saved me, didn't you?" he said. "Saved my life when I would have drowned."

"Never mind that now," Scraps answered. "We do what we must do. You would have done likewise, I'm sure. In spite of our initial differences, I think we've grown quite fond of each other."

Astral started up the steps. "But you did. You saved me. I remember now. It's coming clear to me. We were riding our horses, trying to outrun the tide. My horse stumbled and I went head over teakettle and... ."

"Hush, now," Scraps scolded him. "We must be quiet. We have to listen. If this is the Time Vagabond's castle—if we have made it to the island in spite of everything—we don't want him to know it."

Astral reached the top step and stood next to Scraps. "If it *is* his castle, we need to find Dag-gar and Sonoria. They should be here, and—"

Scraps reached into the top of his tunic and pulled out the leather bag that hung around his neck, the bag that contained the Amber Teardrop. He finished Astral's sentence. "—and Dag-gar's father, Captain Jarl."

Astral looked at it with wide eyes. "You still have it? You didn't give it to Dag-gar?"

"No," Scraps said. "We neglected to make that important transfer, I'm afraid."

"So, you forgot. Well, that's just grand. So now what?"

"Now we must find Dag-gar and Sonoria—or Captain Jarl. Don't forget, the purpose of this quest is to get this into his hands." Scraps walked the perimeter of the room looking out the arrow slits. "Wherever we are, there's a lot of fog out there—and low, scrubby trees."

Astral was shivering. "I'm cold," he said.

Scraps continued moving about the room. "Come then, start moving. It will warm you up." He headed down the passageway leading from the chamber.

"Where are you going?" Astral asked.

"I want to look down here first. Or we can go up the stairs. Or you can try to go out the way we came in."

"No, no, that would *not* be a good idea."

"Then, boy, we have just these two choices. Get out your sword and follow me."

With Astral close behind and his own sword at the ready, Scraps moved slowly down the passageway that led away from the chamber. The stone floor was wet and slippery with mud and scum; Scraps kept one hand on the wall to keep from falling, and Astral kept one hand on Scraps. Light from the arrow slits allowed them to see, yet it was dim and they moved forward slowly.

The passageway curved slightly to the right and Scraps, with Astral clinging to his tunic, continued without hesitating. Rounding the corner, they could hear the sound of water sloshing and gurgling from up ahead, and a few paces later they saw the source of the sound: Ahead lay a vast chamber whose ceiling arched up and was lost in darkness, and in the middle of this chamber was what appeared to be a huge pond or lake, and floating on this lake—was a large, fully rigged, three-masted sailing ship.

The sight stopped them cold where they stood.

They both gazed silently at what they beheld, their swords hanging limply from their hands. Then Scraps began walking toward the incredible vision, but Astral hesitated, letting go of Scraps' tunic.

"What are you doing?" he asked.

"We're going to see the ship."

"I don't think that's a good idea."

"And why not, pray tell?"

"Why, there might be sailors aboard. One never goes aboard a ship without asking permission. It simply isn't done. Protocol, you know."

"Blast the protocol. You're frightened."

"No, I'm merely being respectful."

Scraps' face began to turn red. "Listen, boy wizard, there is nothing about the Time Vagabond we need to respect. Now, I'm going aboard. You either stay here or come with me."

"It might not be a bad idea if I kept a lookout while you go aboard," Astral said.

"Of course, of course, that's fine. But come on deck with me while I explore down below. Keep them from sticking me in the back, you know?"

Astral sighed but followed Scraps, who now led them around the bow of the ship. Here again, standing under the bowsprit, they stopped and stared, for the bowsprit was carved into the image of a racing horse—a stallion, whose eyes were gleaming, reddish amber.

"What does that mean?" Astral asked.

"I have no idea."

"The horse is—it's the same bluish color as Sonoria's stallion, Spiritus. And its eyes, too, are the same."

"Well, imagine that, little wizard. Perhaps that's the name of this ship, then," Scraps said. "Spiritus."

"But how could that be? I mean... ."

"Shush, now. Pay attention. And stop hanging onto me. You're supposed to defend me, not cling to me like an unweaned pup. We must be ready to defend ourselves if we need to."

"But why do we need to go aboard?"

"Think now, boy! Dag-gar and Sonoria could be here, gagged and tied up in the hold of the ship. What better place to hide them away?"

They walked around to the other side of the ship and found a gangway leading up to the deck. They stepped onto it and moved up slowly. There seemed to be no one else about; they heard nothing but the gurgling water and the echoes of their own breathing.

When they reached the deck, Scraps said, "You wait here. I'm going down below and take a look."

"But—but," Astral stammered, "What if you don't come back?"

"Then, my boy, use your magic to get out of this place. Lest you forget, you're a wizard. Conjure something up. That's what I intend to do if I meet with untoward difficulties."

Astral sighed. Scraps ignored him and examined the door to a companionway. It hung on heavy bronze hinges and its latch, also wrought from heavy bronze, was in the image of a stallion. He lifted the latch, felt the cold of its metal on his fingertips, pulled the door open, and disappeared down the steps.

On the side of the companionway just inside the door hung a small oil lamp on a gimbled bracket. Scraps pushed the lever that lifted the glass chimney, and with a snap of his fingers, lit the wick.

The lantern cast a pool of yellow light by which he could see down the steps to another door. This one was carved with a bas-relief scene of a green valley surrounded by snow-capped mountains. Around the valley was carved a herd of running horses, and leading the herd was a stallion whose eyes were inlaid with amber. The bronze door latch was shaped into a spiral and decorated with a floral pattern.

Scraps stopped here. He had heard something—a whispering, perhaps—a low voice. He waited. The whispering stopped. He lifted the latch and, holding the lamp up in front of him, pushed the door open.

Upon stepping into the room he saw a table, broad and heavy, made from some dark wood; on the table a candelabrum held five long yellow candles. He set his sword and the lamp on the table, snapped his fingers again, and with the blue flame that came from his fingertips, lit the candles.

Somehow he had expected to see what he now beheld, somehow it had to be this, had to be them: Before him, on a broad, wooden catafalque, lay two mummified bodies, one with a head, the other headless. They were dressed in blue silk robes embroidered with gold thread.

"My young ones," Scraps whispered, for he knew who they must be. "Such is our fate, all of us, for eternity."

But then there was a scream from up on deck: Astral.

The sound of struggle, scuffling and grunting, came down the companionway. There was another yell and a hard thud. Scraps grabbed his sword and ran back up the stairs. He leaped out onto the deck, his sword up.

Astral was standing in the middle of the deck, his bloody sword clutched in one hand, his dagger in the other. And before him, lying in a widening pool of blood, lay a dead monster: a man with a grotesquely distorted face that was covered with oozing sores and whose muscular body was dressed in the raw skins of animals.

Astral's face had gone pale. He was staring down at the creature he had just killed and then he looked at Scraps.

"So now, my ancient friend, after all that worrying! You had me worried, too—worried that you were incapable of defending yourself. But congratulations: you've killed the Poong."

"The Poong," Astral repeated, his voice weak and flat.

"A horrid creature, really. The epitome of savagery. The result of poor breeding by a once and future master race."

"He jumped down from the rigging," Astral said. "He—he attacked me with his sword! I think he meant to kill me."

"Indeed he did," Scraps agreed. "That, it would seem, is the Poong's only purpose. Killing and death, killing and death."

"What are we going to do now?" Astral asked.

"We are going to find Dag-gar and Sonoria. But we must remember, the Poong—and there is only one of them—will not stay dead for very long. He no doubt works for the Time Vagabond and when he regains his life, he will most assuredly let the dark one know we are about."

Still staring at the dead Poong in disbelief at what he had done, Astral said, almost absentmindedly, "What did you find down there? Down there in the ship?"

"Dag-gar and Sonoria, both."

This brought Astral out of his shock. He pulled his eyes from the Poong's sprawled body and stared at Scraps. "Dag-gar and Sonoria? They are down there? Then why do we have to go searching for them? What are they doing down there? Why don't they come up?"

"Because the Dag-gar and Sonoria down there are from a different Time-Place. They are not the lovely, living, breathing young people we know—in fact, these are just their mummies, dried-out husks. I suggest," and now Scraps looked at Astral with that condescending expression that Astral found so annoying, "I suggest that you go down and look for yourself. It will be instructive."

"I don't understand," Astral said. "Mummies? Of Dag-gar and Sonoria?"

"Ah, you don't yet understand Time and how she folds over herself like Mother Mar folds her bread dough while kneading it. If the gods' handmaiden decides to do it—and who can know what Time will do from one moment to the next—she can make the same people, their living selves and their dead selves, be present at the place at the same moment. Our dead remains are somewhere, too. Somewhere out there—or maybe right here in the castle. We might yet trip over them. But never mind that now. If you are not going to go down and see their dead selves, we had better get out of here and see if we can find their living ones."

Chapter 41

Scraps led Astral back the way they had come, back into the chamber where the water whirligig had deposited them. He stood at the bottom of the staircase that led up into the castle proper, looked at Astral, shrugged, and began to climb up it. Without a word, Astral followed him. The middle of each step was worn deeply from the tread of untold numbers of feet. As they climbed, the staircase grew brighter, until finally they came to a window.

Scraps peered out. "I think you were right," he said. "I think this is the Time Vagabond's castle. We are on an island and I can see, off in the distance, a land that looks like the one we rode away from today."

Astral came up beside him and peered down. Below them the ramparts of the castle dropped precipitously toward a forest of low bushes and scrubby trees, and then there was the rocky beach and the ocean that spread outwards. In the distance was the mainland.

"I think," Scraps said, "that our dear Mother Mar had a hand in getting us here. Else the water whirligig might have dropped us off a millennium hence, in some remote, uncharted civilization. It's happened to me before."

"What will we do now?" Astral asked. He was shivering again and had moved close to Scraps' skinny body for warmth.

"Move, of course, lad. Move. No one ever got anything but cold by sitting still. Be ready, though—as you were with the Poong. You comported yourself in quite a heroic manner. Likely saved both of our lives."

They continued upwards until they came to a closed door. Like the other door, it was made of thick wood, had three big, iron hinges, and bore a heavy iron ring.

Scraps looked at Astral and Astral nodded. Scraps took hold of the iron ring and pulled. With a great squeaking sound, the door began to open. When he had it opened far enough, he peeked around it and then, without saying anything to Astral, he stepped past it and disappeared.

Astral waited for something to happen, some cry of fear or anguish. Hearing nothing, he slowly put his head up against the edge of the door and peeked beyond it with one eye. To his great consternation, there was no sign of Scraps, just a large room filled with assorted armaments. There were racks of pikes, piles of swords, axes, flails, halberds, maces, and strange suits made of metal that looked like men.

He heard Scraps' voice. "Suits of armor," he said.

"What?"

"That's what they are. Suits of armor. To protect the body from arrows and spears and such—during battle. Have you not seen them before?"

Astral stepped into the room. "Of course I have," he said, "I've seen all such things in my many Time wanderings."

"There's something different about these, however," Scraps said.

"And what is that?"

"Look closer at one of the metal suits. What do you see?"

Astral walked up to one of them and touched the face of it. The visor fell off, hitting the floor with a loud clattering, and Astral found himself staring into the empty eye sockets of a skull. He let out a yell and jumped back.

"Shush!" Scraps whispered, "you'll let everyone know we're here."

"There is a dead man in there," Astral said. "Or at least his bones."

"Yes and it might be you or it might be me—our dead selves from the distant forever. And there's one in every suit of armor you see here. 'Twould seem this is an armory and an ossuary, both."

"What does it all mean?" Astral asked.

"I have been alive a very long time," Scraps said, now scratching his head, "and I know many things. But there are many more things that I don't know—and this is one of them: Why the skeletons of dead men have been left inside suits of armor."

Then he turned and began walking along the wall of the room. He started to say something when again there came the sound he had heard while in the bowels of the ship: a whispering, faint but real; not the wind, not the humming of his own ears. "Can you hear that?" he asked.

Astral listened and said, "Someone is whispering—or so it sounds."

"I heard it when I was down in the ship. Did you hear it then?"

"No. I just heard the Poong breathing—just before he jumped on me. And I smelled him, too."

"But you do hear it now?"

"Yes, of course. It's coming from…" He turned around once and then again, wetted his finger in his mouth, and held it up as if he were seeking the direction of the wind. "… down there."

He pointed toward a broad staircase on the other side of the armory that curved downwards and disappeared in darkness. Scraps immediately walked across the armory toward it, his sword at the ready, his long legs taking great strides, his hat flopping on his head, his quiver of arrows rattling against the bow that still hung across his shoulders.

When he reached the staircase he stopped, looked down it, and listened. Motioning for Astral to follow him, he began descending the stairs.

Astral, arriving at the staircase, looked down after Scraps. He could see his gaunt and awkward figure moving slowly down the steps, his body casting shadows on the walls, and beyond him he could see the premonitions of flames, the flickering of firelight. Rising up from this uncertain darkness was the smell of cooking food, and now came the certainty of what they had heard: a whispering, someone chanting, susurrations loud enough to be distinct from the damp echoing of bat wings or the scratching of rats.

Chapter 42

Dag-gar and Sonoria found themselves in a small chamber lit only by the daylight filtering in through arrow slits. Their voices echoed against the stones of the walls, and for just a moment they thought that what they heard was the sound of their own breathing or the scraping of their own feet.

But no. It was something else. Dag-gar glanced at Sonoria and she shrugged.

"It sounds like whispering," she said, her own voice a whisper echoing against itself.

Dag-gar nodded. He moved across the chamber and entered a long hallway that led from it and moved in a long curve into more darkness. He stopped and, when Sonoria had caught up to him, said, "It's too dark to see."

"Then we will have to feel our way along. Be careful. Keep your hands on the wall and feel with your feet lest you fall into a pit."

So they proceeded along the hallway, one hand on the rough stones of the walls, the other held out into the darkness ahead, sliding each foot forward before stepping. The stones were damp and they heard the scurrying and squeaking of rats around their feet and their heads brushed against bats hanging invisibly in the darkness.

And they still heard the whispering. It grew louder and then diminished. It came to them with a paced rhythm, as if some long and sacred ceremony was being played out just beyond them, and yet they never seemed to reach it.

Then they saw light ahead of them: a fire—orange and yellow glimmerings on the wet, uneven stones of the walls. They began to be able to see now, see the corridor curving away before them, see the silhouettes of scurrying rats and the fluttering bats. The whispering grew louder and they moved more slowly, watching, listening. Then, along with the whispering and the smell of smoke and the soot of millennia of long-dead fires, came the smell of rancid meat and fat cooking over smoldering flames.

They came to the end of the passageway. Dag-gar moved slowly. He reached the last of the wall where it fell away to reveal the chamber. Then together, he with his sword at the ready and Sonoria with an arrow notched in her bow, they stepped around the corner.

What greeted their eyes as they strained to see against the uncertain light, was not immediately identifiable except that from the sound of its whispered chanting it was human. It was covered with a tattered brown robe and it huddled over a fire as if tending its food. Long gray hair, filthy and matted, hung down around its face and skeletal arms and hands were visible where the sleeves of the robe ended.

"Old one," Dag-gar called out. "Who are you?"

The figure did not move nor stop its whispering to indicate it had heard him. Instead it continued on, chanting and worrying the meat with a desiccated hand.

Dag-gar and Sonoria walked across the room until they stood just a few paces from the fire and the spectral old man that hovered over it. They lowered their weapons.

"Old one," Dag-gar said again, this time with a softer voice, "are you Jarl, the captain of the good ship *Mother-of-Pearl* and father to a boy named Dag-gar?"

At these words the chanting stopped and the figure lifted his head from his work. He did not look for the source of the voice but only looked upwards at the ceiling of the chamber lost above in the darkness. He seemed to wait for something and then looked back down at his fire. He began whispering again, chanting and now rocking his body in rhythm with the song.

"Father!" Dag-gar cried out and he dropped to his knees next to the man and took him by his shoulders. "Father, I am Dag-gar. I have come to take you away from here."

The old man stared at Dag-gar's face. There was, at first, no recognition. Captain Jarl stopped whispering his song. He gazed into Dag-gar's eyes, then reached up and touched Dag-gar's cheek with his fingertips. His eyes were cloudy and red-rimmed, his face gaunt and deeply lined. Across these features came an expression of disbelief. "If this is truly you, my boy," he said, and his voice was still but a coarse whisper, "though I trust you are but an illusion sent by the Time Vagabond to torment me—if this is truly you, you must go. Go now. Take your young life with you and leave this cursed place."

"You are coming with me," Dag-gar said.

The old man laughed a hoarse, cackling laugh. "Escape? Nay, nay, for me there is no escape—no leaving this chamber where I have spent an eternity and where I shall spend another."

"But you must merely follow us," Dag-gar said. "We can take you out of here straight away."

"So you would think, yes," Captain Jarl said, waving his hands about, "yet all passages out of here, while open to you, are closed to me—until I surrender the Amber Teardrop to the Vagabond of Time. For that is the price—yes! That is the priceless price I must pay to live again."

"We have it," Dag-gar said. "We have the Amber Teardrop... ."

He stopped. The old man grabbed the front of his tunic and pulled him close. "The Time Vagabond must never have it! You understand this. Keep the Amber Teardrop from me lest I weaken and surrender it to him. Keep it hidden, keep it safe. Or there will come an end to Time—for that is what he wants—to end sweet, sweet Time—and so, destroy the gods and bring about the Rule of Nothingness."

"Where is he," Dag-gar asked, "Where is the Time Vagabond?"

Captain Jarl let out a moan and rocked back away from Dag-gar. "He is everywhere and nowhere, gone and not gone, he exists and he vanishes. He is a warp in the being of Time, you see, a dent in the armor of the past, future, and present; a crack in the barricades of what will be, what was, what is."

Then the old man stopped and looked beyond Dag-gar, past where Sonoria stood watching them. "There," he said, lifting his hand and pointing, "there he is."

Dag-gar and Sonoria spun around. Standing at the bottom of a broad staircase was the now-familiar black-cloaked figure.

Dag-gar stood up and faced him. "Captain Sorrow! I have come for my father. I will take him with me."

Captain Sorrow raised his arm and pointed at Dag-gar with a fat finger on a baby's hand. "Oh, pity you! Pity you, young man, for you have deceived me! I entrusted the Amber Teardrop to you and you have thrown it away—thrown it into a fire. Just when I had learned the secret: a drop of wizard's blood and a bit of moonlight and it will tell me all it knows. But now—now there is nothing left. The Amber Teardrop, the key to the control of Time, is gone. You see then that nothing now matters? Nothing? And so, you all then must die—for what does it matter if you go on living?"

The Time Vagabond then raised both arms and looked upwards, and inside the cowl of his robe there was again the howling void of his face. This must have been a signal, for an instant later came the sound of footsteps and the rattling of weapons. From the dark corners of the chamber appeared a man, a short, powerful man whose skin was covered with sores and who was dressed in filthy rags. He carried a sword in one hand and a shield in the other.

Sonoria recognized him: It was the man who had strangled her in the forest when they had faced the Time Vagabond and exorcised him from Dag-gar's soul. With a single movement, she took an arrow from her quiver and notched it into her bow and let it fly. It struck the monster in the chest and with a scream, he fell to the floor.

The Time Vagabond laughed, "You think you have killed him, hey? But no, he is, after all, the Poong and the Poong can never be killed. For he, poor creature, is doomed to suffer an infinite number of deaths while he does my bidding."

Indeed, no sooner had the Vagabond uttered these words than the monstrous Poong was once again getting to his feet. With a snarl of rage, he ripped the bloody arrow from his chest.

At the same moment Captain Jarl staggered to his feet. Drawing himself up to his full height, he addressed the Time Vagabond in a voice that rasped from his throat. "You have kept me here, in this horror, for an eternity. For this place, this dim and ruined castle, is the nexus of the dark forces of the cosmos, the demon's navel, the gateway through which the doomed must pass to reach their fate. But now I will escape this madness through the infinite forgiveness of death. Take me, then; I accept my freedom." With that, the old man rushed at the Poong, his arms spread wide apart, beseeching him to kill him.

But Dag-gar stepped in front of him and stopped him with one arm while he raised his sword with the other. "We will not go so easily, my father," he said.

"Kill them now!" the Time Vagabond shrieked, and the Poong lifted his sword and attacked.

* * * * *

Scraps held up one cautionary hand. Astral hesitated.

"What is it?" he asked, "What do you see?"

"Hush!" Scraps whispered, and he began backing up the staircase until he reached Astral. "They are down there," he said.

"Who?"

"Them! Dag-gar and Sonoria—and an old, old man and—"

"It must be Captain Jarl," Astral said, interrupting.

"Of course!" Scraps whispered. "And the Time Vagabond, too, whom Dag-gar calls Captain Sorrow—and the Poong you thought you'd killed."

"What should we do? If the Poong cannot be killed, it will kill them." Astral said.

"We are wizards!" Scraps said, "We can do great things."

"Well—what?"

"What time of day is it?"

"I don't know. Well past the noontide, I should think."

"Too early for a moon, then," Scraps said.

"I should think so, yes."

Scraps reached inside the top of his tunic and pulled out the bag that held the Amber Teardrop. "So then, while you're thinking, think of some other way to wake up the immaculate lady in this amber bauble other than moonlight and flames from magical wood."

"Well, I don't know."

"What would happen if we used a drop of wizard's blood and sunlight— sunlight instead of moonlight? Would it still work?"

"I have no idea—perhaps it would double, or even triple the Amber's power, or more than that. It might be very dangerous. Or it might not work at all."

Scraps looked upwards at the arched stone ceiling above them. No sunlight was visible. "How can we get sunlight? Just a momentary sunbeam would be enough, I should think."

"The arrow slits!" Astral cried, pointing behind them.

They moved quickly back into the armory. Daylight flickered through an arrow slit. Scraps peered out. The clouds and mists that hovered over the castle roiled around them. Below, the sea waves broke against the rocks of the beach.

He turned to Astral. "Help me now, boy! We need to conjure up a break in these blasted clouds. Perhaps by combining our powers we can manage it."

Astral grasped one of Scraps' hands and squeezed it. He closed his eyes and began muttering.

But Scraps pulled his hand away. "No, not yet," he said. "First we'd better have a drop of wizard's blood. Give me your hand. It's your turn."

Astral opened his eyes and saw that Scraps had already pulled his dagger from its sheath. He looked at Scrap's face, winced in anticipation, and then surrendered his palm. Scraps made a quick jab and a big drop of blood immediately formed in the middle of Astral's hand.

"Now," Scraps said, "do you remember the incantation for sunlight?"

"Of course I do."

"Good. We must chant it together."

Scraps raised his sword and swung it in a circle over his head. As the blade cut the air, a blue flame once again came from its tip. Then both wizards closed their eyes and began muttering in unison words from a long dead tongue. In a moment the room began to brighten and then a single ray of sunlight came in through the arrow slit and then through all the arrow slits until the armory was aglow with bright light.

"Quickly now," Astral said, "drip some blood on the Amber and then hold it in the sunlight!"

Scraps did so. He held the Amber in the palm of his hand while he reached for Astral's wrist and turned his hand upside down. A big drop of blood hung for an instant, then fell on the Amber. Scraps held it in a ray of sunlight.

There was a moment when they thought nothing would happen. For too long the Amber Teardrop with its smear of blood sat unchanged in Scraps' palm in the full flood of sunlight.

Astral started to say, "So, I suppose it does take moonlight after all—" But his words were cut short by a high-pitched wailing, a rising ululation that was in a few moments too much for their ears. The sound was coming from the Amber and Scraps could feel the Teardrop vibrating and see it shimmering and changing colors from its bright glowing brown to red and then a deep blue. It then began to grow and it grew larger and larger, swelling until it doubled and then tripled in size.

Scraps looked down at Astral and over the wailing din said, "What do we do now? It's working!"

"Why do you think I know what to do with it?" Astral said, flapping his hands at his sides.

It was then that they heard the loud clamor of desperate struggle coming up the staircase: the horrible sound of the Poong screaming and of swords clashing, steel on steel. Scraps cupped the now shrieking and incandescent Amber in both hands and ran for the staircase. Nor did he stop when he reached the top, but began running and leaping down the steps with Astral right behind him, his sword at the ready.

Halfway down, without looking at the scene below him, Scraps threw the Amber into the air and watched it spin and tumble into the chaos of the battle. As it fell, the shriek became a scream, the incandescence a raging storm of blue-white fire that spread and engulfed the chamber from wall to wall and ceiling to floor.

Astral yelled out, "Look! The water! It's coming in from everywhere!"

And indeed, a great flood welled up through the stones of the floor and the walls opened up and a swirling tide came sweeping in from all sides, carrying everything before it. While Astral managed to race back up the steps and escape the raging torrent, Scraps was caught up in its whirlpools. As Astral watched, he was sucked down into its vortices and disappeared. And so, too, did all of them—Dag-gar, and Sonoria, and Captain Jarl and the Time Vagabond and the Poong.

Chapter 43

Astral sat huddled by Mother Mar's fire. He was shivering, his face pale.

Mar handed him a cup of hot tea. She pressed the palm of her hand against his forehead. "You are feverish," she said. "This tea will help. But drink it slowly. It's hot."

Astral nodded and put the cup to his lips. He took a tentative sip and then another. Mar took the cup from him and set it on the broad wooden table where she had been kneading dough to make bread. "Now, tell me, what happened out there on the island in the clouds?"

Astral, his voice uncertain and shaking, related his adventures as well as he could remember: They had begun riding out toward the island, racing the tide. His horse had tripped. Scraps had come back for him, had rescued him. But the flood tide overtook them and swallowed them up and they were certain they were doomed. But no—they were caught up in a whirlpool of Time and carried right into the castle itself. There they had first found a strange and wonderful ship on whose prow was carved a magnificent stallion the same blue-roan color as Sonoria's stallion, Spiritus, and with the same glowing, red-amber eyes. Scraps had gone down into the ship and said he found the mummified remains of both Dag-gar and Sonoria. And then they had found a room where suits of armor were filled with the bones of dead knights or perhaps of themselves. And then they had found a dungeon and in that dungeon—here he hesitated and began to stammer as if what happened next was truly unspeakable—and in that dungeon they had seen an ancient specter of a man, a filthy, emaciated man who must have been Captain Jarl. And there, too, were Dag-gar and Sonoria and they were engaged in desperate combat with the Poong, who cannot die.

But worst of all was the demon—the fiend—whom Dag-gar called Captain Sorrow, also known as the Time Vagabond. He hung in the air dressed in his black robes, his face not a face but an infinite void, a hole in the universe, into which he sucked everything—the air and all its energy, the sky, the living flesh off the bones of those in the room.

Astral stopped talking. Mother Mar handed him the cup of tea and he drank again, this time not sipping, but taking a gulp. She took the cup from him and took his hand in hers, though hers were still covered with the flour from her kneading.

"And so, then?" she said softly, gazing into Astral's eyes as if to read in them the things his voice and words could not tell.

So he went on: They had come up with an idea to use the Amber Teardrop without moonlight—for what is moonlight but the reflected sun? They had co-joined their wizardly powers and conjured a hole in the clouds for the sun to shine through and had dripped his own wizard's blood onto the Amber—here he stopped and looked at the palm of his hand and the bloody scab that had formed on it—but then, he said, things began to go awry. Perhaps the sunlight was, as they had feared, too strong. In any event, the Amber Teardrop had reacted differently than it had in the moonlight. Instead of a lovely and inscrutable lady floating up out of it and dispensing wisdom and magic, the Teardrop began to make a shrieking sound and to glow and then to grow until it was many times its original size.

Astral stopped again, and again Mar gave him more tea. She put her hand on his arm and squeezed it, but said nothing.

He continued: They had had no idea what to do next and so, in desperation, with the sounds of murderous battle coming up from the dungeon, a battle Dag-gar and Sonoria and Captain Jarl must certainly lose, Scraps had run with the Amber Teardrop down to the last step on the broken staircase and flung the now-exploding Amber into the dungeon.

Astral stopped, but this time, after taking a deep breath, he went on: The rest he said, was hard to remember. The vibrations from the Amber seemed to shake the very walls of the castle. Water began rushing into the dungeon from everywhere. He had yelled a warning to Scraps, but Scraps was too far down the staircase to escape. The raging water and the wind it caused knocked him off the steps and into the dungeon with the rest of them. Astral had then run up to the top of the stairs and looked back and had seen that the dungeon was now a great, swirling whirlpool of foaming water that had taken everything away before it. He had then turned and run for his life.

Somehow he found his way out of the castle, but how, was a miracle he would never understand. He ran out into the fog, the cloud having re-formed over the island after their magic had dissipated. He was confused and dazed but he could hear the sea below him and he ran toward it down one of the many paths that meandered through the trees and bushes. But what to do once he reached the sea?

As he was coming out onto the stony beach a great bird swooped in low and nearly crashed into his head. It was a seabird with long white wings and bright orange-and-black eyes. It flew in tight circles around him and made him understand he was to follow it. This was not an easy thing, because stones on the beach were loose and rough, but follow it he did, and it wasn't long before he came to a clearing where there was a pool of clear, fresh water and a thick growth of green grass. And there they were: Dag-gar's horse and the great stallion, Spiritus.

"And then," Mother Mar said, "you rode the stallion back here again, racing the tide and this time winning that race."

"Yes, yes. This time I won. On the great stallion Spiritus, I won," Astral said. Then he looked past Mar and realized for the first time they were not alone in her small cottage. There were four others, young men and women, all dressed the same in rough woolens and leather tunics. They were watching him and listening to his story. He ignored them and looked at Mar questioningly. "What do I do now? What happened to them? Where are Dag-gar and Sonoria? Are they lost—are they dead?"

"I think not," she said. "I think that Time, which is, as you know, the handmaiden of the gods, became very angry—angry with the Time Vagabond. She had had quite enough, it seems, of his meddling, of his busybody tampering with things, and decided to put an end to it. A drop of your blood and the sunlight was all she needed and, poof! She was free to deal with him."

Mar turned again to her bread dough. "So," she said, "she swallowed them all up in a whirlpool of Time, which you know all about, having been caught up in one yourself. But Time is not just a spinning whirligig. Look here." Mar took the dough up into her hands. "Think of Time as this dough. I can twirl it, and twist it, and I can even fold it over and into itself. And such is a nature of Time. Don't worry about your friends. They are fine— safe somewhere inside its folds."

"And as for you, my ancient boy wizard, you see these young people around us? They are Thrangs, and they are searching for the answer to the Great Mystery. They rode in here after you left this morning. I would think you could travel with them. They will give you a horse and you can ride with them. Go where they go, live the way they live. You will learn a great deal, and, perhaps with your help, they will actually find that which can never be found. But as for right now, drink your tea and have a slice of my bread."

"But what about the stallion, Spiritus?" he asked.

"It is best to leave him here with me. He is a wild one and he belongs to one woman—Sonoria. She will come for him someday and I will keep him sleek and fat for her."

Mar cut a thick slice of bread from a loaf that sat on the table. "Here now," she said, smearing it with butter, "finish your tea and eat this. Then get some sleep, for tomorrow you are off with these young barbarians."

Epilogue

So, the child's tale had been told. It was late. The stars had moved across the desert sky since she began talking, yet she had not seemed to tire of the telling. Now she stopped and watched what little remained of the fire. The old wizard watched her and then he, too, looked at the lingering flames. Behind them was the sound of insects and the camel's perpetual chewing.

"But what happened to me—to the old wizard?" he asked and he stretched his awkward body out on the blanket he had spread in front of his tent.

"You were carried here, by the Time whirligig," she said.

"But I remember nothing of this. Not a thing."

"That is because it has not yet happened."

"Ah, yes, of course, it hasn't. And I assume Astral, the Ancient Boy, is still riding with the Thrangs searching for the answer to the Great Mystery. But, what, my dear, became of Dag-gar and Captain Jarl?"

The girl-child smiled and the firelight played off her fine features and her white-blond hair glowed a dark yellow in the dying flames. She said this:

"There is a castle on a lonely island in a lonely sea. One evening a handsome young sea captain calls at the gate of the castle. He carries something in his arms and he says something to the guards at the gate—and it is a great and heavy gate with big iron hinges—and the guards open the gate and it creaks horribly when it moved on the hinges, but they let the handsome young sea captain in."

The child paused and looked up at the stars, as if reading the rest of the tale in their pale glimmerings. She looked at a particular star that glowed red in the heart of the celestial Scorpion and said, "The princess and the prince who live in the castle greet the sea captain and he shows them what he carries in his arms. It is a baby boy, and he says he believes it is their baby boy because he is dressed in a robe of golden silk and one of his sailors had found it in a hay wagon.

"And the princess and the prince are overcome with joy and they thank the sea captain and take their baby boy back up to his nursery and put him back in his cradle."

"So," the old wizard said, "that's all well and good. But what happened to the young warrior, the proud Sonoria who has loved Dag-gar forever?"

Now the child did not hesitate, as if it should have been obvious to anyone who had heard her tale. "In this castle lives a beautiful white cat whose mewing sounds like silver bells tinkling. When the princess and the prince put their baby boy back in his cradle, they put the beautiful white cat in the nursery with him and the cat curls up with the baby boy and watches over him forever."

But there was something that the girl-child did not tell the old wizard that night in the oasis in the desert with the sounds of insects and the camel munching his endless supper. It was this: The swirling, tumbling waters, the awful storm of foam and spray that took them into its vortex, had taken them somewhere else before spitting them out, finally, in this place in Time. She had been with him, with Dag-gar. They were aboard a great ship with a great blue roan stallion carved into its prow, and they were exceedingly ancient and more than ancient—decrepit and desiccated by an eternity together. And they were dying and their death was being attended by a boy wizard who was nearly as ancient as they were, yet still a boy.

He had dressed them in robes woven finely from gold and blue threads and, in preparation for the end, had instructed them to lie on a catafalque in the belly of the ship. He had placed crowns of ermine and amber on their heads and had helped to make them comfortable. Then he sat and waited, sat down at a table on which he had placed a candelabra with five candles, which he lit with the blue flames he conjured from his fingertips.

How long the ancient boy waited she did not know, for then she was lifted off the catafalque and carried away again by the whirlpool and brought back here, to the old wizard and his camel. She was a child again, but like all children, filled with a child's wisdom—and more than that, for now she knew the truth of Time and so she knew, too, the answer to the Great Mystery. It was this: Time meanders and flows and folds back upon itself like Mother Mar making bread, kneading her dough, and there was no beginning, and there will be no end.

About the Author

Douglas Arvidson grew up on a farm in New England. After serving in the military and finishing graduate school, he spent nearly thirty years overseas, teaching, traveling, and writing. His inter-national prize-winning short fiction has been published in Paris, Prague, and in literary magazines in the United States. He lives on the Eastern Shore of Virginia. Visit his website at douglasarvidson.com and his blog at douglasarvidson.blogspot.com.

About the Cover Illustrator

See more of the illustrator's work at www.scarboroughconcepts.com.